A Stolen Woman

Catherine Lea

For my beautiful girl.
You're forever at my shoulder and in my heart.

PROLOGUE

He was out by the incinerator in back of the house, burning the last of the clothes when his phone rang.

What now? He'd promised his wife he'd be home early. Cursing the thing, he dug it out of his pocket and checked the screen. The second he saw the number, sweat flashed on his forehead.

What did they want from him now? Hadn't he done everything they'd asked? Would they never leave him alone?

For a moment, he considered ignoring the phone—letting it ring out and go to messaging. But what good would that do? If the facts came out, he'd be hunted down. Just like Westrum. Westrum had gotten in out of his depth; wound up with a target painted on him. Next thing, he was just another body in an inner-city dumpster with his throat cut and only a bunch of sordid photographs to identify him.

He couldn't let them do that to him, to his wife. Yes, he'd made mistakes, but he'd worked too hard, done too much to go like that. So he swiped the icon on the screen and held the phone to his ear without speaking.

The response was immediate. As if the man could see him. "Good evening, my friend. I have a request."

A bolt of fury seized him. "A request? Or another order?" he demanded. Then he wondered why he even bothered.

"My friend, you understand the terms of our agreement. Did we not discuss this?"

How could he forget? Ever since the Westrum fiasco, the screws had tightened on him. Giving up that first girl was a no-brainer. It was her, or him. Now here was the Man, demanding more.

Without a hint of emotion in his voice, he asked. "What is it this time?"

"The information you provided me was of great value. Thank you."

"You called to thank me?" He couldn't disguise the sarcasm.

"Oh, my friend, how I wish that could be so. But that little bird we caught tells me you have something of mine. Just send me the address where I'll find her. You can leave the rest to me. And we can pretend this never happened."

His heart sank. This was worse than he'd ever imagined.

"And if I tell you I don't know what you're talking about?"

"Oh, my friend, we both know that is not true. Just give me what I want. Let us just say, it would be in your best interests."

Ever since the day he met her, he'd known this day would come. Giving her up now tore his heart out. But what else could he do?

"And when do I get my files back? The ones you promised me?" He stopped short of adding, *The ones you stole from me.*

Despite the warmth in the Man's tone, the threat was patently clear. "Oh, I can see why you're eager to get them back. Your escapades were… let's say… adventurous. But our arrangement has not come to an end."

He clenched his teeth, felt the vein in his neck thump. There was no way out. If those photographs made it to the Internet, they would ruin him. The press would have a field day. The company would be dragged through the mud and his wife would disown him.

"You haven't told me what I have to do to make that *agreement* come to an end."

"It ends when I have no more use for you."

The inference couldn't be plainer. The day the Man had no more use for him would be the day he was dead.

He had to find an escape.

He had no idea how, but his very life depended on it.

"You'll find her at Sunny Springs," he said and hung up.

CHAPTER ONE
DAY ONE—7 PM—LANEY

Laney couldn't have picked a worse night for a tragedy if she'd asked for it.

She'd been driving for over half an hour now with the rain hammering on the windshield swirling all the lights along I-480 into a blur and no sign of a letup. All she could see were shards of light reflecting off blacktop in front, and the blaze of headlights as cars sped up behind and swerved around her, spraying up sheets of water that pounded on the doors like a prison riot hose.

In rain like this it might have been smart to pull over, to seek shelter. Laney didn't have time for that. The second she'd gotten the phone call from the night nurse over at Sunny Springs, she'd dropped everything and jumped in the car.

Given the choice, Laney wouldn't have put a dog in Sunny Springs Facility for the Disabled. But at the time, choice was a luxury Laney didn't have. She'd spent the last six months in Carringway Women's prison. Turned out that the shipment of electronics she was helping to move eight months back didn't actually belong to Lyall Chessmire like he told her it did, the lying asshole. The police said it'd all been stolen two weeks before.

Laney had tried to explain, pointing out she was just helping a friend. But from the minute the cops glanced over Laney's police record with all the misdemeanors and arrests, O.J. Simpson's defense team wouldn't have gotten her off. As a result, she'd been sentenced to a six-month stretch at one of Ohio's private prisons—Carringway Women's.

Laney spent that six months swearing she'd do right by her sister, promising she'd turn her own life around and be the sister Kimmy needed. So, the second she was released, she had found an apartment—or at least, she'd found an ex-con who had one—and moved in with her.

The plan was to save enough money for a proper apartment, then bring her disabled sister home so she could care for her like she'd promised her mother she would. She'd vowed that she'd quit screwing up for once in her life.

Everything was working out. She'd gotten a job; paid off her debts.

Then, that phone call came in.

The night nurse had been almost incomprehensible—words tumbling out so fast Laney had had to tell her slow down so she could understand her. She told Laney she was one of the night nurse aids at Sunny Springs Home for the Disabled. Through the jumble of words, Laney picked up "hurt Kimmy" and "in terrible danger."

Laney didn't even stop to find out what the danger was. She'd dropped everything, jumped in the car, and headed straight over. Now she was wondering if she should have taken a second longer to find out because frankly, she found herself debating over whose ass to bust first—David Whitcliff, the smartass facility manager, or Elizabeth McClaine, the rich bitch who'd put Kimmy there in the first place.

But that would have to wait. First, she had to bust her sister out of that place.

The instant she turned into the tree-lined avenue that formed the entrance to Sunny Springs, her eyes were searching the lit-up windows across the front of the place. Through the sheets of rain obscuring her view, the place looked like a space ship. Sunny Springs was the latest high-class facility for the disabled. It boasted state-of-the-art equipment, top-rated nursing staff. Any minute now you'd expect some fancy doorman to step out and ask if he could park the car for you.

Laney didn't care if the place looked like Buckingham Palace where the Queen of England lived. Everything about the place set her teeth on edge. If it hadn't been for Wendy, the nurse aid caring for Kimmy, Laney would have kicked up such a storm from inside Carringway, they'd have had to brick up the cell. But six months—that's all she'd had to endure. And besides, what good would it do for her to spend another minute in Carringway on bad behavior?

As determined as she was pissed off, she put her foot flat to the floor, tore down the driveway, and swerved to a halt in front of the main entrance, eyes searching for paramedics or cops, anything that might give her a clue as to what had happened.

Instead of parking in the assigned visitor spaces around the back, Laney stopped at the front doors, jumped straight out leaving the car door open, and ran up the four wide-sweeping front steps. When the sliding doors failed to open, she pounded on the glass with the flat of her hand until a passing cleaner spotted her. Looking a little bemused, he hit the inside button and the doors parted enough for her to slip inside. Marching past the reception desk, around past the dining area, she headed to Kimmy's room.

She'd just turned into the second hallway when she heard a shout behind her.

"Excuse me!"

Velma Stanford—the residential manager of Sunny Springs, the two-faced bitch. Laney recognized her voice but didn't turn around.

"Miss Donohue! Laney!"

Without breaking her stride, Laney called over her shoulder, "Where's my sister? Where's Kimmy?"

"Laney, will you please calm down? Kimmy is perfectly safe. Please, have a little respect for our other clients."

Laney stopped short and turned a razor-edged glare on the woman. "I got a call saying Kimmy's been hurt and she's in trouble. Or are you saying that's all bullshit?"

Velma stammered a few words, no doubt searching for the "company line."

"Yeah, thought so." Laney marched off again, leaving Velma gulping air.

She scurried after her. "Laney, there was a minor incident that's been dealt with. You should have called us. We could have put your mind at ease.

Kimmy's in bed now. You don't want to disturb her, do you? Why don't you come back tomorrow during visiting hours?"

Laney paused at the elevator and punched the button with the side of her fist. The moment the elevator doors opened she got in, followed by Velma. "Screw your visiting hours. I'm sick of this place. I'm sick of your smartass manager and everyone else in this dump. I'm taking Kimmy out of here right now."

On the second floor, she got out with Velma still trotting along at her shoulder. At the corner she turned down the corridor, striding along until Velma reached out a hand and grabbed her by the shoulder and jerked her back.

Laney's eyes went from Velma's hand up to meet the woman's gaze and the hand dropped.

"Laney, please will you just listen to me?" Velma said.

"I just got a phone call from someone here saying Kimmy was in trouble and that she'd been hurt. Now I want to know what the hell's going on in here."

Velma folded her arms tightly across her chest. "I've been trying to tell you. The night nurse came to me and told me she'd called you. But it was a mistake. We tried to call you back, but you didn't answer. Check your cell phone."

"Where's Wendy?"

"She's gone."

"Gone where?" The hesitation told Laney that the next words out of Velma's mouth would be a lie. So she marched on.

Velma caught her up, speed-walking next to her. "She's been fired, Laney."

She angled a sardonic grin across at the woman. "Fired? Only decent person in this shithole, and you go and fire her. What did she do? Be nice to someone?"

Before she could reply, Laney stopped dead in front of Kimmy's room. She gave the door panel a gentle knuckle-tap and pushed it open.

"Kimmy?"

No sign of her. Bed unmade and crumpled, pens and papers all over the floor, a broken lamp next to the dresser. Laney's heart flipped.

"What the hell happened here? Where is she?"

Velma followed her into the room, looking around with a puzzled expression.

"She was here, I promise you. She can't be far away."

With a rising wave of terror looming over her, Laney shouted, "Kimmy, baby? Where are you?"

A muffled sob.

Laney spun around. Another sob—coming from the closet.

Crossing the small room in three quick strides, Laney yanked the closet door open and peered into the line of faded dresses and coats that made up Kimmy's wardrobe.

"Kimmy?"

A whimper this time.

Laney shoved the hangers back to find her sister sitting at the very back of the closet, eyes red with tears, nose streaming. Eighteen years old with all the innocence and non-worldliness of a child. Laney's heart filled with sorrow that flashed to anger.

A gasp from Velma as Laney crouched to reach for her sister.

"Come here, baby." Laney gently eased Kimmy from the folds of fallen clothing and helped her to her feet. "That's it. I'm here now, sweetie."

Kimmy slowly got to her feet and folded into Laney's arms, still sobbing as Laney turned a dangerous look on Velma, who was already protesting.

"I swear, Laney, I had no idea she was in there. I'll write up a report and find out what happened."

"Write whatever you want. I don't give a fat rat's. She's not staying here a second longer."

And with her arm protectively around her sister, Laney ushered her disabled sister out, leaving Velma with both hands clapped to her mouth, and staring after them.

CHAPTER TWO
DAY ONE—8:17 PM—LANEY

It took them twenty minutes to get to the rundown two-family house on East 86th Street she'd been sharing with Jody Gaskill, until Jody moved out. Might have been helpful if Jody had told Laney she was leaving—or that the rent was six weeks overdue. But no, despite having paid up half the rent like they agreed, Laney had gotten home one day to find all Jody's belongings gone, the front door lock busted off, a pile of eviction notices amongst the crap all over the floor.

Not that that was any great surprise. Jody had never been what you'd call reliable. Her idea of dealing with a problem was taking off before it blew up in her face. She'd made her way through life writing bad checks, stealing anything that wasn't nailed down, then blaming someone else for all her troubles. Which was why she wound up in Carringway Women's Prison with Laney. But she'd given Laney a roof over her head when she needed it, so it wasn't like Laney was in any position to complain, was it?

Laney slowed, checking the street back and forth, then pulled into the gravel driveway and cut the engine. While Kimmy stared straight ahead at the house, Laney reached back for her jacket, then turned to Kimmy.

"So, this is my place, okay? It's only for a couple of nights. Just till I get some things worked out, okay?"

"Go home?" Kimmy asked her in a teensy voice.

She turned to follow Kimmy's gaze across the two broken front windows that were boarded up and the busted-up railing on the porch, the leaky down-pipe that had broken away from the side of the house and gushed water out across the scrappy lawn where it collected in pools and ran to the gutter. "Yeah, I know. It's not exactly a palace, but it's dry, and there's a warm bed. And it's not for long, okay? You'll be safe here."

Sitting there waiting for the reaction, Laney was suddenly struck by just how alike they were: Kimmy with that same mousey brown hair—although you wouldn't know it since Laney had dyed her jet black for the past six years—those same high cheekbones, the almond-shaped green eyes. Would Kimmy have been smarter than Laney if she hadn't gone head-first into that empty swimming pool all those years ago? Would she have grown up and made more of herself than Laney ever had?

Laney snapped herself back to the present. She couldn't go there. Not now. So, she undid her seatbelt and gave Kimmy a reassuring smile as she opened the car door.

"C'mon, let's go in before we both end up with pneumonia."

After getting out, Laney checked the street each way—no sign of David Whitcliff, the douche-bag manager out there at Sunny Springs. This was bound to be the first place he'd look.

That didn't matter. What was he going to do? Bust down the door? Drag Kimmy back without any explanation of how she got those bruises all over her?

Like hell.

She rounded the car and opened Kimmy's door, and squeezed her eyes heavenward at the thunderclouds overhead. Cleveland rain. That's all she needed now.

"C'mon, babes. There's only a few steps we gotta get up. Then we'll get you in some clean clothes, a hot drink, and some food. I think I've still got some casserole left I can heat up."

Kimmy sat rigid in the car, fists clenched, then threw back her head, keening like a frightened child as the first drops fell. Huge and fat, they splattered on the car and popped as they hit Laney's scalp and cut tiny trails through her hair.

"Come on, sweetie. You're gonna have to help me here. I can't carry you." Laney hunched her shoulders against the worsening weather as she unlatched the seatbelt and tried to turn Kimmy.

"Come on, I'm getting wet here," she growled, then cursed herself for getting frustrated. What was the point in getting mad at her? That would only make matters worse.

Tentatively, Kimmy slowly twisted towards her, setting one sneakered foot to the ground, then the other as she leaned out and scowled accusingly up into rain. Laney eased her to the edge of the seat, then dropped to circle an arm around Kimmy's waist. When she felt Kimmy lift, she eased her up, closed the door, then hugged her close as they made her way across to the stairs. By the time they made it to the top step, the heavens had opened and they were both dripping wet.

"Wait just a second while I get the door." She released Kimmy and raked her dripping hair back from her face while she dug in her back pocket for her house key. As she inserted it in the lock and twisted it open, she turned to find Kimmy with the front of her thin gray sweater pressed to her mouth as she cast a beseeching look out across the street.

"Wendy?" she whimpered.

Laney felt that old familiar ache of failure as she followed her gaze out across the dismal surroundings. "Yeah, I don't know where Wendy is right now. Let's get inside out of the rain. Then I'll call her up and find out what's going on, okay?" Looping her arm around her sister again, Laney eased her to the doorway.

Just before entering, Kimmy stopped to turn a searching look back out into the street. Laney gave her a little squeeze, urging her on, and Kimmy moved again. She guided Kimmy through the tiny living room to the battered sofa, brushing aside newspapers and the laundry she'd been folding to clear a space for her to sit.

Kimmy gingerly perched on the edge of the seat, running a scornful gaze around the room then back up at Laney. "Wendy?"

"Don't worry, I'm gonna find her. See if she knows what the hell happened back there." Laney took out her phone and found the number Wendy had once texted her on.

"Wendy?" Kimmy asked with aching hope.

"Yeah, I heard you. I'm doing my best here, okay?" She hit the key, then turned away, running her frozen fingers through her hair as she waited for the line to open. What came back were the three familiar tones, followed by a message that the number was no longer in service.

"Super," she said, and hung up.

Kimmy stared up at her, brow furrowed into an accusing look.

"I tried. It's the wrong number, okay? But I'll find it."

No response. Just that same despairing gaze.

"How about I get you something to eat, huh?"

Out of nowhere, Kimmy's face crumpled, breaths sputtering between pursed lips. Tears welled and burst and raced down her cheeks. Then a tiny, brokenhearted squeak. "Wendy."

Laney let out a long, weary sigh. "I don't know where she is. I just tried to call her, didn't I?"

Devastated, Kimmy folded over with her fists clenched at her mouth, rocking back and forth and keening.

How many times had Laney seen this? One wrong word, one mistaken look, and Kimmy would become inconsolable. She'd rock and wail like she'd been physically wounded. Took ages to calm her down.

Exhausted, confused, Laney tossed a look upward, then took a screwed-up tissue from her back pocket, dropped to a crouch in front of her sister. Using one finger crooked under Kimmy's chin, she gently lifted her sister's face towards her and dabbed away the tears.

"Hey, what's all this about, huh? I thought you'd be happy to come stay with me. Huh?"

Kimmy held her breath, a moment, then pulled her face away, lower lip jutting, chin crumpled. So Laney sighed deeply and took her sister's hands in hers. Holding them close to her heart, she tipped her head to catch Kimmy's attention. "So, listen, babes. Are you listening?"

Kimmy took a hiccupping breath but kept her eyes pointedly averted.

"I really need you to look at me, babes. Turn this way." Laney angled her head a little more and this time caught Kimmy's attention.

"Listen, I know I'm a crappy sister. I shouldn't have left you in that place so long. But that's over now. I'm out, and I'm not going back. From now on, I'm gonna take care of you again. Like I used to. Only better this time," she conceded a little guiltily. "And this time it'll work out. I promise you."

When Kimmy turned a woeful expression on her, Laney squeezed her hands.

"How about we get you out of those wet clothes, into something dry?"

In the absence of a response, Kimmy tugged a clenched fist from Laney's grasp and held it up, like a kid playing a guessing game.

A little surprised, Laney blinked at her. "What's this? You got something here?"

She folded her hand around Kimmy's, cupping it gently as she watched those long fingers unfurl to reveal a tiny scrap of paper crumpled in the center of her palm.

Laney looked up, frowning as she gently took the note.

"What's this, babe? Is this for me?"

Kimmy held her gaze, the intensity like an electrical charge as Laney teased out the crumpled note, pressing out the creases with her thumbs, flattening it.

The script was immediately recognizable as Wendy's, those back-sloping letters, the loops and whorls. Laney stared at it for some seconds, shocked at the three words written there. They simply read:

Please find me!

CHAPTER THREE
DAY ONE—8:17 PM—ELIZABETH

Elizabeth had foolishly worn the four-inch heels to match her chiffon dress. She'd been standing in them, moving from foot to foot, watching the guests slowly circulating around the room. Anyone could see they hadn't come to see her. They were seeking out whoever they could corner to cut deals with, or lobby for support, or negotiate with for the sharpest investment details. All of them fully engaged with each other. None of them was even talking to her. Now her feet were killing her.

Just off to her left, Greg Peterson, the chairman of her father-in-law's board of directors, had just emerged from a tête-à-tête with a suave-looking young man in a suit. Some tough negotiations going down, if the look on Greg's face was anything to go by.

Elizabeth tipped her glass as he approached. "Greg, nice seeing you again. Still on the clock, I see." She nodded, indicating the young man behind him with her glass.

"Say what?" He glanced back, as if he didn't know. "Oh, that." Again, that dimpled grin. The guy thought he was God's gift. "I should thank you for inviting me to a great party, Elizabeth. I have some solid investment opportunities coming up so running into Jim there was a real stroke of luck." He turned and scanned the room behind him. "Looks like you've got anyone who's anyone here."

"Yes. And you can thank my PA, Penny Rickman, for that," Elizabeth told him with a cool smile.

He turned back to her and nodded toward the champagne flute in her hand. "You still on the candy water? Or have you succumbed to a real drink?" He gave her a conspiratorial flick of the eyebrows.

"Still the good old lemon-lime and bitters. Nice and sharp. Just the way I like it," she replied, widening the fake smile as she raised her glass. "It brings out the best in me."

"If you can't join 'em, fool 'em, huh?" He chuckled at his own joke and touched her briefly on the arm. "Will you excuse me, Elizabeth? I see Charles is free and I need to talk to him about some upcoming business opportunities. Good seeing you." And without waiting for a reply, he turned and cut his way through the crowd toward Elizabeth's father-in-law.

"And thanks for all the happy birthday wishes," she said sourly, toasting his departure.

"You having a great time?" a voice said behind her.

Elizabeth turned to find Penny Rickman, her PA, cutting through the crowds behind her.

Penny beamed around. "Great turnout, huh?" she said and took a swig from her glass.

Elizabeth ran a bilious eye over the crowd. "Yeah, great."

"You don't sound like you think it's great. You sound put out."

"Do I?"

"Yeah. I would have thought you'd be thrilled someone put on a birthday party like this for you."

Elizabeth narrowed a stare at her. "Oh yeah, I'm thrilled. And when I find out who that someone was, I'll kick her thoughtful butt into the middle of next week for arranging my fifty-second birthday party three months early, *and* calling it my fiftieth."

Penny's shoulders dropped. "It isn't *three months* early. It's only a few weeks early. And bear in mind that *that thoughtful person* had to send out invitations three months ago to get every eligible bachelor worth a damn in this town into the same room at the same time. And who says they have to know your age to the day? So quit pouting and enjoy yourself."

Elizabeth drained the glass and placed it on the tray of a passing waiter.

"And did *that thoughtful person* think to invite anyone I actually care about? Like Stacy and Bear? Or Nancy? Or Diana? Hm?"

"Oh, c'mon. Stacy and Bear are home with a kid. And what do you want a reporter here for?"

"Diana happens to be a friend. Or didn't it occur to you to invite friends?"

"Holy crow, next thing you'll be telling me I should have invited Delaney."

Elizabeth arched one brow.

Penny's shoulder's dropped. "You're kidding, right? He's a cop, for cryin' out loud. You don't need that kind of guy in your life. You need to spread your social net. Find guys who hang in the same social circles." When all Penny got back was a narrow-eyed look, she grabbed Elizabeth's elbow, and wheeled her around. "Come on, let's get you out there meeting people before you completely ice over."

Guiding her through close-packed groups of what looked like Cleveland's social upper echelons, Penny nodded and called out greetings. After a few "Hellos" and "Great party" comments from those they passed, they came to four couples who were clearly in serious discussion.

"Excuse me," Penny butted in, causing them all to look around.

A gap widened in the circle and Tyrone Chesterton raised his glass to her.

"Happy birthday, Mrs. McClaine."

Tyrone was the youngest son of a couple who were once Elizabeth's and her ex-husband's closest friends. After the Chestertons, Tyrone was probably the last person she'd have invited to her party.

Elizabeth tipped her head and smiled. "Thank you, Tyrone. Nice to see you here."

"Great party," he said, grinning. "I just hope I look half as good as you when I get to your age."

Elizabeth widened a forced smile on him. "And I hope you get to live that long," she replied before Penny wrenched her away.

"Quit being so snotty. It's a party, for cryin' out loud."

As the circle closed behind them, Elizabeth glanced back at Tyrone. "Who invited that twerp?"

"His folks…who are looking right this way," Penny replied with fake joviality through clenched teeth, while offering a flutter-wave at the couple now shuffling uncomfortably on the spot and nodding their way.

"Oh, terrific. And just when I didn't think it could get worse," Elizabeth groaned.

"Shut up and try and look like you're having fun. I've got tons of guys for you to meet." Penny tightened her grip on Elizabeth's elbow to the point where it was almost painful, then dragged her between circles of suits deep in discussion.

"Grant," Penny cried out, hand extended as they closed in on several older businessmen standing in a loose semi-circle, each of whom was scanning the room like barracudas watching the stray minnows.

But at least Elizabeth knew these people. She turned her head, offering her cheek to Grant Alders, who leaned forward to brush a quick kiss on it.

"Elizabeth, you're looking lovely," Grant said with a smile. Grant was in his early sixties, wealthy and intelligent. He had been Elizabeth's family's legal counsel for as long as she could remember.

"Lovely to see you again," Grant's mousey wife Marjorie piped up from where she clung to him, both arms looped around his like a human bracelet.

"I couldn't agree more," said Judge Roth, who also leaned in to touch his cheek to hers. A close family friend of the McClaines, he'd presided over many a court case regarding building permissions. The fact that Charles McClaine's construction conglomeration was more often than not the successful defendant wasn't lost on her. How anyone could see him as impartial was a mystery. But that was life in the upper reaches of the Cleveland social circles. Everyone knew everyone else. And your case was only ever as good as your legal counsel and your social connections.

Kyle Hendry, Charles's trusted VP of Finance, also leaned in to give her a peck on the cheek. "Happy birthday, Elizabeth. You don't have a glass."

"I've just finished one. But thank you for noticing," she replied. "By the way, who's the guy talking with Greg Peterson?"

Kyle ducked this way and that, searching through the crowds, then smiled. "I'm sorry, I didn't see."

"No matter," she said flatly, then searched her immediate surroundings, looking for a way to extricate herself from the group.

"Phone call for you, Mrs. McClaine." The voice came from just behind her—one of the concierges.

Grateful for the interruption, she said, "Thank you, I'll take it out in the lobby. Will you gentlemen excuse me, please?" And she peeled away.

"Damn nerve calling this hour," Penny grumbled as she cut through the crowd, trailing Elizabeth to the door. "Why can't they let you at least have your birthday party in peace?"

Elizabeth closed the door to shut out the noise and put the phone to her ear. "Elizabeth McClaine."

On the other end of the phone was a young woman—she sounded distraught.

"Mrs. McClaine, it's Caroline Judemire over at Sunny Springs. I don't know if you remember me—I'm one of the nurse aids. I'm sorry to call you this time of night, but I didn't know who else to talk to."

Sunny Springs—of course Elizabeth knew the place. It was an enormous group housing project for the disabled that Aden Falls Corporation had built based on the principle of elder care retirement villages. In theory, the project seemed like a good idea, but those who had fought for community living for the disabled had vehemently opposed it, citing a return to the institutional living for the disabled they'd just gotten rid of. As one of the key critics, Elizabeth had been one of the most vocal.

She glanced back at Penny, who frowned and mouthed, *Who is it?*

"Yes, Caroline, of course I remember you. What can I do for you?"

"I'm one of the caregivers here…well, for Kimmy Donohue. I think you know Kimmy."

"Of course I know Kimmy. My foundation supports her temporary accommodation at Sunny Springs."

"That's what I heard. Which is why I'm calling you. So, anyway, you already know she's high-needs and her communication is really limited. Anyway, her sister came to visit today. We've had trouble with her before because the last time she came, she took Kimmy out and never came home all weekend. We were worried sick."

Elizabeth frowned, wondering where this was going. "I can imagine."

"Who is it?" Penny whispered. Elizabeth gave her a quick head-shake and turned away while Caroline went on.

"Yeah, so Laney—that's the sister—she came to visit Kimmy unexpectedly tonight, and she took Kimmy. Now we don't know where they are!"

"She took her off the grounds? Without permission?"

Penny stepped around to hiss up at her. "Who's taken who? What's happened?"

"That's right," Caroline said. "I'm so worried and I didn't know what else to do. I know I shouldn't have called, but I had to do something."

"What's David Whitcliff, the residential manager, doing about it?"

"Well, that's the thing. He told us we're not to tell anyone or go to the police or anything."

"Do you know why?"

"I have no idea."

"Is David there?"

"He's been out looking for them. The charge nurse just told me he's on his way back but from what she was saying, he hasn't got Kimmy with him."

Elizabeth checked her watch. "When he gets back, tell him I'm coming over and I'll be in his office in…" She checked her watch again. "Twenty-five minutes."

Penny's mouth dropped open. "Whose office? When?"

"Please don't tell him I told you," Caroline said. "I'll get in so much trouble. I just didn't know what else to do."

"Don't worry, I'm leaving now. I'll call him from my car."

"Thank you so much," she said, and hung up.

"My coat and purse, please," Elizabeth asked the concierge.

Penny grabbed her arm and tugged her around. "You cannot leave this party. I forbid you to go."

"Penny, I appreciate everything you've done here…"

"Do you? I mean, *do you?*"

Elizabeth considered it with a tip of the head. "Okay, I appreciate the thought. But sweetie, you're my PA, not my mother. And I'm sorry, but I'm leaving now. If you want to do something for me, call Katie, tell her I'll be late home."

Penny pointed back to the ballroom. "What about the guests? We haven't even cut the cake."

"Tell them to save me some." Elizabeth reached across, took her coat, then her purse, from the concierge. "That's if they remember I was here."

She swung the coat around her shoulders and headed for the front door.

CHAPTER FOUR
DAY ONE—8:45 PM—LANEY

Please find me.

Why? Had Wendy seen what had happened to Kimmy? So, why didn't she just call her? Why write her a note? Or had she gotten herself into some kind of trouble that had prevented her doing so?

Ever since she'd been assigned as Kimmy's main nurse aid, she'd been the only one Laney could trust. From the handwritten reports she'd regularly sent Laney, she'd treated Kimmy like family. She'd stayed late to care for Kimmy when she was sick; brought her books and treats. She'd been there when Laney couldn't. So, if Wendy had gotten herself into something she couldn't get out of, and had no one else to go to, then Laney would step up to the plate. Like family would.

After cruising the street for a few minutes, Laney found a parking space in front of the rundown apartment building that, as far as she knew, was the last known residence of Pinky McCorline.

Laney had met Pinky eight months earlier. Pinky was soon to be paroled from Carringway Women's Prison about the same time Laney was coming in. When they found themselves both stuck at the same future employment planning session, Pinky had told Laney how she'd gotten a job. Didn't pay much but that didn't matter, she'd told her. All she had to do was *take care of a bunch of retards*, as she'd put it, until Laney backed her up against the wall half an hour later, smacking her against the cinder blocks with such force it had made Pinky's eyes roll back. Then she'd set her straight, telling her that, as a matter of fact, Laney's sister was one of those so-called *retards*, and putting it in such a way that Pinky had undergone a rapid shift in attitude and told Laney not to worry about her sister, that she'd look out for her.

And while Laney wouldn't normally ask Pinky to "look out" for her worst enemy, choice wasn't something she had. As it happened, a month later, Pinky was fired for a little misappropriation of certain pharmaceuticals from the meds cabinet. Turned out, she managed to escape another six months in Carringway due to a technicality. But by then Wendy had come along, so Laney didn't need to rely on her any more.

Despite the two women having worked together only a short while, Laney was hoping Pinky might know where Wendy might have gone.

From down here she could see all the third-floor windows were in total darkness. That didn't bode well. And even if the elevator was working, what was the point in dragging Kimmy all the way up there? Especially just to find Pinky wasn't even home.

She checked the street front and back, then turned to Kimmy.

"I need to go upstairs and see my friend Pinky, okay? You remember her?"

Kimmy tensed up, threatening to pitch another fit, so Laney added, "Okay, that's fine. You don't have to see her. I just have to ask her if she knows where Wendy lives, and then I'll be right out again. It won't take more than a minute. So I need you to stay here while I do that. Is that okay?"

Kimmy said nothing—just scowled at her with her mouth bunched in a knot.

Laney yanked the keys from the ignition. "Yeah, well, I don't have much of a choice right now. By the time I got you out of the car and across the street, I coulda got up there and back again. Now, I won't be long. I'll just be upstairs there a minute," she said, pointing. "Then we'll go find Wendy."

Ignoring the reproachful scowl on her sister's face, Laney got out and locked the car door. A quick tap on the window to get Kimmy's attention. Then with a reassuring smile, a quick wave, she ducked her head against the rain, and stuck her hands in her pockets. As soon as there was a break in the traffic, Laney shrugged her shoulders against the weather and hurried straight across to the street level entrance, where she pushed her way into the narrow ground-floor lobby to find the elevator out of order.

"See?" she said, flipping a hand at the tape across the doors, as if Kimmy could hear her. "Out of order. What did I tell you?"

Laney knew this neighborhood. It wasn't the kind of place you hung around on your own. Stick around on the street for any length of time, chances were good you'd wind up losing a kidney. Or get shot. Maybe both. So, after taking a second to check that she could still see Kimmy sitting there in the car out front, she pulled open the door leading to the stairs and hurried up to the third-floor landing.

Panting after the exertion of climbing the stairs, she peered through the grimy glass panel in the third-floor door. No one in sight. So she pushed the door open and stepped through. Overhead, the flickering lights showed the dingy hallway carpeting, scuffed by years of use, and sickly green paint on the walls, graffiti scrawled along its length. Checking the hallway back and forth, she hurried in the direction of apartment 3F where Pinky lived, counting off the battered apartment doors as she went. When she got to Pinky's place, she paused, checked the hallway again, then knocked.

When there was no response, she put her ear to the door. No sound from inside. So she tried the handle. It turned. Cautiously, she pushed the door open and peeked inside. Flashes from the TV lit up the room like a mini indoor storm.

"Anyone there? Pinky, you home?"

There was a leap of movement from the sofa and Pinky jumped up, headphones clamped over her ears, straight black hair with a shock of pink bangs over her eyes, hand on her heart.

"Holy shit," she said, leaping up and ripping the headphones off. "You scared the crap outta me."

"I'm sorry." Laney motioned back. "The door was open."

"Oh man, that lock sucks." Pinky pushed past Laney and went straight to the door. After peering out, she closed it, slamming her shoulder into it until it clicked.

"Jeez, you could have given me a heart attack sneaking in like that." She ambled back to the sofa, flopped down again, and pointed the remote at the TV to pause the movie. "I only heard you because the last zombie just got wasted."

"I'm sorry," Laney said, wandering over, nodding around and wondering why she herself had been living in squalor for so long. "Nice place."

While dingy, the apartment was tidy. A coffee table showing ring stains on the surface sat perched in front of a worn sofa over which a crocheted throw had been carefully laid. The TV she'd been watching was angled into the corner, an overflowing magazine rack next to it. Pinky was no angel, but she'd obviously made the effort to put down some roots, make the place into a home. Which was more than could be said for Jody.

Pinky drew her feet up and wrapped her arms around her knees. "So, what are you doing here? I didn't know you got out yet."

Laney jammed her hands in her pockets. "Yeah, a few weeks back."

"Huh, nobody told me." It came out like an accusation. Like Laney should have looked her up the minute she got out. "So, where are you living now?"

"Ah, I ended up staying with Jody over on East 86th. Place is a dump. Then Jody ran out on me. Left me with six weeks rent owing."

Pinky rocked forward and chuckled. "Holy shit. You shoulda known not to trust her. Not after she stole Valerie Spackmire's Fitbit that time, and tried to blame Julie Hester."

Laney couldn't help but smile at the memory. She could still see the prison officer holding the Fitbit up and Jody pointing directly to Julie—not a word said. "Yeah, I shoulda known. Julie bounced her off every wall of her cell two nights later. Ended up with a busted nose and five stitches across her eyebrow."

"She'll never have to pluck that eyebrow again, huh?" Pinky chuckled. "Julie's motto was: 'If you can't fight clean, fight dirty. Go straight for the eyes.'"

"Yep." Laney grinned wider, then looked away and drew a breath. She let the grin drop and turned back, serious now. "Listen, I'm just wondering if you know where that Wendy chick lives? You know, the one from Sunny Springs."

"You mean the one that looked after Kimmy? The foreign one?"

"She was foreign?"

"Oh, yeah, you never got to meet her, did you?"

"Wendy worked the day shift. Only time I got to see Kimmy was at night. That's *if* they let me see her."

"Well, after that shit you pulled, are you surprised?"

"Jeez, I took Kimmy out for *one* day. Got back at six. You'da thought I'd murdered someone."

Pinky sniggered. "You shoulda seen David Whitcliff's face. Man, he was pissed."

"Yeah, I got that, too. So," said Laney, directing the conversation back to where she'd started. "What do you know about this Wendy chick?"

Pinky raised one shoulder. "She was nice…well, way nicer than most of them there. Oh, and hey," she said, wiggling excitedly in her seat and patting the spot on the sofa next to her. "Did you hear who else is working there?"

Laney remained standing. "No. Who?"

"Kiddy Leishman—you know Kiddy? She was in B-block. Well, guess what: she's the cleaner over there now. How about that?"

Laney's head jerked forward and her mouth dropped open. "Kiddy Leishman works there now? What the hell is wrong with those people? They want a whole staff of ex-cons?"

"Don't knock it," Pinky said, sounding a little offended. "We're cheap. We do a good job." When she noticed Laney's eyebrows go up, she added, "Okay, so sometimes we're not so honest. But we're *cheap*. What do they expect?"

"No wonder the place sucks," Laney muttered.

"So anyway, like I was saying, Kiddy calls me up, tells me some fancy guy drives in in a totally cool car, and asks for Wendy."

Laney frowned, a little confused now. "He asked Kiddy?"

Pinky rolled her eyes. "No, she got this from Dorothy, the old lady who does the afternoon shift. So anyway, she told Kiddy—who told me—that this guy is, like, sex on a plate. Like he's got this tight little butt you could totally…"

"Hold on. Does this guy have anything to do with where Wendy is?"

"Keep your pants on, I'm getting to it. So anyway, this guy's wearing an Armani suit and expensive Italian shoes—'cause Dorothy knows about this shit, 'cause she used to work in some fancy menswear store, right? And he's got, like, this little yellow diamond ring on his pinky finger that must be worth, like, some serious moolah. So, anyway, he comes in and asks Dorothy—he says, 'Excuse me,' in this voice that's like, *sexy as shit*, and he says, 'Can you point me to where a lady named Wendy is?'" Pinky's eyebrows went up as she gave a deep nod, ensuring Laney was following the story. "Right?"

"Yeah, so then what happened?"

Pinky shrugged deeply. "He went and got her and she left with him."

"Who?"

"Geez, keep up, will you? *Wendy.* Who else am I talking about? She left with Mr. Armani, right? So, anyway, Dorothy—that's the old lady—she said she didn't look too happy about it—Wendy, that is. She looked like she was going to cry. But Mr. Armani told Velma—"

"—that sour-faced bitch," Laney put in.

"Oh man, isn't she, though? When she accused me of stealin' stuff, I said, 'You know what, lady?' I said—"

Laney could see this going right off on a tangent. Suddenly aware she'd left Kimmy in the car way longer than she'd intended, she cut Pinky off, saying, "So, where'd he take her? This Armani suit, diamond-ring guy— where'd he take Wendy?"

Pinky looked a little crestfallen that the gossip session had ended so abruptly.

"Oh. She didn't say. Just said she was going back to her old job."

Laney huffed. "So, you don't know where she lives?"

A deep shrug. "If I did, I woulda told you, wouldn't I?"

Downstairs Laney exited the side door of the building and waited to cross the street. However, as she stepped out, she squinted through the rain to find the car was in darkness—no silhouette of Kimmy sitting in the front. Ignoring the traffic, she raced across without even looking, and circled around the back of the car. The passenger's door stood open, no sign of Kimmy.

Laney checked the front, the back, even the trunk. Nothing. She stood on the sidewalk in the pouring rain with her mouth agape and her heart pounding, searching the empty street.

"Oh, Kimmy, where the hell have you gone?"

Laney ran down the street splashing through puddles, searching alleyways and side streets, frozen rain lashing at her face and blurring her vision. Rivulets of water snaked over her scalp forming trails that dripped down her cheeks and off her chin. Laney barely noticed. There was no sign of Kimmy.

Two blocks from the car, panic flared hot in her chest. Surely Kimmy couldn't have come this far. So she turned, retracing her steps and heading off in the opposite direction, hands cupped to her mouth, screaming over the passing traffic that splashed by.

"Kimmy!"

On the edge of despair now, she stopped in the middle of an empty side street, turned full circle, and shouted again. Down here all she could hear was the distant hum of traffic and the sound of her own voice echoing off the abandoned buildings, boarded-up windows, and crumbling entranceways that surrounded her. Dread tightened in her throat.

How far could she have gotten? What if she'd wandered off down one of the streets Laney hadn't checked?

But which one?

What if she never found her? What if someone else did…?

No, she couldn't let herself even think that.

In desperation, she crossed into a joining street. Right at the very end, she spotted a distant light and heard the thump of music. If Kimmy had come this far, maybe she'd seen the lights. Maybe she'd been lured by the music.

Laney's heart rate kicked up a notch. Hope and fear bloomed simultaneously as she trotted down towards it, determinedly ignoring the worsening condition of the neighboring buildings. This wasn't a part of town to get lost in at any time of day. For someone with Kimmy's challenges, it was a death wish.

When she got to the place, she stood back, looking it over. Four beaten-up cars were parked in front, two across the street. The place was two stories high, front windows replaced by sheets of graffiti-strewn plywood, the entrance spray-painted with the words *No Entrance* and a swastika.

Laney hesitated. The adrenaline coursing in her veins told her to run. Every nerve screamed that she was walking into a death trap.

But if Kimmy was in there, what choice did she have? So she stepped across the broken bottles and busted-up garbage bags lined up at the front door, wiped her hands on her jeans, and with her upper teeth sunk into her lower lip, she knocked. Inside the music was so loud she figured no one would have heard. So she pounded on the door with the side of her fist and kept pounding until the door opened.

The guy looked in his late twenties, thickset, neck like a bulldog, tattoos up and down his arms. Behind him, lights flashed and raucous laughter and hoots filled the room.

"What do you want?" he yelled over the music.

"I'm looking for my sister. She's about my height, mousy brown hair, gray sweat pants, and a sweater with a kitten motif on it. You know if she came by here?"

He stepped outside and closed the door, shutting the noise inside while he inspected the deserted street.

"How old is she?"

"She's eighteen." Laney folded her arms and kept her distance, wondering just how much she should tell him. Wondering if she'd made a mistake coming here. "She's disabled," she said. But seeing the dubious look on his face, she tipped her head in concession, adding, "Well, not physically disabled. Obviously."

"And she came this way?"

She turned to follow his gaze up the street. "I don't know. I left her in the car just for a second and when I got back she was gone."

"Why did you leave her in the car?" The tone was one of bewilderment coupled with blame.

Breaking eye contact, Laney hugged herself a little tighter, cursing herself and wondering the same thing.

"I just need to find her. You didn't see her, that's fine."

He hesitated a second, then shrugged. "I didn't see anyone. Hope you find her soon."

But what if he was lying? What if they had seen her?

As he turned back for the door, she called, "You sure she didn't come by here? Maybe come inside?"

For a second she thought he was going to come back, maybe hit her. She took a step back, waiting. But he glared at her a second, then opened the door, and yelled, "Hey! Turn the music down." Twice he yelled for the music to be turned down, and when it died, he called, "Anyone seen a disabled girl, maybe five feet three, mousy hair? Long or short?" he asked Laney.

"Um, cut in a bob. To her shoulders. And she's wearing sweats," she called over his shoulder.

A general mumble came back, then a guy with dreadlocks and the glassy-eyed look of a long-time drug user came to the door. "I seen a girl. About ten minutes ago. Walking that way." He pointed. "I asked her if she wanted to come party, but she said something about some chick and just kept walking."

"Wendy?"

A salacious grin widened on his mouth. He leaned against the door and looked her up and down. "Yeah, maybe."

"Which way did she go?"

"You wanna come in? Have some fun?" He jerked his head back, indicating the noise behind him.

"Yeah, maybe another time," she said in a deadpan tone. "So, which way did she go?"

He pointed, snorting like she'd made a bad choice.

Laney barely noticed. She was already moving, running in the direction he'd indicated.

With her heart thudding in her chest, she ran to the corner, and stopped. Four streets intersected, north, east, west, and the one she was on. Derelict buildings in each direction. Broken glass, boarded-up windows. Only two streetlights. She walked a few steps, then turned on the spot and shouted, "Kimmy! Where are you, dammit?"

At least in this weather the druggies and the weirdos and the mentally disturbed were probably inside, staying out of the rain. Or at the party back there. That was one small mercy. At least that's what she told herself.

Pausing only to check alleyways and boarded-up building frontages, she pressed on with her heart frozen in fear.

Then she heard it. If the rain hadn't let up, she might have missed it. A whimper. Maybe ten yards down the street. She moved cautiously down the darkened street, past dumpsters, past stacks of collapsed cardboard boxes and shapes that might have been people, ducking and peeking between.

"Kimmy!"

Then she heard it again. She slipped her phone from her jeans pocket, switched on the light, shone it into what looked like a black hole between two abandoned buildings. And there she was—dirty, saturated, hair plastered to her face, Kimmy sat huddled in a corner, head down on her knees, sobbing.

Laney moved towards her, one eye watching for movement from the shadows.

"Hey, babes, what are you doing down here?"

When she crouched in front of her, Kimmy looked up. Laney had never seen her so forlorn.

Her mouth was drawn down at the corners. "Wendy?"

Laney felt her heart seize up. She reached out, stroked a saturated strand back from her sister's face. "I'm gonna find Wendy, okay? But I can't do this with you. I'm sorry."

Kimmy smeared away the trail under her nose with the back of her hand and sniffed. Even in the gloom of this dingy alley, Laney could see her face light up. She scrambled to her feet, took Laney's hand in both of hers and tugged her towards the mouth of the alleyway. "Wendy."

Back at the car, Laney picked up her phone. She found the number for Sunny Springs and cleared her throat. As soon as the call picked up and a voice announced that she'd reached Sunny Springs, Laney lowered her voice to a terrible disguise, and said, "May I speak to Wendy, please?"

As she waited for the woman at the other end of the line to check the number, Kimmy's eyes stayed riveted on her.

"I'm sorry, ma'am, Wendy left our employment today. Can someone else help you?"

"Ah, I see. This is her credit card facility calling. Do you have a forwarding address for the woman in question?" she asked, rolling her eyes and wondering how bad it really sounded.

"I'm afraid not, ma'am. Is there anyone else I can put you through to?"

"No, it's fine. Can you tell me her other name?"

"You don't have that information?"

"Uh, no. I don't."

"I'm afraid that's confidential. Is there anything else I can help you with?

Irritated, she dropped the snooty accent, Laney said, "You haven't actually helped me with anything now."

"Then I'm sorry," came the reply, and the line clicked dead.

Laney hung up with a feeling of dread solidifying in her chest.

Why was Wendy fired? Was she the one who'd hurt Kimmy?

Only one way to find out. She hit redial again, scrolled through until she found the last known number for Kiddy Leishman, hit the little phone icon. If anyone knew what was going on in that place, it would be Kiddy. An empty ring tone sounded down the phone. It rang five times, then beeped to indicate messaging. Annoyed, frustrated, she hung up, suddenly aware of the silence emanating from Kimmy, aware that the smile had evaporated. Sure enough, her sister was watching her, mouth dropping at the corners, brow forming a peak on her forehead.

Oh please, not again.

Laney drew a deep breath. "Babe, she's not there. I'm sorry."

Kimmy sucked in a ragged breath and shrank back in anguish. Any minute now, she'd go hyper. Laney gently placed a hand on her shoulder.

"No, wait, wait. Wendy's probably gone home. I'll find her, okay? You trust me?"

A single tear broke and ran down Kimmy's cheek. Her lip quivered but at least she was listening.

"Okay, so that's the plan, right? But I can't leave you in the car, can I? So, first up we gotta get you in some dry clothes. Then we're going to someone's house. She can take care of you while I go find Wendy, okay?"

Kimmy reached for her, long fingers gripping her arm. "Come?"

"No, you can't come with me. You might run off again. And then what'll I do?" Smiling, she tucked a strand of Kimmy's hair back and felt the grip loosen.

"Wendy?"

"Yes. I'll find Wendy, okay? Wherever she is, whatever trouble she's gotten into, I promise I'll find her." Laney started up the car. "And boy, she better have a good explanation for all this."

CHAPTER SIX
DAY ONE—11:54 PM—ELIZABETH

From the street, the Sunny Springs Residential Care Facility might have been mistaken for just another private hospital. That was no coincidence. The construction conglomerate, Aden Falls Life Care, had built the place on the blueprint of their other elder care hospital and nursing homes.

"A safe and peaceful environment for your disabled love ones," the blurb had read.

Which might have sounded good. But Elizabeth had been one of the loudest opponents of the scheme. She'd lobbied hard and used what influence she could to halt the project. After all, wasn't shuffling the disabled out of the community and into institutions what they'd fought to abolish only a few years before?

Consequently, she'd been aggrieved when the project had been green-lighted. She'd made her views known to anyone who'd listen—including the local media. Not that that had changed anything.

Now, driving in through the automatic gates and down between rows of beautifully tended garden beds, widened and easily accessible front doors, she wondered how David Whitcliff would remember her—the woman who almost single-handedly brought the project facility to a halt? The woman who'd publicly called him "a money-hungry miser bent on chiseling cash out of the most vulnerable in society?"

A warm welcome was the last thing she was expecting.

Lights were low in the reception area as she pulled into the visitor parking slot. The place looked closed up for the night. But as she got out of her car, the wide glass double doors that led into the front foyer slid apart and a woman appeared, arms tightly folded, peering over at her.

As Elizabeth closed her car door and walked towards her, she recognized Velma Stanford, David Whitcliff's PA—a dowdy-looking woman in plastic-rimmed eyeglasses and wearing her customary box-pleat skirt, open-neck blouse, and pale gray mohair cardigan slung around her shoulders. She held out her hand, saying:

"Mrs. McClaine, I got your message. David's in his office."

Without receiving anything further by way of greeting, Elizabeth followed her through a dimly lit reception area and on into a wide lounge set with chairs and tables in a restaurant setting to the left, sofas and coffee tables to the right.

Walking one step ahead, Velma glanced back. "We haven't seen you here in a while."

"I wish I could say the visit was strictly social. But it's not. I'm following up an incident with one of our clients—Kimmy Donohue."

A slight falter in Velma's step slowed her a fraction, as though she'd flinched at the name. "Is that so? Well, I'm sure David is doing everything in his power to address the situation."

"That's very reassuring," Elizabeth said without emotion.

"You're probably fully aware how much our organization appreciates the support your foundation offers our clients. I don't know where they'd be if they weren't here."

All lip service, if you asked Elizabeth.

"I'm sure your shareholders lie awake nights worrying about these young people," Elizabeth replied rather waspishly. It wasn't as if the corporation running Sunny Springs was doing it out of the pure goodness of their hearts. Elizabeth had seen the first-quarter profit announcements for the year. The investors weren't short of a dollar or two.

Velma pointedly ignored the comment. "This way," she said, indicating a doorway from which light spilled into the hallway. Elizabeth waited while

Velma placed one hand on the doorframe, and leaned in. "David, Mrs. McClaine's here."

"Fine. Send her in." David Whitcliff's voice. Elizabeth recognized it immediately and felt her hackles involuntarily rise.

Velma stepped back gesturing as Elizabeth entered the office to find David rising from his desk.

"Elizabeth," he said, pointedly checking his watch. "A little late for a visit, isn't it? What brings you here?"

"I'll give you two guesses, David." She hovered a moment and when David sat again, gesturing toward the chair opposite, she also sat, crossing her ankles to one side while she set her purse on the floor beside her. "I want to know what you're doing to find one of your clients who's gone missing."

David's eyebrows rose as if in surprise. "A client? From here?" he asked, pointing one finger to the desk. As if he didn't know.

Elizabeth tilted her head. "Let's cut the BS here, David. I'm talking about Kimmy Donohue. I'm told she was taken off-site by her sister. Without permission."

Seemingly abandoning any pretense of affability, he leaned on his elbows, hands clasped at his mouth. "And may I ask who told you this?"

"No, you may not. Suffice to say I was at my own birthday party where some of the most influential people in Cleveland are still clinking glasses and drinking champagne they didn't pay for."

At this, David nodded once and dropped his eyes to his desk. "I see."

She had omitted the fact that the news came via a phone call. To Elizabeth, his reaction suggested that at least one other person back in the ballroom she'd just left was in receipt of the same information. She did a quick mental checklist of guests, wondering who.

"I've also been advised the police haven't been notified. Is that correct?"

He opened his hands briefly. "That's… correct, Mrs. McClaine."

"Why not? She's a vulnerable young woman who depends on this institution for her care. You've let her down."

David leaned back, placed his pen on the desk, and crossed his arms defensively across his chest. "Mrs. McClaine, I don't consider Kimmy to be in any danger. She left the premises accompanied by her sister, and while I'm not sure of her exact whereabouts at this moment, I'm confident she'll be kept safe, and they'll both be back very soon."

Elizabeth's mouth dropped open. "How can you possibly think this is acceptable? That someone can remove a very high needs client, without permission, and what? You just expect they'll turn up when they're ready? Do you honestly think that's an appropriate course of action from a facility that's been charged with her care and safety?"

"Mrs. McClaine, forgive me, but while I appreciate that you're concerned about Kimmy, there are some extenuating circumstances I'm not at liberty to discuss with you. Now, if you don't mind—"

Feeling her cheeks flash red, Elizabeth said, "Do I need to remind you that my foundation funds this young woman? And several others in this facility?"

"No, you do not."

"So, you're saying this is the level of care we're paying for? And we should just accept that?"

David raised one palm at her. A *Stop right there* gesture. "Can we just calm down a second?"

Elizabeth sat back with her head high, mouth pressed hard, while he continued on.

"For your information, my security people are out searching for them. What do you think I am? Callous? You think I'm not worried?"

"Then why didn't you tell me that sooner? And why haven't you called the police?"

The man hunched over, briefly cupping both hands over his nose and mouth. "I can't..." he began, then took a deep breath before sitting back again.

"Look, we're doing everything we can to find her. It's only been a couple of hours, but if we don't find her by morning, I will bring in the police. Would that satisfy you?"

Elizabeth gave it a moment. "Tell me what you know about this sister of Kimmy's."

He nodded, decidedly more relaxed now.

"Laney had applied for guardianship of her sister. Unfortunately, she had no fixed address at the time. Then she was sentenced to six months in Carringway for distributing stolen items. Since it was your trust that was funding her, Kimmy came here. I thought you, of all people, would have known this."

A little shocked by the backhanded accusation but unwilling to get sidetracked, Elizabeth redirected the conversation. "How exactly did Laney just walk in here and take her? Surely you had security?"

"She arrived outside visiting hours. My admissions manager, Velma Stanford, attempted to stop her, but Velma said Laney became violent. For her own safety, Velma stood down and called security. Of course, by then it was too late. Our security cameras picked up Laney taking Kimmy to her car and driving off with her. But I'm confident she will bring her back."

"This is totally unacceptable, David. Kimmy is under the care of our foundation—"

"With all due respect, Mrs. McClaine," he interrupted. "I'm satisfied the appropriate action was taken under the circumstances, and that Laney Donohue presents no danger to her sister. Now, that's all I can tell you at the moment. It's late, and I have work to do. *If* you don't mind."

Elizabeth felt her anger subside. Shouting at him wasn't getting Kimmy back.

"So, where do you think the sister took her?"

"Last I heard was that Laney was living in some cheap apartment with another ex-con. I've asked my security go over there and check the place."

"And if they're not there? Where else would they go?"

David Whitcliff heaved out a deep, weary breath. "Mrs. McClaine, I wish I knew."

***

The Associate

12:34 AM. He had just gotten home. The party was exactly what he'd expected, all the same white-collar criminals and fraudsters posing as honorable businessmen. He knew what they got up to, what mutually beneficial arrangements they made behind closed doors, the kind of questionable deals they cut when no one was looking. In truth, they were no better than that Albanian thug whose grasp he'd fallen into.

He'd just been preparing to excuse himself and leave when he overheard that conversation coming from somewhere behind him.

He'd turned his head just a fraction, pretending to listen to Charles McClaine spouting off on some political tirade again, nodding intently, but listening in to what was being said by the woman a couple of feet to his left.

From what he could hear, Elizabeth had left the party to follow up a missing nurse aid out at Sunny Springs. Her PA had made a joke of it, but the news sent a chill down his spine. He had immediately excused himself from the group, slipped outside, and called the Man.

"She'll lift every stone," he told him. "Everything will come out."

"Do whatever you need to," the Man said and hung up.

He knew exactly what that meant. It meant he'd have to create a diversion. Like the Westrum one. That would mean contacting that woman again. The very thought of it sickened him.

But until he found a way out of this mess, what choice did he have? So he scrolled through his contacts, clicked on her name, and dialed.

She picked up on the first ring.

"Hello, stranger," she said.

CHAPTER SEVEN
DAY ONE—11:54 PM—LANEY

Laney took Kimmy back to the house and found another pair of sweat pants and a sweater. They hung loose on Kimmy's slim frame, but at least they were dry. Then she'd collected her lock picks and the thirty bucks she'd hidden under her bed, and they'd headed out.

Wendy had left Sunny Springs in a hurry. And with some man. And according to the gossip chain, it didn't sound like it had been her choice. Whoever this guy was, he was rich and Velma Stanford knew who he was. Under the current circumstances, she'd be about as likely to help Laney as she was to fly to the moon. That left Laney only one choice.

But if she had any intentions of following the plan forming in her mind right now, taking Kimmy along was out of the question. Her only option was to swallow a heap of pride, hold her temper, and keep her mouth shut. Three things she wasn't exactly known for.

She pulled the car to a halt right outside the house she'd last visited just over three years back. Not a great part of town, but not the worst. A white picket fence ran all the way across the front of the yard and around the sides. It was the only house on the street that had one. The only house that looked like the owners cared enough to mow the grass and pick up the trash regularly. It still had the same blue shutters on each side of the windows, same carefully tended gardens, same welcome plaque nailed by the front door next to the brass doorbell. Wasn't always money that made folks proud of their homes.

No lights on, Laney noted. Though that wasn't surprising, this time of night.

She crossed the street, stepped up the front stairs, and peered through the medallioned glass in the front door. No sign of life on the inside.

Please be home. Please, please be home.

The first light knock drew no response. She gave it a minute or so, then pounded on the wood panel with the side of her fist. Then she turned on the spot hugging herself while she checked the street again. Right across from her, Kimmy stared back from the front passenger's seat.

"You stay there, Missy," she mouthed, and pointed a mock threatening finger at her sister. She was reaching for the brass bell ready to shake the thing, when a light popped on inside the house and the door opened.

Janelle stood framed in the doorway, fury radiating off her like a heat wave. Wearing a shabby checked bathrobe, brassy blond hair sticking up in the front, scowl on her face, she glowered out at Laney.

"What are you doing here? You know what time it is?"

"Hey, Janelle." Laney shuffled uncomfortably and shrugged. "I was…y'know, passing by."

Janelle lifted her wrist high, squinting at her watch in the dim light of the hallway behind her. "At what, 2:30 in the morning? I don't see you for over three years and suddenly, middle of the night, you're passing by and you have to see me?"

Laney unfolded her arms and slid her hands into the back pockets of her jeans, chewing her lip while she searched for words. "Okay, so that's not exactly accurate. I wasn't just passing by."

When she looked up, Janelle had her arms folded, eyebrows arched, waiting. "Well, go on. And boy, this better be good." She angled her head as if to hear better.

"Yeah, well…um," Laney turned to check the car again, then blew out a breath under Janelle's fiery stare. "I kinda need some help. And I didn't know who else to go to," she said quickly.

Her aunt's shoulders dropped and she huffed into the air. "What did you do now?"

"I didn't do anything," Laney complained. "Why does everyone always think I've done something?"

No response. Just a callous glare.

Laney's mouth dropped open. "Oh, come *on*. That wasn't my fault. Lyall had the key. He said the guy gave him permission to take that stuff."

"Same old story, huh? Always someone else's fault. Elaine Donohue, you are nuthin' but trouble. Were from the day you was born. I don't know what your mom ever did wrong. Things you done these past five years would make her turn in her grave." She shook her head slowly.

"That's not true."

"Oh, really? So, where you been the last six months? The Caribbean? The Bahamas? Or maybe you were spending your days in sunny Honolulu, working on that white prison tan you got there, huh?"

"Geez, and you wonder why you never see me."

"Well, go on, let's have it—what do you want?"

Laney slid her hands into the front pockets of her jeans this time, sucked briefly on her upper lip.

"Okay. I, ah…" She directed her gaze over Janelle's shoulder and shrugged. "I need you to do me a favor."

"A favor, huh? At two o'clock in the morning. You got the nerve of the devil."

"I need you to take care of Kimmy for a while."

"What? When?"

"Like…now?"

Janelle's jaw dropped. "Why? Where is she? I thought she was in that fancy-shmancy care facility you stuck her in."

"I didn't stick her in there," Laney cut in sharply, then turned a glance back at the car, lowered her voice. "Anyway, she's not there anymore. She's in the car."

Janelle lifted a horrified look at the car out on the street, then shoved past Laney onto the porch. "What the hell is she doing in your car? At this time of night?" she asked, pointing angrily.

"I can explain."

Nostrils flared, Janelle stood tall, glaring down at Laney. "You better hope so."

Janelle had left Laney and Kimmy in the living room while she went upstairs. She'd come back with an old pair of pajamas for Kimmy and an old sweater and pants for Laney, while her clothes spun in the drier. Now Laney sat on the sofa with her feet tucked up beneath her, Kimmy curled up at her side, head in her lap, fast asleep with a rug over her.

Janelle reappeared from the kitchen with two steaming coffee cups, handed one to Laney, who reached out and took it.

"Thank you."

"Mind you don't spill it on her."

Laney frowned, annoyed by the implication. "I won't."

Janelle crossed to place her cup on the coffee table, then dropped heavily in the armchair opposite. "Those bruises look like hand marks. Who would do something like that? To someone with Kimmy's disabilities? What the hell is going on in that place?"

"I don't know. But I'm gonna find out." Laney took a sip of the coffee. It was good and hot. She felt it flush her with warmth. She hadn't realized how cold she'd been until now.

"You think it's this Wendy woman? You think she's been abusing her?"

Laney pushed a lock of her sister's hair back from her sister's face, felt the softness of her skin. "I don't think so. Wendy sent me regular letters, telling me how Kimmy was doing. She was the only one really looking after her. When I called Sunny Springs, they said Wendy doesn't work there anymore. Said she suddenly left yesterday." She lifted her gaze to meet Janelle's, gave her a skeptical look. "One of the girls that works there said she left with some rich-looking guy, and it didn't look like Wendy's idea."

Janelle frowned. "Maybe it was her father. Maybe there was some family dilemma and that's why she didn't look happy."

"So why leave me this?" Laney dug in her pocket and pulled out the tiny note. She passed it across to Janelle, who leaned forward to take it, put on her eyeglasses, and frowned down at it.

"Kimmy had it in her hand when I picked her up. It's Wendy's writing."

"You think it was meant for you?"

"Who else? Otherwise, why give it to Kimmy?"

Janelle handed the note back. "So, what are you planning on doing?"

Laney's stroked Kimmy's hair back. "I'm going to find Wendy. She looked after Kimmy when I couldn't. If she's in trouble, I want to help her."

"You make damn sure of your facts. Last thing you need is another stretch for assault."

"I'm not going to cause trouble. Just find her. Make sure she's okay."

Janelle lifted her cup, cradling it in both hands while she watched the two sisters. "So, why's Kimmy even in this place—this Sunny Springs? Why didn't they ask me? If I'da known she needed somewhere, she could have come here."

"I told them that. The day I got sentenced, I told them you'd take care of her. But the lady from social services said the funding application said she had to go there. She said they have all the facilities and therapists and shit…I mean, stuff."

A frown from Janelle. "And you didn't tell them I had all the facilities? That I could care for her?"

"I tried. Seriously, I did. They wouldn't listen. They just made the decision, said it was the best for her. The judge signed the form, and that was that."

Janelle tweaked back one side of her mouth. "I find it a little weird that some care facility gets preference over family."

"So did I. I mean, that's what I told the judge. But seriously, what was I gonna do? Argue, and get an even longer sentence for contempt?"

"Pfft. That's all those smartass bureaucrats for you. Couldn't make a rational decision if you hung 'em by their heels and beat it out of them." Janelle took a thoughtful sip of her coffee, put the cup down, and sat back with her arms laid along on the armrests of the chair. "So, what's the plan? How are you going to find this Wendy woman?"

Laney looked up, held her gaze.

That look must have said everything because Janelle threw up one hand

and said, "Nope. Don't tell me. I don't wanna know. But when you find her, you be sure you don't do anything stupid."

"I know, I know."

"Don't you even think about doing anything illegal, you hear? You'll wind up straight back inside."

"No, I hear you." She did a double take as Janelle angled her head at her, suspicion etched into every crease. "I said I wouldn't, didn't I?"

For a second, Janelle glared at her, then let out a weary sigh. Laney didn't blame her. Knowing Laney's history, even she wouldn't have believed her, either. But Janelle was family. She wouldn't let her down.

And right now, if Wendy was in trouble, she wouldn't let her down either.

CHAPTER EIGHT
DAY TWO—12:54 AM—ELIZABETH

Elizabeth was surprised to find Penny's car parked in the driveway when she got home. Sure enough, as soon as she pulled into the garage, her PA was standing in the doorway with one hand on her hip, and a chastising look on her face. Like the mother of a teen home long after curfew.

"I hope it was worth it," Penny said as she waited for Elizabeth to get out of the car.

Elizabeth closed the car door and started for the house, deliberately ignoring the scowl on her PA's face. "What? The trip? I think so."

"Trip, my sweet patootie," Penny grumbled as Elizabeth stepped past her and into the house. "I'm talking about whatever dragged you away from the party. Kyle was asking after you. Charles called you out for a speech. I had to stand in for you. Do you know how that made me feel?"

Elizabeth marched through into the kitchen with Penny hard on her heels like an attention-starved spaniel.

"Kimmy Donohue's sister took her out of her care home without permission and now no one knows where they are. I thought that was somewhat more important."

Penny's attitude did an immediate shift. "What? Just took her off-site and never told anyone?"

"Correct. Just walked out. A young woman with serious disabilities. I don't know what her sister's thinking." She put her purse on the countertop and went to the coffee machine. "You want some?"

"Sure. Where did she take her?"

"I have no idea. Then David Whitcliff tried to tell me I should just go home and forget all about it. As if I could."

"Of all the nerve."

"I know. Anyway, I've been racking my brain for a connection—trying to think why I remembered Laney Donohue. Then it hit me."

"And...?"

"David told me Laney Donohue was in Carringway Prison. If I'm right, she was one of the women who applied for the early release program."

"Uh-huh," Penny said and briefly drew down the sides of her mouth in a facial shrug. "Small world. So, it turns out you interviewed her?"

"Nope. Come upstairs while I get changed. These shoes are killing me." Elizabeth kicked off one shoe, then the other, and headed upstairs, speaking over her shoulder to Penny, who followed. "If Laney Donohue had gotten through the initial application rounds, I would have interviewed her. But she wasn't eligible because she was applying to care for her sister, not her own child."

"And the program was for young mothers."

"Exactly." Elizabeth entered her bedroom, tossed her shoes into the closet and turned for Penny to unzip her dress. "But I'll go back through the applications when I get a chance, see if I can learn anything from them."

While Elizabeth shimmied out of the dress and picked it up off the floor, a mental light went on for Penny. "Oh, I see. So, you think maybe there's a clue as to where she'd go?"

Elizabeth grabbed a pair of slacks and a cashmere sweater from the closet and threw them on the bed. "It's a long shot but that's what I'm hoping. Wait just a sec." Elizabeth pulled on her pants, picked up her phone, and dialed while Penny held up the sweater like a mother dressing a toddler.

"Who are you calling?"

"Delaney." She held the phone clamped between her shoulder and her ear while she slipped the sweater on, then grabbed the phone as she tugged it down. "No one from Sunny Springs has even bothered to call the police. I don't know what's wrong with these people."

"You talked to David Whitcliff though, right?"

The call clicked through and Delaney's voice came down the line. "Elizabeth, nice to hear from you. Even at…this time of night."

Ignoring the comment, Elizabeth launched straight in with, "I'm sorry, I know it's late but I had a call tonight to say a young woman out at Sunny Springs has disappeared."

A brief silence spooled out over the phone. Elizabeth imagined Delaney's eyes narrowing in thought while he digested the implications.

"Lance, are you still there?"

"I'm here. Are you talking about the residential care facility? The one that looks like a private hospital?"

"Correct. I got a call earlier this evening to say that she was taken offsite, *without permission*, by her older sister, and they haven't been seen since. She's disabled, Lance. No one's done a thing," Elizabeth told him, before he could jump in and tell her that a person has to be missing for 24 hours before the police would issue a missing persons report, which Elizabeth already knew. "She has very limited communication and she's extremely vulnerable. I have no idea why it hasn't been reported."

"Uh-huh."

Elizabeth waited while the silence echoed down the line, then turned a puzzled look on Penny. "Did you hear me?"

He answered, saying, "Can you describe this young woman?"

"Which one?"

"Either of them."

The solemn tone sent a chill down Elizabeth's spine. "Are you opening a missing persons report?"

"Nope. I'm asking because we've just received a report of a young woman found dead a couple of miles from Sunny Springs."

"Oh, my God. And you think it could be Kimmy or her sister?"

"We don't have an ID yet."

"Where was she?"

"Lake View Cemetery. I'm on my way over there now."

"I'm coming, too."

"Where are we going?" Penny whispered.

Elizabeth covered the mouthpiece. "You don't have to."

"There's no need, Elizabeth." Delaney sounded as though he was now regretting telling her. "The whole place is cordoned off. You won't be allowed in."

"But what if it's one of these two young women? I could identify her." Elizabeth let the suggestion hang in the air a second, then said, "It'll take me twenty minutes to get there."

"You could identify her at the morgue."

"Is she in the morgue now?"

A telling silence stretched. Then he said, "The Crime Unit has the area cordoned off. They have to investigate first."

"I'll be there in twenty minutes."

The heavy sigh told Elizabeth she'd worn him down. "If I told you that wasn't necessary, and to stay home, would you listen?"

"I think you know me better than that," she said.

"Why would I think otherwise?" he said in a resigned voice.

***

The Associate

He was exhausted. Ever since this whole thing started, he felt like he was up to his neck in quicksand: the harder he tried to escape, the more he sank.

He'd just gotten into bed when the phone rang. He plucked it up, flung the bedcovers aside, and quickly tiptoed to the bathroom. Just before closing the door, he peeked back to check his sleeping wife. The sound of her soft, regular breathing emanated from somewhere under the covers. Still asleep, thank God.

So he closed the door and answered.

"What now?"

"Let's not get testy," she said. "It's you that wants the favor, not me."

"Then what do you need?"

"You want a diversion? I need some files. I believe you'll have access to them. Can you send them to me?"

"What for? I told you what to do."

"Yeah, well, I've got a better idea," she said. "Or would you like an exposé featuring your name?"

His heart sank. No matter which way he turned, someone was set to destroy him. But he'd come this far.

"What files do you need?" he asked.

"I'll send you a list," she replied. "There'll be a note attached telling you exactly how I want them."

CHAPTER NINE
DAY TWO—12:24 AM—LANEY

Laney had waited until Janelle had tucked Kimmy into the bed in her spare room, where she had awoken briefly, said something about Wendy, then gone back to sleep.

Twenty-five minutes later, here she was, parked on the side of a darkened back street that ran parallel to the western perimeter fence of Sunny Springs. Through the swaying trees lining the driveway, she could clearly see the front of the facility awash in the cold blue light of the exterior floodlights. A few cars were in the parking lot. Probably night staff. Otherwise no signs of life.

She got out of the car, locked it, then dropped into the shadows along the fence line. Ten-foot-high fences. Laney wasn't one of those who had spent their time in Carringway's gym, pumping iron and developing a six-pack. She'd spent most of those six months on work duty, packing work gloves into boxes and sealing them up. Long days and lousy food. Last thing she wanted was to wear herself out on a treadmill. As a consequence, she'd never been so unfit. So even considering attempting the fence was out of the question.

Instead, she moved silently through the overgrown grass edging the street and crept on towards the open driveway. When she got to the entrance, she fell into a crouch and checked the area. No one around. Creeping in through the open gateway, she ducked into the shadows again, following the tree line all the way up the driveway to the east side of the building. Dropping to a crouch under the nearest window, she lifted her head and peeped in to find a communal living area furnished with sofas, a piano in the corner, a large bouquet of flowers on the table.

No signs of life. So Laney moved on, ducking from window to window, brushing past wet shrubs, squelching through rain-sodden gardens, until she got to the corner where she peeped around to take in the front entrance.

Two large double doors. Locked, no doubt. Secure electronic locks. She could pick a standard lock but she hadn't hung around the right cons inside to learn how to pick an electronic one.

Typically, the door would have an exit button next to it on the inside. Or an exit sensor. Only way to open them was from the inside.

That meant she'd need a diversion.

Sticking to the shadows, she followed the gardens in an arc around the front of the building, where she picked up a path leading around back. Out here, overhanging trees formed a darkened archway at the end of which she spotted an outbuilding with a concrete driveway leading up to the front double doors. Like a garage. Or a barn. Grounds like these, you'd need a ton of gardening equipment. A ride-on lawn tractor at the very least. She figured that's where it would all be stored.

Groping her way through water-sodden shrubs she picked her way around the side of the garage, where she peered in through a side window. Pitch black inside but for the occasional flash of red light, indicating an alarm. It flickered on and off, perhaps triggered by the motion of the twigs brushing against the window with a scritching sound.

Wasn't the best, but it was all she had. About a twelve-second walk from the front entrance to here. That's all she'd need.

A quick scout around brought her to a stack of empty flowerpots at the rear of the building. She selected one and checked it for heft. It felt about right, so she went back to the window, swung the pot like a shot-putter, and smashed it against the glass. The window shattered and the alarm immediately burst into life—shrieking into the night with an ear-splitting scream.

Heart in her mouth, she sprinted back down the pathway, ducking under dripping tree branches, leaping over flowerbeds, splashing through puddles, until she hit the shadows out front and stopped. Hands on her knees, breathing heavily, she waited.

"Man, I gotta get fit," she whispered as she watched.

Sure enough, a figure in a blue uniform appeared in the reception area and approached the glass front doors, peering out into the night. Probably a nurse. She stood peering out beyond the glass, turning her head left and right, wondering what to do.

"Open the damn door," Laney urged quietly. "Just come out, see what the noise is."

Then a second figure appeared. The two spoke briefly before the second woman hit the button on the side of the door and both doors slid open. Wasn't till she stepped out into the night with her hair flying in the wind, and pulling the cardigan around her shoulders, that Laney recognized Velma Stanford.

Seven seconds now. Timing was everything. Too slow, she'd miss the door. Too fast, they'd catch her.

Velma moved cautiously out, surveying the area while the doors closed behind her.

"Shit! Okay, hit the button again," she whispered at the figure still inside. "C'mon, you can do it. Just follow her."

Still the nurse remained inside, peering around the doorway while Velma made her way around to the side of the building, angling her head this way and that, searching the pathway. Suddenly, Velma returned, calling to the nurse inside, and pointing in the direction of the garage. Again, the nurse hit the exit button. The doors swished apart and she also stepped out, staring off along the path where Velma had just gone.

"Yes! Now go. Follow her, just go!" Laney hissed under her breath.

…three…

Laney crept to the edge of the shrubbery, rocking on her heel like an athlete ready for the gun while her heart pounded and the seconds passed…

…four…five…

Now, both women were huddled at the end of the pathway, looking down towards the garage. But still in sight. Then they moved on.

Now!

Laney leapt out of the bushes and did a running tiptoe up the two front steps and slid easily in between the doors, twisting into the reception area just before they met. With a quick glance over her shoulder she did a fast-walk for the nearest hallway and headed down it. From behind her came the swish of the front doors opening again, along with the mumble of voices. With her heart still thudding, she slipped into a darkened office doorway to her left, pivoted into the room with her back to the wall, and waited.

Two women, headed this way, wet rubber soles squeaking on the floor. She could hear them talking. Laney held her breath.

The two women moved right on past, one saying, "It was probably a tree branch. I'll call the security company, get them to check it out."

Velma, the snooty bitch.

"I'll get back to the ward," the other woman said. Laney heard footsteps pause outside the door, then double back.

Next, Velma's voice calling after her. "Check the ward thoroughly. Make sure all the clients are still asleep."

"Yes, ma'am."

The squeak of rubber soles receded off around a corner and faded to nothing. Laney gave it a few more seconds, then quietly tiptoed around the door and peeked out, left then right. No one in sight. The hallway echoed emptiness.

The first time Laney had ever come here was five weeks back. She'd been escorted to David Whitcliff's office. At the time he was all sugar and spice, telling Laney to sit down and call him "David," like they were besties, and that Kimmy was safer in Sunny Springs than with her, and that she didn't have any choice but to hand over care of Kimmy to Sunny Springs. After all, didn't they have all the fancy facilities for someone with Kimmy's disabilities? And besides, what did Laney have to offer her? Or at least, that's how she'd heard it.

Her response was fast and fiery.

What the hell did he know about who should take care of her sister? Laney was family, for cryin' out loud. Okay, so maybe she didn't have a fancy house and a new car. But that wasn't what made a family, was it? And what about Janelle? Wasn't she good enough?

Which was met with the same flat response she'd gotten every other time she'd suggested it. Like sending Kimmy to stay with Janelle was tantamount to sending her to work in the mines. So she'd told David where he could shove his facility; that once she was on her feet, she'd take her sister out of this shithole and never come back.

He'd spun around in his chair and dropped Kimmy's file back into the big black file cabinet behind his desk, then had security escort Laney off the premises.

So much for Laney and her shitty temper. But she'd bet anything she liked that along with Sunny Springs's patients' files, that big black file cabinet also held all the staff employment details: who they were, what they did, where they lived. Wendy's included.

She ducked out, and walked quickly along the first corridor, searching the nameplates on each of the doors until she came to David's.

She tried the handle—locked.

No surprises there. So she dug the lock-picks from her jeans pocket and went to work. After a couple of minutes, she heard the satisfying snick of the door lock and the handle turned. Inside, she flipped the wall switch and a cold white light flickered on.

Settling in David's chair, she spun around to the line of black file cabinets behind the desk and started with the top left-hand drawer, flicking through folder after folder. Finding nothing of interest, she went to the next drawer down. That was all the accounts, signed client documents, and legal papers. Nothing about staff.

In the next, she found more legal papers and searched until she located the one Judge Roth and Mrs. McClaine had signed, authorizing Sunny Springs to take care of Kimmy during Laney's incarceration. Laney ripped it from the file, tore it into a million pieces, and cast it into the wastepaper basket next to the desk. They'd have another copy on disc, but it gave her some satisfaction knowing they'd be put out searching for the original. Even if it didn't take long.

The next drawer down was packed with more files, all grouped into sections tagged Nursing Staff, Administration, and Care Staff.

Laney found Pinky's file almost immediately, and opened it.

Patricia McCorline, age twenty-four, after-hours cleaner.

"Pfft, that didn't last long."

Attached was a photo of her: black hair with fluorescent pink bangs—obviously dyed the instant she was sprung from Carringway—clear blue eyes, stud in her brow. Oddly enough, the photo made her look far younger than her twenty- four years. Or was that just because Laney was used to seeing her in the flesh? Regardless, it had DISMISSED stamped across the front in large red letters.

"Better luck next time, kiddo," she said, turning the page to skim over Pinky's dismissal notes and the list of drugs found in her possession. "Man, you don't do things by halves, sister. No wonder they fired your ass." She chuckled and stuck it back in the file cabinet.

Behind her, David Whitcliff's office door burst open. Laney didn't need to turn around. She could smell the reek of self-righteousness overriding Velma's sickly-sweet perfume.

"Miss Donohue, may I ask what you're doing in here?"

Laney put Pinky's file back, and plucked out another and swiveled David's chair to meet Velma, who stalked into the room and stood next to the desk, indignantly tugging her cardigan into place over her shoulders.

"Just checking through all these files." Laney grinned up at her. "Can't seem to find what I'm looking for. Maybe you can help me."

This file belonged to someone who'd been fired for ongoing absenteeism. Which wasn't what she was looking for, so Laney spun in the chair, deposited it back in the drawer in no particular order, plucked out another, and swiveled back.

This one was a loan application form—the name *Velma Roberta Stanford* handwritten into the first box.

Laney leaned back in the chair and let out a soft whistle. "Wow, this is a loan application for twenty-five large. With your name on it. Somebody's spending up a storm, Vel. What's it for—new car, house, luxury vacation maybe?" She waggled the file in the air until Velma reached across the desk and snatched it from her.

"That is private business," Velma said, hugging the file to her chest. "You have no right looking through here. I want you out of here right this minute. I already have a detailed report outlining your blatant disregard for our regulations. Don't make this any worse."

From the look on Velma's face, Laney had hit a nerve. Not wanting to pursue the matter and potentially embarrass the woman, she spun back to the open drawer, plucked out another file, and leaned back in the chair, one ankle up on her knee while she flicked through it. "Matter of fact, I'm not interested in your financial arrangements, Velma. I'm looking for someone named Wendy. Remember her?" Laney whipped the chair around to face her. "Foreign girl, good with people. She used to work here. Until yesterday, that is. Now, where do you suggest I look for her personnel records? 'Cause, for the life of me, I cannot find them here."

Velma's cheeks flashed red. For a second, Laney thought she might lunge at her. Instead, it was like a something inside her head clicked. Her demeanor underwent a chilling shift and she modified her tone.

"Laney, please don't do this. Why don't you just bring Kimmy back and we'll forget all about this?"

"And what? You'll tear up the report you wrote?" She frowned deeply. "Really? After all the work you put into it? Why don't you just tell me? What do you have to lose?"

"Why don't we talk about this? We could come to some arrangement. One that suits both of us."

Laney's eyebrows shot up. "An arrangement? Wow. Like one where Kimmy never gets out of this shithole, and I stay in prison for the rest of my life? Boy, wouldn't that be something."

"You have no right to go through these files."

"Then just tell me where I can find Wendy." She gave Velma a hard stare. "That really would be helpful."

"You know I can't do that. Our policies prevent us from giving out private information about our employees. As you're well aware."

Laney tutted and swiveled back to select another file. "You don't want to help me, then that's fine. Oh, wait a second…what do we have here?" Around she swung once more, this time waving the file at Velma. "In the staffing section—Wendy O'Dell. And look at this: according to your files, she still works here. What's with that, Vel? I thought she was fired."

Velma's nostrils flared. "Please, Laney. I know you have your reasons, I know you think you're doing this for Kimmy, but this is only going to make things very difficult for you."

"Oh, seriously? I love that you care for me so much. So, how come Wendy had to leave so fast? Did she steal something?"

"Wendy left of her own accord. She went back to her old job."

"So, who was the dude she left with? From what I hear, you knew him pretty well." A loaded statement. Feeling out just how well she knew this guy.

With a dead-eyed expression, Velma picked up the phone, savagely punching out the numbers. "That's it. I gave you a chance. Now, you leave me no choice." When the line picked up, she said, "Get me the police."

Bingo. She knew exactly who he was.

Laney sat back paging through the file, grinning and shaking her head while Velma waited on the phone. "I can't wait to hear this."

After a moment, Velma shifted a pointed gaze onto Laney, saying, "This is Velma Stanford from the Sunny Springs residential facility for the disabled…"

Laney got up, rounded the desk, leaned in and whispered, "I'll see you around, Vel."

"Just a moment," Velma said into the phone. "Laney, you stay right here," she called after her. "Running is only going to make it even worse."

Clutching the file to her chest like a schoolgirl carrying books, Laney turned, backing up a few steps. "Oh, I'm not running, Vel. I am definitely walking here. And you will not stop me."

Then she turned and headed quickly for the front door with the sound of Velma's voice shouting after her.

CHAPTER TEN
DAY TWO—1:02 AM—ELIZABETH

Lake View Cemetery lay on the border between East Cleveland and Cleveland Heights. One of the largest cemeteries in Ohio, Lake View was spread over almost 285 acres and boasted architecture and monuments that had seen it rise to become a popular tourist destination.

In the gloom of the night, chalk-white angels and towering monuments rose from the earth like the ghosts of those whose graves they marked, the ground between studded with a seemingly haphazard collection of headstones.

Four police units, plus a car she recognized as Delaney's, were already parked at the side of the narrow street leading through the cemetery grounds. As she eased the car in and parked behind a police cruiser, Penny pointed off to their left.

"That'll be them over there."

Elizabeth tugged the key from the ignition, ducking her head to follow her line of sight. Sure enough, in the distance she could see a pale blue halo of lights through the trees. About halfway between the women and the distant light, two police officers walked carefully between headstones, also headed in that direction.

Penny got out of the car, sweeping her hair out of her eyes and watching them while she waited for Elizabeth to tug her headscarf into place, check her look in the rear-view mirror, and get out.

"I don't know what you think you can do here. Do you even know what Laney Donohue looks like?"

Elizabeth locked the car with a flick of the switch on her key, dug a flashlight from her pocket, and started in the direction of the distant glow, talking over her shoulder. "It doesn't matter. I have to know this isn't her. And I have to know it isn't Kimmy."

"But what can you do here? Delaney told you he had it under control, didn't he?"

Elizabeth stopped short, and turned to face her PA. "What else am I going to do? Go home? Get a great night's sleep while Kimmy's missing? I'm the reason this happened. Me," she said, stabbing herself in the chest. "I put her in Sunny Springs. Now she could be dead."

They quickened their pace, hunching their shoulders and squinting against the wind. It wasn't until now that Elizabeth found herself wishing she'd grabbed the camelhair car coat instead snatching up her hip-length wool jacket in her haste. They picked their way between burial plots and headstones, following the dim circle of light cast by Elizabeth's flashlight before they came to a white tent erected over the site. Despite the shelter of the surrounding trees, the sides of the tent billowed and flapped with each gust of wind. Portable floodlights had been set around the periphery of the area, washing the scene in insipid white light. To the left Delaney stood amid a clutch of police officers, issuing orders, if the gestures were anything to go by.

As they approached the crime scene tape marking off the area, an officer stepped out, cutting them off.

"Ma'am, I'll have to ask you to leave."

"I'm here by invitation." She nodded towards Delaney, who was looking over. He excused himself from the huddle and motioned for her to approach.

Nodding in acknowledgement, the young officer stepped back, allowing her to pass, before returning to his post.

"Elizabeth," Delaney said in grim acknowledgment.

She brushed back a stray wisp of hair that had escaped her headscarf. "Do you know who she is yet?"

"Not yet."

"Do you want me to see if I can identify her?"

With his hands driven into the pockets of his coat and his collar turned up, he switched his attention briefly back to the site, then shook his head. "I'm sorry, Elizabeth. I can't let you see her. She's in pretty bad shape."

Elizabeth switched her attention to where a young officer exited the tent behind Delaney, the expression of horror plain even at this distance.

"Do you know what happened to her?"

Delaney followed her line of sight, watching the officer who was now in hushed conversation with another. "We don't know yet. She wasn't murdered here. The ground's soft. It's slushy underfoot all around here. There's no prints showing a sign of a struggle. But we found a shoe matching the one she was wearing over by the roadway. I'd say someone brought her in, carried her here, and didn't notice the shoe fall."

"Who found her?"

"Some local kids. They said they were playing around in the cemetery trying to frighten each other, and one of them took up the dare and just kept running. Said he tripped over the body. Thought it was one of his friends playing a joke on him."

"And you don't think they were responsible?"

He shook his head. "They're fifteen, sixteen. They reported it straight away. They were pretty shaken up."

"Lance, I have to know if this is either Laney or Kimmy Donohue. Please, can you at least tell me that?"

Penny placed a comforting hand on her arm. "Hey, he's doing everything he can. And they won't necessarily have an ID for her yet, will you?" she asked Delaney.

Delaney broke eye contact for a moment, hesitating before facing her. "Look, I've opened a missing persons report on Kimmy Donohue, and put out an APB. We've got units already searching for her. Elizabeth, go home and get some sleep. There's nothing you can do here. As soon as we get an identity for the girl, or we find Kimmy, you'll be the first to know."

"But you don't—"

"He said he'll let you know," Penny insisted.

Elizabeth wavered a moment, her lower lip clamped between her teeth as she cast a worried gaze back at the tent. "What was she wearing? The girl. What was she wearing when she was killed?"

"Sweat shirt, sweat pants. The sweater was back-to-front. We think she's been changed out of her own clothing. For whatever reason."

"Maybe she was wearing something distinctive—something the police would recognize."

"Could be."

Penny briefly squeezed Elizabeth's arm. "Hey, let's get you home. You heard him—they'll call if they find anything."

"Detective?" This from one of the officers who had just exited the tent. "I think we found something."

"What is it?" Elizabeth asked no one in particular.

"I'll be right there," Delaney called. Then to Elizabeth, he said, "Go home. We'll find Kimmy. I promise." And with that he turned with his hands deep in the pockets of his coat, head down against the wind, and went back to the site.

Elizabeth swept her hair back from her face and narrowed her focus on them, trying to make out whatever it was that the officer was showing Delaney. It was something small, something probably the size of a small book, maybe a phone, but from here it was impossible to tell.

"Come on, hon," said Penny. "What you need right now is a hot drink, and a good night's sleep."

Despite the voice in her gut urging her to stay, to demand answers that no one had, Elizabeth nodded. "You're right. Then you and I will start first thing in the morning."

"Doing what?" Penny asked. "You heard what he said. They've got the whole thing under control. And frankly, we're lucky he told us that much. And what do you think we could we do that they're not?"

"He said they'd look for Kimmy. Nothing about Laney. She may be the only one who knows what happened to Kimmy in Sunny Springs."

"Or the only one who'll tell you."

"Exactly. Come on, let's get back to the car before the heavens open and we both end up sick tomorrow with a head cold."

CHAPTER ELEVEN
DAY TWO—5:15 AM—LANEY

Laney had hurried back to the car and headed towards the central city, eyes skipping up to the rear-view mirror every few seconds in case she was being followed. As soon as she was sure no one was following, she turned down a side street, and parked under a streetlight. Flicking on the overhead driver's light, she picked up the file she'd taken from Sunny Springs, and opened it.

The headshot showed a stunningly beautiful young woman: jet black hair swept back from her forehead and tumbling to her shoulders, startling green eyes under sleekly arched brows, flawless olive complexion and generous mouth, lips slightly parted. How she ended up on what was probably minimum wage in a place like Sunny Springs was anybody's guess. She could have been a model, if you'd asked Laney. It felt strange to finally see the girl she'd put so much faith in, the girl who had cared for Kimmy like another sister, and to have never met her.

"What were you doing working in a place like that?" Laney mused as she dismissed the photograph and checked the employment details below.

She flipped the photo to check the back, then turned to Wendy's personal and employment details. According to the form she'd filled out when Sunny Springs hired her, Wendy was twenty-eight years old, held a Masters in linguistics, and enjoyed running, skiing, tae kwon do, and boxing.

"Sheesh! That's one way to get your beautiful face messed up," Laney muttered, and turned the page. Attached to the back of the file was the brief handwritten background check done by the guy at Employment Pulse, the recruitment agency. No previous employers. Evidently, this had been Wendy's only job.

"Seriously? She's twenty-eight and she's never held down a job before?" She flipped to the front again. Then she found it, in small print below the personal details—Wendy O'Dell's address and phone number.

According to her watch it was still too early. But Laney had one more person she wanted to see before she went to Wendy's mother's. And this was the perfect time.

Kiddy Leishman must have lived in one of the crappiest streets in the crappiest area of Parma. The place was easy enough to find. Kiddy still lived with her parents, Zena and Ptolemy, who were listed in the white pages under their full names. Laney had only to Google part of the name and it had come up with the details. She knew the area wasn't exactly the Ritz, but with the sun spreading the first watery rays of light through the thick cloud cover, it made the place look even more dismal than she'd even imagined.

With the echo of early morning birds ringing down the empty street, Laney plucked the key from the ignition and pushed her seat back, preparing for at least an hour-long wait for Kiddy to get home from work. She was just about to close her eyes when she heard an engine approaching and caught sight of a beat-up red Mustang in the rear-vision mirror. It turned into the street behind her and slowed. As it swerved in off the street and straight into the driveway of Kiddy Leishman's house, Laney caught a glimpse of Kiddy behind the wheel.

Laney checked her watch. "Home early, huh? That figures." Kiddy never was one to overwork herself. Laney adjusted the seat back up and watched.

Across the road, Kiddy got out of the Mustang and slammed the car door. Dressed in a grimy white gauze skirt that flared from the waist like a ballerina's dress, mid-calf-length boots, and a fur-lined puffer jacket, she looked as if she was just returning from a Gothic-themed fancy dress party. After locking the car, she paused to direct a wide-mouthed yawn into the air, then turned for the house.

Just as Kiddy reached the front door, Laney got out of the car and called out.

"Hey, Kiddy!"

Kiddy swiveled around, turning a squint-eyed look out across the street. Spotting Laney, she ambled a few feet towards the front walk and paused in a slouch with one hand on her hip.

"Geez, Laney? Is that you? What are you doing here?"

Aware the whole street could probably hear the conversation, Laney crossed at a trot, then walked up the front path to meet her.

Kiddy hadn't changed one dot since she was in Carringway. Every con who'd met Kiddy agreed she could have passed for an older, world-wearier version of Shirley Temple. Her dirty blonde hair sprang naturally into bunches of ringlets that bounced every time she moved. Her wide blue eyes and rosebud lips lent her the look of a girl half her twenty-six years, but the meth-eroded teeth, smeared mascara, and sickly complexion of a habitual drug user added another element altogether.

Laney stuck her hands in her pockets. "Hey, Kiddy. How you doin'?"

"I'm doin' okay. I don't suppose you're here to ask me how I'm doin' this time of the morning, though. How'd you find me?" she said, her severe dental degradation lending her a slight lisp.

"Your dad's name is Ptolemy. It's not that hard."

"Oh, right." Kiddy chuckled. Then she glanced back over her shoulder at the house. "I'd ask you in but if my folks catch me dressed like this, they'll kill me."

Laney gestured at her clothing. "Why? Because you're planning on running away to join the circus?"

Kiddy looked down at herself. "Ha-ha, you're too funny. I finally got a night out, is why. You have no idea what it's like living with your parents. They treat me like I'm ten years old."

"Then I won't keep you too long." Laney shifted her weight and dashed a knuckle across one eyebrow, trying to come across casual. "I just wanted to ask you about someone back at Sunny Springs."

Kiddy made a face. "And it couldn't wait till like…?" She squinted at her watch. "After breakfast, maybe?"

"Well no, it's kind of urgent. Do you remember talking to Dorothy about a nurse aid named Wendy? Like, the one who was working at Sunny Springs?"

"Oh! You must have been talking with Pinky."

"Yeah, matter of fact I was."

"Oh, man," said Kiddy with a roll of her eyes. "Does she never shut up? I spent two months in the same cell as her. Yap, yap, yap, that's all I got. She's lucky I didn't kill her."

"Yeah. So, ah…" Laney rolled her hand, urging her to continue.

"So, yeah. Dorothy was telling me about this guy that came and took her. Like, Wendy, right? Said he looked like a cross between David Beckham and Johnny Depp."

"I can't even imagine what that would look like," Laney admitted.

Kiddy ignored her. "So, anyway, apparently, she's got a *new job*," she said, making air quotes as she said it. "Well, that's according to that new kitchen hand, if you can believe anything she says."

"What does that mean—'a *new job*'?" Laney said, mimicking Kiddy and also doing air quotes.

"Well, you know what I mean…"

Laney made an irritated face and looked away, saying, "How about you tell me."

"Well, she's a hooker, isn't she? Like, high-class, but a hooker all the same."

A burst of laughter from Laney. "A hooker? Why would a hooker—high-class or anything else—be working at Sunny Springs?"

"Well, I don't know, do I? If you only came here to insult my clothing and tell me I'm talking shit—"

"No, no. I'm sorry, okay. Can you remember anything else Dorothy said about the Armani guy? Anything."

Kiddy gave a moment, then said, "He had Boston Celtics plates on the car. Oh, and one of the guys called him Jerko."

"Jerko? Was that, like, his name or something?"

"How would I know? Was I there? No, I'm telling you what Dorothy said, okay?"

Nodding and wondering how much help that was, Laney said, "Yeah, yeah, I was just asking. So that's it?"

She shrugged briefly. "That's it."

Laney's shoulders dropped. She'd been hoping for more. "Okay, thanks. Hope your folks don't kill you." She pointed to Kiddy's house, where a drape had tweaked back in the living room.

"Kiddy, is that you?" came a bellow from inside. A woman's voice.

Kiddy bellowed back. "No, it's the tooth fairy. Who do you think it is? I better go," she told Laney.

"Yeah, thanks, I'll see you around."

"Oh, and something else," Kiddy said, just as the front door burst open and an angry-looking woman—presumably Kiddy's mom—appeared in the doorway. "Dorothy also said Velma Stanford just about had a heart attack when she saw him. Ran out and met him the second the guy's car pulled up."

"What? Like he was her boss or something?"

Kiddy's mom marched down the path and elbowed Kiddy angrily aside to glare at Laney. "And who the hell are you?"

"Cab driver," she replied immediately. "Have a great day, ma'am," she told Kiddy. With a quick wave, she hurried down the path and speed-walked back to the car without a backward look. By the time she was back in the car, Kiddy had disappeared inside and the front door was closed. Just as she stuck the key in the ignition, the sound of a heated argument and the crash of something hitting an internal wall rumbled from Kiddy's house. It was followed by a scream and a string of language even Laney wouldn't use. It echoed down the street like something out of a horror movie.

"Geez, Kiddy, move out and get your own place, for cryin' out loud," Laney mumbled, grateful for once for her own situation.

So, Velma knew the guy way better than she was letting on. How? And why let him take Wendy when she obviously didn't want to go?

She picked up Wendy's employment file from the seat beside her and went through the details again, this time one by one. The only address she could find listed was that of Wendy O'Dell's mother. Did her mother even know she'd gone missing?

Another bloodcurdling scream emanated from the house.

Eager to get away, Laney plunged the key into the ignition and pulled out.

Mrs. O'Dell's address was less than a half hour away. If she hurried, she could get there before the traffic got too bad. And she could figure out what she'd say on the way.

CHAPTER TWELVE
DAY TWO—6:45 AM—ELIZABETH

Elizabeth had barely slept. She'd woken at 5:00 AM, and lain staring at the ceiling running a hundred different scenarios of Kimmy Donohue through her mind, praying she was okay. Praying Laney would keep her safe—something her own organization had failed to do.

Finally, in an effort to shake off the impending melancholy, she'd gotten up, gone downstairs, and made coffee. She was sitting there, staring into space and fending off those last images when the front doorbell sounded.

Penny walked straight in, handing her the newspaper as she passed, saying, "It's all in there—dead girl, cemetery, yadda, yadda. Nothing we didn't already know. You got coffee?"

"In the pot. I might need another as well." While Penny went in search of her morning Java hit, Elizabeth shook out the paper, checked the front page only to find pictures of a jubilant Indians crowd after a win, then turned to page two.

Beneath an article on welfare fraud, she found it—a few lines outlining exactly what Delaney had said, except the reporter had suggested the body as possibly being one of the many homeless in the city.

"Why would they think she was homeless? Someone had changed her clothing. Or weren't the press told that?" Elizabeth said, as Penny entered the living room carrying two cups. She laid the paper down, took the proffered cup.

Elizabeth went on, "And you know what disappoints me? That a homeless young woman is worth only a couple of lines. Is she, what? Worthless?"

"Delaney said she was a mess. Sounds like someone beat her up pretty bad," said Penny.

"That poor girl. I wonder how her parents must feel."

"Let Delaney deal with that. You've got enough on your plate right now."

Elizabeth looked up sharply. "What do you mean?"

"You didn't see it? Front page, under the Indians win."

Elizabeth put her cup down, lifted the paper again, and dropped her attention to the article in the lower section of the front page. The headline read: *Something Rotten in the State of Ohio?*

The cost of caring for the most vulnerable in Ohio is on the rise, and it seems that those who portray themselves as the champions of the most vulnerable in our society have little care as to who is tending to them.

According to sources, a growing number of disabled young people are being channeled into institutional care using illegal workers, while being funded by organizations such as the Charles McClaine Foundation, chaired by socialite Elizabeth McClaine. Once a vocal opponent of the type of institutional care provided by such organizations as Aden Falls Corporation and projects such as Sunny Springs, it seems Elizabeth McClaine has had a change of tune, and is now happy to sponsor our disabled young people into such situations.

"This is ridiculous. If they've been using illegal employees, how is that my fault? Putting anyone in one of those institutions was against my better judgment. Now they're making it sound like we're funding some underhanded scheme, shoveling people in there for the money. As though I'm some kind of criminal."

Penny arched one eyebrow. "I'd like to know who told them you're funding these young people."

"So would I. *A growing number*," she mumbled angrily. "See if you can find a contact number for this…Jennifer Reels. I'd like to know where she gets her cockeyed information. But first, I want to know if that was Laney Donohue they found dead over at Lake View. If it is, maybe everybody will take Kimmy's abduction a little more seriously." She slid her phone from across the coffee table towards her, checked her watch, and dialed.

Penny also checked her watch. "Awful early to be calling, don't you think?"

"Seriously? You think he'll be sleeping when he's got a dead body and a young woman missing out there?" When Delaney answered, Elizabeth shifted her attention back to the phone and lifted it to her ear.

"Lance, it's me."

"Yes, Elizabeth. What can I do for you?" He sounded tired.

"Any chance you've identified the young woman yet? The one in the cemetery?"

"Not yet. I'll let you know when we do."

"So, you still don't know if it's Laney Donohue."

He paused for some moments. He knew something. Politicians were the most elusive when it came to giving out information. Cops came next in line in that regard. Elizabeth had learned this long ago. She'd also learned it was only a matter of asking the right questions. She turned a hopeful look on Penny, who raised her eyebrows, waiting.

A phone rang in the background and it sounded like he'd switched the phone to his other hand before speaking. "We had a call last night to say that Laney Donohue broke into Sunny Springs and took some files."

"Well, at least we can rule her out as the dead body. I don't suppose she had Kimmy with her while she was doing her break-in?"

"I wish. Would have saved us some time." She could hear the cynical smile in his voice.

"What files did she take? Do you know?"

"I can't make any comment on that, Elizabeth. You know that."

"How did I know you were going to say that?"

Another pause.

"Have you seen this morning's paper?" he asked.

She picked up it, shook it out in disgust, and tossed it back on the dining table. "Yes, I have. I don't know what that Reels woman is insinuating. First thing this morning, I intend to catch up with her and put her straight. I've been one of the most vocal lobbyists, fighting against this kind of institutionalization, Lance. How could they make me out to be...*endorsing* it?"

"Preaching to the converted here, Elizabeth." That smile was back in his voice. In her mind's eye, she could just see the creases each side of his mouth, the faint smile lines forming around his eyes. Then it was gone.

Snapping back into cop mode again, he said, "I'll let you know if anything interesting comes out of our investigations. In the meantime, we've got the girl down at the morgue, awaiting ID."

"Any clues yet?"

"A couple." Still evading her questions, still playing it close to his chest.

"Lance, I'd really appreciate it if you could let me know as soon as you find out who she is. In the meantime, I need to get to the bottom of this story before they start flinging more mud and I find myself waist deep in alligators."

"Good luck with that," he said, the smile in his voice suddenly appearing again. Then he hung up.

"So, what now?" Penny asked, but Elizabeth was already lifting her phone.

She found the number in her received calls list and hit the send button. "I want to find out what files Laney Donohue took. I'd like to have that in my back pocket before I see David Whitcliff. Hello," she said when the girl picked up. "Caroline, it's Elizabeth McClaine. I'm sorry to call you so early."

"That's okay, Mrs. McClaine. I couldn't sleep all night, worrying."

"Listen, I believe Laney Donohue came back to Sunny Springs last night."

"She did? Oh, thank the Lord. Did she bring Kimmy back?"

There was so much hope in the question, Elizabeth hated answering. "No, I'm afraid she didn't."

"Then where did she leave her? She had no family apart from that aunt. And she wouldn't leave her there."

Elizabeth blinked in surprise. "What aunt?"

"Laney's aunt. Oh, golly, what was her name? She used to visit Kimmy every week. Jenny...Jeanette? Janelle, that was it. Janelle Hooper. She lives somewhere out in Garfield Heights. But there's no way Laney Donohue would take her there. One of the girls here told me about her, said there was some family issues or something. Said Laney's aunt wouldn't have anything to do with her. That's why she ended up in Sunny Springs."

"I had no idea Kimmy had other family," Elizabeth said, more to herself than to Caroline, and turned to find Penny frowning up at her.

"Well, that's what I was told."

"Okay, Caroline, thank you so much. If you find out anything, anything at all that sounds unusual, could you let me know?"

"Of course."

"I appreciate it," Elizabeth said and hung up. "Let's go. We've got our work cut out for us."

"What do I do?"

"You're staying here. I want you to follow up on a woman named Janelle Hooper—Laney Donohue's aunt. It's a long shot, but she could know where Laney is. And I'd like to know why she didn't come forward to take care of Kimmy when Elaine Donohue went into Carringway."

"And you?"

Before Elizabeth could answer, her phone rang. She swiped it up and checked the screen—Charles.

"Oh, terrific. That's all I need."

Charles McClaine was her ex-father-in-law. A wealthy construction tycoon, he had wanted to ensure the mother of his only granddaughter would remain living in the manner to which she'd become accustomed, and under his control. After Elizabeth and her husband separated, Charles had set up the Charles McClaine Foundation and placed Elizabeth as custodian. The role meant that whereas she lacked personal wealth, her social standing and political connections kept her in the upper social circles of Ohio, and never far from the McClaines. The fact that Charles probably used the foundation as some kind of tax haven had never escaped her suspicions. But the number of families with disabled children that she'd helped over the years convinced her that some questions should be left unanswered.

No guesses why he was calling, though.

So, with her heart in her mouth, she lifted her chin and swiped the screen to answer.

"Charles," she said, her tone reeking of overblown friendliness. "Lovely to hear from you."

"What in the hell is going on, Elizabeth?"

She could just see him in her mind's eye, sitting at his broad cherrywood desk, newspaper spread in front of him, finger pounding the page. She pressed her lips hard together and absently repositioned a napkin on the table. "Going on? What do you mean?"

"The piece in the paper is what I mean. Who gave them this information?"

"I don't know but I'm working to get to the bottom of it."

"Well, when you do, I want a retraction from that paper, and a public apology. I have some very critical deals on the table right now, and I can't afford to get involved in some public slur campaign. Do you hear me?"

"Absolutely. Loud and clear."

"Call me when you've got the issue ironed out." And he hung up.

"Not so happy, huh?" said Penny, who had obviously heard every word.

"Oh, I intend to find out what's behind it, all right. But I'm damned if I'm going straight to the paper to demand an apology before I have a few more answers." She scooped up her purse and keys and headed for the front door.

Penny scrambled to grab her own purse and hurried after her. "So where are we going?"

"*I* am going to have a long chat with David Whitcliff. I want to know how many people knew about the incident last night, and what axes they might have to grind. And he'd better have the answers."

"And what about me?"

"I want you to find this aunt of Laney's—that's if she even exists. Hopefully, she may be able to give us some answers."

CHAPTER THIRTEEN
DAY ONE—8:45 AM—LANEY

By the time Laney got to the only address she had for Wendy O'Dell, the wind had dropped, and while the rain had stopped, the sky remained overcast and threatening. She found a parking slot two doors down, and sat for some minutes studying the house. A picturesque two-story brick colonial, it sat midway down a tree-lined street of well-maintained houses with neatly trimmed front yards and white picket fences. The drapes were still drawn. At almost nine on a Tuesday morning, that didn't bode well. Folks should have been up and going to work by now.

It was only now as she turned back to the file that the questions began bubbling up.

Why would Wendy leave with the guy if it was clearly against her will? Was he her husband?

"But if you're married to him, why put your mom's address on your resume?"

Unless he was abusive and she had gone to her mother's place to escape him. Which made sense. In which case, why not just go to the police? Why go and work at a dump like Sunny Springs? And what did Velma have to do with it?

Hopefully, the answers lay just behind that front door.

Laney got out of the car, crossed the street, and mounted the four steps to the front door. After driving a finger into the bell press, she turned to view the street, while she waited. No sound or signs of life from inside. She leaned over to peek through the adjacent window but the drapes were drawn. After another minute, she skipped down the stairs, heading back to the car when the door opened behind her and a woman in a bathrobe peered out. She looked like she'd just gotten out of bed.

"Mrs. O'Dell?" Laney said and turned for the stairs again.

The woman bunched the front of her robe in at her throat and squinted out into the light. "What's this about?"

"I'm looking for someone named Wendy O'Dell. Does she live here?"

The shock on the woman's face was immediate. Her color paled visibly and her eyes widened in desperation. "Have you seen her? Do you know where she is?"

The questions came with such urgency, Laney found herself floundering. "Uh, no, I don't. I was kind of hoping you could tell me where she is."

The woman searched out over Laney's shoulder, bewildered, as if expecting to see someone else before coming back to her. "How do you know Wendy? When was the last time you saw her?"

"I, ah…listen, would you mind if I come in a second?"

She considered it for a moment, then widened the door and stood back. "Yes, of course."

Laney found herself in a comfortable living room—flowers on the mantel, deep-seated wingback armchairs positioned on either side of a broad fireplace, waiting while Mrs. O'Dell—who had identified herself as such—went and got coffee. When she returned, she sat on the sofa opposite Laney, pushing her hair back of her face, as if suddenly aware of her disheveled state.

"I haven't heard from Wendy in over six months now. Last I heard from her was just after she went to Boston. A terrific job came up. She has a Masters in linguistics, you know."

"So I heard." The linguistics degree. Boston Celtics plates on the car. That also made sense.

Mrs. O'Dell dropped her head momentarily to run her hand through her sleep-tousled hair. The pain and confusion over her daughter's lack of contact were patent in every worry-line on her face. Though there were no photographs of Wendy among those on the piano, Laney noticed. Or on the bureau. It was almost as though every trace of her had been removed from the house.

In the face of such heartache, there was no way Laney wanted to add to it by telling her what she knew—that her daughter had been so close to home, only to have been taken, possibly against her will. But she had to say something.

For some moments Mrs. O'Dell seemed to go off into her own thoughts, so Laney plucked up courage and broke the silence. "So, where was this job she was sup…that she went to?"

With a quick shake of the head, Mrs. O'Dell snapped herself back out of her thoughts and took a shuddering breath. "It was supposed to be a firm of lawyers. They needed her for their international offices. She'd applied through a site on the Internet. I can't tell you how thrilled she was when she got it."

"You said 'supposed to be'? You mean they weren't lawyers?"

"I've searched everywhere for them. The company had a professional site on the Internet when she landed the job. Then…" She shrugged deeply, hands spread wide, eyes searching before meeting Laney's again. "Then nothing. The day Wendy left, they just disappeared. No mention of them on the Internet or anywhere else. I looked up registered legal entities, the companies register—still nothing."

"Maybe they changed their names. Lawyers do that sh…that stuff all the time. You know, like when they get a new partner and such."

"Then why hasn't Wendy called? Why hasn't she contacted me?"

Floundering under the intensity of Wendy's mother's despairing gaze, Laney opened her hands and scanned the room, searching for an answer. When her eyes lit on a picture of a young woman, she gestured to it, figuring she'd change the subject. "That's a nice photo. Is that her sister over there?"

With her features still cast in that same expression of hopelessness, Mrs. O'Dell blinked, then turned to follow Laney's gesture. Then she met Laney's gaze again, frowning.

"That's Wendy." Her tone was one of near disbelief.

For a second, Laney's brain scrambled. "Excuse me?"

"That's my daughter, Wendy. She's an only child."

Laney blinked hard. "I don't understand. I'm looking for Wendy *O'Dell.*" Then it dawned on her. "Are you saying that's Wendy?"

"Well, of course." Mrs. O'Dell rose from her seat, crossed to pick up the photograph, then stood for some moments, tracing the outline of the image with one finger while staring down at it. Seemingly taking some effort to break herself out of the moment, she wrenched her eyes from it, then passed it to Laney.

"That was her just after she graduated. I have no idea…" she told Laney. She clasped her hands tightly in her lap, desperate to finish, but her throat visibly tightened and the words remained unspoken. Almost at once, her face crumpled. She clapped a hand to her mouth as the first wave of emotion folded her forward.

Laney's heart twisted in her chest as the woman remained doubled over, openly weeping. Quietly rising from her seat, Laney slipped the photograph from Mrs. O'Dell's grasp, and studied the girl smiling out of the frame. She had strawberry blonde hair, blue eyes, and a smattering of freckles over a pale complexion. Even with a good hair dye, there was no way this was the same person as the one whose photo was tucked in her jeans pocket. She was about to say something—anything to ease the woman's pain—but two beeps from her phone stole her attention. She slipped it from her pocket, checked the screen. The message read:

Meet me. Did some digging. Found something yr going to want to see. Kiddy.

"Thank God," said Laney.

CHAPTER FOURTEEN
DAY TWO—9:32 AM—ELIZABETH

For the second time in the past twelve hours, Elizabeth turned the car into the driveway of Sunny Springs. Now, in daylight, the place looked a picture of tranquility. Neatly clipped shrubs lined two of the paths leading around the sides of the building and in front, blocks of brightly colored flowers arranged in patterns flanked each side of the path.

Determined not to allow the façade of the place to stifle her resolve, she parked next to a glazier's van, got out, and strode purposefully to the double front doors. Just as they swept apart, she stepped through into the reception area and marched straight to the desk.

Behind the desk, she was surprised to find Caroline Judemire, who looked up in alarm, her cheeks flashing pink.

"Mrs. McClaine. What can I do for you?" Caroline was the girl who had first called Elizabeth to notify her of Kimmy's disappearance. From her demeanor, she fully intended keeping up the pretense that she had no knowledge of what had happened. In truth, she couldn't have looked more guilty if she'd hung a sign around her neck.

Keeping her manner distant so as not to incriminate the girl, Elizabeth announced, "I'm here to see David Whitcliff, if he's available."

Behind Elizabeth, a woman appeared from a doorway and made her way towards the hallway leading towards the hospital wing. Caroline's eyes followed her until she disappeared down an adjacent hallway before leaning forward, whispering.

"Did you find her aunt?"

"Working on it."

"They still haven't called the police about Kimmy. I hope they do." She looked worried.

"If they don't, I'll make absolutely sure she's found," Elizabeth whispered back.

When a second woman entered the reception area, asking for her messages, the girl scavenged around and found them, telling Elizabeth in a loud voice, "Yes, ma'am. I'll call him and tell him you're here." With which she picked up the phone.

"Thank you," Elizabeth replied with a furtive wink.

Caroline smiled in response and mouthed a *thank you*, as she hung up.

Not two minutes later, David Whitcliff strode into the reception area with his hand extended in welcome. "Mrs. McClaine. Wonderful to see you again. Come through to my office." The look on his face and flat tone of voice totally contradicted the gesture.

Taking a moment to request Caroline hold his calls, he gestured Elizabeth in the direction of where he'd just appeared from, then walked briskly ahead, speaking over his shoulder. "If you'd like to come this way. Although I'm sure you're quite familiar with our facility by now," he added sourly.

"More than familiar," she mumbled as she trailed him down the corridor.

For some moments they walked in silence until he paused at his office, waiting until she'd entered before following her in, then rounding his desk and taking a seat without offering her one.

She took the chair directly opposite him despite the omission, and waited while he busied himself closing a file on his desk and placing it in a drawer behind him.

When he swiveled back to face her, he leaned both elbows on the desk, hands clasped at his chin. "I have a full calendar today, Mrs. McClaine. I hope this won't take too long."

"Then I'll try to make it brief."

"I assume it's about the Kimmy Donohue incident." He shifted something on his desk. "For your information, we've notified the police, but since she was last known to be in the company of her sister, we're not overly worried."

She smiled. "That's good to hear. Also, while I'm here, I'd appreciate a list of all those on your staff who deal with our private funding arrangements. I'd like to track down whoever has been speaking to the press."

For a moment, he looked dumbfounded.

"The press? What press?"

"You didn't see it? There was a piece about how we fund some our clients into private institutions; Sunny Springs in particular. It's on page three of this morning's paper. Under the article on welfare fraud."

His face blanched. "If anyone here went to the press, believe me, I'd also like to know."

"I'm sure you would. Because right at this moment, my father-in-law, Charles McClaine, is asking the same questions."

David picked up a heavy file and spun on his chair to slap it on the black file cabinet behind him. "Leave it with me, will you, Mrs. McClaine? I'll make some enquiries, but I doubt it's anyone from here. It's strictly in violation of company policy for staff to approach the press without authorization. But thank you for letting me know."

Feeling brushed aside and determined not to be discounted, Elizabeth said, "Then just tell me the name of the person who was supposed to be looking after Kimmy."

"I can't give you names. All I can tell you is that the woman caring for Kimmy at the time is no longer employed here."

"She left? When?"

He hesitated. "Yesterday."

Her eyes narrowed. "She left? Or she was fired?"

"Does it matter?"

"Yes, it matters. I can ask our legal team to address this, David."

"She was fired."

Elizabeth said nothing, just held his gaze.

Wilting under her glare, he broke eye contact to lift a file. "We believe she was responsible for some bruising on Kimmy Donohue. Nothing serious, but worrying."

Elizabeth's mouth dropped open. "Nothing serious? Are you kidding? How did you get this woman? Did she have a history of abuse?"

"You don't think we would have red-lighted that?" Obviously regretting his remark, he reached back and plucked a file from a cabinet behind him.

Somewhat calmer now, he said, "I'm not personally involved in the recruitment process, you understand. I leave all that to Velma." He flicked over a few pages, then zigzagged one finger down the page. "I don't know what use it'll be in finding Kimmy, but here it is: Employment Pulse Recruitment." He slammed the file closed and pushed it toward her. "I should add that we will not be using their services again. I hope that satisfies you."

Elizabeth left the file sitting where it was. "Thank you, David. That's all I needed to know. I won't take up any more of your time." She collected her purse and got up.

Seemingly surprised at the ease with which he had placated her, he rose from his seat and smoothed a hand over his head. "My apologies for my abrupt manner, Elizabeth. I'm completely snowed at the moment. I've got reports to get out, and Velma has called in sick."

"That's a pity." It came out a little more coolly than she'd intended. "I hope she's well again soon."

Once again, he rounded the desk, guiding her to the door. "I just hope she's back tomorrow, sick or not. I'm down two admin staff and I've had to leave a junior nurse aid on reception."

"She seems to be doing a fine job."

Elizabeth was just about to step through the doorway when she turned, a tiny frown creasing her brow. "Oh, by the way, you couldn't tell me what files Laney Donohue stole when she broke in, could you?"

His face blanched. "No, I couldn't. I haven't had a chance to review what's missing."

"When you find out, would you mind letting me know?" she said.

"Of course. The instant I'm in possession of those facts, I'll call you."

"Thank you," she said.

He was lying through his teeth, and she knew it.

But she had one more piece of the puzzle.

CHAPTER FIFTEEN
DAY TWO—10:22 AM—LANEY

Tasked now with also finding Mrs. O'Dell's lost daughter, Laney had offered up a few pathetic words of solace. Even to Laney, they sounded empty and clichéd. But she wasn't used to these situations. So, when there was no response and Mrs. O'Dell had continued sobbing into her hands, rocking like a child, she'd touched her on the shoulder, said her goodbyes, and slipped out of the door feeling her spirits as leaden as the overhead skies.

As she made her way back to the car, shoulders hunched against the rain, she'd made herself a silent promise that if she could find anything about the real Wendy O'Dell, about where she'd gone, why she'd disappeared from her family's life, she'd return and pass it on to her mother. Good news or bad, a mother had the right to know.

But if the woman she'd been searching for wasn't the same as the one who'd left the grieving mother Laney had just visited, then who was she?

She was sitting in the car outside Wendy O'Dell's parents' house, trying to put aside the memory of that mother's torment, when a second message came in—this one also from Kiddy. But this one had an address. What the hell had happened that Kiddy needed to see her so badly? Who could she have spoken to at such short notice?

Laney immediately fired up the car and took off.

Twenty-two minutes later, here she was sitting outside the address Kiddy had given her, looking the house over. Drapes drawn, newspapers piled up on the front steps, grass a couple of weeks past cutting, it looked abandoned. Gingerly, she got out of the car and went up the front path, one eye on the street. Instead of ringing the front doorbell, Laney opted to follow a narrow path that led around the side of the house, under an arched trellis over which a bedraggled rose bush had climbed, and around to the back yard. The surface of the pool was strewn with fallen leaves that dappled the dirty blue cement bottom in shadow. Two chairs and a potted plant had been blown over alongside the barbecue, the cover of which had been lifted and twisted to one side by the wind.

Fear stabbed at her gut. It looked like no one had been here for weeks. Maybe months. So why send her here?

Fighting the urge to run, she moved onto the decking at the back of the house, one eye on the perimeter hedging shielding the pool area from the neighbors, then paused with her back pressed to the wall beside a window.

Inside she could see a broad dining room with eight chairs positioned around a long wooden table, behind which stood an ornately carved wooden dresser lined with plates and cups. Through a door to the left of the room, the house was in darkness. Just ambient light from an outside source. Probably a rear window. When a shadow passed the doorway, she sucked in a quick breath and jerked back out of sight.

That was enough. Whoever was in the house must have seen her. She didn't have time for stupid games.

Ducking under the next window, she headed for the front yard and the street again. But just as she reached the corner, she heard the sound of the front door closing.

Immediately, she turned back, walking quickly towards the rear of the property from where she'd just come. When she checked back over her shoulder, she saw a shadow—someone following her. She broke into a trot, and was just about to run for the rear fence when she heard Kiddy's voice.

"Hey, stupid! Where are you going?"

Laney stopped short with her hand to her heart, felt it thudding against her ribs.

"Kiddy? Is that you?"

Sure enough, Kiddy rounded the corner behind her dressed in skin-tight jeans, a *Soundgarden* tee shirt, and the same puffer jacket and boots. She'd wiped the mascara from beneath her eyes but her pallor was still the same washed-out gray of a habitual meth user.

"For cryin' out loud, you scared the bejeezus out of me."

"I told you to meet me here, didn't I? I don't know why you're getting your panties in a bunch."

"Okay, okay." She gestured towards the house. "So, what's the deal with this place? Looks like nobody's been here for years."

"Well, just after you left I got ahold of Dorothy, the old lady that does the afternoon shift, right? So, I asked her if she knew where Wendy lived. And she didn't." She threw up her hands and lifted both shoulders. As if that was the end of it.

Laney made a face. "Yeah, so…?"

"So, anyway, I said, 'Well, do you know where she mighta gone?' and she's like, 'Why do you want to know?' And I'm like, 'You remember Laney Donohue, right? Kimmy's sister?'"

Laney frowned, wondering if she'd ever get to the point. "Yeah, yeah, so what did she say?"

"So anyway, she says there was another girl turned up about a week before Wendy split. Apparently, she was looking for some girl named Katarina something-or-other. Dorothy remembered because this girl had the same accent as Wendy. Anyway, I said, 'So, what happened to her?' And Dorothy was like, 'Oh, yeah, so Velma came out and talked to her. She took her inside and then two guys came and picked her up.' So, Dorothy followed them. You know, to see where they went."

"As you do," Laney said, implying it would be the last thing you'd do.

Ignoring the sarcasm, Kiddy turned toward the house, waving a dismissive hand at it. "So, anyway, this is where they brought her—like, the new girl."

"Was it the Armani guy? The same one who picked up Wendy?"

"Nah, this one was a fat guy. Dorothy said the other one kept giving him orders and the fat one looked totally pissed."

Laney frowned and looked up at the blank windows and unwelcoming façade.

"So, what'd they do when she got here?"

"Beats me. They took her inside, but you'd never know. Looks as if no one's been there in, like, months. There's dust all over the furniture, and the fridge has been switched off."

Laney's jaw dropped. "You broke in?"

Kiddy gave her an incredulous look. "The locks were totally simple. It's like the place was just begging to get burgled." As if that justified her actions.

"And you thought you'd get me out here so I could get arrested along with you? Gee, thanks a bunch."

Kiddy's shoulders slumped and her eyes rolled heavenward. "Nobody's getting arrested, for cryin' out loud. Geez, you've turned into a such a wimp since you got out. But wait till you see what I found inside."

Laney's eyes went back up to the darkened upper-story windows with a welling sense of dread. "What did you find?"

"Come and see."

***

The Associate

A tiny red light blinked on in the bottom right-hand corner of his screen.

Oh please, God, no!

Ever since he installed the surveillance system in the house, he'd dreaded that red light. Movement-activated cameras throughout the house. The sensor set to trigger that red light at the slightest movement.

For months, nothing had happened. Then a week ago, he got that call—the one to say that a girl had turned up at Sunny Springs asking about Katarina.

If they found Katarina, they would take her and he'd never see her again. Giving up her friend made him sick to his stomach. But what else could he have done? So he'd made a call. Was told to let them deal with her.

Within the hour, two men had picked her up and taken her to the house.

Intrigued, wondering what this girl knew, whether she'd talk, he'd turned the video on, tracked the two men as they escorted the girl into the front entrance and down the hallway.

He'd switched the camera angle to watch them pause to unlock the basement door. Even without audio it was obvious she was questioning them, asking where they were taking her.

One of them appeared to give her a brief explanation, then ushered her through the door. Even more curious now, he'd switched the feed to the basement camera that he'd installed high in the corner, angled down across the workbench. It was on a swivel bracket so the camera could pan from one side of the basement to the other.

What he'd witnessed after that had made him sick to his stomach. He'd had to turn it off. Then he'd sat there with the images he'd just witnessed spooling over and over through his head, knowing that while he'd never heard her screams, he'd never obliterate those last images from his memory.

It was that night, while he burned her clothing in back of the house, that he'd gotten that phone call.

Now that little light was on again. This time, there had been no warning.

Reluctantly, he'd clicked on the hallway camera and watched the young woman enter the front door. She looked like a teenager, her hair a nest of blonde ringlets. She wore puffer jacket, jeans, and a dark tee shirt.

With his heart in his mouth and his fist pressed to his lips, he watched her close the door and creep through the house, opening doors and peering into rooms before moving on. He clicked to the second camera, palms sweating, blood pounding in his ears as he watched her try the basement door.

"Don't go in there. Please don't go in there," he begged her under his breath.

Unable to open it, she walked on to the kitchen while he let out a breath. He followed her back in the direction she'd come, then up the stairs. When he lost her briefly, he feverishly clicked from camera to camera, desperate to locate her. He found her on camera four upstairs and tracked her into each of the bedrooms, both bathrooms, then the upstairs office.

"No, no, no," he muttered over and over, slowly shaking his head as he watched her opening drawers, and closets.

Keeping one eye on the screen, he checked there was no one outside his office and lifted the phone.

The second it answered, he said, "There's movement in the house. Someone's broken in." He listened to the response, glanced at his watch, then said, "It's ten minutes away. She could be gone…no, wait…" His heart flipped. "Now there's two of them," he said.

The man at the other end snapped out a couple of orders.

He nodded. "I'll get over there right now," he said and hung up.

CHAPTER SIXTEEN
DAY TWO—11:50 AM—ELIZABETH

No calls. No messages on the phone. In fact, Delaney probably wouldn't even bother contacting her if they found the identity of the dead girl. Why would he? But Elizabeth had more than one string to this violin. She was just lifting her phone when it rang in her hand—a number she didn't recognize, so she kept the greeting cool and brief.

"Elizabeth McClaine."

A woman's voice replied. "Mrs. McClaine, this is Jennifer Reels. I'm a freelance reporter. I believe you wanted to speak to me." Blunt, forthright, she sounded in her late forties, maybe early fifties, with the husky voice of a smoker.

"That was quick, Miss Reels."

"Your PA just spoke to me. What can I do for you?"

No correction on the "Miss," Elizabeth noted. She checked the time. "I'm just on my way out. I'd like to meet with you if I can."

"I'm sure you do." A wry smile came through on her words. As if she was holding the line, waiting for Elizabeth to take the bait.

This was a game Elizabeth knew well enough to be wary.

"What time is good for you?"

Jennifer Reels had suggested they meet straightaway. Which didn't surprise Elizabeth. The woman smelled blood and she wasn't about to let go. By happy coincidence, it turned out Miss Reels was about twelve minutes away. So Elizabeth had proposed her local coffee shop in fifteen.

Despite Elizabeth's making it to the Café St Martin on time, Jennifer Reels had arrived early and was already seated when she walked in. She recognized her the second she saw her—a plump brunette with hair styled in a fashionable swept-over bob with a splash of white over her forehead. Probably in her early sixties, she wore a long-sleeved navy dress with matching shawl tossed over one shoulder, deep red lipstick, long false nails to match, and a glittering array of heavy rings on most fingers. The last time Elizabeth had seen her was at a fund-raising luncheon for the Paralympics. The woman had looked bored throughout the entire event and hardly looked up from her phone.

She waved Elizabeth over and gestured to the seat opposite her. Only now did Elizabeth notice the woman's phone on the table. Set to capture every word, no doubt.

She sat without expression. "I'd prefer you didn't record this."

"If that's what you want." The journalist slid the phone towards herself, swiped through some options on the screen, but left it where it was with the screen blank.

Elizabeth met her gaze with a cool smile. "I read your article this morning, Miss Reels."

A wolfish smile widened on Jennifer Reels's mouth. She leaned forward on her elbows, thick, ring-studded fingers clasped at her chin.

"A call out of the blue, straight after my story? I've been in this business a while, Mrs. McClaine. Wouldn't take a genius to know what brought you here."

Elizabeth broke eye contact while she placed her purse down on the floor next to her. "I'd like to know where you get your information."

"I'm sure you do. And I'm sure you know I'm not obliged to divulge that."

With a mildly condescending smile, Elizabeth relaxed and met her eye. "Unless your information is incorrect."

"Oh, my information is quite correct, Mrs. McClaine. You could say it's right from the horse's mouth."

The smug, self-assured smile irritated Elizabeth. But the last thing she could do was lose her composure.

"I'm sure your sources think they have their facts in order, Miss Reels, but the numbers stated in your article are clearly…" A small shake of the head, as if searching for the word. "…way off the mark."

Try and explain that one way, she thought and fixed the woman with a challenging stare.

Without responding, Jennifer Reels leaned to one side and picked up a file from the briefcase down by the leg of her chair. She flicked through a few of the enclosed pages, stopping on one, then twisted the file on the table to face Elizabeth. The open page showed the electronically signed documents Elizabeth had forwarded back to the court, confirming sponsorship of Kimmy Donohue.

"Is this your signature?"

"This is a confidential document. Where the hell did you get it?" Elizabeth demanded, all pretense at pleasantries gone.

Obviously satisfied by the fact that she'd rattled her, Jennifer pulled the file back, flipped the page, and slid it back again.

Elizabeth blinked at the document now in front of her. It was the same document confirming her foundation's sponsorship, signed in the same way, and also sent to the relevant authorities. This time it was the application of a young man Elizabeth knew well. He had been virtually paralyzed since birth with cerebral palsy, and recently lost his mother who had been caring for him. According to the notes below, one of the conditions of support from the Charles McClaine Foundation was the referral to Sunny Springs for live-in care. She looked up in horror.

"This is a mistake."

"A mistake, Mrs. McClaine? It's right here in black and white. And here's another. Is this also a mistake?" Jennifer Reels flipped to the next document— this time a young autistic woman. Elizabeth knew her also. With help from her social worker, she'd applied for funding from the Charles McClaine Foundation while waiting for her Medicaid Waiver. Elizabeth had sponsored her without question. But the form in front of her clearly stated that the young woman would only be granted the funding if she were to reside at the Ellan Graves Home for the Disabled—the sister home to Sunny Springs.

Elizabeth angrily stabbed the pile of documents with the nail of her index finger. "These documents have been altered. I did *not* authorize these referrals."

"So, you're saying you didn't refer Kimmy Donohue?"

Stumbling for words now, Elizabeth could see a dangerous hole opening up right in front of her. Anything she said now could be twisted into something else. She hesitated, then opted for "That is none of your business."

"Au contraire, Mrs. McClaine. This is very much my business. Your electronic signature is on every document in this file. If you didn't put it there, can you explain how it got there?"

For a moment, Elizabeth was lost for words. She'd been around politicians and the press for long enough to know that whatever came out of her mouth next could cause the finger of blame to point to some even more diabolical act of treachery she was supposed to have carried out. In fact, she'd probably done quite enough damage now.

Keeping her lips firmly pressed together, Elizabeth got up and tucked her purse under her arm, trying valiantly to hide how shaken she was. "I have nothing more to say to you, Miss Reels." She pushed in her chair. As if that punctuated the end of the conversation.

"Until what? You speak to your lawyer?" The woman smiled up with that slimy grin again.

"I think this meeting is over." Elizabeth turned to leave, but behind her, Jennifer Reels called after her.

"And what about Kimmy Donohue's abduction, Mrs. McClaine?"

Elizabeth spun around, her nostrils flared.

But Jennifer Reels wasn't done. The grin faded into an expression of fake bewilderment. "Or are you telling me that it's sheer coincidence that one of the clients *you* referred to Sunny Springs is missing? A young woman that could be dead because you put her into an institution rather than allowing her to stay with her aunt?" She cocked her head. "So tell me, Mrs. McClaine, because this is your opportunity to set the story straight. You've referred fifteen young people into these places in the last four months." She passed her a sly sideways smile and winked. "What's in it for you?"

The words sent a blast of fury through Elizabeth. She took one step towards the hateful shrew. "I don't know where you get your facts, but you'd better start looking for your shit under someone else's rug. My foundation was set up to help these young people. You keep printing your lies, you'll have my lawyer banging on your door. And you won't look so smug when I sue you for libel."

And she walked out.

As soon as she'd gotten into her car, she took out her phone with shaking hands and dialed. Penny answered almost immediately.

Elizabeth took a measured breath, an attempt to keep the tremors from her voice. "How did you get on?"

Penny sounded immediately concerned. "Are you okay?"

For a long moment, Elizabeth pressed her lips together so hard they hurt. Then she swallowed back the welling urge to cry.

"I never want to see that woman again."

"That good, huh?"

Elizabeth sniffed back the tears. "Not even that good. What did you find out?"

"Well, it sounds like I did better than you."

CHAPTER SEVENTEEN
DAY TWO—12:45 PM—LANEY

Laney had followed Kiddy in through the front door of the house, noting the heavy Yale deadlock on the front door and wondering how long it had taken Kiddy to pick it.

Inside, shafts of late morning light cut through the gaps between the closed drapes, picking out a sea of dust motes that swirled in the unseen air currents. The place smelled stale, like old books. Feeling every ounce the intruder, she followed Kiddy through the living room towards the back of the house and paused at a basement door under the stairs. It bore a recently installed lock of solid new brass set into the door.

Kiddy dropped to one knee and got to work on it.

"How long have you been here?" Laney asked, wandering past her towards the kitchen to peer out into the back yard where she'd been a short while ago.

"Not so long. I checked the upstairs but there's nothing up there. Like, there's furniture and everything, but there's no clothes in the closets or nothing. I haven't looked down here, though."

Laney watched her for a moment, her ear turned to the lock, fingers working like a surgeon, lock-picks twisting this way and that in infinitesimally small increments.

Whereas Laney could pick locks, Kiddy was clearly a pro. Another skill she'd picked up in Carringway.

Laney folded her arms and leaned a shoulder to the wall while she waited.

"That's some lock. I wonder what's down there."

Kiddy grinned up at her. "Yeah, you can bet whoever put it on here was protecting more than the water heater. Oh, hey, I think I got it."

There was a faint click and Kiddy tried the handle. It opened to a dark set of stairs leading to the basement.

"You wanna go first?" asked Kiddy.

Laney gestured. "Nah-uh. You opened it. You get the honor."

"Chicken." With a wider grin, she pocketed her lock-picks and gingerly stepped through onto a small wooden landing.

Laney peered over her shoulder. "What can you see?"

"Nothin' without lights." She scuffed her hand up and down the wall on each side of the doorframe until she found a switch. She flipped it and a pale, yellow light snapped on down below.

With her hand on Kiddy's shoulder, Laney moved gingerly down the stairs.

"Jeez, it smells like something died down here."

"You're not kidding," said Kiddy, who trod her way carefully down the ten wooden steps, pausing to blow out a breath on each one that creaked under her weight. "Jeez, I hope these stairs hold. We fall down here, no one's coming looking for us."

"Yeah, thanks for that."

The single overhead bulb illuminated a typical basement set with water heater, pipes snaking up the walls and across the ceiling, washer and drier at the foot of the stairs, furnace in the corner. Directly across from the stairway was an old wooden workbench, dark oily stains over the surface, vise screwed to one side. Beside it sat a wooden kitchen chair. Laney moved straight to the bench while Kiddy walked the perimeter of the room and paused to open the washer.

"There's nothing but shit down here. Why would you go to so much trouble to lock it all up?"

Kiddy snapped open the drier and leaned in. "There's clothes in here."
"What kind?"
She pulled out a narrow pair of women's jeans that she held up against

herself, then tossed them onto the washer. Next, she drew out a grubby-looking tee shirt and tasseled shawl. Finally, a pair of women's underwear which she held pincered between her finger and thumb.

"Nothing fashion-worthy, that's for real."

Laney snorted. "Like you'd know."

She tossed the underwear back into the machine. "You're just hilarious. Remind me to ask you over next time I need a laugh."

"At least I'm not still living with my parents," said Laney.

"Hey, don't knock it. It's free and the meals are pretty good." She held up the sweater then consigned it to the heap. "Well, whoever washed this stuff must have forgotten to come back for them. Hardly surprising—they're not missing much. Although it does make you wonder what she left in." She stuffed everything back into the machine while Laney returned her attention to the array of screwdrivers, pliers, wire cutters, and a coil of wire that littered the top of the workbench.

Wrinkling her nose, Laney searched the area. "What's that stink? It smells like something's gone rotten."

Kiddy moved up next to her and absently picked up a pair of pliers. When she opened the grips a pale pink, oval flake fell out. She picked it up, turning it in her fingers, then threw it down and stepped back. "Oh, shit."

"What is it?"

She wiped her hand on her jeans. "It's a freakin' fingernail. That's what it is."

"What? In the pliers?"

Already Laney was picking them up, studying them. Then she picked up the section of fingernail. "Oh jeez, this is blood."

"Somebody was tortured down here. That's why the locks on the door. Let's get out of here." Kiddy headed for the stairs.

Laney spread her hands, watching her. "So that's it? You're just out of here?"

Kiddy spun around. "Are you kidding? You know the kind of people that do this shit? You mess with them, you'll be the next one disappears."

"I'm not done till I find out what happened to Wendy."

Kiddy pointed. "And all this doesn't put you off?"

"All this just makes me want to find her even more."

Kiddy snorted. "Good luck with that. Close the door on your way out," she said and scurried up the stairs, leaving Laney alone in the basement.

"And thanks a bunch," Laney yelled after her. Kiddy's footsteps creaked overhead on the wood floor, then she heard the sound of the front door closing. That was fine. It was better to do this alone. Whatever had happened down here had everything to do with Wendy. Her gut told her there was a connection.

All she had to do was find it.

CHAPTER EIGHTEEN
DAY TWO—12:50 AM—ELIZABETH

"You told her to find her shit under someone else's rug? Seriously? You said that to her?" Penny grinned in awe.

Elizabeth didn't exactly share her enthusiasm. They were on their way to the address Penny had found for Janelle Hooper, Penny gripping the wheel with palpable zeal as she wove in and out of traffic—something Elizabeth usually pulled her up on. But right now, her mind was back at the café, still picturing that smug, self-assured grin on Jennifer Reels's face.

She turned her gaze to the passenger window, mentally kicking herself. "I was stupid. I let her goad me. And I knew exactly what she was doing. She laid those documents right in front of me, then smiled like a barracuda, waiting for me to jump into the pool. And I did. With both feet."

"Meh, don't let it worry you. What's she going to do now? Accuse you of saying she's full of shit?" She chuckled. "Man, I wish I'd been there."

Penny hit the turn signal and swerved around the next corner so fast the momentum threw Elizabeth sideways. She grabbed the dashboard to prevent herself falling against Penny.

"Uh, can we slow down a little? Thank you," she said when the car slowed to within the limit. "I know her type. She'll start digging, that's what she'll do."

The corners of Penny's mouth went down. "And what's she going to find? That you're offering young people help when they need it? Wow. You are evil beyond words."

Elizabeth lifted her purse and checked her phone, running her thumb down a mark on the screen, momentarily annoyed to discover it was a scratch. She switched it on. "I don't trust her. She's one of those people who'll dig up anything she can for a story. It doesn't have to be true."

"Yeah, but you've got nothing to hide. Have you?"

She cut a sharp look at her PA.

Penny noted it. "I'm just saying you've got nothing to worry about. So quit stressing."

"You know, if this woman wants to get ugly, truth be damned, she will. And where did she manage to dig up all those documents from? Ones I didn't sign. And if I didn't sign them, who did? And why? What's there to gain? A few measly bucks for..." She stopped mid-sentence while the implications circled in her brain. Then it hit her.

"You've got that look."

"Who would gain the most from having new clients admitted? Clients with guaranteed funding already in place?"

"If we're talking Sunny Springs, then Sunny Springs, I guess. Or the Ellan Graves Home for the Disabled. You said one of the young people had gone there."

"Exactly. Both of those places are owned by Aden Falls Corp."

"I don't buy it. Why would a huge conglomerate like Aden Falls start cooking the books to make, what? A few hundred bucks? That would be ridiculous."

"Then why? That's what I don't understand."

Penny pulled the car to a stop and cut the engine. "Try to understand it later. We're here."

CHAPTER NINETEEN
DAY TWO—1:00 PM—LANEY

Laney started with the clothes. The tags were a brand she'd never heard of, the jeans for someone tall and slim, and the shawl somewhat ragged after washing. But when she drew out the tee shirt and held it up, she could clearly see darkened marks across both the back and front. In light of what she'd seen so far, there was little doubt what those marks were.

She put the clothing back, and was just about to head upstairs when she noticed a tiny corner of white peeking out from behind the work bench. Wedging the tip of a screwdriver in behind the bench, she gently eased it out.

It was a tiny photograph, same as the one on Wendy's employment file. The girl in the picture was just as beautiful—large green eyes, long black hair, smooth olive skin. On the back, a line of tiny letters in pale blue read, *Pierre Porter Photos.*

Upstairs again, she stuck the screwdriver in her pocket and followed the hallway to the front of the house again, heading for the second floor. Whoever owned the house must have left something that would identify them. Third doorway down, just as Kiddy had said, she found the office.

Brightly lit with nursery motifs over the walls, it must have once served as a baby's room. Now, under the window that looked out into a huge Cleveland Pear tree, sat a broad oak desk set with a writing set, ink blotter, and phone. After closing the door, she plopped down in the black leather office chair, and slid out each of the drawers. Nothing in the top three. The fourth one down was locked. She rattled it, then pushed the chair out to lean down and study it. It looked like one of those big file drawers and had a tiny keyhole in the top right corner. She spun in the chair left and right, checking the room for anywhere that might hold the key.

"Shit! You're hiding something in here, I just know it."

So she got to work on it with the screwdriver. Wedging it into the gap along the edge of the drawer, she pressed down hard, levering the gap wider until the metal buckled and the lock finally gave way. She opened it.

The drawer was heavy and stiff, like it had been overfilled. Inside was a line of bulging files. Placing the screwdriver on the desk, she picked the first file out and opened it. It looked like a bunch of legal documents, each one written in a language that looked like Russian, or Bulgarian, or whatever, and each marked with an official-looking red stamp.

She laid it on the desk and plucked out the next one. All in the same language. She was about to discard it when she ran her eyes down to the final line on the page. According to the text in English, it had been signed by someone from Aden Falls Corporation but the signature was indecipherable. Didn't Aden Falls own Sunny Springs?

At the back of the drawer was another set of files. She pulled it out to find a dossier with the name *Employment Pulse* written across the front. It was stacked with what looked like employment files, each pinned with a headshot photograph of a young woman who stared blankly into the camera, a barcode beneath. Each of the women was perhaps in her teens to early twenties, dark-haired and attractive.

So, assuming these were employment profiles, then it followed that the top line next to the photograph, "emër," was probably the woman's name. Below that, each field had been completed in the same language. All the way down.

She thumbed through the pile. Stapled to each girl's file was a small newspaper clipping in some foreign language.

Laney would have bet her right arm these were employment advertisements.

The final four profiles each had a large red line running corner to corner. Like they'd been crossed off. Or they were no longer available. Then she came to the last one.

She recognized her straightaway—the woman she'd known as Wendy. It was exactly the same photo as on the file she'd lifted from Sunny Springs. And on this one, the name on the second line down was in English.

"So, your name is Katarina. Katarina Novak." She studied the photograph closely, noting the blank look in her eyes, an expression of utter despair. "How'd you wind up working in Sunny Springs, Katarina? And if you're working under Wendy O'Dell's name, what happened to her?"

Laney leaned down and pulled the rest of the files forward. At the very back of the drawer, she found a stack of passports, all bound together with a rubber band. She slipped the band off and shuffled through them. Each bore a banner of six stars over the jagged outline of a country, and the words, "Republic of Kosovo" printed on the front.

Was someone running an employment agency out of here? And if so, what kind? These girls all looked more like magazine models. Why would they come all the way from another country to take low-paid jobs for places like Sunny Springs?

Unless…

Laney lifted the corner of the first photograph on the first employment file. A tiny line typewritten in blue read: *Pierre Porter Photos.* Same with the next two. Same as the one on the photo she'd found downstairs.

Her gut told her if she didn't join the dots and figure out what was going on and where, Katarina would disappear forever.

Laney had to find her. For all she'd done for Kimmy. She owed her at least that much.

She was so engrossed in studying each of the passports that when she heard the front door close, she physically jumped—then grinned.

Without even turning around, she shouted, "I knew you'd come back."

For some seconds, she sat there expecting a smart remark in response. She swiveled on the chair, ready with a smug remark to Kiddy about running off like that. When no response came back, her grin faded.

Footsteps echoed up from downstairs.

She frowned. "Kiddy? Is that you?"

A creak from the stairway sent her heart into a gallop and her stomach dropped.

"Kiddy, will you quit screwing around?" she called, although everything in her gut told her to run. That this wasn't Kiddy. That whoever it was, she didn't want to be there.

At the sound of footsteps approaching, she leapt out of the chair and backed up, eyes wide, heart in her throat.

The footsteps halted. Just on the other side of the door. A matter of feet from her.

"Kiddy?" she asked under her breath.

The door swung open.

CHAPTER TWENTY
DAY TWO—1:00 PM—ELIZABETH

Elizabeth and Penny both peered across the street at the house. Neatly manicured lawns, huge tree in the front yard. If you asked Elizabeth, it was the kind of warm-looking family home every American deserved. But life wasn't always fair.

As she followed Penny up to the front door, Elizabeth couldn't help casting an admiring eye across the gardens. Why on earth had Laney Donohue refused to allow her sister to live here? Why would she have opted for a place like Sunny Springs instead?

The door opened a matter of seconds after Penny's knock. Janelle Hooper must have been waiting since they'd called.

"Come on in," she said by way of greeting as she widened the door.

Penny slipped a look back at Elizabeth, then stepped on inside. Elizabeth followed, giving the woman a brief smile that must have appeared as cool as the chill she felt in her heart as the door closed behind her.

"Come on through this way." Janelle gestured to a neat living room off to the right, then strode off past them, leading the way. Dressed in blue jeans, checked shirt under an Indians sweater with the collar pulled up, bare feet, she sat heavily in an armchair. "Take a seat."

Elizabeth sat and made a slightly more in-depth assessment of the woman: short, spiky brown hair around a weathered face, dirt-stained hands, callouses down the sides of her fingers. Signs of a woman not afraid of hard work.

Janelle Hooper cocked her head. "So, tell me what this is all about."

Elizabeth spoke. "It's about your niece, Kimmy Donohue."

"Yeah? What about her?"

Before Elizabeth had a chance, Penny jumped in. "How did she wind up in a place like Sunny Springs? Why didn't she come and stay with you while Laney Donohue was in prison?"

Janelle raised her eyebrows, looking a little taken aback by the bluntness while Elizabeth slipped Penny a withering gaze for the same reason. But Elizabeth was mildly surprised when Janelle answered.

"Whoa. Straight to the point, huh?" She drew a deep resigned breath and thoughtfully shook her head. "If I'da known Kimmy was gonna end up in that shithole…excuse my language—"

"You're excused," Penny said without a second thought. Or without considering Elizabeth.

Janelle continued. "Well, I would have had her come stay here. For cryin' out loud, she's family," she said, gesturing widely. "That's what you do with family, right?"

Elizabeth jumped in next, cutting off Penny, who was probably going to ask the same question. "I'm sorry to be so blunt, but why didn't you?"

Again, Janelle considered the question, this time tilting her head back and groaning mildly, as if in self-recrimination. "We weren't on good terms, me and Laney. Shouldn't have been that way, but that's how it was. Laney's mom—my sister—she, ah…" Janelle shifted in her seat while she found the words, then she swallowed hard and looked up. "She took her own life three years back." She paused and bit her lip, clearly fighting back a wall of emotion, then cleared her throat and swallowed hard before meeting their gazes again.

"I'm so sorry."

Still fighting to contain herself, she rubbed a knuckle at the corner of one eye. "Well, I told the powers-that-be after the funeral that I'd take Kimmy. No way was I gonna let the kid down. I was more than happy to have her come live here. She'd have been happy. I'da made sure of that. But by then, Laney had already applied for guardianship. I was pissed, I can tell you."

"But, surely since Laney was her sister, that made the most sense.

Especially if that's what she wanted. And I know that you may not agree, but I think that's a very noble gesture—a young woman determined to care for her disabled sister."

Janelle blinked at the floor a couple of times. When her gaze came up, it was flush with regret. "Ah, geez." She rolled the back of her hand under her nose and averted her eyes briefly before answering. "Laney was always trouble. Ever since Kimmy fell in that pool and wound up with head injuries. Soon as they declared her brain-damaged for life, Laney went right off the rails. Gave her mom hell; did things I don't even want to think about. She stole, acted out, stayed out all night worrying her mom sick." She dropped her head, squeezed a finger and thumb to her eyes, then looked up, fighting back that welling emotion again. "I blamed her for my sister's death."

An agonizing silence fell, neither Elizabeth nor Penny knowing what to say. Janelle broke it, saying in a low voice, "It wasn't her fault. I was looking for someone to blame. Then, when she got custody of Kimmy, I was pissed as hell. I refused to talk to her. Refused to go near her. I thought she'd just screw it up. And then when she got herself arrested…" For a moment, she sat blinking hard against the welling tears, knuckles white as she wrung her hands in her lap.

"When she got arrested, I thought, 'There you go. I knew you'd screw up.' Then a while after, I found out Laney had lost her job. She'd refused welfare, the stupid girl." A tear broke, ran down her cheek, and dropped from her chin. "I thought, 'Why didn't she come to me? Why didn't she ask me for help?' But she couldn't, could she? I'd cut her off. Didn't even offer to help her when she had Kimmy. What kind of family does that? What kind of family turns their back on their own?"

She sniffed hard and turned her face away to press the heel of her hand to each eye, then sat there, staring into her hands.

"Have you seen Kimmy since?" This from Penny, her voice soft with sympathy.

Janelle nodded, short and sharp, then met her gaze and sucked in one long, ragged breath. "I went to visit her every second day in Sunny Springs. I kept telling her that she'd be home soon, that I'd make sure she was okay."

"So, what did you do?"

"I applied for guardianship. Got turned down. Then I went to see that judge that signed all the papers. He said his hands were tied, said he couldn't do anything. I felt terrible for Kimmy. All I wanted to do was help her. But all she wanted was to be with Laney."

"I'm sorry. But it's kind of understandable she'd want her sister. Especially if Laney had taken over caring for her, been like a mother to her. And it's always tough on siblings. They get the short end of the straw. They always come in second in the family. Which is why so many of them act out."

"Oh, don't get me wrong. Laney adored Kimmy. Always did. And that love went both ways. Kimmy followed Laney around like she was the second coming. Far as Kimmy was concerned, she was the perfect sister."

"So, what made her go so far off the rails?" Elizabeth asked.

"Because Laney was the one who pushed Kimmy into that pool. She never forgave herself. Truth be known," she said and swallowed hard, "neither did I."

They sat for some minutes while Janelle left the room, ostensibly to check something upstairs. But when she returned, her eyes were visibly red and swollen. She sat down, pulled herself together, and laid both arms along the rests of the armchair as if steeling herself against further emotional displays. "I don't know what else I can tell you. I don't know where Laney is now."

"Have you contacted David Whitcliff?"

Janelle let out a derisive snort. "Call him? Pfft. I wouldn't spit on that conniving skunk. Saw him when I was there visiting Kimmy. Swaggering around like with his ass-wipe cronies, making out he was king of the hill. And all the time allowing someone to leave bruises all over my niece." The moment the words were out, she dropped her eyes to her thumbnail, as if a split in it had suddenly caught her attention. Then she got up. "Anyway, I gotta get on. Gardens don't weed themselves."

Elizabeth rose from her seat, eyeing her. "How did you know Kimmy had bruises on her?"

Janelle was halfway to the front door, and stopped to busy herself, straightening a picture. She looked back in fake surprise. "Excuse me?"

"I asked how you knew Kimmy had bruising if you hadn't seen Laney." Elizabeth waited, head cocked. "Or did you speak to her?"

At the sound of a door closing somewhere upstairs, Janelle huffed and her shoulders fell. The three of them moved to the foot of the stairs, waiting. After a few soft footsteps, Kimmy Donohue appeared on the landing peering down at them, nibbling her thumbnail and looking utterly forlorn.

"Laney?" she asked in a tiny voice.

"Oh, Kimmy." Janelle moved straight up the stairs towards her and took her by the hand. "I told you to stay upstairs, honey."

"Laney?"

"Well, at least we know where Kimmy is." said Elizabeth.

On their way back to the car, Penny said, "I'd still like to know who put those bruises on her."

"You're not the only one. It's one thing to blacken my name in the papers, but when you start abusing my clients, I'm not sitting around on my hands. But there's something more going on than what we see. And I intend to get to the bottom of it."

"You're going to see Jennifer Reels again?"

"Not right now. I need to get a few more facts straightened out. I'll drop you back at the office. I need you to hunt out anything you can on Jennifer Reels. I'll be making a surprise visit on Ryan Halverston. I want to know exactly how they processed my recommendations. And he'd better have some good explanations."

CHAPTER TWENTY-ONE
DAY TWO—1:32 PM—LANEY

Even before the door was fully open, Laney was in motion. Shoulder leading, she barged forward like a linebacker, crashing into his midriff.

But he was ready for her. She caught a fleeting glimpse of him, ducked under his arm to make a beeline for the stairs. But before she could get her footing she felt something crack her hard on the back of the head, and she went down, her head reverberating like a bell.

When she blinked open her eyes, he had her gripped under her arms, her feet thudding from one step to the next, vision blurred and her head thumping. He lowered her to the floor and she realized they were at the basement door. He had one hand clamped to her shoulder while he fumbled in his pocket for the key.

Gathering whatever strength she could, she twisted and turned in his grasp until he lost his hold on her and she stumbled into the opposite wall. She got to her hands and knees, but he was already on her, standing astride her, both hands around her throat. She clawed at his fingers, desperate to pry his hands open, but he lifted her and swung her around, then shoved her. She threw out both hands, but tumbled forwards through the open doorway, down the stairway, rolling over and over until she hit the concrete floor below, and came to a halt just in time to hear the door slam shut.

The click of the key confirmed she was locked in.

Every bone in her body ached. Her head felt like it was twice its size. But she didn't have time for sitting around feeling sorry for herself. If these people had taken Katarina, who knew what they'd do to her? To find her, she had to get out of this basement. So she dragged herself to her feet and began searching.

Same basement. Everything where it was when she was last down here. Instinctively, she patted her jeans pockets while she checked the area—no phone. She tried her back pocket—no keys. He must have taken them.

It was only now as she scanned the place for them that she caught a tiny red light up high in the corner above the drier. She moved closer, squinting up at it. A camera. Probably motion activated. That's probably how he'd seen her. She glared into the lens, tossed her head dismissively—then began to search for a way out.

A dirty orange curtain covered a narrow basement window high over the workbench. She climbed up on the bench and drew it back. Bars had been bolted to the outside. No way out there.

Next, she turned her attention to the workbench, searching for anything she could use. In the bottom drawer, she found a hammer.

After testing the heft of it, she gave the camera a sneering look and headed for the stairs again. At the top she stood back, took careful aim, and swung the hammer with all her might—like a baseball great, swinging hard and wide. The hammer hit the lock with a clang. It jarred her arms and shoulders and rang like a bell through her head. She waited for the vibrations to stop ringing through her skull, then studied the lock. The wood around the door held fast.

"Shit!"

In a flash of fury she smashed at the lock over and over, screaming curses at it until her energy gave out and she slumped back against the wall.

This was hopeless. All she was doing was wasting time and energy. Standing there bent over with her hands on her knees, she could feel him watching her, laughing at her.

She straightened, defiant. "Screw you!" she yelled at the camera, and flipped him the bird.

It wasn't until she turned that determined look on the door that she noticed the hinges. Old brass ones, attached with six screws on each side of the hinge, each of them. Each hinge holding the door fast.

Casting the hammer aside, she skipped down the stairs again, giving the camera another *I'm-not-done-yet* look, and began raking through the workbench drawers. This time she came back with a screwdriver and headed up the stairs, flicking a smug grin at the camera. Starting with the top one, she fitted the screwdriver into the first slot. It was tight. At first it wouldn't budge, but she wasn't giving in, so she put all her might into it and the first screw began turning.

After a couple of minutes, the first screw dropped onto the floor, so she started on the next one.

Three screws out, only six more on the other two hinges. Halfway down, the second hinge let out a groan and the door dropped a fraction. By the time she'd gotten the first couple of screws out of the lowermost hinge, the door was beginning to lean inward. She eased her fingers into the crack down the side and pulled. When it creaked and fell towards her she nearly went backwards down the stairs but she jumped aside just in time to watch the door fall inwards with the crack of wood, held now by only the last screw.

She looked up, caught the camera on her.

"Adios, asshole," she said, and headed for the front door.

Right across the street Laney found her car exactly where she'd left it. Dropping to one knee by the right-hand fender, she found the spare key duct taped to the underside of the wheel arch, right where she always kept it. Still no phone. But that didn't matter. She was on her own anyway.

So she got in the car, plunged the key into the ignition, and started it up.

She had no idea where that mystery man would have taken Katarina. No idea if he'd harm her, or if she'd get to her in time. But she'd made a promise to herself, that she'd find her, so she had to try.

And she knew exactly where to start.

CHAPTER TWENTY-TWO
DAY TWO—2:05 PM—ELIZABETH

Ryan Halverston must have been in his early forties, if Elizabeth had to guess. With sparkling blue eyes and a pleasant smile, he'd once been one of the most eligible bachelors in Ohio, until a former Victoria's Secret model had convinced him to put a ring on her finger. Since then, he'd all but completely slipped from the society pages.

"Elizabeth," he said in greeting as she entered his enormous seventeenth-story office set in a fashionable corner of the downtown area overlooking the city. He got up, offered his hand, which Elizabeth took as she leaned in for the perfunctory peck on the cheek.

"Wonderful to see you again. I think you just keep getting lovelier every time we meet."

Despite the overblown flattery, the smile she felt widening on her lips was genuine. It was that old familiar attraction she'd always harbored for Ryan. He was what her mother would have called a dandy. She'd have said he was "smiling in your face while picking your pockets down to the lint." Elizabeth acknowledged her own fickleness for a good-looking man, and took the offered chair while he rounded his desk and sat down again, leaning comfortably back with one ankle resting across his knee.

He briefly lifted one finger in acknowledgement. "Nice party, by the way. And thanks for the invitation."

Elizabeth felt her cheeks warm. For all her bluster on the night, she hadn't even realized he'd been there. "My pleasure. I was…disappointed that I was called away in the middle of it."

He smiled showing perfectly formed white teeth she guessed had to be expensively constructed crowns, while he straightened his tie over his impossibly white shirt. As if not wanting anything to break the spell his good looks cast.

His focus fell to a small bronze paperweight which he repositioned. "Matter of fact, I spent most of my time talking with David Whitcliff, one of our facility managers. I wouldn't blame you if you'd avoided us altogether."

Elizabeth felt her smile drop.

"Is that so? I didn't know David was at my party."

"I have to say, I was a little surprised you'd invite him. Told me he'd come as someone's guest. Then I got stuck with him, talking shop. Couple of times I thought I'd fall asleep." He grinned at his own quip, then fell serious as he moved something on his desk.

"But at the risk of sounding blunt, I doubt you wanted to see me for a guest appraisal." His smile widened, confirming why he'd been so much in demand by all the debutants of Cleveland. Suddenly serious again, he sat forward, leaning on his elbows. All business. "So, what can I do for you, Elizabeth?"

Elizabeth made a mental note to check David Whitcliff's movements on that night, and find out why he didn't tell her he was at the party. She crossed one ankle behind the other under her chair and addressed the point in hand. "Aden Falls. Or more to the point, Sunny Springs Home for the Disabled."

"Sure. What would you like to know?"

"I've just been in a meeting with a journalist. Not an experience I'd like to repeat anytime soon."

He chuckled, moved the paperweight an inch on his desk, then folded his arms and looked up again. "I don't blame you. I try to keep out of their sights these days. Too many tar pits to fall into."

Getting straight to the point, Elizabeth said, "She tells me I've authorized funding for fifteen young people in some of your…housing facilities."

He made a dismissive face. "Is that a problem?"

"Not if I signed them. Which I didn't."

He dropped his gaze a fraction, frowning. "Then it must have been someone in your office."

"There's only me and my PA. And she didn't sign them."

He narrowed his eyes on her, head slightly inclined. "Are you saying that someone in my organization falsified these documents?"

"I'm not making any accusations, Ryan. I'm trying to find out who signed these documents and how these young people ended up channeled into your facilities. To do that, I need to follow the trail back. And it ends with your organization. That's all I'm saying."

Again, he absentmindedly reached across and shifted the file again. Elizabeth lifted her chin a little, trying to read what was written on the front. Apparently noticing that small movement, he lifted the file, opened a drawer, and stuffed it in, leaving Elizabeth feeling like some kind of peeping Tom spying on their business.

He gave her an empty smile. "The best person to talk to would be Emma Waits. She's our admin who deals with all the legalities of funding applications."

"So, where do I find her?"

He fixed her gaze for the longest moment, perhaps assuming Elizabeth wouldn't actually follow through and speak to her.

Finally, in resignation, he lifted his phone, pressed a button. "I'll have my secretary find her."

Elizabeth waited in the outer office for several minutes before a young woman appeared. Eyeglasses, knee-length checked woolen skirt, white blouse slightly open at the throat to show a gold cross on a fine chain, flat-soled shoes—she approached Elizabeth with her hand out.

"I'm Emma Waits. Mr. Halverston tells me you wanted to talk to me about the application system."

Taking her hand and rising to her feet, Elizabeth said, "That's correct. If you could just walk me through your systems, I'd be grateful."

They walked along a brightly lit hallway, eggshell blue painted walls with artwork tastefully displayed on each side. Elizabeth eyed a couple of works by local artists she found herself coveting, but snapped herself back to the task at hand when Emma paused at a doorway, indicating for her to enter, saying, "This way."

Inside was a desk stacked with files and ledgers, papers and reports. She offered Elizabeth a seat, then rounded the desk to sit opposite her. "They say it's a paperless world. Imagine if it weren't." She smiled, stacked the files directly in front of her onto another pile to her left, then turned on her computer.

"Ryan told you what I was looking for?" Elizabeth asked, a little surprised.

"Your funding application consents. Why else would you be here?" Another smile as she narrowed her focus on the screen and clicked the mouse. "Ah, here we are. I'll print them out."

Behind Elizabeth, a printer whirred and groaned into life. Emma got up, went to the machine, and held her hand out, ready to receive the documents as they rolled off. When the last one peeled out and the printer beeped and powered down, she returned to her desk, stacked the pages to square them off, then handed them to Elizabeth.

The top page was the application for funding for Kimmy Donohue. In a textbox at the foot of the page was the note outlining the conditions of funding, that Kimmy temporarily reside in Sunny Springs Home for the Disabled, and that all necessary funding would continue until reassessed.

Emma nodded at them. "Of course, they're all electronically signed."

"Yes. I sign them on my phone."

Then she turned to the next one. The young man paralyzed with cerebral palsy—her same electronic signature—which she checked for similarity—same name, date, same condition noted below…

Elizabeth blinked at it. Check the next one—the same. And the next one.

Had she left that condition on all these applications? Was that why her clients were being sent into institutions in the Aden Falls conglomerate? A critical electronic error on her part?

An instant wave of horror crashed over her leaving her so shocked she felt ill. What the hell had she done?

Attempting to hide her rising panic, and probably failing, she gathered up the paperwork, restacking it on the desk, and smiled. "Do you mind if I keep these?"

Emma shrugged. "Not at all."

And that's when her phone rang—Penny.

Elizabeth excused herself and answered.

"Can you talk?" said Penny.

"Go ahead."

"I've got news I think you're going to want to hear."

She turned a sideways glance on Emma, then stepped a short distance away with her back turned. "Give it to me."

"I did some digging. You're not the first hatchet job Jennifer Reels has done. Not by a long shot. Some go a ways back, but one was more recent—Gate Westrum. He was a young, up-and-coming realty broker. Young, single, good-looking. Had everything going for him."

Another furtive glance at Emma. She was busying herself with some files, obviously trying to look disinterested.

All the same, Elizabeth cupped her hand around the mouthpiece and dropped her voice. "Wasn't he the one that was murdered a few months back?"

"That's the one. Found in a dumpster with his throat cut and his face pulverized. All kinds of dreadful photographs and some pretty incriminating financial documentation thrown in with him. They all indicated he'd been making deals with very unsavory characters. Apparently, he'd met them while frequenting a Boston-area nightclub called *The Hyde Park Luxury Rest Stop*."

"Is that what it sounds like?"

"Not even close. Sources I found say it's a tightly run brothel with a high-roller casino in back. The police have been trying to close it down for years."

"A little inside info going on, you think?"

"That's what the article inferred but didn't go so far as saying. But, even if Gate Westrum had survived the attack on him, Jennifer Reels made damn sure he'd never have been able to show his face in this town again. But here's the thing—are you sitting down?"

"Assume I'm sitting."

"Gate Westrum was on last night's party guest list."

"Are you kidding? How could you not have known he was invited?"

At the rise in her voice, Emma looked up. Perhaps realizing her presence was no long needed, she smiled and excused herself. In response, Elizabeth gave her a tight smile and nodded, then waited for the door to close before resuming the conversation.

Penny's voice rose in defense. "It wasn't *me* who invited him. He was listed as somebody's guest."

"You remember who?"

"You think I wouldn't have told you by now? All I have is the main guest list. Mister and Mrs.? Blah Blah. Then a bunch of single names. *I'm sorry.*"

"Okay, so we have to figure out who invited him."

"Yeah, but here's where it gets really weird: according to the list of attendees at your party last night, guess who managed to turn up and was living it up at your party."

"Gate Westrum? So, either he came back from the dead, or someone else used his party invitation."

"Correct."

Elizabeth chewed her lip while she turned it over in her mind. "There has to be a connection between Gate Westrum and whatever happened out at Sunny Springs. Where are you now?" Elizabeth asked.

"I'm in the office."

The fact that Penny's tone had suddenly become guarded wasn't lost on Elizabeth.

"What is it?"

A brief hesitation.

"Penny, what's happened?"

"Breaking news on the radio…"

A black hole opened up in Elizabeth's stomach. "Saying what?"

"Oh, dear lord. They're saying the McClaine foundation is involved in insider trading."

Elizabeth's jaw dropped while the words sank in.

"*What?*" She drew a couple of ragged breaths, then said, "That's ridiculous.

I don't know where they get their information, but I'm calling them right now and putting them straight. What station was that?"

"Hold on, I just switched over. Crap, it's on at least two stations. Probably more. Hold on a sec."

In the background, Elizabeth heard the office computer switching on. "What are you doing?"

"Checking the…uh-oh. That same story's gone live all over the Internet."

Elizabeth rolled her head back and drew in an infuriated breath. "Who's behind this one? As if I need to ask."

"You guessed it—Jennifer Reels, reporter extraordinaire."

One side of her upper lip curled in fury. "Reporter extraordinaire, my foot. Wait till I get ahold of that woman. Next time her name gets mentioned in the papers, it'll be in the obituaries."

"Whatever you're gonna do to her, you gotta promise to let me help. Oh, dammit, the switchboard's lighting up like a Christmas tree. I'm gonna have to go."

"Thanks, Penny. If anyone needs me, tell them to leave a message. I've got a reporter to put in her place."

CHAPTER TWENTY-THREE
DAY TWO—2:35 PM—LANEY

The photographer's studio was located in a strip mall on the outskirts of Old Brooklyn. Pierre Porter Photos looked like a failing, one-room outlet with dusty props in the window and the company name in chipped gold lettering on the glass.

An overhead bell jangled as she pushed open the door, and a balding man with a greasy comb-over looked up from the newspaper he had spread out on the counter. Probably in his sixties, beer belly, wire-rimmed eyeglasses, he looked nothing like Laney had imagined. He gave her a bored look then made a point of closing the newspaper and straightening.

"Can I help you?" He didn't sound like he wanted to help anyone.

Laney gave the place a mild once-over as she crossed to the counter. It didn't look like the kind of place you'd go for your wedding snaps. The shop itself was small and dismal, a multi-colored bead screen covering the exit to a room at the rear. Next to him the dusty counter held an aging computer, a phone, and a pile of Manila envelopes, each with string tied over the front in a cross. Lining the walls were a series of faded photographs that looked like they'd been taken some time in the last millennium.

Laney leaned one hand on the counter, wondering if she was in the right place. "Are you Pierre Porter, the photographer?"

He dropped his chin, regarding her over the top of his glasses. "Depends who's asking." He drew the newspaper toward himself, folded it once, and leaned on the countertop.

She slipped the tiny photograph she'd removed from Wendy O'Dell's file from her pocket and pushed it across the counter to him.

"Are you the one who took this?"

He picked up the photograph and tipped his head back, mouth turned down at the corners while he studied it through the grubby lenses of his glasses. Then he slid it back to her. "Like I said, who wants to know?"

"A friend of a friend."

He snorted mildly. "Gee, that's original."

"Okay then, I want to know."

He regarded her sourly. "You want answers, you're going to have to be a little more specific."

"A friend of mine's gone missing. I'm looking for her. Last I knew, she had a photograph taken by you. Or at least," she conceded, "by someone from this photo shop."

He gestured widely. "Look around. How many photographers you think we got working here?"

She shrugged. "Then I guess it must have been you. Her name was Wendy."

This time he raised both hands theatrically and looked heavenward. "Wendy? Wendy who? You know how many Wendys I shot over the last thirty years?" He saw the look she gave him and gave her a deadpan look. "With a camera, is what I'm saying."

The guy was deliberately playing dumb. Laney tucked both hands in her back pockets, lips pursed, nodding around the place while she decided on a different tack.

"Okay, let's do this another way, shall we? These little photographs— when was the last one you took?"

He made a dismissive gesture. "Last time someone came in for a passport photograph, I guess."

"And when was that?"

The corners of his mouth turned down while he thought. "Two, maybe three days ago? As you can see, the place is so busy it's hard to remember."

She gave him a long, blank stare. "So, these are passport photos. Is that what you're saying?"

"You're pretty quick on the uptake."

Laney ignored the comment and tapped the photo. "Did you photograph this girl?"

He lifted one corner of the snap, checked the stamp on the underside. "It's got my name on it. I guess I must have."

"Do you remember her?"

"How would I know? I get all kinds in here."

"I'm not asking about all kinds. I'm asking about this girl."

"Ah, geez. How would I know who she is? They don't tell me their names. It's not like they come here for the scintillating conversation or nothing. They come, they go. That's all I know."

She turned to the front window, noting the narrow parking lot out front, and the lack of foot traffic. "Do they come in by themselves? Or does someone bring them in here?"

The guy picked up the newspaper, folded it again, and tucked it under one arm like he was about to leave. "Listen, while I'd love to stand here and chat, I got a business to run. So, if you don't mind…" He indicated the front door.

Laney fixed her gaze on his and squared up to him. "Fine. Thanks for all the help."

"No problem," he said.

They stood eyeing each other for a moment. Then she left.

Outside in the car, she sat watching the place. Between the gold lettering on the window, she could see him on the phone and glancing up every now and then. With the dark-tinted car windows, he wouldn't have been able to see her. After about a minute of what looked like an animated conversation that included a lot of hand gestures, he hung up, shook his head angrily, and disappeared out the back.

She gave it a second then jumped out of the car and trotted straight to the door. Again, the bell jangled as she pushed her way in. This time, she made straight for the phone and lifted it. By the time he appeared through the beaded screen and registered what she was doing, it was too late. She'd already lifted the phone, hit redial, and noted down the number that popped up on the screen.

"Hey!" he said and scrabbled to get to her. "Hey, hey, what do you think you're doing?"

He snatched at the note with one fat hand and missed. "Hey, gimme that."

"Thanks again for the help," she told him, pocketing the note as she scurried for the door. Behind her he'd already rounded the counter, coming after her. She threw open the door and bolted for the parking lot. It wasn't until she got back to the car that she chanced a look back. He was standing at the door glaring after her.

She got in, twisted the key in the ignition, and started it up while he retreated inside and shut the door.

Whoever he'd dialed was about to get another phone call from him. That didn't matter. All she had to do was wait. Sooner or later, he'd leave.

And she'd be right behind him.

CHAPTER TWENTY-FOUR
DAY TWO—2:49 PM—ELIZABETH

It took a matter of seconds for Elizabeth to hit the redial on her phone and find Jennifer Reels's number. Which was also how long it took for the woman to pick up. Elizabeth suspected she'd been waiting for the call. The tone confirmed that, along with the fact that Ms. Reels was not only more than happy to meet with Elizabeth, big surprise, she could do it right away.

Twenty minutes later, she walked into the same café they'd met at not two hours earlier to find Jennifer Reels sitting in the same seat with the same shark-like grin on her face. Elizabeth couldn't wait to wipe that smug look off the woman's face with the news she'd be consulting her lawyer.

As Elizabeth approached, Jennifer one-handedly wrenched out the chair alongside her.

"Mrs. McClaine, nice to see you again."

Elizabeth deliberately took the chair opposite and sat with her back ramrod straight and her features tight.

"Ms. Reels. I want to know what grounds you have for accusing my foundation of insider trading. And don't bullshit me. I have other ways to find out. I'm simply giving you the courtesy of telling me first, before I consult my lawyer to discuss what charges to lay against you."

The woman sat back with a look of mild surprise before one side of her mouth curled into a snide smile.

"Whoa, Mrs. McClaine. You sound unhappy."

"Don't come at me with that holier-than-thou crap. I have no idea where you got the idea I or anyone at my foundation has been involved in insider trading, but it's as far from the truth as you could get, and I expect a full retraction in your sordid rag tomorrow morning."

"Or…?"

The woman was baiting her. Elizabeth wanted to slap that smug look off her face. Instead, she said, "Or I promise you, I will be taking legal action."

Far from backing down, Jennifer Reels's grin widened. "Ah but, *Methinks thou dost protest too much,* Mrs. McClaine."

"Meaning what?" Elizabeth responded, knowing full well that the quote was intended to humiliate her.

"Meaning I have solid evidence that you *knowingly* bought shares two years ago in a venture you had a personal interest in. So, before you go running off to your lawyer, I suggest you think very carefully about what's going to come out of the woodwork in the wake of a full investigation."

Elizabeth felt her lower lip tremble. She sputtered a few opening responses, then said, "Are you blackmailing me?"

"Blackmail is a very dirty word, Mrs. McClaine. And I would not call this blackmail in any sense. You see, I want nothing from you. All I'm looking for is the truth." That shark-like grin again.

Openly fuming now, Elizabeth spoke between clenched teeth. "You think dragging the name of my foundation through the mud for a two-bit story is truth finding? I'd like to see your evidence of this…so-called insider trading."

Just as she had earlier that day, Jennifer Reels leaned down and removed a single file from the briefcase on the floor next to her. With an aura of smugness surrounding her, she opened the file, spun it on the table, and slid it across to Elizabeth.

Sitting on the other side of the table, Elizabeth felt her heart thud once in her chest and her cheeks flare red.

What the hell has she found?

Already feeling sick, Elizabeth drew it towards her and scanned the files. They were copies of her share certificates for several companies she'd been advised to invest in over the years. These proved nothing. In a flash, that illness in the pit of her stomach turned to relief. Without wanting to show her hand too soon, she looked up and straightened in her seat.

"Where did you get these?"

"Oh, didn't you know? This is all public information, Mrs. McClaine. You just gotta know where to look."

Elizabeth shoved them back. "You're going to have to try harder than that, Ms. Reels. And as for that retraction, I'll send you a draft of what I'd like to see in it. You've wasted your time."

As she went to get up to take her leave, Jennifer Reels pushed the papers back across the table again. "I'd suggest, Mrs. McClaine, that before you go off half-cocked, you take a good look at these papers."

Straightening with her purse tucked under her arm, Elizabeth cast the woman a withering glare, then dropped her eyes back to the documents on the table.

Jennifer smiled up at her. "Like I said, Mrs. McClaine…Elizabeth…may I call you Elizabeth?" Her tone was mild, patronizing.

"No, you may not."

"That's a pity. But before you charge off to defend your honor and waste your lawyer's time, can I just point out a few notes of interest?" She angled her head. "Just bear with me a moment."

They locked eyes for a moment. Elizabeth felt a flash of sweat bead her brow. Whatever this woman had in that file—whatever she'd found—Elizabeth didn't want to see it. All she wanted to do was flee. But something in the woman's manner twisted that knife of terror into her chest. Wisdom from years of dealing with politicians and all the hangers-on had taught her never to back down; never to run. First find out what the angle is, what's to be gained, and who stands to benefit. So, with her nostrils flared in fury and fear, she stepped closer to the table and passed a bilious eye across the files. As she did, Jennifer leaned across and pointed to the top certificate.

"You recognize this one?"

"Do you think the money we have in our trust just sits there doing nothing? For your information, we *invest* it. We make it work for us. That's how we generate more funds for our clients. As for Peyton Healthcare

Training, they provide training for caregivers. They're a small company that bid for our funding and won. What of it?"

"So, you're admitting that you pay them? Through applications by clients to your funding scheme?"

It was a trap. Elizabeth knew it. But she had to know.

"Just get on with it, Ms. Reels. What are you driving at?"

"So, I suppose you're going to tell me that you no idea that Peyton Healthcare Training is a subsidiary company of Aden Falls Corporation? And that your big announcement in July this year…" She paused to lift out and unfold a newspaper clipping which she held up like a kid at show-and-tell. "…praising Payton Healthcare for their successful bid to supply client assessment services exclusively for your foundation had nothing to do with the sudden rise in share value for Aden Falls?"

That news hit her like a hammer to the chest. But how was that insider trading? How could it be?

Time to call the woman's bluff. Elizabeth held her eye, lifted her head and squared off to her.

"Ms. Reels, I still don't see what my investments have to do with anything."

The reporter arched one eyebrow in surprise. "Again, bear with me a moment, Mrs. McClaine." She lifted the top certificate from the pile, swiveled it with two fingers, and pushed it across to Elizabeth again. "Are you telling me that this next certificate with an investment amount of fifty thousand dollars in Aden Falls Corporation—the very corporation your father-in-law does construction for, the very same corporation that claims funding via Payton Healthcare from your foundation—can't be considered insider trading?"

The shock hit Elizabeth like a brick wall. For a second she thought she was going to pass out.

Nausea welled in her stomach, but she had to keep going; had to know. She stammered a moment, then gathered herself. "As I said, Miss Reels, my foundation invests widely. And I still don't see what that has to do with anything."

The woman let out a snide chuckle as she gathered the papers and put them back into the file. "You're going to have to do better than that when the FBI come sniffing around. Shouting 'I'm innocent' doesn't exactly fool them these days."

Tucking the file documents and newspaper clippings into her briefcase, Jennifer Reels casually added, "By the way, this is just a heads up, Mrs. McClaine. I'm doing you a favor. Giving you time to get all your ducks in a row."

"If you're trying to insinuate that you've done this just so I can scramble to cover up whatever fake deals you've dreamed up, you can think again. I'll expect that retraction on the front page first thing tomorrow morning. Or next time you see me, I promise you, it will be with legal counsel."

And she walked out.

Outside in the car, Elizabeth gripped the steering wheel with both hands to stop them shaking. This had to be a mistake. There was no way she would ever put the foundation in such a position.

How could they have invested fifty thousand dollars in Aden Falls without her even knowing? Compared to the total asset fund of the foundation, it was a pittance. But that wasn't the point. She was just wondering how this situation could possibly get worse, when her phone rang—Charles.

"Oh, yeah. That's how," she whispered. She steeled herself, and picked up.

***

The Associate

The story had been out less than an hour and already it had hit the headlines.

Of all the stupid things to do. He'd told her what he needed. A diversion, that was all. Easiest assignment yet, wouldn't you think?

But no, that wasn't enough. She'd started digging and gotten greedy, come back demanding more money, telling him she had others to pay. Now he had no choice. He had to take action. Before she let his secrets out and he wound up the next one found in a dumpster.

He got up from his desk and went to the door of his office, peeked out to ensure no one was around, then closed it. Back at his desk, he dialed her number and waited. With every unanswered ring, his heart beat faster. How could he have gotten into this mess?

After six rings, she picked up.

"I gather you've seen it," she said without preamble. She sounded pleased with herself.

He modified his tone to sound equally impressed. "I have. We need to meet. I have one more thing I need from you."

"More files? Another story?"

"Something like that."

"You know this will mean more money."

"You'll get it," he assured her.

He gave her directions, told her to make sure she wasn't followed.

Then he hung up. Took the pistol from his lower desk drawer. And left the office.

CHAPTER TWENTY-FIVE
DAY TWO—3:03 PM—LANEY

Even if Laney still had her cell phone, a number alone wasn't going to be any help. So, instead of leaving, she'd sat back with her arms folded over her chest, watching the photographer's store front from out in the parking lot.

No more than a minute later, the venetian blinds snapped shut across the front window and the sign on the door flipped to Closed.

A thin smile of satisfaction snaked across her lips. Her instinct had been right on the button. The guy was heading out. She had her next lead. She snapped her seatback upright and started up the car, drove out of the parking lot, and waited on the street.

Sure enough, a few minutes later a blue convertible pulled out with Pierre at the wheel, the slicked-over hank of hair immediately coming loose and trailing in the wind like a streamer. The car wouldn't be hard to tail. All she needed to do was hang back.

She pulled out, watching him three cars ahead, turned left when he did, right when he did. When they hit a back street, he was certain to spot her, so she drove on to the next intersecting street and turned down, expecting to see him there.

Nothing. She slowed, turned into the street he'd gone down, and pulled over, checking the street front and back.

"Where the hell did you go?" she muttered.

After what felt like an eternity, she pulled out again, assuming she'd lost him. Then she picked him up in the street she'd crossed into. She followed him, traveling parallel to him one street to his left, dropping back every now and then so he wouldn't pick her up at every intersection. After three more cross streets, she glanced across to see him pulling right. She slowed as he did and pulled over when his turn signal indicated a left-hand turn into the parking lot of a single store set on a scrappy lot way out in the boonies. The sign out front showed a computer and a cell phone, suggesting they sold or serviced both.

Laney cut the engine and sunk down, watching Pierre get out, glance both ways, and hurry into the store. She folded her arms, sat back and waited, wondering where Katarina could be now—hoping upon hope she was still alive.

How had she escaped them? And how had she come across the real Wendy O'Dell? Were they friends? Was Wendy dead?

Ten minutes passed. Each one felt like an hour. Laney glanced at her watch and huffed. Frustrated, she grabbed the jacket from the back seat, slipped into it, and pulled the hood up. She got out, locked the car, and casually ambled up the street towards the store. But just before she got to the door, she noticed the closed sign was up and the lights were off.

Pierre must have left with whoever was in the store. She turned full circle then walked quickly down the side of the store to find a second parking lot—a dust bowl surrounded by a chain-link fence with knee-high weeds growing up through it. No cars.

She'd lost her only lead.

Furious, she stuck her hands on her hips and scanned the parking lot. "Dammit!"

Now what?

To her left was a set of three stairs leading to a back door. With no other options available, she made her way up and checked the lock. It was an easy one. Another glance around, checking the area. No one in sight, so she got to work on it.

It took less than thirty seconds to pop. But the instant she opened the door, an ear-splitting alarm went off like a siren, wailing loud and long while several red lights flashed through the store.

Knowing this area, Laney figured she had about fifteen minutes before the police arrived. That gave her plenty of time.

"Dumbasses," she told the system as she moved through a tiny workroom and headed for the front counter.

The store looked typical of any backstreet computer stores she'd been in—several laptops chained to displays, cell phones on the walls with prices shown below. With a palm pressed to one ear to block the noise, she checked the number on the store phone. Same one Pierre had called. That confirmed she was in the right place. Next, she hit redial and checked the last call. It had been made three minutes previously—a Boston number. She made a note of it, slipped it into her pocket, and retreated back to the office, where she checked the time.

Thirteen minutes to go.

All at once, the alarm shut off and the store fell into silence. Her hand dropped. All she could hear was the residual ringing in her ears. No idea why it had switched off. It could mean the alarm was monitored. Any minute, security might call in. So she started at the top desk drawer and moved down, checking each. Nothing out of the ordinary. A quick glance out through the front windows of the store. No cars in sight. No one here. So she switched on the computer. The guy must have been in some hurry, because he hadn't shut it down.

"Thank you, thank you," she muttered as she hit the email icon and waited.

A flood of emails pinged into the inbox. As they did, a title snagged her eye—"*Cleveland Assignment Completed.*"

With her heart ratcheting up a notch, she tossed another glance at the front windows and clicked on the message. It was cc'd to four other recipients. Laney recognized one of the names and the hairs stood up on the back of her neck.

Contract Completed. Employee 634 terminated. Records deleted, was all it read. It had been sent by Julia Nosovich at Employment Pulse.

A knot tightened in her stomach. Nosovich—the employment agent—that was the one who'd referred Katarina to Sunny Springs.

She sat at the desk and typed "Katarina" into the search field in the email inbox. Seconds later, it came back with a list of emails, all containing a reference to Katarina. Most were advertisements. She added "Nosovich" to the search, and the list was pared down to a series of seven emails. Each was cc'd to the same four names. All replies from Julia Nosovich. One included an address she recognized—the house she'd just come from.

No wonder she'd found employment records at the house. Whoever Julia Nosovich was, she was running some kind of international recruitment agency out of that address. And from what Laney could see, the job prospects wouldn't be every college girl's dream.

If Katarina had been brought into the country under false pretenses, how did she wind up in Sunny Springs? And if she'd escaped, why not go to the police?

She deleted "Katarina" from the search bar and added in the word "recruitment."

What seemed like a million emails popped up.

Same results for "Sunny Springs."

There had to be something more specific.

On a hunch, she typed in the words "Sunny Springs + Boston."

Another stream of emails emerged. Most were advertisements, so she added "Nosovich."

Two messages came up in English. The first read:

Models and Actresses Wanted. Two-Year Contract. Guaranteed $US200,000 per year.

Two hundred replies.

All trimmed down to twenty-seven. All beautiful. One was from Katarina Novak. The last message was dated six months back.

Then, an address. Somewhere in South Boston.

She Googled it, then copied the address into Google maps.

Her gut told her that's where Katarina was.

A nine-and-a-half-hour drive. She checked the time. It would be almost midnight by the time she got there.

So she grabbed a phone and charger out of the drawer, and left.

CHAPTER TWENTY-SIX
DAY TWO—3:50 AM—ELIZABETH

Elizabeth walked straight into her office, dumped her keys on her desk, briefcase on the floor, then turned to Penny, who had followed her in. Before Penny could open her mouth, Elizabeth jumped in, counting items off on her fingers.

"Number one: Laney Donohue walks into Sunny Springs and takes Kimmy. Two: a dead girl turns up in the cemetery…" Noting Penny's dubious look, she conceded the point, and added, "…a murder victim whose identity has yet to be established, I'll give you that."

"And may have nothing to do with anything."

Elizabeth also let her have that one. "That's entirely possible. Then three, Janelle Hooper tells us Laney is searching for one of the care workers from Sunny Springs, right?"

"Gotcha so far."

"Four, I get some newspaper hack from out of the back of nowhere accusing me of falsifying documents. And what happens when I start looking into events at Sunny Springs? *Whoa!* Suddenly, I'm insider trading, and I'm all over the news."

Penny dropped her gaze to the floor while she thought it through, then said, "Sheesh! Sounds like something out of a movie."

Elizabeth pointed a finger at her to punctuate the point. "*Exactly.* So, what does all this tell you?"

Still frowning, Penny chewed a lip while she gave it some head space. "That…Laney Donohue found something? Maybe she doesn't know it yet?" She lifted her shoulders briefly and gave Elizabeth an apologetic look. "Y'know, this hatchet Jennifer Reels is doing on you…" She hesitated, trying to frame the suggestion. "Have you even stopped to consider it may have nothing to do with Kimmy and Laney?"

Elizabeth stalked over to the window and stared out over the city—her city. She knew this place like the back of her hand; knew those who protected it, those who thought they ran it. They weren't always the same.

With a glance back at her PA, she said, "Is that what you think? That I'm barking up the wrong tree?"

Penny stared at her, unblinking. "Um, is 'yes' the correct answer?"

"No, it isn't the correct answer. I may not be in the political arena any more, but I know a smear campaign when I see one. This is a diversionary tactic. It's what the good old boys do. If anyone gets one whiff of their dirty slush funds or their nasty little illegal operations, they pick that person out, make up all kinds of stories about them, and throw them under whatever bus happens to be passing. By the time the media's done, it doesn't matter if it was true or not. That person's reputation is in the toilet and there's no coming back."

Penny frowned, clearly dubious.

Exasperated, Elizabeth turned to her. "Don't you see? That's what's happening here. I was thinking about this all the way over here. Seriously, yes, trust funds may have inadvertently been invested into Aden Falls. But how is that insider trading? Unless I benefit *personally*, and *financially*, from the deal. Or if whatever I've done has been at the expense of someone else. So, investing a few measly bucks into a healthcare facility—with no personal financial gain coming my way—tell me how that could be illegal?"

"Well," Penny began and put up both hands, "just playing devil's advocate here, but don't you think it's a little close to home? I mean, I know the trust needs to invest its money, but some could point to the fact that we do, indeed…benefit."

Elizabeth threw up one hand. "And there you are. You're doing it now.

You're focusing on my suspected *wrongdoing* instead of what's really going on here. You're stuck in that debate of whether I've actually committed a crime or not. You're not focusing on why the issue has suddenly become relevant in the first place."

One corner of Penny's mouth drew back briefly in confusion. "I'm sorry, I don't see the connection."

"Precisely. That's the point. It's a well-used political tactic. And even if I was arrested for insider trading—which I doubt I would be—with the time it would take for lawyers to get involved and me to defend myself against the charges, then whoever's behind it—the real culprit—would have had enough time to dig a hole and bury the crime before anyone even knows. Meanwhile, I'm the one in the public square having rotten tomatoes thrown at me."

"You really think that's what this is? That someone's trying to blacken your reputation? Just to cover something up?"

"I can smell it. You don't hang around these people and not see all the dirty tricks they'll pull when they think someone is getting too close to the truth."

Penny spread her hands. "What truth? We don't even know what's happened."

"Exactly. So, let's go back. Something happened. Something someone thought was safe. When did all this start?"

Still unconvinced, Penny frowned at the floor, then said, "When Laney Donohue took her sister out of Sunny Springs? That's when all this began, right?"

"Exactly. And at what point did I get involved?"

"When…" Penny jutted out her lower lip. "…you went to see David Whitcliff, I guess."

Elizabeth tapped the side of her nose and pointed at Penny. "Give the lady a prize. David Whitcliff was at my party. Why didn't he tell me?"

"Um…he was embarrassed?"

"No, because he was trying to make out he was out searching for Kimmy. That's why he didn't call the police. Because David had no idea Kimmy was gone. So, who else would have known about Laney taking Kimmy?"

"No one but the staff there, I guess."

"Caroline called me. And evidently, someone else called Laney."

"Do we know who?"

"Not yet. But there's a chance that whoever called Laney told someone else who had an interest. So, who else was there who knew I was involved?" When she saw Penny still struggling, she said, "This isn't about me being paranoid. Something is going on here."

"Okay. Well, I guess…maybe not David Whitcliff, but how about the Admissions Manager?"

"Velma Stanford. There's something about that woman that gives me the creeps," Elizabeth muttered as an aside. "Who else?"

"Caroline, of course."

Elizabeth blinked. "Oh my gosh. If anyone found out she called me, she could be in danger. I'll let Delaney know."

Penny shifted uncomfortably. "I'm still not convinced all this is connected with the Jennifer Reels stories. I mean, surely it would have to be someone who had access to your financial information."

Ignoring her, Elizabeth let her gaze range out across the office. "Or maybe this nurse aid has something of someone's, and they want it back. And that was the stone that caused the first ripple."

"Who is this girl she's looking for, anyway? The nurse aid—what's the big deal?"

"Apparently, she's the one who took care of Kimmy while Laney was in prison."

"But that could also be a coincidence, right?" Penny asked, still obviously unconvinced.

"Look, this nurse aid disappears from Sunny Springs, a dead girl with no identification turns up in Lake View Cemetery, and suddenly, the instant I start looking into what's happened, my name hits the headlines for all the wrong reasons. That's no coincidence. That's a reaction. I think this nurse aid knows something or has seen something someone doesn't want made public."

"Maybe it's to do with whatever Laney took when she broke into Sunny Springs," Penny offered, although still without conviction.

Elizabeth slowly turned a wide-eyed look on her PA while the pieces fell into place. "Of course. Laney inadvertently picked up something from those files no one wanted her to see."

"So, what would that be? I mean, all they have out there are the files of their disabled clients or their employees, don't they?"

"Exactly," said Elizabeth, this time with a little less conviction.

Penny gave it some deep thought. "I'm sorry, I'm totally lost," she finally admitted.

"Stick with me, kid. There was something in those files someone doesn't want made public. Who would that someone be?"

"Um…Velma Stanford?"

"David Whitcliff, that's who," Elizabeth corrected her. "Well, if David Whitcliff thinks he can lie to me about his whereabouts, then bushwhack me with a few fake media reports so he can hide his dirty deals or whatever he's doing, he can think again."

Penny grabbed her purse and scuttled after Elizabeth as she left the office.

"You think he's doing some dirty deals? Wait up, Elizabeth, I have to lock up."

Elizabeth wasn't waiting. She had already marched down to the elevators and stabbed the down button repeatedly with her finger. By the time Penny caught up, Elizabeth was huffing up at the light panel and impatiently checking her watch.

"So that's where we're going? To see David Whitcliff?"

"What's the point? He'll deny everything. And I doubt he's calling the shots here. I'd get more going to his boss."

"Then we're going to see Ryan Halverston?" The delight in Penny's tone made Elizabeth turn a skeptical gaze on her PA.

"Don't let that blue-eyed smile and those dashing good looks fool you. If he's planning to put my ass in a sling and boot it all the way to Texas just because he's got something to hide, he's got another think coming. But there's one person I need to see before I confront him again."

As soon as the elevator opened, Elizabeth stepped straight in and punched the button for the basement parking.

"That being…?" Penny said.

"Grant Alders. He's the one who signs off on all these investment deals. He can tell me if they're legit."

They both stood staring up at the light panel, watching the numbers count down. Finally, Penny said in a quiet voice, "I thought you weren't worried."

The bell pinged and the elevator doors opened. Elizabeth regarded her PA for a second. "It's one thing not being worried. It's a whole different matter not being prepared."

CHAPTER TWENTY-SEVEN
DAY TWO—4:38 PM—ELIZABETH

Grant Alders was in court when Elizabeth arrived. His legal assistant asked her to wait in his office, telling her that he wouldn't be long. Almost thirty minutes later, the door opened and he walked in, all bluster and apologies as he hung up his jacket behind the door.

"I'm sorry I kept you waiting, Elizabeth."

"It's me that should apologize, Grant. I know this is short notice."

Grant Alders had been a family friend and had spearheaded the legal department of Charles McClaine's construction company since the beginning. A big man, with deep-set brown eyes and a kindly demeanor, it was generally thought that his business acumen and legal expertise had formed the backbone of Charles's empire, and that without him the company would never have survived those early days.

He gestured her to a comfortable leather chair opposite him. "Can I get you coffee?"

"Not for me, thank you. I don't want to hold you up," she said, noting the pile of files on his desk.

He sat back, arms along the armrests of his leather chair, assuming a relaxed position. His furrowed brow and tight features, however, contradicted any ease he tried to portray. He seemed tense, anxious to get on with it. "Now, what can I do for you?"

She fixed his gaze. "The investments for the trust."

A little shrug. "What about them?"

"I assume you sign off all the paperwork?"

"You know I do." Grant shifted in his seat, his brow furrowing slightly. "Is there a legal problem you're worried about, Elizabeth?"

"It's the funds that we have invested with Aden Falls."

He opened his hands briefly. "What about them, Elizabeth?"

"I have a rogue reporter claiming that we're—well, my foundation—is guilty of insider trading."

He smiled widely. "By investing in a large company that happens to be in the same industry? How could that be insider trading?"

"Payton Healthcare just won the tender to supply all our client evaluation services for funding."

"That's correct."

"Jennifer Reels is claiming that Payton is a subsidiary of Aden Falls. And that as a result of that deal, the share price of Aden Falls increased and that could be construed as insider trading."

Grant tipped his head, clearly amused. "That's quite a long shot, Elizabeth. Companies often invest in the same industry because they understand it. And according to my records, the share hike wasn't exactly earth-shattering."

"So, there's nothing to worry about?"

"This reporter is hunting for a story. I'm sorry it's upset you so much, my dear."

She gave it a moment while she mentally put all the facts together. "Okay. Gate Westrum," she said. "Do you know him?"

His eyebrows went up while he took a dubious breath. "That's a name that hasn't surfaced lately."

"I hear he was murdered."

"So I believe."

"What do you know about him?"

He looked away and opened his hands, perhaps considering how to frame the explanation. "The way I heard it, he got into some financial difficulties."

"What kind of financial difficulties?"

"He'd become involved in some illegal dealing. But that's all I heard." He frowned. "Elizabeth, I can see why you'd be concerned about charges of insider trading, but what's your interest in Gate Westrum?"

She shifted in her chair. "I suppose you saw the article in the paper. About the Charles McClaine trust, and my recommending our clients into Sunny Springs—which is owned by Aden Falls."

"I did, as a matter of fact. I guessed you must have had your reasons. I suggest if you have an issue with the client funding you should see Kyle Hendry in the finance team. He's the one responsible for client authorization sign-offs."

"Thank you, I will." She met his eye, held it. "There's something else. This reporter, Jennifer Reels, the one who's dragging my name through the mud. Turns out, she's the same one who wrote the articles on Gate Westrum."

He lowered his gaze for a moment, then looked up, puzzlement obvious in his expression. "I'm sorry, Elizabeth, you've lost me."

"I was hoping you might know what incriminating evidence Gate Westrum was found with. In the dumpster, I mean. I thought if I can find a connection between my foundation and whoever Gate Westrum was dealing with, I could figure out what the angle is."

The smile on Grant's face deepened the crease lines each side of his mouth. He dropped his head briefly again, maybe a little embarrassed.

"The way I heard it, there was a significant amount of photographic evidence proving that Gate Westrum had had a wonderful time in the company of some very dubious ladies on his trips. With all due respect, Elizabeth, I can't see how that could possibly be connected to you."

"You think someone was blackmailing him?"

"Blackmail was never suggested in the articles I read about him. But I guess that's possible. Gate held a lot of highly sensitive information about his clients." Grant scratched at the corner of his eye. "Whatever that information was, he must have somehow used it to manipulate someone. And that didn't end well for him."

"What was found with him?"

"I wouldn't know."

"So where were the photos taken?"

"The police said they were from a nightclub, I believe. They were following up, but that was the last I heard."

"Did you know him? Personally, I mean?"

He shook his head, made a dismissive face. "I met him twice. He was still trying to build his business as a realty broker. He approached us with some business opportunities, but they weren't what we were looking for. Otherwise, I only know what I read in the papers."

"Have the police followed up on his murder?"

Mouth down at the corners, he gave another head-shake. "I have no idea, Elizabeth, but I'd assume so. What's this got to do with the article on your foundation? You want to initiate an allegation of libel against her?"

"No, no." She shrugged. "I don't know. It's a gut feeling, that's all. I believe someone put Jennifer Reels up to writing the article in order to sidetrack me from looking into why a nurse aid from Sunny Hills disappeared."

He blinked at her. "And you think there's a connection. With this young woman." Not questions. Statements of disbelief.

Elizabeth could hardly blame him.

She sighed. "Okay, I admit, there may be no connection," she said. "I'm simply trying to establish why this article came out the minute I began looking into the incident at Sunny Springs. Like I said, it may be coincidence. If Gate Westrum had been murdered in some random attack, as unfortunate as it would be, I could see that. But he was found in a dumpster with a bunch of sordid photographs. To me, that was done to humiliate. But why would anyone do that? The guy is dead. The only reason I can think of is that someone wanted to send a message to someone else."

"I have no idea, Elizabeth. I can only tell you what I heard."

"Then I discovered someone invited him to my party."

His head jerked forward. "Your birthday party?"

"Correct."

"Elizabeth, if anyone had seen him, I can guarantee at least *someone* would have recognized him. He's been dead for months."

"I know, I know," she said, feeling foolish for even suggesting it. "And I appreciate anything you have told me." Sensing she'd gotten everything she could, she gathered her purse and searched in it for her key. "Oh, can I ask one more thing?"

He smiled. "Sure."

"Where was the nightclub he was visiting?" When he frowned, she added, "You said Gate Westrum was on some kind of business trip."

He gave a small shoulder shrug. "Boston, I think. But don't quote me on that. I could be wrong," he admitted.

He could have been, but a tiny voice echoed through her head telling her he wasn't.

"Do you know the name of the nightclub?"

"I'm sorry, Elizabeth, I don't." He grinned. "It's not somewhere I'd go. But like I said, maybe Kyle can shed a little more light on the client funding for you."

"Thanks, Grant. You've been a terrific help."

CHAPTER TWENTY-EIGHT
DAY TWO—5:09 PM—ELIZABETH

Grant had called ahead to find that Kyle was in a meeting, but promised he'd be there as soon as he could. Ten minutes later, he emerged from the elevator with his hand out, and a welcoming smile. He threw one arm gently around Elizabeth and affectionately pecked her on the cheek, then escorted her straight to his office.

After rounding his desk to sit facing her, he lifted a stack of files from the desk, set them aside, then swiveled back to face her, leaning on both elbows, chin rested on his bridged hands, eyeing her fondly.

"I'm sorry to interrupt you like this, Kyle."

"My dear, you have no need to apologize. In fact," he said with a conspiratorial wink, "you've given me a good excuse to take ten minutes out."

A nice remark, although Elizabeth knew full well that the only thing that would interrupt his schedule would be an imminent threat to the company, or his own death.

"Oh, and I forgot to tell you how much I appreciate your inviting me to your party. Just a shame I didn't get to spend more time with you. I was looking forward to at least one dance."

"I'm so sorry, but I got an urgent call and had to rush away," she said. "Promise me you'll come to the next one, and the first dance is yours."

"Wild horses wouldn't keep me," he said and chuckled. Clasping his hands on the desk in front of him, he let the smile drop. All business now, he frowned at her. "Now, what can I do for you?"

"My clients—the ones I support through the foundation—"

"Of course. You need some funding signed off?"

"Not exactly." She broke eye contact and shifted uncomfortably in her seat. "Did you, by any chance, see the article in the paper?"

"About the referrals? Indeed I did. I have no idea what they're making a fuss about."

"So, you knew all fifteen of those applications came to you with the clause referring them to Aden Falls' facilities, and no others?"

His mouth went down and he looked away as if confused by the question. "Well, of course. Those were the conditions of funding."

"So, you knew that each of the clients was placed in a facility run by Aden Falls."

"If they're searching for accommodation and choose to accept funding, then yes. Is there a problem, my dear?"

"My funding applications are supposed to include a list of *available* accommodations. They're supposed to suggest *alternative* accommodations should they be needed. What's gone out looks like some kind of ultimatum. That if they don't go to an Aden Falls facility, they don't get funding."

"I can't see a problem here, Elizabeth. If that's what they choose, that's what they choose. And we all know that accommodation for the disabled isn't exactly easy to find these days."

Ignoring the comment, Elizabeth stuck with her line of questioning. "So, you're saying that's how the documents arrive to you? With that clause attached?"

"Well, of course." He frowned, perhaps a little puzzled by the question.

"And then what happens?"

"I sign them, arrange for the funds to be allocated, and then forward copies to Grant, and each of the agencies involved."

"And you've never…" She shook her head briefly, searching for the right words. "You haven't changed anything on them?"

The smile might have looked genuine to anyone who didn't know Kyle Hendry. Elizabeth recognized it as a sign of utter offense. "Elizabeth, they're legal documents. Yes, I sign them. But I'm not authorized to change the content of them. That would be—"

"No, no."

"—illegal, not to mention unethical."

"No, please, I didn't mean to suggest that you'd do anything of the kind. I was just…" She shook her head, then met his gaze. "It doesn't matter."

Despite the confident response, her heart was in the pit of her stomach. Why hadn't she checked each one? How could she have made one stupid mistake that had been replicated over and over without her knowledge, and impacted the lives of at least fifteen young disabled people? Right now, she wanted to hide herself away somewhere.

On the other side of the desk, Kyle tipped his head, trying to catch her eye. "Is there anything else I can help you with?"

She took a shuddering breath and picked up her purse. "No, that's all I needed. Thank you."

She was about to get up, when he said, "Can I just ask you, Elizabeth…"

She looked up, dreading his asking for further explanation.

"If I'm reading this right, I'm guessing some of your clients ended up being referred to those facilities in error."

Sitting again and fumbling with her purse on her lap, she nodded. "I've done something completely stupid, Kyle. I attached that clause referring one client to Aden Falls. It just happened there were no community homes available, and there was no choice. But I didn't delete it." She blinked at a spot on his desk just in front of her, not wishing to meet his gaze. Finally, she looked up, met by a look of sympathetic warmth in his eyes.

"Now fifteen young people have been sent to the very facilities I abhor, just because of my own stupidity." She sat ready to take her medicine, self-reproach burning in her chest. "I have no idea what I should say to their families."

"Elizabeth." He reached a hand out across the desk, palm up.

Reluctantly, she responded by placing her hand in it. His big fist closed on it and squeezed. A fatherly gesture.

"My dear, most of those young people didn't have families. Which was why they needed your help. They were fortunate to have had you there for them."

"It still shouldn't have happened. And if that ghastly reporter hadn't pointed it out in her article, I'd never have known."

"Have you taken the clause out of the documents on your phone now?"

Still mentally kicking herself, she shook her head again. "No."

"Why don't you do it now?"

She plucked the phone from her purse and swiped the screen. After a moment or two, she drilled down and found the template. Looked it over. Then frowned.

"This is the template I use. But the clause isn't on here."

"And that's definitely the one you use?"

"Of course. I have it on my computer in my office, but if I'm visiting a client, this is what I use."

"Hm," he said and plucked a pair of gold-rimmed eyeglasses from his shirt pocket, which he slipped on. "May I?"

He reached out a hand and she passed him the phone.

She watched as he scrolled through various apps, squinting into the screen, swiping and stopping, then swiping again. "How do you normally send your documentation? For example, how do you send me the applications for funding?"

"Just hit send, I guess."

"And then where does it go?" He swiped again on the screen.

She lifted her head, trying to see what he was doing. "To my office. It saves a copy, then goes out to you."

He paused, eyeing her over the top of his eyeglasses. "So, I'm assuming you use the company intranet?"

"Are you suggesting someone from the company is tampering with the documents before they get to you?"

He continued searching from screen to screen. "Not at all. I just want to make sure it doesn't go anywhere else. Ah, here it is." He tapped a finger twice on the face of the phone. "There, all done." He handed it back.

She studied the screen, which now showed the home page. "What did you do?"

"I simply marked an option on the document to not include attachments."

Her shoulders dropped in relief. "You are such a sweet man. Thank you. I wish I knew more about these things. The last time I spoke to someone from the IT department, he might as well have been speaking Swahili."

He smiled. "No problem."

Keeping her eyes down as she put her phone into her purse, she cautiously said, "By the way, what do you know about a guy named Gate Westrum?"

She looked up to gauge his reaction.

Kyle sat back, his expression doubtful, and took a deep breath before answering. "Well, I've heard of him, of course. Apparently, he decided to try his hand at blackmail. Unsuccessfully, it seems."

"So Grant said."

"That's all I heard. I couldn't give you any more details than that."

Right then, her phone rang, cutting him off.

"Sorry, I should have muted that." She leaned down to switch the phone to mute, noticing the call was from Charles.

"It's Charles. I'd better take this. Will you excuse me a moment?"

The minute she answered, Charles barked down the phone, "Where are you?"

"I'm with Kyle, as a matter of fact."

"Then I want you here, in my office, in five minutes."

She'd never heard him sound so furious. She wanted to make up an excuse. She wanted to run and hide until he'd calmed down. Or at least stay out of the firing line until she had something to give him.

Instead, she plucked up courage, and said, "May I ask what it's about?"

"I'll give you two guesses," he said, and hung up.

CHAPTER TWENTY-NINE
DAY TWO—5:54 PM—ELIZABETH

Charles McClaine left her waiting outside his office for ten minutes, sitting there with only his PA, who made a point of ignoring her. Clutching her purse close on her lap and letting her gaze waft across each of the paintings on the wall, she felt like a kid sent to the principal's office. But what had she done? Made one mistake, that's what.

Then she thought about those fifteen young disabled people—people who had depended on her trust in times of need, people who had been told they wouldn't have access to her help unless they chose Aden Falls to accommodate them.

Manipulation, that's what it came down to. Blackmailing them into institutional living, no matter what they might have chosen.

The tide of fury had just risen in her gut again, when Charles's PA rose from her seat.

"Mr. McClaine will see you now."

She led Elizabeth to the door, opened it, then stood back while Elizabeth crossed into Charles's inner sanctum.

No invitation to sit. For some moments, she stood in front of his desk. He didn't even look up. Just continued writing something on a notepad. It wasn't until she took a deep breath and let her eyes wander around his office that he finally put down his pen, plucked his eyeglasses off, and glared at her.

"What the hell is going on?" he asked.

"That's what I'm trying to find out."

"Do you know what damage that woman is doing to my foundation?"

Oh, *his* foundation now. Normally it was referred to as *our* foundation.

Elizabeth steadied herself. "I believe this has something to do with a nurse aid from Sunny Springs. From what I gather, Laney Donohue found her sister beaten and left in a closet, and went off to find her—the nurse aid, that is."

His brow creased in utter disbelief. "What's that got to do with us? And why are you dragging my name through the mud?"

"I'm not dragging your name through the mud. As I said, I'm trying to figure out why this woman is even writing these stories." Realizing her voice had risen, she modified her tone. "I believe it's something to do with a realty broker by the name of Gate Westrum."

"Gate Westrum? What's he got to do with anything? No, don't answer that," he said, swatting it away with one hand. "Just stay out of it, Elizabeth. Just do your job. That's what I pay you for."

That hurt. Only rarely did he remind her that the foundation and her livelihood depended on him.

"I still need to investigate what happened to Kimmy Donohue, and find out how she was left with bruises all over her."

He blinked at her. "No, you don't. Whatever has happened over at Sunny Springs is nothing to do with the foundation. Just leave it."

"Then what about this woman—this Jennifer Reels? The one who's writing these stories. How does she have access to the foundation's investment information? Where did she get copies of the funding agreements? You can't tell me she just happened to dig around and she found all this. Someone is feeding her all this information. Doesn't that worry you?"

By the time she'd finished, she realized her voice had risen again. Shouting, in fact. She touched a knuckle to her lips and cleared her throat.

Charles sat rigid in his leather chair and fixed her with a stare. "Just. Stay. Out of it."

"And what about Kimmy? And what about those fifteen young people who are living in Aden Falls institutions just because…" She stopped short while a couple of boulder-sized realizations came loose in her brain and tumbled to the ground, leaving her without words. She swallowed hard and hugged her purse in tight.

"You built them," she said calmly. "The Charles McClaine Construction Company built all those institutions."

He stared at her. Kept staring. Saying nothing. Daring her to continue.

"All the time I was lobbying against these…these medieval housing developments, these insane asylums from the dark ages—"

He waved her off, saying, "Oh, now you're just getting carried away—"

"—you were in the background, scheming and planning to construct more and more of them, the hell with what I thought."

"Don't give me that, Elizabeth. We're a construction company. You think I'm going to turn away good business just because it doesn't suit you?"

"And what if that isn't a part of our philosophy?"

Charles lifted his head, his steely gaze fixed on hers. "Then you're welcome to offer up your resignation from the trust. And we both know what that means, Elizabeth."

She knew very well what that meant. It meant losing her home, her maid, and her income. The threat was like a smack in the teeth.

"You're telling me you'd throw your own granddaughter out on the street? Is that really what you'd do?"

His response was immediate, and brutal. "No, Elizabeth. Only you."

Shocked to the core, she stood in front of his desk with her mind reeling and tears threatening.

"You can't take Holly away from me. She's my daughter."

"Then don't push me," he said in a harsh voice. "We take care of our own here, Elizabeth. If you want to be a part of this family, you do as you're told. Stay out of it, and I promise you all this will go away."

CHAPTER THIRTY
DAY TWO—7:42 PM—ELIZABETH

"He threatened to take Holly away?" Penny's face was frozen in horror. "And what? He thinks you'd just walk away? Ride off into the sunset without her?"

"He knows how much money he has, and how much I have. It would be no contest."

"But the law wouldn't—"

"Oh, don't be ridiculous," Elizabeth snapped at her. "They've got Grant Alders. Do you know how many legal battles he's lost lately? None, that's how many."

How could she lose the daughter she'd fought for—the child whose love was the only thing that kept her going some days? How could she let her be torn from her grasp? Used as a bartering chip?

Unbidden tears suddenly sprang up. She squeezed her eyes closed and dropped her head into her hands. When she blinked away the tears and looked up, Penny's brow was wrinkled, her lips pressed together so hard they were white. Elizabeth had never seen her look so wounded.

"Oh, Penny, I'm so sorry. I didn't mean to take it out on you. I just…" Shaking her head slowly, she was searching for words, when Penny said,

"It's okay. I know how I'd feel. Let's get a coffee and we'll come up with a plan."

Elizabeth took the steaming cup and held it between both hands, peering into it as if looking for answers.

Penny was first to speak.

"You know what I think? I think you should call up Laney, tell her we'll do our best to help her find a good, safe place for Kimmy. Just until she's got herself in a better position to care for her. Tell her to forget about finding that nurse aid. She's probably got a new job by now, anyway. In fact, she's probably forgotten all about Kimmy. And what's the point in dragging it all up again? It's not going to change anything. Just tell her we'll help her move forward."

Turning a sideways look on her PA, Elizabeth said, "You mean whatever's going on, stay out of it. Get on with my job. Like I've been told to."

"I'm not saying that. But hey, what else can you do? Charles has told you to drop it. So, drop it. Why would you risk everything you've worked for? Why would you risk losing Holly? Just for one girl you haven't even met?"

"And what about these articles? Jennifer Reels?"

"Charles said it would go away, didn't he? He has one heck of an amount of clout. He'll fix it."

Elizabeth blinked into her lap. In all her darkest times, she'd never felt so powerless. But if she fought back, how much did she have to lose? Everything, that's what.

"Maybe you're right. I have my home. I have my job. I have my daughter."

"Exactly."

One nod. Decision made. "Okay, I'll step back. Do me one favor first, though: get Janelle on the phone for me. Tell her I need Laney's cell number. I'll call her up, tell her we'll do whatever we can to help her and Kimmy. If they need funding, they'll have it. If they need a home, we'll find them one."

"That's our job, after all, right?"

"You're right. That's our job."

"I think that's a good decision." Penny placed her hand on Elizabeth's arm, gave her a gentle squeeze. "I'll call Janelle, then I'll make us another pot of coffee."

While Penny lifted the phone and dialed, Elizabeth turned her gaze back to the window: Cleveland, her home. Holly's home. They'd be okay. All she had to do was what she'd always done—take care of her own. Just like Charles had said.

Then, why did she feel so empty?

Behind her, Penny hung up the phone but said nothing.

"What did Janelle say?"

"Nothing. I didn't call."

Penny was staring wide-eyed into her computer screen.

Elizabeth moved over beside her, also gazing at the screen. "What is it?"

Despite the fact that Elizabeth could see it herself, Penny read from the screen:

"'Breaking news: At 4 PM today, a woman was found dead with a single gunshot wound to the head. Shortly afterwards, police formally identified the victim as Velma Stanford, residential coordinator of Sunny Springs, the facility recently named in articles pointing to anomalies in the Charles McClaine Trust's funding practices. Mrs. Stanford was seen only the day before in a heated debate with Elizabeth McClaine over client applications.' It goes on about funding, blah, blah. Written by the inimitable Jennifer Reels."

In shock, Elizabeth read the article over again, pausing on quotes by alleged witnesses. "This can't be right…"

Penny's hand was still on the phone when it rang. She shot a pensive look up to meet Elizabeth's gaze.

"Take it," said Elizabeth, steeling herself.

"This could be bad."

"Take it," Elizabeth said again.

Lifting the phone, she said, "Charles McClaine Trust, you're speaking with—" She stopped short, nodded, then said, "Sure, I'll pass you over." She covered the mouthpiece and whispered, "It's Delaney."

With her heart in her throat, Elizabeth took the phone, sucked down a breath, then put it to her ear. "Lance."

"I need to see you," he said.

"When?"

"Now," he said.

CHAPTER THIRTY-ONE
DAY TWO—9:23 PM—ELIZABETH

Explaining to Delaney that her housekeeper, Katie, had to leave early, Elizabeth had requested he meet her at her home. Assuring her that while the visit would be official, she wasn't under arrest and therefore she could decide where they met.

All the same, Elizabeth couldn't help but note the change in his tone, this one of authority, this one the cop's.

She had duly driven straight home, put Holly to bed with a story, then showered and changed before his arrival. By the time the doorbell rang and she emerged from her upstairs office wearing casual gray slacks and a pale pink cashmere sweater, he was standing in the living room with his hands clasped behind his back, his steely gaze directed out over the garden through the large picture window in the sitting room.

"Thank you, Katie," she told her housekeeper as she saw her to the door on her way out. "I appreciate your staying so long."

"No problem, Mrs. McClaine." Just as the housekeeper was about to leave, she shot a worried glance back at Delaney. "Is everything okay?"

"Everything's fine. You take care." She watched Katie go to her car, then closed the door, and returned to the living room.

"Lance…or should I address you as *Detective*?"

He dropped his head a moment, acknowledging the situation. "I know this is official business, Elizabeth, but I just need to get a picture of what's going on here."

She walked briskly across to the sofa and sat with her legs crossed, one knee up and her hands clasped it to conceal the tremble she could feel radiating through her.

"I guess it's pretty obvious, isn't it? I get a hatchet job in the local papers about my funding recommendations, then the woman responsible for client placement is murdered."

"So, you admit you did have an argument with her."

Elizabeth snorted and rolled her eyes skyward. "I had nothing of the kind, Lance. I was looking for information. I wouldn't say she stood in my way, but she wasn't exactly helpful, either. I'm sorry she's dead, but I wasn't the one who did it. Why would I? Seriously," she said flippantly, "if I was going to kill anyone, it would be that Jennifer Reels."

When his eyebrows shot up, she added, "Strike that. Bad joke."

"Consider it stricken."

He was still standing, she noted. Still in his official capacity. As a cop. A detective, determined to get at the truth. And she, whether he admitted it or not, was now a suspect.

He let his eyes range out just above her head. Maybe not wanting to meet hers. "Do you mind telling me where you were today?"

Switching her position on the sofa, she tucked one foot up under her and rested one arm along the back. Trying to look composed. Unsure if she conveyed the demeanor of the innocent. "Good Lord, I've been all over the place. What time, exactly?"

His eyes met hers. "Three-forty-five this afternoon."

"Three-forty-five?"

"Or thereabouts."

She placed a knuckle to her lips and frowned. "Let me see. That'll be when I met with Kyle. At his office. I'm sure his secretary would confirm that."

"She already has. When did you last see Velma Stanford?"

"Yesterday morning. Our meeting didn't last long. Perhaps five minutes."

"One of the staff said ten."

She flipped a hand and huffed. "Okay, ten."

"Did she say where she was going straight afterwards?"

A shard of annoyance lanced through her. "Lance, do you honestly think I killed the woman? Okay, anyone would tell you I wasn't her biggest fan. All I wanted was an explanation of what had happened to Kimmy Donohue. You'd think I'd asked her for secret military codes."

"This is my job, Elizabeth. I need to get to the truth."

"Then tell me something: what do you know about Gate Westrum?"

His demeanor switched; his curiosity piqued. "What does Gate Westrum have to do with this?"

"I have no idea. But Jennifer Reels gave Gate Westrum the same hatchet job she's been giving me. I've been trying to find a connection. There is one, Lance. I know it. The second I started looking into why Kimmy was left bruised in Sunny Springs and a nurse aid left, I touched a nerve. I just don't know whose."

The concern was obvious on his face.

"Mind if I sit?"

She gestured to a chair, and he perched on the edge, elbows on the rests, hands dangling.

"Gate Westrum was a young property developer we'd been investigating."

"For what?"

"Fraud. Syndicated money laundering. To mention only a few. We had a solid case against him. We were close to taking him down when he was murdered."

Elizabeth wasn't expecting that. She blinked at him. "Are you saying he was involved in some kind of organized crime? Who did he work for?"

"Our connections tell us he'd been dealing with a syndicate that sprang up in Boston a few years ago—illegal casinos, nightclubs, high-ticket prostitution—all rackets owned by the Veluccio family."

"And you think they killed Gate Westrum?"

"Looks like. We think he found out something he shouldn't. My guess is he tried to blackmail them, and he wound up in a dumpster with his throat cut."

"Why would they do that? Surely, they could have come up with a better way to get rid his body," she said.

"That's exactly what we thought. But his lawyer identified him so we had no choice but to close the case."

"But I still don't understand what this has got to do with me—unless…"

"Go on."

She sat forward. "It's a long shot, but the girl—the one who was caring for Kimmy. She suddenly left Sunny Springs that very day. Now Laney's trying to find her."

"What girl is this?" he asked, urgency sharpening his tone.

She gasped as the pieces slotted into place. "They young nurse aid who was caring for Kimmy. Oh my lord, why didn't I think of it until now—she could be your dead girl."

He said, "Will you excuse me a second?" and immediately got to his feet, dredged his phone out, and walked to the window while he dialed.

"Callaghan, get someone from Sunny Springs over to the morgue first thing in the morning. Make sure it's someone who can identify the nurse aid who left Sunny Springs yesterday morning…what was her name?" he asked Elizabeth.

"Wendy something…Laney didn't get her last name. She said she was foreign."

He relayed the information, then said, "Correct," into the phone, listened, then hung up.

Stuffing his cell back in his pocket, he turned to Elizabeth. "I beg you not to get involved in this, Elizabeth. If it's who I think it is, these people are dangerous."

"But why would they kill her? She wasn't doing anything wrong, was she?"

"I have no idea," he admitted. "Listen, I have to go. I've got another line of inquiry opened up." He got to his feet, dug out his car keys, and fumbled with them for a bit, head down.

Elizabeth also got up. "So, I'm not under arrest?"

"I didn't come here to arrest you. I came because I…" He cut his attention to the window, then back. "Because I wanted to make sure you were okay."

Her cheeks warmed as she dropped her gaze to the floor. Then looked up. "What about Laney? She's gone off to find this girl."

"Where did she go?"

"Right now, I have no idea. But according to her aunt, she's on her way to Boston."

Worry lines deepened on his forehead. "When did she leave?"

Elizabeth checked the time. "Hours ago, I'd say."

"I'll see what I can do. In the meantime, don't speak to the press, and…I just have to ask you…"

"Not to leave town?" she asked.

He tipped his head. "Something like that."

***

The Associate

At last, she was gone. For months now, Velma Stanford had been like the sword of Damocles, hanging over him.

Ever since he'd secured the job for Katarina at Sunny Springs as a nurse aid, Velma had asked about his interest in this girl, tried to find out the connection. He'd fudged the answers, not exactly lying, but not telling her the truth, either, and ultimately, she'd done as he'd asked. From that moment, he had planned to leave Katarina, let her get on with her life.

What he hadn't counted on was how intense his infatuation had become, how deeply in love he'd fallen. He simply couldn't bear to be away from her. Just the sight of her made his blood run hot in his veins, gave him a spring in his step. When he was with her, he felt like a man thirty years his junior. The flush of youth was euphoric, something he'd never felt before.

So, against his own better judgement, he'd visited her at Sunny Springs. That was when Velma had seen them together. Almost at once, she had clicked as to the nature of their relationship. That wouldn't have been a problem. It was only when she spotted the tattoo on Katarina's wrist that she knew exactly who she was; knew where she had some from. And exactly who to call.

So she came up with her plan to wring every penny out of him that she could. She'd threatened him with exposure, told him exactly what she knew and who she'd tell.

158

How much money had he paid out to her since that day? He didn't even want to think about it.

Now Katarina was gone, far beyond his reach. He'd never get her back. Heartbroken, he'd had to accept that fact.

But Velma still wasn't done. All that time she'd been waiting in the wings with her hand out. He had to deal with her once and for all. Because as long as she was there, he'd never be safe.

With virtually no planning, he'd called her, told her to meet him somewhere quiet. She was the one who had suggested the quiet lane not far from Sunny Springs. Probably to save her the time of driving anywhere else, the miserable shrew. But it suited him. Almost no traffic at that hour. No one for at least a mile. And no way to connect the location to him.

She was already sitting there in her car when he arrived, mentally counting out the money she was about to squeeze out of him, no doubt.

He had parked behind her, checked the street back and forth, and gotten out. When he walked up alongside her, she looked up, that conceited grin curling her lips. Careful not to touch her car, he'd motioned her to lower the window.

She'd looked a little hesitant, but did so.

Without a word, he'd pulled the pistol from his coat pocket and shot her once in the forehead. It was so fast she didn't have time to react. Blood spattered through the car behind her and she fell back.

Checking the area once more, he'd quickly pocketed the pistol, gone back to his car, and sped away.

All he knew was that she was dead. Now there was only one more to get rid of, and his troubles would be over.

CHAPTER THIRTY-TWO
DAY TWO—11:23 PM—LANEY

The drive had been exhausting. Particularly after the day Laney had had. She'd stopped twice for gas and to check the best route to Boston. A can of Red Bull and a stale hot dog from a truck-stop café were all that kept her going. That and the determination that she would find Katarina, that she'd keep her promise. But now it was more than that. Somehow, in her determination not to fail, not to back down against a few short odds, her resolve had strengthened. Something in her gut told her that if she gave up now, everything her aunt had believed about her would be true. And that was something she couldn't accept.

When she got to the outskirts of Boston, she turned on the GPS in the phone she'd snagged at the computer store, and entered the address she'd found. Turned out it was somewhere in the area of Hyde Park .

This time of night the traffic was sparse, but her eyes were bleary. A couple of times she nearly missed the turn, but after another half hour of twisting through streets of enormous Victorian houses with latticework fences and roses in the front yard, she found what she was looking for.

She pulled over to the side of the street and looked it over.

From the outside, it looked like the perfect set for a historical romance—a stately four-story Victorian home, dark gray with white-painted windows, and stained-glass panels in a front door that stood at the top of ten broad front steps. A wide verandah ran around the lower floor with tall white plant holders visible even in this light at each corner, each carved into a ring of cherubs supporting the base with a large palm sprouting from the top. Two identical turret-shaped additions on either side of the house completed the postcard-perfect appearance, as did the gaslight-style posted down the walkway. On a metal sign that swung in the breeze, she could just make out the ornate lettering that spelled out the word, *Hyde Park Luxry Rest Stop.*

If it was what Laney suspected, resting wasn't what patrons had in mind, and the inside offered no luxury for the occupants.

She got out of the car and trotted across to the front gate. Still wondering what she was going to say, she stepped straight up to the front door and knocked. A shadow crossed the glass on the inside and the door cracked open. The musky scent of incense rolled out on a wave of warmth, and a sloe-eyed girl with tousled brown hair peeked out.

"Oh hey, I'd like to spend some time with one of your girls—name's Katarina. Hers, I mean, not mine. I was recommended her. By a friend," she added, hopefully.

The girl blinked confusion at her.

She drove her hands into her jacket pockets. "Yeah, well that's what I was told. Y'know, that I could come here for a little girl-on-girl…that kinda stuff. He said I could find it here."

The girl ran her eyes down Laney's battered leather jacket and tatty jeans.

"I am sorry. No one here," she said and closed the door while Laney put her hand on the wood panel making desperate noises to stop her.

"Dammit," she said as the door clicked closed. Cursing her stupidity, she knocked again. The door cracked open almost immediately. Same girl.

"Okay, I'm not looking for…whatever it is you do here. I'm just looking for a friend. Her name is Katarina, okay? I just need to know where she is."

"I cannot help. Please go." And she closed the door again, this time followed by the sound of the key turning in the lock.

Laney muttered a few words Kimmy would pitch a fit over and went back to her car.

She was sitting looking the place over in the yellow glow of the streetlamps, considering her options, when a sleek black car hummed down the narrow road from behind her and slid into the parking slot in front. Some fancy-ass car: shiny executive thing, late model. The inside light popped on as the driver's door opened, and a man in a black coat got out. Perhaps in his fifties with hair graying at the sides, dark suit pants, and shiny, expensive-looking loafers, he furtively checked the street, and crossed to the house. Just before making for the front steps, he scanned the street once more, straightened his lapels, then hurried up to the porch to press the bell.

"Dirty bastard," Laney sneered to herself. Just the sight of him made her want to spit. But then she had an idea. Might not get her in, but it would give her some satisfaction.

While he stood on the front verandah, hunching into his coat and waiting to be let in, she got out of the car, slammed her door, and called, "Oh, hey! Excuse me, but I wonder if you can help me."

The man shot a scowl back over his shoulder, buttoned the front of his coat, and cautiously moved to the edge of the steps, checking the street again.

"Are you talking to me?"

She drove her hands into her jacket pockets and walked quickly towards him. "Yeah, I'm kinda lost. Can you tell me if I'm at the right place? I'm looking for a girl—name's Katarina—Katarina Novak. She told me she lived around here. And you know what?" She snorted and shook her head. "I'm damned if I can find her."

This was met with a stony glare. For a second he seemed to weigh his response, then he said, "I'm sorry, I'm not from around here. I don't think I can help you."

When he moved back to the door, she approached, going as far as mounting the two bottom stairs while she addressed him again. "But you know who lives here, right? Maybe they'll know."

Slowly, deliberately, and radiating impatience, he turned back to her. This guy clearly wasn't used to answering to anyone.

"Believe me, the people who live here won't know her. I suggest you recheck your address."

Behind him, the door cracked open and a dim yellow light knifed across the porch. He leaned towards whoever was on the other side of the door, and muttered something. Then to Laney, he said, "Good luck finding your friend," and he disappeared inside.

"Good luck, my ass," she muttered after him.

There had to be another way. Back at the bottom of the steps, she spotted a narrow, overgrown path leading around the side of the house. She dropped into the shadows and followed it. Pale warm light glowed from behind the heavy drapes across the first-floor windows. Even around the back, every drape was drawn. But around here, it was so dark she could barely see the path.

She groped her way past some kind of climbing plant and rounded the back of the house. Out here, a rear light shone a dim circle over the back steps where a young woman sat in a silky pale-colored kimono smoking a cigarette, her long auburn hair bundled into a disheveled knot on top of her head.

Laney watched her for a moment. The lighted end of the cigarette glowed bright as she drew on it, then allowed wisps of smoke to trail into the air as she hugged herself against the chill of the night.

Seeing no one else around, Laney stepped from the shadows and the girl gasped. She pulled the kimono around her, and immediately stubbed out the cigarette, preparing to flee back in through the door behind her.

"Wait! I need to talk with you," Laney called in an urgent whisper.

The girl's eyes were wide with fear, but she paused, arms folded tightly across her chest. She cut a look back to the house behind her, then said, "Who are you? What do you want?" An accent. Eastern European. Maybe Russian. Or Kosovan, if Fatso could be believed.

Laney moved slowly towards her, one cautionary palm up to her. "I'm not gonna hurt you. I just need to talk."

The girl dashed another look back to the house, her lower lip tucked between her teeth, caught in indecision. "I cannot. I am sorry."

Laney jumped in before she could leave. "I just need a little information. I'm looking for someone. I could really use your help. *Please.*"

Seemingly still weighing up her position, the girl shifted slightly to allow her focus to trail up the covered verandah to a point just behind her.

Laney followed her line of sight to a small security camera fixed to the corner of the house.

"Sit down and I'll move out of range."

The girl pensively perched on the top step and waited while Laney stepped back far enough that she figured she'd be out of shot.

"That far enough?"

The girl pretended not to notice. "I think so."

"I'm looking for a girl named Katarina—Katarina Novak. Do you know her?"

The girl squeezed her eyes shut. As if the very name brought pain. An almost imperceptible nod.

"Is she here?"

The slightest shake of her head.

"Where is she?" Laney asked.

"Gone. She ran. They went and got her. Brought her back. But not here."

Laney's heart sank. If these people were even half as vicious as she suspected, she hated to think where Katarina was now. "So, where did they take her?"

"I don't know. One of the other establishments, I think."

"Which one?"

The girl checked the camera again. It had swiveled towards her. "Please, you must go. They'll…"

"They'll what? Kill me? They gotta catch me first."

A flutter in her voice. "It is not you I that I worry about." A quick glance at Laney. "I'm sorry."

A noise from inside—the slam of a door. The girl gasped. "Someone is coming. You must go."

"Where's Katarina? I'm not leaving until you tell me."

Panic flared in her eyes. She got up, pulled the kimono in around her, and went for the door.

Laney went to the side of the stairway. "Please!" she begged. "I just need to know where she is."

Just as she opened the back door, the girl paused, cut a frightened look back at Laney and hissed, "Go back to your car. Wait there."

Then she disappeared inside.

***

The Associate

"Do you recognize her?"

The Man had called him. Middle of the night again. Did this bastard think he had nothing else to do but be at his beck and call?

Just before calling he'd emailed a section of the security footage taken a short while ago.

Of course, he recognized her. She was the one he'd locked in the Cleveland house basement. The Man had to know that. Especially since he'd also seen the same footage of her breaking out, that arrogant look on her face as she'd flipped him the bird. He'd taken that personally, felt the insult down in his gut as if she'd assaulted him physically. Then he'd sat helplessly watching her escape.

He'd hoped that was the last he'd see of her. No such luck. He should have known she'd turn up again. But how the hell she'd found the place in Hyde Park?

Watching her now, he could see the determination in her expression as she stalked around the back of the Hyde Park address, skulking in the shadows, thinking no one could see her.

In a flat tone, he told the Man, "Yes, I know who she is."

"Her arrival here is a consequence of your failings, my friend," he said. "You are a slave to your emotions, my friend. This time, you must deal with her. Once and for all."

Deal with her. The way he had dealt with Dijana? Or maybe even Katarina? He swallowed back the thought, praying that wasn't the case.

"What do you suggest?" he asked, an edge of anger creeping into his voice.

"Use your initiative. Use the people you know," the Man said and hung up.

How many had to suffer or die just to hide this despicable Man's secrets?

But what could he do? He was caught in the jaws of the devil.

Given his few options, he hung up the phone and opened his contact list. The number was fifth from the bottom.

When the phone picked up, he asked for her by name. She'd know who he was. And she'd do exactly what he asked.

Such was the power of fear.

CHAPTER THIRTY-THREE
DAY THREE—12:07 AM—LANEY

It was only fifteen minutes but it felt like a lifetime. Laney had sat out in her car, eyes glued to the front door of the house when movement in the bushes at the side of the property caught her eye.

And there she was. Clearly recognizing the range of the security cameras, she moved far across to the hedged boundary, and disappeared. Next thing, the lower foliage in the hedge rustled, then parted, and the girl crawled through. Now she was wearing a black turtleneck sweater, jeans and sneakers, a puffer jacket pulled over the top. Probably why she'd taken so long. Head down, hands in pockets, she walked quickly down the street a few yards, then waved Laney over.

Laney started up the car, veered around the Jaguar, and cruised quietly down the street until she was alongside the girl. After a quick glance each way, the girl dashed over to the car. With one hand on the hood, she rounded the front and got into the passenger's seat.

"Anyone see you?" Laney asked, glancing back.

The girl twisted in the seat, ducking and shifting, eyes fixed on the front of the house for some moments before relaxing. "I don't think so." Turning to Laney, she rubbed her upper arms of her jacket as if to warm them. "Drive."

Laney fired up the engine and pulled out. "Are you okay?"

"I'm okay."

"What's your name?"

At first, the girl seemed reluctant. Then she said, "Gordana is my name."

Laney took the first right, meaning to circle and come back to the house. "What do you know about Katarina?"

"You will not find her here. They brought her here when she first came, but I have not seen her since she ran."

"Who brought her here?"

"The man. I do not know his name. They call him Njerku. It means, the Stepfather. He has many businesses here. Also, back home. He is a very bad man. Please, you cannot stay here. It is dangerous."

"Home being where?"

"Most of us are from Kosovo. Some from Bulgaria. Others from Russia. Njerku has many brothels across Kosovo, hundreds of women and girls stolen from their homes and forced to work in dreadful conditions. All of them fear for their lives. Or the lives of their families. That's why they stay. Njerku tells them they must pay off debts he claims they owe. But none of the women can understand how they incurred such debts."

"But why are you here? In America?"

"A new boss came to our city in Kosovo. It was becoming overcrowded, and Njerku saw more potential in America. He lures young women here from our country with the prospect of good jobs and big money, and safety. Every woman I have met has the same story. They believe they have a wonderful life ahead of them. They think they have left the corruption and danger behind. It's not until we arrive that we discover we're caught in the same trap that we were so desperate to escape."

Checking the rear-view mirror and turning down yet another random street, Laney shook her head in disbelief. "That's terrible. So, why don't you go to the police? Why don't you tell them what's happening?"

Gordana let out a cynical snort. "Because there is nothing the police will do. Njerku pays them well. He had many contacts here. And he has diplomatic immunity. So the police just send us back. The fortunate ones live to warn the rest of the consequences of trying to escape. The others..." She shrugged heavily. "We don't see them again."

"And this is how Katarina ended up here? She was lured by a job?" This was sounding remarkably like the story Wendy O'Dell's mother had told her. "But how did she escape?"

"Katarina is very beautiful. One of her clients fell in love with her. He took her away, found her a job." Gordana dropped her head in remorse and swiped a tear from her cheek.

"We were all so jealous of her. We thought she had escaped to the perfect life. But then, Njerku found out. He killed my friend Dijana just to find out where she was." Tears welled in her eyes and slid down her face. "Please, if you find Katarina, tell her…wish her well for me. Tell her…tell her I am sorry. Turn right here. I have to get back before they miss me."

"Do you have any idea where they would have taken her?"

"If she's still alive? I have no idea."

Laney turned back into the street and eased to a stop behind the Jaguar again.

"Just tell me somewhere. I gotta have a place to start. Please."

Gordana scraped her teeth along her lower lip while she searched the quiet street. Her eyes flashed up to the house, then she quickly said, "Maybe they would have taken her to the North City Hotel club. It has an illegal casino where men come to gamble."

"Where is this place?"

"It is very remote. It has a bar and gambling house. Maybe Katarina is there. Maybe not." Suddenly, she swiveled around, peering back down the road. "I must go. I'm sorry I cannot tell you more. And they will start looking for me." Gordana opened the car door and swung her legs out, pausing to regard Laney. "You are a good person. I may never see you again. Please careful."

Laney reached out and grabbed her arm.

"Then help me. Stay in the car. Come with me," said Laney. "You and I—we can bust this whole thing open, help those women in there."

"Why would you do that? Why would you risk your life for people you don't even know?"

"Because I know what it's like to be in prison. I know what it's like to leave your loved ones behind. Or would you prefer to go back? Keeping your mouth shut until you're past your use-by date? And then ending up dead?"

Gordana shot a fevered look back at the house. Her ragged breaths and trembling hands radiated the terror racking her tiny frame.

She swung a determined look on Laney, steely resolve in her eyes. "Promise me you won't die. Promise me that if there is any danger, that you'll run."

Laney blinked at her in surprise. "I promise I'll do my damnedest."

She pulled her legs in and slammed the door. "Then let's go."

CHAPTER THIRTY-FOUR
DAY THREE—1:16 AM—LANEY

Gordana had told Laney that they would have missed her by now.

"I was supposed to meet a client ten minutes ago," she said, turning in her seat to scan the street behind them. "They send someone after us."

"Did you tell anyone where you were going?"

"Never. I wouldn't endanger another woman there. But they'll be out looking for me."

So Laney had snaked around the backstreets, up this way and across to the next, to avoid detection. After fifteen minutes and seeing nothing obvious in the rear-view mirror, Gordana visibly relaxed.

"Take the next left," said Gordana. "We are close."

They had come to an intersection where a street sign indicated they were entering the Boston neighborhood of Dorchester. As they drove, Laney let out a low whistle at the massive four-story houses on each side of the street, all recently renovated with front yards of clipped hedges and iron-railing fences.

"Njerku owns many properties here. That is how he makes most of his money."

"In property?"

Gordana nodded. "He makes plenty with the casinos and girls, but in America, he found greater wealth in property development. But when he buys his properties, he has to make an income from them. If you leave a property empty for too long, drug addicts and homeless people move in, ruining it and dragging down the property prices. In a strange way, he is actually benefiting the neighborhoods he buys into.”

“And that's why the police leave him alone.” Laney snorted at the irony of it. “How do you know all this? About the property development and such?”

Fidgeting with the zip of her jacket, Gordana dropped her head a moment. “You probably do not believe it, but I have a Master's degree in city planning. I came here believing I would be contributing to the gentrification of districts around Boston.” A grim smile tweaked her lips back. “I suppose that is what I ended up doing. But not in the way that I had expected.”

“Don't your parents wonder where you are?”

Again, she lent her attention to the clasp on her jacket, clipping it into place then unfastening it. “Each week, we are forced to write a letter to our loved ones, telling them how happy we are, that we have good jobs and are making money. The letters, of course, are all read before they leave the country.”

“That stinks,” Laney spat out. “What happens if the woman's parents start asking questions? I know I would.”

“One girl called her mother on the telephone. Njerku beat her to death in front of us. I heard he had her family killed.” As if to wipe out the memory, she switched her attention to the side window, watching the passing houses bathed in the yellow glow of the streetlights. “No one tried to call their parents after that.”

“What a bastard,” said Laney, hardening her eyes on the road ahead.

“Slow down. We're almost here.”

“Where?”

“Turn right down there,” she said, pointing. “It's that big place down there.”

Sure enough, an enormous four-story house loomed into view. Much like the one they had just left, it was a large Victorian home, ivy trailing up the south wall, black turrets and circular extensions to the upper-level stories, a broad balcony across the front.

Gordana folded her arms tightly over her chest and shivered.

"You been here before?" Laney asked her.

Without taking her eyes off the house, she nodded. That same fear she had radiated earlier had returned.

"You wait here. I'll go knock on the door."

"They won't let you in. If I'm with you, I can explain."

They both looked up at the house again.

"Sitting here ain't doing the job," said Laney. "What are we going to say?"

"If one of the girls answers the door, I can ask her if Katarina is here."

"And if someone else answers?"

She looked away. "No one else will."

"Then let's go."

At that moment, Gordana reached across, briefly touched Laney on the arm, looked her in the eyes. "You are a good person, Laney."

A little taken aback, Laney said, "So are you."

The moment broke and they both got out of the car. Laney locked it, then unlocked it, figuring they might need a quick getaway. She rounded the car and followed Gordana up the five front steps to the verandah, where they paused.

Gordana went to knock, but hesitated.

"I can do this," Laney told her. "You go back to the car."

A quick shake of the head. Gordana took a shuddering breath, then rapped her knuckles on the glass. Almost immediately, the door swung open.

At the sound of footsteps Laney swung around. Behind her, a big man in black pants and a white shirt raced up the steps and grabbed her, wrapping her in a bear hug with one arm across her throat, while a second man burst from the house and put a gun to her head.

"What took you so long?" the man with the gun asked.

"We took the back streets," Gordana replied.

Laney's eyes went to Gordana, questioning. But Gordana stepped back, hands clasped at her mouth and her face crumpling. "I am so sorry, Laney. I'm so, so sorry."

The pressure on Laney's throat intensified until she couldn't breathe. She kicked out, fists pummeling at him, desperate to wriggle free, but he slapped a stinking cloth over her face and her limbs went numb. Black dots appeared in her peripheral vision and spread.

Her brain did several flips, nausea welled. She closed her eyes, and the world around her disappeared.

CHAPTER THIRTY-FIVE
DAY THREE—7:42 AM—ELIZABETH

Elizabeth had spent a sleepless night trying to put all the pieces together in her head before coming to a decision and making the call. By 6 AM, when she'd intended to get up, she felt drained. At the sound of a tiny knock at her bedroom door, she called, "Yes?"

The door cracked open and Holly peeped in. As soon as she saw Elizabeth, she burst into the room, running on tiptoe to the bed to peel back the covers and slide in against her mother.

Feeling a smile widen on her lips, Elizabeth shuffled back into the warmth of her bed to give her room. Holly slipped down under the covers wriggling until she'd molded to the shape of her mother's body. In response, Elizabeth enveloped her, pulled her in. She could smell the sleep in her daughter's hair, feel the warmth of her body against hers.

"What are you doing here, Missy?"

"I wan' a tuddle."

With her head propped up on one elbow, Elizabeth brushed back a wisp of Holly's soft blonde hair and placed a kiss on her ear. Holly giggled and snuggled in closer, so Elizabeth did it again, firmer this time.

Holly chuckled and clapped her hand over her ear. "That tickle, Mommy."

"I know it does. Lemme kiss you again and again," she said, playfully wrestling her while planting kisses all over her face and neck, causing Holly to squeal in delight and kick her feet under the covers.

Pausing to lift her head and check the alarm clock on the nightstand, Elizabeth sighed. "I have to get up, Sweetie." She went to roll to the other side of the bed, but Holly threw a restraining arm around her.

"Nooo. Stay with me."

"I can't, Sweetie. I have a meeting to go to."

Elizabeth lifted Holly's hand, kissed it, then got up. Plucking up her bathrobe from the end of the bed, she slipped into it and paused next to Holly. Leaning down, she placed a hand on either side of her daughter's face on the pillow. When Holly looked up at her, Elizabeth touched her on the nose. "I love you to bits, Missy."

In response, Holly reached up, soft hands gently cupping Elizabeth's face. "I love you, too, Mommy."

Standing there, gazing down at Holly, Elizabeth wondered how she'd ever live without this child. When Holly was born with Down's syndrome and a cleft lip, Elizabeth thought her world had come to an end.

How foolish could she have been? She'd only learned how precious her daughter was when she almost lost her six years ago. How could she lose her again? Even to the McClaines? What knife-edge would she have to walk to ensure that never happened? Then again, how long could she dance to Charles McClaine's tune? And what would she have to do to keep the status quo? After all, she had to be able to get up and look herself in the mirror each morning.

Elizabeth kissed Holly firmly on the cheek. "You stay here, and stay warm until Katie comes, okay?"

"When will you come home?"

"Soon as I can."

Holly snuggled back down among the layers of Elizabeth's bed once more. "Okay, Mommy."

No sooner had Elizabeth gotten ready than the doorbell chimed through the house.

"I'll get it," she called to Katie, her housekeeper, who was now bustling in the kitchen making Holly's breakfast.

As soon as she opened the door, Penny pushed in past her with a newspaper under her arm, looking her over.

"You're up early."

Elizabeth checked her watch. "You're here early." She closed the door and followed Penny into the kitchen while Penny talked over her shoulder. "Seen this morning's papers? Morning, Katie."

"Good morning, Miss Rickman. Coffee?" Katie replied.

"You speak my language," Penny said and slapped the paper on the table.

"Don't tell me," Elizabeth said. "More news stories?"

"Yeah, but thankfully, only what we already know—that Velma Stanford was shot dead in her car." She unfolded the paper and twisted the front page towards Elizabeth, who gave the article a brief glance.

"Y'know, I had a thought," Penny said. "I lay awake all night thinking about how all this crap started and how it's escalated to the point where you're getting threats from your own family."

Elizabeth shrugged into her coat, adjusting it as she listened. "Uh-huh."

"And I think you're right."

"Oh, just for a change?"

"Yeah, okay, don't get all holier-than-thou on me."

Elizabeth smiled. "I'm sorry. Go on, I'm listening."

"Well, I was thinking—it's like, everywhere you go, this guy Gate Westrum's name keeps popping up, but no one seems to know anything about him. All we know is he's some property broker who got himself murdered. For what? Why does his name keep coming up. So, I'm thinking: who's the one person who seems to know the most about this Gate Westrum guy? And who's the person who brought his name into it in the first place?"

"It was actually you," Elizabeth said. "But I know what you mean. Jennifer Reels seems to have all the inside info."

Penny nodded once in agreement. "Exactly. So, then I started thinking, why don't you go see her? Why don't you ask her what she knows about him? And, I mean, why wouldn't she tell you? The guy is dead. It's not like he's going to sue her."

"Two steps ahead of you, Sweetie," Elizabeth told her as she hoisted her purse under her arm and brushed down the gray box-pleat skirt she'd chosen for the meeting. "I've got a meeting with her in twelve minutes."

"Oh, so you weren't planning on telling me this? And my rushing over here was a total waste of time?" Penny said, a little put out.

"Not a bit," Elizabeth told her with a smile. "Holly's been asking when she'll see you again. She misses you. I thought maybe you two could spend a bit of girl-time together over breakfast. Then maybe you could do me a huge favor and take her to school."

Penny's face lit up. "Well, as a matter of fact, I think I could manage that."

***

The Associate

Word came back almost immediately—they had her. Through the bad English and the background echo, one of the Man's braindead goons had called, telling him that Gordana had done exactly as he'd requested. She'd taken her to the other house, straight into the trap.

Turned out her name was Laney Donohue. The sister of the young woman Katarina had been caring for at Sunny Springs. And now they had her. *In the Studio*, he'd said.

The Studio. It sounded like something artistic. That couldn't be further from the truth. It was merely a torture chamber. The first time he'd seen it, he couldn't understand how anyone could subject another human being to such atrocities. He'd nodded around during the tour, then gotten out of there as fast as he could.

Now, here was this Albanian thug asking if he should dispose of Laney Donohue in that place.

In his mind's eye, he could still see her giving him that hand signal as she escaped the last basement she was in. That smug look of determination in her eye. She'd seen him; could identify him.

He could not let her escape a second time. The only way she was getting out of this one was wrapped in a roll of heavy-duty black plastic.

He dragged his mind back and swallowed back the bile that had risen. The thought of what they'd done to Dijana made him sick to his stomach. He didn't want to think about that ever happening to anyone else. But right now, it was her, or it was him.

Then, in one of those blinding flashes of inspiration, he realized something: this could be the opportunity he'd been waiting for. The fact that this nuisance girl had followed the trail this far; the fact that she could have led him to where they were holding Katarina—that had planted a seed in his mind. Already it was germinating into a plan.

He told the thug on the phone to hold the Donohue girl, that he didn't care what they did as long as she was still capable of answering questions when he got there. Then he told him to call Njerku, the boss—the asshole who'd been holding a gun to his head for too long now. He told the thug that this Laney Donohue had important information that Njerku would have to hear in the girl's own words.

The dopey thug's confusion echoed down the phoneline. In fact, even to him, the explanation didn't make sense. That didn't matter. It was the only way he could set his plan up.

As soon as he was sure the Albanian idiot understood what he had to do, he hung up and checked the airlines. If he hurried, he'd catch the next flight out to Boston.

He closed down his computer, snatched his coat from the stand, and called his wife as he left the building. He told her he'd been called away on business, that he'd be back tomorrow. Just in case it was the last time he ever spoke to her, he told her he loved her, then went straight to his car.

If he played this situation correctly, if he got his timing just right, and the gods were with him, he'd not only free himself of this nuisance girl, but he'd finally rid himself of his cold fish of a wife, and that sadistic Albanian thug. All in one clean swoop.

And finally, he could save Katarina.

CHAPTER THIRTY-SIX
DAY THREE—9:24 AM—ELIZABETH

Jennifer Reels was at the same table in the same café when Elizabeth arrived. Her hair was pressed flat on one side as though she'd slept on it, and her makeup had settled into the creases on her face like a topographical roadmap. In stark contrast, the deepened lines and bags under her eyes made her look as though she hadn't slept in a week.

"Nice to see you again, Mrs. McClaine," Jennifer Reels said in a flat tone. Both hands were wrapped around a steaming cup of coffee as if it were a lifeline.

"We keep meeting like this, they're gonna start charging us rent," she said, watching Elizabeth pull out the chair opposite. Despite the warmth of the café, she shrugged into her jacket as if she was cold.

Elizabeth perched on the seat and signaled the waitress. "Cappuccino, thank you," she told the waitress who approached; then she switched her attention back to the reporter. "You look tired."

"Oh, really? You get me out of bed this hour of the morning and you think I look tired? Color me shocked." She took a sip of her coffee and set it down again, hands still cradling the cup.

"I think you probably know why I'm here."

Her bloodshot eyes lifted to meet Elizabeth's in amusement. "Why don't you tell me? Just in case I missed a memo."

"Gate Westrum."

Her eyes flickered in surprise. "Gate Westrum? What's he got to do with the price of fish?"

Elizabeth's coffee arrived. She cleared her throat and shifted in her seat while the waitress set it down. Both women waited in silence until the waitress had retreated before continuing the conversation.

Elizabeth leaned in, voice lowered. "Who was he?"

"What makes you think I'd know?"

"The article you ran four months ago makes me think you'd know. From what I read, it didn't paint a particularly flattering picture of the deceased."

Jennifer lifted a world-weary gaze to the ceiling before releasing a tired sigh and meeting Elizabeth's gaze again.

"Gate Westrum was a psychopathic property developer who got himself killed trying to outmaneuver the wrong guy. He was a swindler and a thief who got what he deserved. What else do you need to know?"

After that description, what *didn't* she want to know?

She started with: "Who was the guy he was trying to outmaneuver and how?"

"I don't understand. What's Gate Westrum got to do with anything?" Jennifer asked again.

"It just seems strange to me that you did the same hatchet job on him as you did on me. I took a look at the article on my phone just before I left. It felt…" She lifted both shoulders briefly. "I don't know…personal. Intentional. That's the feeling I got with both articles."

"So, I'm assuming you've read everything I've written?"

Elizabeth smiled. "I'm sure I've missed some literary greats penned by you, Miss Reels, but no, I'm sorry, I haven't." She gave it a moment, then said, "Look, why don't we quit the dance of the seven swords here and get straight to the point? Who was it put the target on my forehead and set you out to do your worst?"

Jennifer Reels sniggered and lifted her cup, grinning across at her.

"Whoa. That's a bunch of interesting mental images you just conjured up for me, Mrs. McClaine."

"And yet…?" Elizabeth spread her hands.

Again, Jennifer sighed and placed her cup down. She propped both elbows on the table, stubby, ring-encrusted fingers clasped at her chin, steely eyes on Elizabeth.

"Mrs. McClaine, I told you once that I don't give out the identities of my sources. That's the truth. You may think me a little low on scruples, but it goes against every fiber of my being. In this case, I decided to meet you here because I'm making an exception. You wanna know why?"

Elizabeth angled her head in suspicion. "I can't even guess."

"Because I want you to get to the bottom of who shot my sister in the face. I want you to hunt that bastard down and make him pay. That's why."

The shock hit Elizabeth like a rock. "Velma Stanford was your sister?"

"And my information source. She's the one who called me. She didn't want you sniffing around Sunny Springs. She wanted you out of there."

The news had Elizabeth reeling with even more questions as the implications hit her one after the other. "So, she's the one who gave you the paperwork on my clients?"

"Some of it. She got the rest from someone else. And before you ask, I don't know who. I think Velma was in some kind of trouble. I asked her. I said, 'Whatever it is, this can't be the answer.'" A shake of the head. "I don't know what the hell she'd gotten herself into, but she didn't intend confiding in me."

"And the story about Gate Westrum? She put you up to that as well?"

"She did. First, I thought it was a great story. Young, snappy, up-and-coming property developer hits the big-time, pisses off the wrong person, ends up dead. A real eyeball-grabber. I thanked her with a decent-sized check."

"But she never let on why she gave it to you?"

"Not a word. You have to understand, Mrs. McClaine, my sister and I were never close. But last year, her husband went into the hospital and came out with cancer and a use-by date. She was looking at debt that'd make your eyes water: doctors, nurses, medication lists as long as your arm, the whole kit and caboodle. That's why I came back here to Cleveland—to see what I could do to help her. Time I got here, she'd booked him into Fair-Skies, the elderly care facility. He's in the hospital unit there."

"Fair-Skies? That's the new state-of-the-art facility overlooking the lake, isn't it?"

"That's the one. All privately run. The fees are horrendous. I wondered where she got the money. One point, I even asked her. She said she was doing okay. Said she was using their savings."

"You didn't believe her?"

"Pfft. They didn't have savings. Or if they did, it wouldn't have been enough to pay for that level of care. At the time, I figured she'd borrowed the cash and was too ashamed to say so."

"And then she was struggling to pay it back," Elizabeth surmised, now feeling dreadful for the way she'd spoken to the woman.

"Or not," said Jennifer. When Elizabeth's eyebrows went up, Jennifer added, "You know who owns the place, I assume."

She waited with her brows raised until the penny dropped.

"Aden Falls," Elizabeth said like it had been punched out of her.

"Same owners as Sunny Springs."

"So, where does Gate Westrum come into it?"

"I have no idea. When Velma first called me in, I did a ton of research on Gate Westrum. There was no stone I left unturned. And yet I could not find one thing on the guy before he turned up in Boston four years ago. A guy who just appears out of nowhere, and yet my sister seemed to know him inside out. There's something dirty going on at Sunny Springs. I can smell it. Velma knew what it was. I think someone was paying her husband's care to keep her mouth shut."

"Someone at Aden Falls?"

"It would seem so."

For a moment, Elizabeth let the information run around her head. Yes, she'd already suspected something was going on at Sunny Springs. Hadn't she said that all along? But what was so bad that someone would pay the care of Velma Stanford's husband, then murder her? And what did it have to do with the young woman Laney was searching for? If anything.

"What do you know about the young woman who disappeared from Sunny Springs—the nurse aid?"

"Only that her name was Wendy O'Dell. That she disappeared and hasn't contacted her mother in over a year. That Mrs. O'Dell's a mess over it."

"You visited her?"

"No point. Yeah, Wendy O'Dell worked at Sunny Springs. And no, she didn't bother telling her mother where she was. Families have fall-outs. Shit happens. But how could that have anything to do with Velma's murder?"

"Have you told all this to the police?" Elizabeth asked.

"Not yet. Oh, they'll come see me. Sure as God made little apples. But if the secret of Sunny Springs is dirty enough to murder for, and well-hidden enough that even I couldn't get to the bottom of it, you can bet the cops are gonna meet a brick wall."

The image of Delaney popped into her mind. That rugged determination. How hard he'd worked to find Holly when she was taken. "The police here are pretty good."

Jennifer let that smirk slide across one side of her face again. "Only if they know what they're looking for. And even I couldn't figure that out."

"Then why are you telling me all this? What makes you think I can do any better than the police?"

"Because when you started asking questions, you hit a nerve. Because you rattled someone enough to have my sister call me in. Whether you're aware of it or not, Mrs. McClaine, you're right at the epicenter of this shit storm. When you started asking about Gate Westrum, you frightened someone enough to murder my sister. And I sure as hell don't want to be next."

CHAPTER THIRTY-SEVEN
DAY THREE—9:24 AM—LANEY

Laney had no idea where she was when she awoke. Sometime in the night she'd felt the pinch of a needle in her arm. Since then she'd wafted in and out of consciousness until she found herself lying on her side in a fetal position, enclosed in what looked like a small dog cage, dim light all around. With her head still spinning, she levered herself up on one arm and blinked back the haze to clear her vision to take in her surroundings. Screwing up her face, she licked her parched lips.

She was in what looked like another basement—windows blacked out all around, stairs leading up to what looked like a steel freezer door at the top with a padlock looped through the handle. But this wasn't a basement like the last one. This one sent a chill of terror down her spine.

All around a pale blue light glinted off white tiled walls and floor. Icy air blowing from an AC unit on the wall next to her had dropped the temperature to a chilly 45 degrees, according to the LED figures on the gauge. A steel surgical table sat center-stage, same wispy blue light picking out a white, five-drawer medical trolley standing alongside.

Over on the wall were hung a line of black rubber suits—like diving suits. Next to them, three sets of manacles dangled from where they'd been bolted into the surgically clean white of the tiles. A variety of whips and studded collars, were displayed along with instruments, the uses of which she couldn't even begin to guess. Even the air smelled of antiseptic. Like a surgical theater.

Next to her were two other crates, both the same size as the one she was in.

"What the hell…?"

In such a confined space, she could barely move. Holding her knees in tight, chin tucked in, she managed to swivel herself around onto her butt. Working her arm down to her feet, she reached for the bars and rattled the cage door. Then she spotted the padlock down there. On the outside. Which she should have expected.

Nausea twisted and rolled in her stomach. She remembered being dragged out to the car, regaining a swirling sense of consciousness every now and then, only to have a stinking rag clapped over her mouth and nose, dropping her straight back into that same oblivion. Each time she'd come to, she'd noted a series of images: the guy—the thug that grabbed her at the house, the car—Celtics plates, ditto; being shuffled into the back seat, the drive, watching trees slide by, a green freeway sign: *Boston South*. Slumped in the back seat between two men, she'd kept slipping in and out of consciousness, every now and then taking in the passing scenery. Nothing she could recognize.

Every conscious moment wondering how she would ever escape.

Next thing, she'd awoken in this stinking cage.

Automatically, she squeezed a hand to her back pocket for her phone— her only hope.

Gone. Of course it was.

Steadying her back against the side of the cage, she raised one foot as far as she could, used all her strength to strike it against the cage door. It sent a metallic vibration throughout the frame, but the door held fast. This time, she twisted around, shifting position slightly. Again, she struck the door. Flats of both feet this time, every bit of her fury charged into the strike. Still the door held.

From somewhere behind her came the distant sound of a door closing. Someone was up there. Coming this way? In desperation, she pounded the cage door again and again. Each time the cage rocked and clanked on the glossy white floor.

The upstairs door opened and a shaft of yellow light sliced into the open space. A click, and blinding white light flickered on from somewhere overhead.

A sound like a freezer door. Then footsteps. Coming down the stairs.

Laney gripped both sides of the cage, drew her legs up as far as she could, and using all her weight landed a powerful strike at the cage door, slamming it so hard the cage lifted at one end.

But still it held.

The click of shoes on the white tiled floor. She didn't even turn around to see.

She let out a scream of frustration, a guttural cry of determination, and smashed at the cage door again. In her peripheral vision, she could see him standing there.

"You will not break that," he told her calmly. Foreign accent. Maybe Russian. Or Bulgarian or Albanian. Something like that. Laney could never pick them out.

"Is galvanized iron. Very strong." He leaned over, put his fat hand down just above her head, fingers through the grille, rattling it as if to prove its strength. "See? No break."

Furious, she grabbed one fat finger, clinging to it with both hands, and tried to bend it back. He yelped, tugged at it but she clung on, drew her mouth up to it, and sunk her teeth in, tasting the trickle of blood in her mouth.

"Bitch!" He lifted one knee onto the top of the cage, let go a string of obscenities, now using his other hand to extricate his finger. Finally, he whipped his free hand behind his back, came back with a gun, pressed the end of the barrel hard to her cheek.

"Let go, or I blow your brains all over floor." The instant she released his finger, he snapped it back, holding it cradled with the gun hand while he inspected it.

In a flash of rage, he aimed the gun straight at her head. "You will pay for that. You wait. I make sure you pay." The tension of the moment broke when the upstairs door opened again and a second guy entered from the top of the stairs. He sauntered across with an elongated handgun pointed at the floor. A silencer on the barrel, from what Laney could see. An authoritative jerk of the head. "Bring her."

When the second guy retreated back through the doorway, the fat guy grunted, like he didn't like taking orders. All the same, he took a key from his pocket and unlocked the padlock on the cage door. He grabbed her by both ankles, hauling her out so the ridge below the opening scraped painfully across her butt and then her back as she came out.

Still sickened by the stink of that sharp-smelling liquid they'd used to knock her out, she leaned on one hand, trying to get to her feet. The guy hooked her firmly under one arm and hoisted her up. She winced at the pain in her back and the fug still clouding her brain. When she opened her eyes, he had the gun an inch from her face.

"One move, you die."

"Who are you? What do you want?"

Ignoring her, he roughly jerked her around, half carrying, half dragging her to the bottom of the stairway. Her feet felt like lead. She stumbled, almost falling, but he yanked her to her feet and shoved her at the stairway.

She stumbled, grabbed the metal rail, leaned heavily on it. She'd never felt so awful. He shoved her in the back.

"Move."

She took one step up. "I'm moving. Where are you taking me?"

"Shut up and go. You will find out."

She lifted her head, straightened as well as she could, and turned side on to him. "Listen—" she began in a reasonable tone.

But he whipped his hand around, backhanding her across the face so fast it sent her sprawling. Lying face down on the stairway, she tried to get up. But he grabbed her by the back of the shirt, hoisting her until she regained her footing. He shoved her.

"I'm moving, dammit." Now she could taste her own blood in her mouth. Her face throbbed from the blow and her forehead smarted from where it had hit the edge of the step.

When the door above her opened again, a wedge of yellow light hit her eyes, made her blink.

The second guy in the doorway. "What are you doing? I said bring her."

The one holding her responded angrily. "I am bringing her." Then muttered something in his own language.

There was only one way she'd get out of this now. And that was to go along with whatever they had planned, then look for an escape wherever she could. She gripped the rail and clambered up towards the second guy, who waited on the top step, glaring down at his compatriot in disgust until she passed in front of him. Then he pointed down at the first guy.

"You get your attitude straightened out. Boss coming. Wants to question her."

Fatso replied sourly as he stomped up behind her. "When do I get money?"

The response was an angry outburst from the second guy. Laney didn't have to know the language to know what he'd said. It was a string of insults, if the response was anything to go by. Second guy came down the stairs, grabbed her arm, yanked her up the last step and out the door. They took her one on each side, and dragged her to a waiting car. Same car as the one she'd seen out at the house with the Celtics plates. She was sure of it.

While the first guy held her arms behind her back, muttering bitterly, the second guy opened the back door and swiped up a roll of clear tape from the back seat. He peeled off a length, bit through the edge, and tore it from the roll. Then went to stick it across Laney's mouth. She twisted this way and that, fighting the grasp Fatso had on her.

Second guy barked something. Fatso huffed, gripped both her hands firmly in one of his, fingers digging painfully into her flesh, and used his injured hand to grab a handful of her hair. While she was held motionless, the second guy slapped the tape over her mouth, sealing it down each side with his thumbs. Then he turned her around and wound a length around her hands before drawing her back, then pushing her head-first into the rear seat of the car. She twisted around to a sitting position, scowling out at them as they blabbered in their own language.

Who was this boss they were talking about? What could he want with her? And how had they found her?

Didn't matter. Right now she had to get out. Her gut told her if she didn't, she wouldn't see the end of the day. She was searching the car for anything she could use as a weapon when the second guy's phone rang.

She watched them through the open car door as he answered, turned to face away from the car a moment, nodding as he listened. After a few brief words, he hung up and stuck it in his pocket and turned back, speaking to Fatso.

"Njerku is coming here," he said.

Fatso huffed.

"Put her back."

CHAPTER THIRTY-EIGHT
DAY THREE—9:24 AM—ELIZABETH

"Well, that's very nice," Penny told Elizabeth, indignation souring her tone. "Jennifer Reels doesn't want to get knocked off, but she doesn't care if we are."

"She's scared. Something about Gate Westrum scared her."

"Why? The guy's dead. What's he gonna do? Come back and haunt her?"

"I don't know. Reporters have died defending the identity of their sources. The fact that she's given me Velma's name tells me she's even more frightened than she lets on."

Penny snorted. "Frankly, I can't see her dying for anyone else. More likely, she'd use them as a human shield."

Elizabeth was listening with only half an ear. In her mind, she was still trying to piece together what seemed an impossible puzzle. She tore the top sheet from her blotter, pinned it over the budgetary plans on her whiteboard, and grabbed a Sharpie.

"So, this is the timeline of events, starting from the beginning." She drew a single line from left to right, bisected it with several vertical strokes, then started with the first one. "Gate Westrum turns up here four years ago. He's a young property developer who came to Cleveland to secure construction deals."

She turned a blank look on Penny, then dropped her shoulders. "Dear Lord, I am so stupid. Gate Westrum was the one who secured all the property deals for Charles. He's the one who brokered all the property deals between Aden Falls and Charles McClaine Construction. How dumb could I be?"

"Given you were lobbying against the old-fashioned state-run facilities for the disabled, I'm surprised you missed that," Penny mused.

A defensive knot formed in Elizabeth's chest. "Four years ago, I was still trying to get this trust fund off the ground. I was lobbying politicians, government departments, trying to—"

"I know, I know," Penny said, patting the air.

"—set up charity events, sucking up to whoever I could to bring governmental departments on board," Elizabeth continued, using the end of the Sharpie to count the items on her fingers until she did a double-take at Penny, then stopped. "Yes, I know you know. I'm sorry."

"This is not your fault. You were doing your job. The one Charles McClaine asked you to."

Folding her arms across her chest, Elizabeth dropped her head and sighed. "So, why do I feel responsible?"

"I'm sorry if it sounded like an accusation. It wasn't."

"I know you weren't accusing me."

"I'm just saying they must have played their cards pretty close to the chest for you to have not even noticed."

"At the time, Charles had me running in circles, demanding I get this done, and that done. I remember crashing a meeting he was in. I was mortified. He was so furious, I backed out of his office like a scolded kid."

"But if Charles has already fessed up that his company did the construction for Aden Falls, why would he lie about dealing with Gate Westrum?"

"Keep the company name clean?" Elizabeth suggested. While it was possible, it didn't gel.

Penny made a face. "I guess if it's a multi-million-dollar deal, he's gonna protect himself, right?"

Still not convinced, Elizabeth said, "I guess so. Or maybe he dealt with someone else."

"That's also possible."

Feeling they'd come to a dead end, Elizabeth said, "So, let's move on. Next thing that happens is Laney Donohue comes out of prison and takes her sister from Sunny Springs."

"Who's been beaten." Noting the possible confusion, Penny added. "Kimmy, that is—not Laney."

"Right." Elizabeth drew an arrow pointing upwards where she wrote *Kimmy and Laney*.

"As a result, Laney goes looking for the nurse aid who left that day." Another line pointing to the words *Nurse Aid*.

Penny nodded. "Correct. Though who knows why?"

"What do you mean, 'who knows why'?"

"Well, you don't just take off hunting for someone without good reason. Maybe this girl had something of hers. Maybe she was the one who left the bruises on Kimmy."

Blinking at the revelation, Elizabeth said, "You're right. After all, that's where this began. And that means Laney knows something we don't. I need you to call Janelle. Ask her if she's heard from Laney since she dropped Kimmy there, and get Lanie's cell number. I need to ask her a few questions."

Penny made a note. "Will do."

Again, Elizabeth turned to the timeline. "So, what happens next is that Laney breaks into Sunny Springs. Velma Stanford catches her. In light of what's happened, I doubt it was David Whitcliff who was worried about those files like we originally thought. It was Velma. She thought Laney had inadvertently picked up something that'll incriminate whoever she's been hiding a secret for."

"A big enough secret that the concerned party would cough up for her husband's medical care."

"Which…" Elizabeth turned to Penny with pointedly lifted brows. "…may not be that big of a deal if you owned, or even just ran, the place he was put into."

Penny clutched a hand to her heart. "Oh, not Ryan Halverston. Please tell me it's not Ryan Halverston."

"Eye on the ball, Penny, eye on the ball," Elizabeth said, and turned to look over the notes. "What the hell are they hiding?"

Penny threw up both hands and dropped them. "Exactly. We already know Gate Westrum made some deals with Charles and wound up dead. Maybe he was stiffing the property seller. Maybe he was…I don't know, fixing the price so he got a bigger commission."

Elizabeth snorted into the air. "Yeah. Because that would never happen." Narrowing her eyes back at the timeline, she said, "No, it's something else. Something we're missing. Okay, Gate Westrum cuts a deal with Charles, ends up dead; nurse aid leaves Sunny Springs, Laney breaks in and steals something, someone thinks she's got something important and kills Velma."

"Yeah, that makes no sense," Penny said flatly. "Unless they're worried about some kind of illegal employment practices coming to light. And frankly, killing Velma is a little drastic, don't you think?"

"Maybe we're looking at this from the wrong angle. Maybe we should start with the girl Laney is looking for. What was her name?"

"O'Dell, Wendy O'Dell."

"Get David Whitcliff on the phone. Tell him I'm coming to see him again. I want to know why she left. I want to know what went on that day. And while we're at it, I want to know why he neglected to tell me he was at my party."

While Penny made the call, Elizabeth lifted her own phone and dialed.

It rang twice and she felt the coquettish smile tweak at her lips as he picked up.

"Lance, how are you?"

"I'm doing okay. But you don't often call to see how I am."

She smiled down at her desk, feeling a little foolish. "Caught," she admitted. "I'm actually calling to see how you've gotten on with the girl in the cemetery."

"Still looking."

"Okaaay. Am I allowed to ask if you're working on the Velma Stanford murder?"

"If you mean the *alleged* murder of Velma Stanford, then yes." She could hear the smile in his voice, indicating he was fully aware she was digging for information.

"What I'm wondering is how you IDed Velma so quickly. How could you be sure it was her?"

"She was in her car, with her driver's license, credit cards, and her work files. She had just left the office, and one of the officers knew her. There's no point in running a DNA match when the evidence is so compelling."

"Uh-huh. Is there anything else you might be able to tell me?"

That smile again. "I can tell you that the investigation is ongoing."

"Well, I guess that's telling me. So, what do you know about the disappearance of a girl named Wendy O'Dell?"

A pause while he made the connection. "The girl in the cemetery is not Wendy O'Dell, if that's what you're asking."

She was taken aback, but tried not to convey it. "I'm not suggesting it is. I'm asking what you know about her."

A long breath while he racked his memory. "Mother called us last year, said her daughter had disappeared and hadn't been seen since."

Elizabeth's eyebrows shot up. "And that was it? You didn't try to find her?"

"We called her cell phone. She told us she was fine, that she'd secured a good job in Boston, and that she'd had some kind of disagreement with her mother."

"And you're sure it was her?"

"Positive ID made. Her mother identified her voice on the recording. Plus, she gave us her social security number, and sent a photograph."

"And again, you didn't follow up because the evidence was compelling."

He tipped his head. "Out of our jurisdiction. We filed the case with the FBI, left it with them. We don't have time to chase every single case where we've exhausted all efforts and come to a satisfactory conclusion. That's not to say everybody's happy. But that's police work."

"Okay, thanks. Can I get a copy of that photograph of Wendy O'Dell?"

A suspicious pause. "I'm not sure. Why?"

"I don't know. I just want to know how she could be working at Sunny Springs only a half hour away, and her mother had no idea."

"Sometimes, that's what happens," he said. "People lose touch. I'll send you the photograph used when she went missing. Hold on."

"I'm holding." After a moment, her phone beeped. She opened it to find a headshot of a sweet-looking blue-eyed, strawberry-blonde girl gazing out at her. Freckles dotting her nose and cheeks. Not classically beautiful, but pretty.

"Got it. Thank you."

"That was taken a couple of years ago." In the background, she heard someone speak to him. "I'm sorry, Elizabeth, I have to go."

"That's fine. And thank you," she said.

She hung up and turned around to find Penny had also hung up.

"That's a no-go. Apparently, David Whitcliff went out of state for a meeting."

"One of his employees is shot dead and he's off to a meeting?"

Penny shrugged. "That's what the girl said."

Elizabeth tsked. "What in the heck is wrong with people? Okay, so here's the plan from here: See if you can dig up any information on who the shareholders of Aden Falls are. Maybe there's something we missed…and yes, I know," she said when she saw Penny's face. "Jennifer Reels would have already raked over that pile with a fine-toothed comb. But with a little hindsight, you might find something she missed."

"And what are you doing?"

"I'm following the Laney angle. I'm calling the only other person who knew Wendy O'Dell. Chances are it's another totally dead end. But it's the only loose thread I've got. And that makes it worth a shot."

CHAPTER THIRTY-NINE
DAY THREE—10:16 AM—LANEY

"Do I at least get something to eat?" Laney called out.

She'd been back in the dog cage in the white-tiled room for over an hour now. This time on her elbows and knees, no room to move. Just across from her, Fatso leaned with his back against the wall, picking at his fingernails while he stood guard over her.

Still acting dumb, he folded his arms, huffed, and looked away.

"Listen, I know you're probably not supposed to talk to me, right?"

A quick glance her way.

"I haven't eaten in a while. I mean, a cookie? A pack of Doritos? Where's the harm?"

Still nothing. She groaned and dropped her head to the floor.

"Man, you must get paid a lot," she mumbled.

Fatso snorted.

She *knew* it. That was the raw nerve to work on. But where to go from there…?

"Have you been working for this Jerko guy a long time? Like, how do you get into this business? Did you answer a want ad in the local paper?"

"Shut up!"

"Listen, I'm just asking, aren't I?" No response. "Who is this guy, anyway? Where'd he get the money for all this shit? I mean, look at these places. He must be totally rolling in cash." She watched him. "Did he steal it? Is he, like, some kind of criminal mastermind like you see in the movies?"

"I told you, shut up."

"Okay, you're scared of him, I get it," she said. Noting the slight flinch, she said, "Is that why you keep working for him? Has to be, I guess. 'Cause no one's stupid enough to do what you do if you're not getting paid."

Obviously irritated, he pushed off the wall and strode to the door to check the lock. Finding it secure, he walked back, leaning his shoulder into the wall this time, with his back to her.

"I bet old buddy boy out there's getting paid. The guy who keeps kicking your ass. I bet he's rolling in it. And he thinks you're stupid enough—"

Without warning, Fatso spun around, flashed over to the cage, and kicked it—flat of his foot inches from her face. The cage jolted back with a clang, slid a couple feet on the tiles, and stopped.

Laney could feel her heart beating in her chest. She was walking a fine line. The plan—the only one she'd come up with—was to piss him off enough to open the cage. But not enough to kill her. It was the crappiest plan she'd ever come up with. But that's all she had.

"Listen, I'm sorry. I didn't mean to piss you off. But it's cramped in here. Can you just let me out long enough to get my blood moving in my legs again?"

"You stay where you are."

She gave it a second.

"Where are you from, anyway? Are you Russian?"

A caustic snort. "Russian? Every American think someone with accent is Russian." He shook his head.

"So, where are you from? Yugoslavia?" Man, she was really reaching. She shook her head, muttering, "Shit, I don't even know where that is."

"You don't know anything. Kosovo. That is my home."

"So, why'd you come here? To America? Must have cost a lot just to get here."

A sardonic grin. "Employment opportunity. Good money. Health benefits." He chuckled at his own joke.

At last, an opening.

"Is that where Katarina was from? From Kosovo?" she asked, knowing full well she was.

"Yes. From Kosovo."

"Why did she come here?"

Another sour grin. "Same as me. Employment opportunity."

"But they lied to her, didn't they? The job wasn't what she thought. They told her she'd landed some terrific job, earning great money."

The corners of his mouth went down. "That is luck. Sometimes good, sometimes not good."

"Is she still alive?"

He looked her in the eye. "She is back at work. Good luck for her. Not so much good luck for you."

"Can you at least tell me where?"

No reply. He looked away.

"She took care of my disabled sister. I just wanted to thank her. That's all I came here for." When he still said nothing, she said, "How about Wendy O'Dell? She's a smart girl. Pretty, too. Did she come looking for a job?" And watched for a reaction.

"Her, too," he said.

Bingo! At least now Laney knew she was on the right track. Wendy had been here. Could still be.

"Is Wendy working here? Like in this place? Or somewhere else?"

This time he ignored her. But at least she'd gotten that much. And he hadn't told her she was dead. She tried shifting position, trying to relieve the ache in her knees. Failing, she gave up.

"Aw, c'mon, please just let me out for a second. My back's killing me in here. You've got a gun. What am I gonna do?"

"We wait for Njerku."

"Well, if he's coming from Kosovo, we've got a long wait."

"Not Kosovo. From Cleveland. Not so long to wait."

More information. She had to keep him talking.

"Still could be hours. And you gotta eat, right?" A hunger pang twisted her stomach. "A nice big burger, maybe? Juice running down your chin. Big slice of cheese, all that crisp lettuce—"

"Shut up!"

"Yeah, I know. I can't stand it either. But you can't kill me until Jerko's here. How about you just let me out, walk around a little, maybe get a drink of water? Then I promise I'll get back in the cage."

Furious now, he rushed across to the cage, whipped out a gun, and shoved it through the grate, barrel pressed hard to the back of her head.

Laney's heart almost stopped. "You're not allowed to kill me," she shouted, desperation and fear squeezing her throat.

"That is what you think," he said and clicked back the hammer.

CHAPTER FORTY
DAY THREE—11:24 AM—ELIZABETH

Caroline Judemire was standing outside her college, hugging a stack of schoolbooks to her chest and looking back and forth down the street, worried frown creasing her brow. As soon as she saw Elizabeth pull up on the other side of the street, she checked for traffic and stepped out, head down, walking quickly to the car.

With a snap look around as though she was afraid of being seen, she opened the passenger's door, slid in, and closed the door.

Fastening her seatbelt, she said, "Thanks for picking me up, Mrs. McClaine."

Elizabeth hit the turn signal and pulled out. "No problem, Caroline. You might need to give me directions to your house, though."

Caroline lifted her head, looking out the windshield. "Turn left up here."

Elizabeth did so. "I guess you know why I wanted to talk with you."

"About Laney?"

"Actually, it's about Wendy, the nurse aid at Sunny Springs. What can you tell me about her?"

Caroline focused on the dash and tried to think. "She was nice. Really beautiful. I mean, drop-dead gorgeous. Old guys used to come in to see their disabled kids and end up with their eyes glued on her instead."

"Really?"

"Absolutely. I wondered why she wasn't a model or actress or something. But she was foreign."

That surprised Elizabeth. "She was foreign? Like French or something?"

Caroline shook her head. "Eastern European. I think she came from one of those Slavic countries."

"It never made anyone wonder why someone so beautiful was working at Sunny Springs?"

Caroline's eyes widened. "Oh, man, we get all kinds working there. Mostly women out of prisons, or…" She tipped her head, searching for the correct term. "…minorities, immigrants. That kind of thing. But not gorgeous ones. Not like Wendy."

Running on a hunch, Elizabeth said, "Can you describe her? Like, how tall was she? Her hair color?"

Caroline turned her attention to the window while she raked through her memory. "She was taller than me. Long hair—really dark. Beautiful olive complexion. Green eyes. That's the thing you noticed first about her—she had beautiful eyes. I'd give my right arm for eyes like that."

A crash of realization sent vibrations through Elizabeth. *It's not the same girl.*

"Anything else? What was her English like?"

"It was good, but you know, she left out quantifiers. Like 'the' and 'an.' So, it wasn't perfect."

"Did Wendy ever tell you where she came from?"

"She kept to herself. The only one she really connected with was Kimmy. Maybe if she'd made more friends she could have asked for help when that man came and took her."

Elizabeth nearly ran off the road. "A *man* took her? Where? What man?"

"The story we got was that It was her old boss and he'd offered her a new job. But I saw her when she left. She was crying. If it was some great new job, she didn't look too excited about it."

"She didn't want to go?"

"No way. But she didn't look like she had a lot of choice."

"Who told you she was going to a new job?"

"Mrs. Stanford. Nobody really believed her, but Wendy didn't ask for help, so what else could we do? We let her go. Should we have done something else?"

"No. Not at all," Elizabeth said, wondering if she were eighteen and impressionable, working in her first job, if she'd have done the same thing. Doubtful. Even at eighteen, Elizabeth challenged everything. She'd have been out there, cutting between them and asking questions. "So, you're saying Velma Stanford was there when she left?"

"Uh-huh. She's the one who told the man where to find Wendy. Afterwards, Dorothy—that's an old lady that works there—she said the guy must have been real rich. She said he was wearing a really expensive suit and a diamond ring on his pinky finger. I saw the car. Man," she said and widened her eyes briefly, "It was a nice car. Boston Celtics plates. I recognized them right away. My dad used to be a fan. Take a right up here," she said and pointed.

Elizabeth slowed and made the turn. So, whoever took her was from Boston. That's where she probably was now.

"Do you know how she got the job at Sunny Springs?"

"Not a clue. She just turned up one day."

"Do you know where she lived?"

"That's my house just down there," Caroline said, pointing again. "She never said."

Elizabeth could have cursed. She had too many more questions to ask.

As they pulled to the curb, Caroline began gathering her backpack and books, ready to get out. "Is there anything else you want to know?"

Where do I even start? Elizabeth thought. But Caroline had probably given her everything she could. So, instead, she said, "You've been a great help. Thank you."

Caroline swung her legs out and hitched up her books. As she got out and went to close the door, she leaned down. "Oh, there was one other thing I almost forgot. Wendy had a tattoo on her wrist."

"A tattoo? What of?"

"A weird one. Like a barcode. You know, with lines and a number. I remember thinking, 'Why would you get a barcode for a tattoo?'" She jerked one shoulder. "I guess people do weird things."

Elizabeth blinked at her. "I guess they do. And thank you."

The dead girl at the cemetery had had a tattoo burned from her wrist. Delaney had confirmed it wasn't Wendy O'Dell. How did he know? Or was Wendy just another missing girl, taken by a different man? Was it a coincidence?

There was only one person who might be able to tell her. As Caroline walked on up to her house, oblivious to the relevance of her last words, Elizabeth pulled out, hit the gas, and took off.

If luck was on her side, he'd be in his office. Yes, she could phone. But she wanted to gauge the reaction to this news. And while she could outline most of what she now knew, she'd have to hold some cards close to her chest and watch every word.

Because this whole mess of lies and dirty deals could spring up and hit her right in the face.

CHAPTER FORTY-ONE
DAY THREE—12:19 PM—LANEY

With the gun still pressed to the back of Laney's head, Fatso mumbled something in his own language, then jabbed the end of the barrel into the base of her neck before stepping back.

So she'd been right. He wasn't allowed to kill her.

What a dumb way to find out, she thought. Despite the chill of the room, sweat ran down her temples, dripped off her nose. Relief flooded in so fast she felt dizzy.

After several minutes, he appeared to have calmed down. She couldn't just crouch here and wait for whatever was coming, so she bit back her fear and tried again.

"Hey, listen. Can you hear me? I'm sorry but I really need to pee."

Then she silently cursed. What was supposed to be a plan had now morphed into reality. The mere suggestion had triggered pressure in her bladder and now she really did need the bathroom.

"I haven't been all night. Now I really gotta go. Can you let me out?"

Fatso sniffed and looked away.

"You know who'll be cleaning up if I pee my pants, don't you? Ain't gonna be buddy boy out there."

Fatso shifted uneasily. He hadn't left the room, so she figured he also had to pee by now.

"Listen, I'm busting. There must be a bathroom down here. Can't you just let me out? It'd take, like, a minute. And I don't feel like being cooped up in here with wet pants."

His eyes had gone from a dead stare to shifting this way and that. After checking his watch, he sighed, pushed off the wall, and strolled over.

"You can go to bathroom, then back in cage."

"I will, I promise. Just let me out before it's too late."

He took out his gun, finger looped through the trigger guard while he unlocked the cage.

Sheesh! If I'da known it would be this easy, I would've yelled this out sooner, she thought wide-eyed, as she shuffled backwards, reversing out of the cage. Knees out first onto the cold floor, she paused, feeling every creaking muscle. She could barely move. As soon as her head cleared the cage, she straightened, flexing her back and rubbing her elbows.

He gripped her under the arm and jerked her to her feet. "Get up."

She grunted in pain. "Careful, will you? I been folded up in there so long I've gone stiff."

He spun her towards the door and shoved her. Next thing, she felt the cold barrel end of the gun pressed hard to the back of her head.

"No stupid moves."

Both hands up, she moved ahead of him to the bottom of the stairway.

"Up."

One sharp jab in the back of the head with the gun.

"Ow. I'm going, I'm going." She rubbed at the back of her head where two lumps had now risen. Up ahead was the freezer door, a padlock snapped shut through a hole in the handle.

Dammit!

The sound of keys being shaken out jingled from behind as she cautiously moved up the stairs. Next thing the gun lifted from the back of her head and the jingle became muffled. She figured he was counting through a keyring, searching for the right key.

Now!

She swung around, knocking his hand aside, and the keys went flying. Just as his aghast expression came up to meet hers, she drove the flat of her foot into his chest. But as solid as he was, he hardly moved. Instead, fury flared in his eyes and he grabbed her ankle and tugged so hard her standing leg buckled. To keep from falling, she snatched the rail with both hands. Already she could see the gun coming up. Using the rail for support, she leapt from the stairs, kicking out at him with her free foot.

He ducked back and she missed. Following the momentum of the kick, she twisted on the stairs and fell flat on her face. He grabbed her by the back of the jacket, hoisted her up like a rag doll, and flung her around. She hit the floor on her shoulder. For a split second she slid on the polished floor and came to a stop with her arms and legs thrown wide. Like a raging bull, he charged across and dropped on top of her, legs straddling her, gun pressed hard to her cheek. She stopped flailing and stared up into his hate-filled eyes.

Furious, lips drawn back into a mask of hatred, he grabbed her shirt at the throat and lifted her, jabbing the gun repeatedly into her cheekbone, using it to punctuate each word he spat through clenched teeth.

"You think I am a fool. I will *kill* you…*kill* you right here." Nostrils flaring, eyes burning with outrage, breaths coming short and hard, he shoved her back. "But not now. When Njerku is done with you, you will be mine."

Rising from his position astride her, he stepped back, gun pointed at her. "Get up. You try stupid move again, I will shoot you and take consequences. Back in cage."

"I still need to—"

The closed-fisted blow hit her so hard across the face, she gasped and fell back sprawled across the floor.

He followed. "Get up. Get up!"

With her heart pounding, and her face and head throbbing, Laney got to her feet. "Okay, okay. I'm going."

Cursing herself, but seeing no alternative, she crawled back into the cage and flinched as he slammed the door closed.

He bent down to secure the padlock. "No more talking. No more stupid lies—" he began, but the sound of his phone cut him off. Wiping the sweat from his forehead with the upper arm of his shirt, he dredged it from his pocket and turned away to answer.

She heard him make a few clipped replies, then hang up.

When he turned back to her, he seemed more at ease. He wiped the sweat from his forehead on the sleeve of his shirt.

"Almost over. Njerku is here. Soon, you can get out of the cage." He bent over, looking her in the eye as a vicious grin cracked his face. "But trust me, you will want to be back in cage again."

Terror welled in her chest. The one chance for freedom, and she'd blown it.

Now she had to wait. Crouched in that cage with her face aching and her head spinning, her body stiff to the point she could hardly move. Her face crumpled and she cursed herself again.

Then, for the first time in many years, she prayed to God to help her.

At the sound of a gentle knock at the freezer door, Fatso went up the stairs and she heard the jingle of keys, then the click of the padlock. It was followed by the sound of the door opening. Every beat of Laney's heart felt like it was going to burst out of her chest. All she could see from this vantage point was a pair of shiny black loafers descending the stairs. They ambled casually across then rounded the cage until a man in a well-cut suit stood looking down at her.

He peeled off his suit jacket and handed it to Fatso, who folded it over his arm like a waiter. Then the man dropped into a crouch in front of her, elbows rested on his knees, hands dangling between. His dark hair looked expensively cut and slicked back. Green eyes fringed by long black lashes. Perfect cheekbones, flawless skin, and teeth so white and even, they couldn't be natural. Diamond ring on his pinky. She didn't even have to guess—Jerko, the guy Dorothy had told Pinky about.

His smile creased a dimple into both cheeks. "Miss Laney Donohue, I presume." An American accent, she noted. Not from Boston, though. The grin widened. As if he were addressing an old friend. "My name isn't important, but my friends here call me The Stepfather. We're going to get to know each other a little better. Unfortunately, this won't be a long-lasting relationship. Also unfortunately for you, it won't be one you'll enjoy." He straightened and stepped back. "Get her out," he told Fatso.

"With pleasure," Fatso replied.

CHAPTER FORTY-TWO
DAY THREE—1:17 PM—LANEY

For the third time, Fatso dragged her out of the cage, scraping her knees over the bottom bar, only this time banging her head on the top of the cage, as well.

Didn't matter. She was so terrified she hardly felt it. When she got to her feet, the Jerko guy sauntered across to a row of pegs and selected a heavy rubber apron hanging from one of them. He slipped the strap over his head and secured it at the back.

"Do you like what I've done with the place?" he asked her. "I call this the Studio. I saw it in a movie once. I thought it was the perfect addition to our services here."

When she didn't reply, he moved across to a display wall of terrifying tools, running his hand over a selection of gadgets until he came to a heavy pair of cutters like a pair of pruning loppers. All she could feel was the pounding of her heart in her chest and the prickle of fear down her spine. All she could hear was her own shuddering breaths.

Testing the scissoring mechanism of the tool, he ambled across to her, paused, and smiled

She stood immobilized by terror as he reached out a gentle hand, using a crooked forefinger to lift her chin.

"You're trembling," he said widening the smile. "I like that."

Gently, he ran the knuckle of his forefinger down her cheek, watching.

Why couldn't she move? Why couldn't she react?

Why hadn't she learned to fight in prison? All she ever did in there was pack gloves.

Gloves, huh!

Where did that ever get her? The image of the prison workroom flashed into her mind. The image of Jody's bulging eyebrow after Valerie Spackmire had finished with her over the Fitbit debacle. At that, a well of deep-seated fear bubbled up into her throat, emerging in a fit of giggles that rapidly turned to violent sobs that racked the air from her lungs.

She sucked in a ragged breath and whimpered, "Please, please don't."

His hand dropped and his smiled widened.

The prison. Valerie Spackmire. That goddamn Fitbit—if you can't fight clean…

Laney blinked the tears from her eyes. The guy was relaxed, exchanging knowing looks with Fatso, who was standing back, waiting for the show.

Dredging every morsel of hatred she could gather, she leapt, both hands going for Jerko's face, but his right hand blocked her left hand while her right found its mark, her thumb driving hard into his eye. He snatched at her hand, tried to shake her off, but she stepped in to follow him, thumb driving even harder until he shoved her off and stepped back. Instantly, Jerko folded over, hands clapped over eyes squeezed shut, groaning in pain.

Fatso straightened aghast, mouth in a perfect O, not knowing whether to go help Jerko or grab Laney.

She didn't waste a second. Shoving Jerko aside, she raced for the stairs, flew up, and slipped the loose padlock from the handle. She wrenched the door open and slipped out, just as Fatso hit the bottom step. Same padlock hole on the outside of the handle, but before she could lock it, the handle jerked—Fatso on the other side. She leaned her shoulder into the door, put her foot against it. He shoved from the other side but the second she felt him release for a second shove, she fed the arm of the padlock through and snapped it shut, just as he slammed into it from the other side.

Now she was free. But where? Corridors ran left and right, a maze of doors. It looked like a hotel.

Jerko had a cell phone. It wouldn't take long for him to call for help, have his goons out searching for her. She had to get out.

She walked quickly to the first corner and peeped around. No one there. So she followed the hallway until she heard voices—urgent, calling out orders—so she swiveled on one foot and backtracked, heading the other way.

Man, Jerko was fast. She swung around the next corner but heard rapid movement up ahead. Nowhere to go, so she ducked into a room on her right, closing the door quietly, and stood with her ear to the wood until the voices passed.

As soon as they faded, she turned to check out the room she was in—and jumped when she saw someone staring at her. Then she realized it was a full-length mirror on the opposite wall that showed her gaping back in horror with one cheek bulging out, hair sticking out in all directions, and a terrified look in her eyes. Immediately, she folded over and let out the breath she had burning in her lungs.

"Oh, thank God, thank God."

But now what? It wouldn't take long for them to come looking for her. She had to move on; had to get out of here.

Sucking in a deep breath, she quietly cracked the door and peeked out. No one in sight, so she stepped out into the hallway.

Voices shouting from the direction she'd come. Armani's voice.

Shit!

On tiptoes, so as not to make any noise, she trotted to the end of the corridor and was about to round the corner when the ding of an elevator sounded. She stopped short and ducked back, shoulder pressed hard to the wall, heard the doors open and more voices. Men, talking urgently in the same language. With her pulse pounding in her ears, she glanced behind her. Jerko was approaching from that direction. Panic flared in her chest until the voices ahead receded hurriedly around off in the other direction. As soon as they were gone, she made a beeline for the elevator, then realized if the door opened to a bunch of thugs, she'd have no chance. So instead, she opted for the door in the corner marked *Stairs*. She hauled it open, slipped into the stairway, and eased the door shut. Empty. Just the sound of her breathing echoing off the white-painted walls.

Stairways led both up and down. No numbering. Just an arrow pointing up, indicating the roof.

Like it would be anywhere else, she thought.

She leaned over the railing and looked down. Miles of stairs wound down and down. So she crossed to a window on the landing.

Looking out, all she could see was a vast view across the city from about twenty stories up, if she had to guess. She hadn't been in a basement at all. She was near the roof.

"What?"

She'd gone down two floors when the sound of a closing door echoed up from somewhere below. Then rapid footsteps clanging on the stairs. No telling if they were going up or down. But she couldn't stay here.

Gently easing the landing door open, she stepped out into an empty corridor. Then she trotted down the carpeted corridor, passing hotel room doors and potted palms in huge urns, until she reached a corner. From somewhere down the next corridor came the sound of men's voices, so she stopped short.

Shit!

She backed up a couple of feet, then spun on her heel. With the pressure of her heartbeat aching in her chest, she doubled back to the stairs at a run. Halfway along, the elevator up ahead dinged and she stopped. More voices. They were searching the whole floor.

Heading back down the same corridor, she tried door after door, finding every one locked until she came to one that opened. She shouldered her way in to find herself in some kind of storeroom, sheets and towels folded on shelves to the ceiling and a full laundry hamper on wheels at the back. Without thinking twice, she stepped up onto a crate and leapt into the hamper, and burrowed down, ass first, pulling sheets and towels from beneath her, nestling into the folds.

The stink of the sheets hit her nose in a fog of body odor and perfume. She shut her eyes, trying not to think of where they'd been. In the distance she could hear the voices approaching. Shouted orders in the same language were followed by the sound of opening and shutting doors.

When the door to the storeroom clicked open, she felt her throat tighten. She held her breath, felt the vein in her neck throb as footsteps slowly entered the room. Squeezing her eyes closed she sent out a silent prayer.

Silence.

He was still in the room. The two of them as still and silent as the crypt. All she could hear was the thumping of her heart in her temples. Then another man spoke from the doorway.

The one in the room replied. A gruff response, and the second man retreated.

In her mind's eye, she could see the remaining man searching the shelves, the ceiling. Allowing herself a cautious breath, she opened her eyes, peering up as if she could see him through the layers of fabric.

Then she heard a sniff followed by footsteps, and the door closed.

Nothing but silence followed. Even the sound of closing doors in the hallway had faded.

Heaving out the breath swelling and biting into her lungs, she flung back the sheets and towels and took a big breath. Fresh air.

At the sight of the grinning face peering down at her, she gasped.

"I told you," Fatso said. "You must think I am fool."

In a snap, he grabbed her by the shirt front with both hands and wrenched her from the hamper. The hamper twisted on the spot, then toppled over, and she fell onto her forearm, but he lifted her again and threw her to the floor.

Then he pulled out his gun and aimed it straight at her head.

"This time, you are mine."

CHAPTER FORTY-THREE
DAY THREE—2:13 PM—ELIZABETH

Elizabeth had been sitting in Delaney's cramped office for almost a half hour now. For the umpteenth time, she checked her watch against the grimy clock up on the wall over the line of battered black file cabinets. She was just beginning to think he wasn't coming when the door opened and he bustled in, all apologies.

"I'm sorry, Elizabeth. I was called out," he said by way of explanation as he rounded his desk and sat. "What did you need to see me about?"

"The girl at the cemetery."

He paused for a second, perhaps considering his response. Then said, "Okay."

"I think the tattoo on her wrist could have been a barcode."

The nod was almost imperceptible. "And why do you think that?"

"Because I spoke to one of the staff over at Sunny Springs who worked with Wendy O'Dell, and she said Wendy had a barcode for a tattoo. Across her wrist."

"Well, thank you for that. I'll keep it in mind." He shifted a few files on his desk, then leaned on his elbows, fingers steepled at his mouth.

She drew a breath, then said, "Lance, I don't believe it's the same girl."

"Neither do we."

"No, I mean the girl at Sunny Springs calling herself Wendy O'Dell. It's not the same Wendy O'Dell who went missing."

He nodded. "Okay."

"I'm saying, I think she could have stolen Wendy O'Dell's identity."

"What makes you think that?"

"The photograph you sent me. She's a blue-eyed blonde. The person I spoke to said she was a green-eyed brunette."

He nodded thoughtfully and drew a small notepad across, scribbled some illegible note on it, then looked up. "Thank you."

Elizabeth couldn't decide whether she'd just given him new information or whether he'd already known this.

"So, what do you think?"

His lower lip jutted and he looked away briefly. "I think you could be right."

"So, maybe the girl in the cemetery is the same one who worked at Sunny Springs."

"We don't believe so."

Which indicated the police knew more than he was letting on.

"But why would both these girls have the same tattoo?"

"We get all kinds come through here with tattoos. And not just the bad seeds. Barcode tattoos aren't exactly original, either. Kids these days seem to think having a barcode tattoo symbolizes individuality. Or maybe conformity. I don't know which." He waved a dismissive hand. "Last thing I'd want is a product code permanently stamped on me."

"So, it doesn't seem strange to you that this girl calling herself Wendy and an unidentified corpse both have the same barcode tattoo?"

Again, he jutted his lip and shook his head. "Could just mean they went to the same tattoo artist."

For a moment, Elizabeth felt like the one small light she'd had, had just been extinguished. Grasping at the only thread she now had, she said, "How's the Velma Stanford case going?"

"Good."

Blood from a stone, she thought.

"Are you any closer to finding who killed her?"

"We're making progress."

Exasperated, she said, "Oh, c'mon, Lance. Can't you tell me more than that? Something. *Anything?*"

He spread his hands. "It's too early, Elizabeth. We're reaching out for potential witnesses, running fiber analyses, DNA tests—"

"I thought you didn't need DNA tests."

He gave her a long-suffering look. Like she'd implied he didn't know his job. "We're searching to see if anyone else was in the car at the time of her death."

"And were they?"

"We don't have the results back." He sighed gently and turned his attention momentarily to the window. "Look, I get that you knew Mrs. Stanford. I get that your trust has been put under the spotlight—"

Her voice rose, aghast. "Under the spotlight? Lance, it was a bunch of lies."

"But why are you so interested in this case?"

"Because whoever left bruises on Kimmy Donohue is up to their armpits in this. And Kimmy is my client. Someone I happen to have a great deal of responsibility for."

"Then I'll keep that in mind."

After allowing the rising frustration to settle, she huffed. What was the point in yelling at him? He was doing his job. It wasn't his duty to report to her.

"Thank you. I guess you've already got a handle on this and I've just wasted your time."

The creases in his cheeks deepened into a genuine smile. "You never waste my time. You know that."

In return, she smiled, a little coy now. She was about to get up when he spoke.

"Oh, by the way, I got you another photograph."

"Of what?"

He reached for his laptop, twisted it on the desk, and opened it. Without elaborating, he hit a couple of keys and the printer set on the desk next to the file cabinets whirred into life.

"Wendy O'Dell. It's not the picture her mother gave us. It's the one we distributed when we first began looking for her." He got up and waited for the paper to roll out. When it did, he took it from the tray and handed it to Elizabeth while he waited for another.

"It was the most recent picture we had of her."

The photograph showed the same pretty strawberry blonde with blue eyes and a smattering of freckles across her nose. A palpable innocence radiated from the image, the expression conveying vitality and humor.

"She's pretty."

"And smart. She's a linguist. Speaks seven languages fluently, plus a couple her mother said she can converse in."

"Seriously?"

He nodded and lifted his head to view the photograph in her hands. "When I spoke to her she said she'd gotten tired of living in Cleveland and wanted to be in Boston. Once we had a positive ID, we left it at that."

"And you're sure she's not the girl in the cemetery?"

"Positive."

Elizabeth lent her attention to the photograph. "What could have gone so badly wrong?" Elizabeth asked quietly. "That a girl could just up and leave her mother without a word? Knowing it's breaking her mother's heart?" She looked up to find Delaney's eyes soft with empathy. He'd known as well as any what Elizabeth had gone through to get her own daughter back.

"I guess we may never know." He lifted the second photograph. "Oh, and here's another one you may not have been able to find. It's a photograph we got of Gate Westrum. It was taken not long before he died. We were in the throes of building a solid case against him when he was first brought in on money-laundering charges. Then he turned up dead." He handed the photograph over.

The instant Elizabeth saw it, she felt her breath catch and an electric current of recognition and fear zap through her.

Delaney noticed. "What is it?"

"Um, nothing. He's a great-looking guy. I mean, he was. I didn't expect that."

Angling his head slightly, Delaney watched her. In a heartbeat his demeanor had cooled significantly. "I wouldn't know. But whoever murdered him did us all a favor."

She tried to smile. "That's not like you to wish someone dead."

His expression hardened. "Elizabeth, from what I've learned, Gate Westrum moved in some very dubious company. Everything we discovered after his death pointed to the disappearances of not just him, but several other people as well. It's a shame we couldn't nail him with that information before his killer got to him. If you know anyone that has the slightest association with Gate Westrum, give them a very wide berth. I mean it."

"Absolutely." No conviction in her tone. Again, he seemed to notice. She could feel his gaze boring into her. She was never a good liar. Her cheeks had already flashed hot. No doubt he could see every mistruth bubbling under the surface of the thin façade.

"May I keep these?"

"Sure."

Folding the two photographs, she rose from her seat—deliberately avoiding his gaze.

"Wait."

She looked up.

He faltered for a second. "Elizabeth, is there something you're not telling me? Something you've seen? Something—"

"No—"

"—you think I should know?"

"No, no. Nothing." The fake smile she turned on didn't fool him, either. She could tell by the way his manner was closing up. "When you had Gate Westrum's body identified, you took fingerprints, right?"

"And dental records," he said.

"And?"

"Let's just say, he was tortured in such a way that he was never going to be identified by his prints."

"And yet they left a bunch of photographs of him?"

"Yep."

"What about dental records?"

"Nothing that we could find. All we know was that he came into this country five years ago."

"From where?"

He hesitated. Perhaps wondering how much he should tell her. "Kosovo. His mother was Kosovan, his father American."

"I see."

"The people Gate Westrum was working for had links with Albanian organized crime in Boston. We found evidence this girl in the cemetery could have been connected to these people. And I believe Velma Stanford's death was also somehow connected. If there's anything more you know that could help us, you'd tell me, wouldn't you?"

"Of course." She snatched up her purse, eager to get out. "Absolutely. You'd be the first to know. And thank you. I'll bring these back—"

"No need. They're yours."

She hesitated in the doorway, turned back, and lifted her eyes to meet his. "Thank you."

"For what?" He stepped forward. Watching her. Waiting.

"For trusting me."

His voice softened with genuine regret. "I wish that cut both ways."

Jerko was waiting at the elevator with three muscled-up thugs wearing dress suits and razor-cuts, all standing with their hands behind their backs. At least she had the satisfaction of seeing Jerko's left eye red and angry from when she'd gouged him. If only she'd done more damage.

"Welcome back," he said, and gestured toward the open elevator. "I should have advised you that the security in this building is second to none."

"You won't get away with this. I have family out looking for me. They'll call the police," she said, and bit the inside of her cheek because it came out sounding like every clichéd cop movie she'd ever seen.

He shoved her into the elevator ahead of him. Each thug including Fatso stepped in, two either side of her, two in front, Jerko next to her, all standing with their eyes raised to the lighted-up number panel.

"I only came looking for Katarina. I just wanted to thank her for looking after my sister. That's all I wanted."

"So you said."

The elevator bell dinged at the next floor and all four of the thugs shared a questioning look. When the doors opened, a girl standing outside blinked wide-eyed into the elevator car. Laney knew her immediately.

"Wendy! Wendy O'Dell. I talked to your mother," Laney shouted as Jerko shoved her aside and pounded the close button. At once, Wendy moved back, still wide-eyed. But recognition of Laney's words had registered in her expression. Laney had seen it.

"I'm sorry, I'm sorry," Wendy called just as the doors met.

"Her name is Wendy O'Dell," Laney told Jerko. "Her mother wants her home."

Nothing. Not the bat of an eye.

"Why are you doing this? These are people. They have parents and people they love who are looking for them."

The elevator bell went again and the doors slid open. Same hallway with the freezer door. An elegant sign pointing in the direction of *The Studio*, a second pointing to the roof.

Laney had no idea how she'd ever get out of this. Her steps slowed as they approached the freezer door until someone shoved her in the back and she stumbled forward.

"Will you quit shoving me?" she snarled.

Fatso stepped forward and opened the freezer door, his pudgy face set in a cruel grin. "Inside."

Surrounded by these four orangutans in dinner suits and Jerko still in his shirtsleeves, she petulantly stepped across the threshold and into the Studio, looking all around. Wondering what kind of monster would use such services, determined not to let her mind wander to the instruments hanging on the wall or the surgical table, she dug deep, scanning every inch of her mind for a plan.

Just as she got to the bottom step and Fatso relocked the door, she turned to Jerko. "Listen, I have a deal I want to make."

Amusement filled his expression. "A deal?" He grinned from one orangutan to the next before coming back to her. "And what is this deal?"

She hadn't thought this far ahead. So she said the first thing that came to mind. "You let me go, let Katarina and Wendy come with me," she said, desperate to make it sound compelling, "and I promise I won't say anything about this place. I *swear*. Just let us go."

Jerko half-folded his arms and placed a crooked finger at his lips, narrowing his eyes as though considering the proposition.

Hope leapt in her chest.

"Hm. And what do I get out of this bargain?"

"Well…um." Her mind went blank.

"You see? I do not see many benefits for me out of this arrangement. You must understand, I am a businessman. I made my name as a negotiator. And when I negotiate, I leave the table with what I want. So, here is your problem, little bird: you have nothing I want."

He went to turn away. So, in irritation and desperation, she blurted out, "I know something you don't."

He hesitated one long moment, then turned to face her again. "And what's that?"

Right then, his phone rang. For the longest time, he stood with her fixed in his steely gaze. Finally, he huffed, stepped back, and snatched the phone from his pocket. After checking the screen, he handed it to Fatso.

Fatso turned away and answered it. A few hushed words, then he addressed Njerku.

"It's him."

"Tell him to call back."

"He says it's urgent."

***

The Associate

This was the third time he'd tried calling. This was the first time the arrogant pig had picked up. Of course he knew who it was. His name was in his directory, wasn't it?

"What?"

"I'm at the airport. My plane was delayed," he explained. "Do you still have the girl?"

"Why do you need to be here?"

"Keep her at the Studio. I don't know all the details, but she knows something about a police sting. And I know exactly how to make her talk."

"I know exactly how to make her talk."

Frustration needled him in the chest. "But you won't know the right question to ask. I've discovered something she doesn't know."

"Then tell me." The impatience was leeching through.

"Not on the phone. I'm two hours away. And make sure the Studio is free. You won't be disappointed."

A long pause, then he said, "I better not be." And hung up.

At least that had worked. For how long was another question. If he was to rid himself of both of these problems at once, he had to ensure they were in the same place at the same time. Two birds, so to speak. Otherwise, he could never be sure. That bastard had wriggled out of more traps than anyone knew.

The plan wasn't a great one. If he'd had more time to plan, he could have engaged the aid of a couple of contacts he'd made through his line of work. With the benefit of hindsight, he could see how much easier this could have been. Without it, he'd just have to make do with what he had.

Oh, if only he could see the look on that bastard's face when he realized who had brought his reign of terror to an end. How much he'd give just to be there and say, "Didn't I warn you?"

But by then, he'd be halfway back to Cleveland. So he'd just have to be satisfied with his imagination.

He hailed a cab, got in, and gave the driver the Hyde Park address.

First, he had to find where they'd hidden Katarina. And only one person would tell him that.

CHAPTER FORTY-FIVE
DAY THREE—1:49 PM—ELIZABETH

Elizabeth returned to the office and immediately fired up her computer, relaying her visit with Delaney to Penny in snatched sentences as she did so.

Penny's mouth dropped open. "And you didn't tell him?"

Elizabeth threw up one hand. "And what was I supposed to say? 'Oh, you mean *that* Gate Westrum? The dead one? Yeah, well guess what? I just discovered the guy managed to rise from the dead just to attend my party. Isn't that a hoot?' And what do you think would have happened next?"

"He would have quizzed you about why he was there. And who invited him."

"Exactly."

"Which we still don't know."

"More's the pity," Elizabeth muttered. "Although I'm developing a sickening suspicion I could be related to him."

"And you're sure it was him? Gate Westrum?"

Elizabeth gave her a deadpan look. "Sweetie, I'm surprised you weren't glued to his side, drooling over him all night. He was the best-looking guy in the whole room."

Penny picked up the photograph and gazed mournfully down at it. "And I didn't even see him. You could have at least pointed him out to me."

A cynical snort burst from Elizabeth's lips. "Oh, yeah, I can just see you two making sweet music together. You offering him your heart. Him leaving your dead, battered body down some alley for the cops to find. My apologies for making you miss out on that," she added sarcastically. "Why didn't I think to ask who he was? Or what was he doing there? What's more," she added soberly, "it's left me wondering who the dead guy the police found in the dumpster was."

"He can't have been there long. Or I would have seen him. Gate Westrum, I mean. From what I read, the guy in the dumpster didn't have too many looks left."

At that, Elizabeth stopped typing. "You're right. He can't have been there long. So, he must have come especially to see someone. And left early. Call up the local cab companies. Tell them you've offered to reimburse a pickup at the address but you need a receipt."

"You think they'll buy that?"

"Who knows? But see if you can get the address he was picked up from, and taken to after. Then get ahold of the party venue. See if they have a list of cars they parked that night."

"Will do." Penny made a note, then leaned over to see the screen. "What are you doing?"

"I'm searching for flights to Boston. If Gate Westrum really is still alive—which looks almost indisputable—and Laney's gone off chasing the nurse aid who seems to be connected with him, I need to find her before she gets herself into any trouble. Did you get her cell phone number?"

Penny plucked a note from her desk and handed it over. "Janelle gave me this one. But she said no one's answering and she didn't get any reply to text messages."

"Are you kidding? A millennial who doesn't answer her phone or reply to texts? Never happens. I have a bad feeling about this. Here's one," she said, pausing on the details for a flight on the screen and highlighting it. "It's showing a delay. If I catch it, I should get there at around…" A quick calculation. "Three, if I hurry."

"And where exactly are you going?"

"The last place we heard of was that casino. What was it? The Hyde Park Luxry Rest Stop?"

"That's the one. But why you? Why not call the police? Get them to go."

"Because Delaney has no jurisdiction there, and you said it yourself; if the local police have been trying to shut this place down, the owners could have someone on the payroll."

"What about the FBI? Why can't they go?"

"Why would they? Because Laney hasn't been seen in the last twelve hours? Because she's looking for a girl who left her place of employment of her own free will? And besides, Charles wouldn't exactly relish the FBI sniffing around, would he?"

"Right. And if you mention Gate Westrum, they could start making connections with Sunny Springs and Aden Falls. And that'll lead them straight to McClaine Construction."

"Correct."

"And they'll discover that the McClaines have invested in some very dubious shell companies that are also connected to Gate Westrum."

Elizabeth blinked up at her. "I doubt I'm going to like the answer to this, but what shell companies?"

"The ones I found when you asked me to trace back all the shareholders of Aden Falls." Penny puffed out her cheeks and blew. "Wow, forget needle in a haystack. This was locating every straw and trying to figure out where it stood in the field."

A sense of dread settled in Elizabeth's stomach. But she had to ask. Clenching both hands in her lap, she said, "And…?"

"McClaine Investments came up as a stakeholder or shareholder in four cases."

"But they may not have known the connection with Gate Westrum, right?"

"If that explanation makes you feel better, then yes. They would have had no idea of his connection. None. Zilch. Nada," Penny said, cutting the air with her hand.

"Because if that information suddenly comes to light after all this time, Charles will immediately think it came from me."

"Which it would have," Penny added.

Elizabeth's shoulders slumped. "I'm stuck between a rock and a hard place."

"Why not just tell Delaney? He's not going to jeopardize your position, is he?"

"If he thinks the McClaines are up to their eyeballs in a bunch of dubious deals with organized crime syndicates that are linked with Gate Westrum, he may not have a choice. My foundation has already been implicated in insider trading—"

"You said it wasn't."

"Kyle said it wasn't. But maybe he was just telling me what I want to hear."

"How likely do you think that is?"

Elizabeth said nothing—just gave her PA a look that insinuated the worst.

"Right. And I guess there's no point in poking the hornet's nest."

"If we only knew who invited Gate Westrum to my party. With all the deals he'd been doing, surely you'd think someone else would have recognized him?"

Penny drew back one side of her mouth and shook her head. "Checked and rechecked. The guy seems to have appeared out of thin air, then vanished back into it. Oo, that reminds me, though. For a while, there was a photographer taking group photos for some kind of Cleveland high society magazine. Let me see if I can find him."

Elizabeth's phone buzzed—confirmation of her flight. "Great idea. In the meantime, my flight leaves in twenty-two minutes. If I get my butt moving, I'll just make it."

"What about Delaney?" Penny asked. "What if he asks me where you are?"

With her purse tucked under her arm, Elizabeth paused at the door. "Take a message and tell him I'll call."

CHAPTER FORTY-SIX
DAY THREE—2:38 PM—LANEY

Jerko had paced the floor for all of three minutes before turning on Fatso and gesturing impatiently. "Where is he? He said he'd be here."

As if Fatso would know. "Boss, he said two hours. It's only been a few minutes." He tapped the face of his wristwatch, as if to prove it.

Njerku's expression soured. He walked over to the cage Laney was curled up in and crouched to look her in the eye.

"What is it you know, little bird? What is it you'll tell him, but you won't tell me?"

A tough question. If she told him *nothing*, he would have no reason to keep her alive. If she told him she did know something—which she'd already done—he could decide to beat it out of her. Doomed whichever way she answered.

"Do I need to loosen your tongue a little?" he'd asked with a sly glance across at the surgical table.

"Boss, he said she doesn't know until he asks the right questions," Fatso told him.

Infuriated, Njerku had straightened, and sneered at Fatso.

Almost at once, his phone rang again.

He snatched it from his pocket. "What now?"

After listening for a few seconds, his expression grew serious. "Are you sure it's her?" A nod. "I'll be right there," he said and hung up. "Call me when our visitor arrives," he told Fatso, then left with the three orangutans, who followed him in a line, still pretending to be deaf.

Now, here was Laney once again stuck in the cage with only Fatso in the room.

"Who's coming?" she asked in a soft voice.

"One of our Cleveland operatives."

She already knew that. "What does he think I know?"

Fatso turned a sneer on her. "I don't know. But, you don't figure out, it will be very bad for you."

***

The Associate

Wasn't it just typical? Life and death in the balance and the flight was a half hour late. People were milling around the gate, waiting to get on the damn plane when he spotted her—Elizabeth McClaine.

His heart almost ceased and his face flashed hot. How would he explain this? Worse yet, who would she tell?

He was considering leaving, abandoning the plan when the boarding announcement was called.

Two choices: to turn around and go home, hope no one had seen him there? Maybe even rebook on the next flight out?

Or to go ahead with the plan, go to Boston and get rid of all his troubles at once?

There were certainly enough passengers that he could safely get on without her spotting him. All he had to do was keep his back to her. If he boarded after her, and got off before her, he wouldn't have to cross her path. Then again, she was bound to be flying first class. Same as him. There was no way she wouldn't see him.

But what if she did see him? He could simply say he'd been called to Boston for business.

Yes, of course. That would be entirely feasible. Didn't the company have business contacts in Boston? He'd have every reason for being there. But the elderly woman in line gave him an idea.

So he made his decision. Waited until Elizabeth had gone on ahead and disappeared through the tunnel with the first-class passengers to the plane, then approached the gate with his boarding pass. He handed it to the attendant.

"Sir, you're in first class. Have a great flight."

Stalling to let Elizabeth get to her seat, he said, "Ma'am, I believe this lady behind me would benefit more from the extra room than I would. I'd like to take this opportunity to swap seats with her, if I may."

Both the attendant and the old woman looked mildly shocked.

"Why, that's so kind of you, sir," the old woman told him.

The attendant took both boarding passes and advised each of them of their new seat numbers and noted them on the tickets. She checked him onboard, and while the attendant checked the old woman on, he made his way down the tunnel to the plane. The second he stepped aboard, he glimpsed Elizabeth in his peripheral vision. She was sitting in one of the front seats on the port side of the plane, a matter of a few feet from him, fussing with her seatbelt.

"Your seat is down this way," the boarding attendant said, gesturing toward the aisle Elizabeth was sitting in.

"Would you mind if I went down the other aisle? I have a business partner sitting down there and I just need a quick word with him."

"Absolutely," the attendant said, and stepped back for him to pass by.

As he dodged people in the narrow aisle, he kept one eye on Elizabeth. She'd settled back in her seat, staring out the window while she waited for the flight to take off.

He was just passing through the doorway from first class into coach when the old woman called out. "Oh, sir! Thank you so much." When people in first class shuffled in their seats, giving her curious side-glances, she said, "I have terrible arthritis and that man over there changed seats with me so I could have more room. Now, that's a real gentleman."

A smattering of applause followed and passengers turned and craned to see this mysterious benefactor. But by that time, he had stepped through the dividing curtain, out of Elizabeth's line of sight. When he finally located his seat, he found an ill-tempered teenaged boy in the aisle seat who was listening to an iPod. The kid gave him a long-suffering look and barely moved while he squeezed past him to his seat. Ignoring the brat, he settled in next to the window, snapped his seatbelt into place, and turned his attention to the tarmac.

At least back here, he could wait until the entire plane had emptied before getting off. That would run what little time he had even tighter. But that was easier than more explanations.

So, despite his height, he hunkered down in the seat as far as he could, and waited.

If things went the way he'd planned, he'd be on the six o'clock flight home and his wife would be none the wiser.

If he failed, he'd pay the ultimate price. And then nothing would matter.

CHAPTER FORTY-SEVEN
DAY THREE—4:02 PM—ELIZABETH

The second the seatbelt light snapped off, Elizabeth unlatched her seatbelt and grabbed her purse. Everyone around her was on their feet, locating their luggage and waiting at the door before the plane had even stopped. That meant the aisle was already clogged with passengers waiting to get off.

Trapped in her seat, there was nothing else she could do, so while the airline crew readied the exits and did whatever they had to, Elizabeth got out her phone and ordered a cab to meet her at the terminal doors. Finally, the aircraft door opened and the lines of people began inching up the aisles. She waited until the line thinned and departing passengers began moving freely, then rose from her seat and followed.

Outside the arrivals door, she found her cab waiting. When she got in and gave the driver the address, he shot her a quizzical look in the rear-view mirror.

"You sure that's where you wanna go?"

"That's why I gave you the address," she said. When he tipped his head as if to say, *Whatever, it's your call,* she said, "You obviously know the place."

He twisted the key in the ignition, and without turning around, pulled into the flow of traffic.

For some while Elizabeth watched the city streets slide by, wondering whether she should have made more effort to contact Laney before leaving; wondering if she'd made just one too many assumptions. She was biting her lip and chastising herself for her impulsiveness when she noticed the driver's eyes flick up and meet hers in the rear-view mirror.

When the light they'd stopped at turned green, he kept his eyes on the road ahead, saying, "I gotta say, I wouldn'ta thought The Hyde Park Luxury Stop was the type of place a lady like yourself might wanna go."

"And why do you say that?"

Another quick look in the mirror. "Just things I heard. Y'know. Stories."

"And what kind of stories might those be?"

A tip of the head with the brief chuckle of dubious past experience, he said, "It's a whorehouse, if you'll excuse my expression. It fronts as a gambling house. Illegal, o' course. I don't know how the cops keep letting it run. I guess they got their reasons."

So, is that where the girl Laney was following had gone?

Determined to encourage him to keep talking, she said, "What kind of girls work there?"

"Ooo, they got some beautiful girls workin' there. I seen 'em. They don't hang around the street corners like the usual kinda street whores. Oh, yeah, they're high-class, those girls."

"But the place doesn't exactly seem a secret. Why would the police allow it to keep going?"

He did a deep shrug and met her gaze again with a meaningful look.

"I see. So, who owns the place?"

A one-sided smirk reflected in the rear-view mirror. "The kind of guy whose name people don't mention too much. He has a habit of making people disappear. Cops here say they're working on it."

"And the girls who work in his establishments? Where do they come from?"

"All foreign." He lifted his head and did a squint-eyed look in the mirror. "Are you meeting someone else there?"

"No, why?"

"There's a cab been following us for the last couple miles."

Elizabeth turned in her seat. Sure enough, not far behind them was another cab.

"You think they're following us?"

Another check of the mirror. "Maybe. Maybe not. They just been right behind us for a while now. I gave it some gas and watched to see if they stayed with us. And they did."

Her heart did one large thud. "How far is it to the address I gave you?"

"Should be around another ten minutes. You want me to go faster?"

Elizabeth glanced back. From here she could just see the driver and the outline of someone in the back seat. "No, keep at this speed. Just let me know if it keeps following us."

"Will do."

***

The Associate

Elizabeth McClaine wasn't among the first passengers off the plane as he'd hoped. He'd waited until the last of the stragglers were still collecting their bags from the overhead lockers and begun moving freely down the aisle. Then he got up, inched past the snack wrappers the surly teen had left on the seat, and made his way slowly toward the front of the plane. When he got to the partition between coach and first, he saw her. She was just easing her way out of the seat, so he dropped back and waited until she'd exited.

"Sir? Is there a problem?"

He looked up to find a concerned cabin crew member approaching from behind.

"No…well, yes. I think I left my paperback book in the seat pocket. Would you mind if I went back for it?"

"Not at all," she said. She watched him return to the seat, and search the pocket.

Conscious of her attention on him, he placed his briefcase on the seat, opened it, then looked up and sheepishly smiled. "Oh my gosh. I must be going crazy. It was in my briefcase all along."

Her smile widened as he approached and left the plane.

"Have a great day, sir."

"I certainly will," he replied, stepping from the exit and striding up the tunnelway.

Walking quickly toward the arrivals lounge, he would have bet his life Elizabeth McClaine wouldn't have luggage. She would have just brought her purse, so the chances were high that she'd already left the terminal.

Just to be sure, he gingerly stepped into the arrivals lounge and searched the area. No sign of her. So he stepped onto the descending escalator feeling like a deer on open ground during peak hunting season, then headed straight for the door.

Outside, he spotted her just getting into a cab. He ducked back, waited until her cab had pulled out, then hailed the next one along. He immediately got in, gave the driver the address, and sat back. It wasn't until they'd been driving for almost twenty minutes when he looked up ahead and spotted that same cab—the one Elizabeth had gotten into—he was sure of it. When they stopped at the lights, he could clearly see her sitting in the back seat, yapping to the driver.

Where the hell was she going?

As soon as the lights turned green, the car in front sped off. After a couple of miles, it was beginning to dawn on him that they could be going to the same address.

If they were, the last thing he wanted was to turn up right behind her.

"Slow down a little, will you?"

"I'm not a betting man, but I'd put money that the car in front is going to the same place as you," the driver said.

"Probably one of my colleagues," he said.

The driver chuckled. "Yeah, for a top-level business meeting, I s'pose." And he shook his head as if his passenger thought he was stupid. "Government think tank on the Syrian crisis, maybe," he added and chuckled.

All he could do was shoot the idiot a sour look. He had no time for imbeciles and their stupid jokes. He had bigger fish to fry.

Like where the hell Elizabeth McClaine was going. And why? Had she discovered something? All those questions she'd been firing around about Gate Westrum had unsettled him. But at the time, he wasn't worried. He'd been confident that all the dirt and everything connected with Gate's murder had been buried.

Now he was wondering if he'd missed something.

The cab slid around the final corner and pulled to the side of the road. Up ahead, he could see Elizabeth's cab parked outside the huge Victorian house. Outside the small sign hanging from the wrought iron post announcing *Hyde Park Luxry Rest Stop* rocked back and forth in the breeze.

She'd gotten out and was bent at the driver's door. He knew what she'd be doing—quizzing the driver, asking him what she knew about the place.

"Drive straight by. I can't make out if it's my colleague or not."

The driver sounded amused. "Yeah, sure you can't. But if I get any closer, I'm gonna run her down."

"Just drive by," he snapped.

They took off again, swerving out and around the car in the narrow street. Just as they passed, he ducked down in the seat, resisting the urge to look back to see if she saw him.

"Park around the next corner."

The cab came to a rest just within sight of the house.

"No, farther along."

The driver gave him a world-weary look in the mirror, but pulled out and did so.

As they came to a halt, he reached into his jacket pocket, dredged out a hundred-dollar note, and passed it to the driver, whose world-weary look morphed instantly into eager obedience.

"Wait here until I come back. There'll be another one."

"How long?" the driver asked, as if the promised "one" might become a point of negotiation.

"For as long as I need," he replied, irritated.

The driver folded the hundred, tucked it in his shirt pocket, and slouched back in his seat as though he'd just been robbed.

Incensed by the greed of the driver, he got out and moved cautiously back to the corner of the street. Through the branches of a straggly shrub, he watched the cab pull away, leaving Elizabeth walking up the front path, her purse tucked under her arm.

She climbed the stairs, running an admiring eye over the front of the house, going as far as smoothing a finger across one of the cherub urns out front. After a quick glance up and down the street, she moved to the front door and knocked. Almost immediately, the door opened and his heart flipped.

It was only a glimpse. But that's all it took. Now he needed a new plan.

CHAPTER FORTY-EIGHT
DAY THREE—5:36 PM—ELIZABETH

The instant Elizabeth saw him, her knees almost gave out. Those chiseled good looks, the startling green come-to-bed eyes, his hair expensively cut and slicked back, tailored suit over an impeccably crisp white shirt. Only now did she note the diamond ring on the fourth finger of his left hand. Under any other circumstances she might have smiled, might have run an appraising eye over him. Might have felt a flood of attraction. Instead, all she could hear were Delaney's words echoing through her mind—*Give them a wide berth.*

"Ah, Mrs. McClaine," Gate Westrum said, widening the door and gesturing for her to enter. "Do come in."

The perfect gentleman. The appealing demeanor and welcoming attitude. None of it real. None of it fooling her.

She crossed the threshold, looking all around. A tastefully decorated lobby with black and white marble floor, deep burgundy walls, with ornate, white-painted plaster architraves. Four high bay windows set in the front to look out over the street were topped with deeply embroidered pelmets and hung with heavy brocade drapes, each drawn aside to reveal thick gauze window shades beneath.

Had she not known the purpose of the building, she would have given her right arm just to take a tour.

After standing back like the proud father of a newborn, watching her as she took in their surroundings, he gestured her towards the next room. As she entered, Elizabeth almost groaned aloud in awe. In here was the same deep burgundy wall color, but it was accentuated by enormous oil paintings in lavishly ornate gold frames overlooking groupings of deep-seated leather chairs. Central to the room was a glass and intricately turned gold coffee table that sat square on a thick, richly woven Turkish rug.

He showed her towards one of the chairs "Please, Mrs. McClaine…or may I call you Elizabeth?"

She stood where she was. "I'm afraid I won't be staying long."

"Then, please, sit." He dropped into one of the chairs and crossed his legs, watching her with an appraising eye.

Feeling as if she'd awoken onstage to a packed theatre, she perched gingerly on the edge of the chair opposite and lifted a solemn gaze to him. "Thank you."

"By the way," he said with a casual hand gesture. "I should also thank you for the invitation to your party. It was…most enlightening."

So he was prepared to put that out in the open. At least that saved her some time. But it also left her feeling vulnerable.

"I'm sorry I didn't get a chance to speak to you," she said.

A gentle frown furrowed his almost perfect brow. "No. And sadly, I wasn't able to stay for long, either. Otherwise I would most assuredly have made your acquaintance." He shifted comfortably in the chair and laced his hands across his midriff, showing it was time to get down to business. "Now, tell me how I may be of service to you."

Such panache. If she didn't know better, she could easily believe he was a Russian aristocrat. Or a member of royalty from some far-flung East European nation. A diplomat intent on the business of foreign trade.

If she didn't know better.

"Then I hope you can help me. I'm looking for a young woman that may have come calling here."

Hands spread wide, an overblown expression of wonder, "Who came here?" he asked, as if the very notion were inconceivable. "I'm sorry, Elizabeth, I have no knowledge of any such person. Can you tell me what she was looking for?"

This was a charade. She knew it. He knew it. All she could do was play along and hope she discovered something.

Gathering every atom of patience and courage, she lifted her chin and replied. "Her name is Elaine Donohue. She was searching for a nurse aid who worked for an establishment which I believe you do have knowledge of—Sunny Springs. It's a facility for the disabled in Cleveland."

That dashing smile flashed again.

"Well, of course I know of Sunny Springs. As I imagine you're fully aware, I have many investments in that, and a number of other such establishments."

"Then you may know of the young woman Elaine was searching for—the nurse aid—brunette, green eyes. Very beautiful. She was going by the name Wendy O'Dell."

A bemused expression accompanied by the shake of his head. "I'm sorry, Mrs. McClaine, but I know of no such person."

"Then I'd be grateful if you asked someone here. Perhaps Elaine came and no one told you."

From the look on his face, Westrum obviously wasn't used to being challenged.

Reaching for the phone on the table next to him, he said, "If you would care to wait just one moment."

After a few sharp words in what Elizabeth assumed might be Albanian, he hung up. Almost at once, a knock came at the door and a heavy-set man in a suit and tie entered the room.

Westrum turned to him. "Can you tell me if a young woman arrived here?"

Without even acknowledging Elizabeth's presence, he said, "No."

"Thank you. You may go."

The man left, quietly backing out of the room and pulling the door closed with him.

"Then what about the young woman she was searching for—the one who worked for your establishment, Sunny Springs? Wendy O'Dell?"

"Wendy…? I don't believe I know of such a woman."

"I believe she was working at Sunny Springs, the facility for the disabled in Cleveland."

He searched the room, incredulous. "But why would she come here?"

"I don't believe she came of her own accord. She was taken. And coincidentally, the man who picked her up answered to your description. Down to the ring on your finger."

Again, he opened his hands, his expression now a picture of bemused innocence. "Then I can only assume that somewhere in Cleveland I have a doppelganger—that is the expression, I believe? Because my employees here will tell you that the only time I left Boston was to attend your party. And I returned immediately after."

"And you're quite sure you didn't pay a visit to Sunny Springs on the day of your arrival? Perhaps it slipped your memory. Because my contact tells me that Mrs. Stanford, the admissions manager, pointed you in her direction."

"Perhaps if you ask this Mrs. Stanford exactly what time this person was there, I would be more than happy to provide proof of my whereabouts at the time."

I'll bet you could, thought Elizabeth.

Tiring of these games, she said, "I'd be happy to ask Mrs. Stanford, but unfortunately, someone murdered her."

This time a look of mock surprise. The widespread hands again. Fake innocence radiating from every pore. "I'm so sorry to hear that. But I'm afraid I knew nothing about Mrs. Stanford's unfortunate demise. And I know nothing about this girl. I'm sorry, Mrs. McClaine, but it would appear you made this journey for nothing."

"Then perhaps, before I go, you wouldn't mind telling me who invited you to my party."

Westrum didn't even blink. But in the matter of a heartbeat, his charming, amiable façade chilled into something else. In that split second, he morphed into the real Gate Westrum: the cold, calculating snake hidden beneath the layers of money and charm.

"That would be a business associate, whose name I'd rather not mention, Mrs. McClaine. Now, if you'll excuse me, I have urgent business to attend to." He got to his feet, indicating their meeting was at an end.

Elizabeth also got to her feet. If Gate Westrum thought he could outdo her, he had seriously underestimated her determination.

Because on the ride to this den of corruption and filth, she'd discovered she had one more arrow in her quiver.

And now she meant to use it.

CHAPTER FORTY-NINE
DAY THREE—6:23 PM—ELIZABETH

"Guess who I just met?" Elizabeth told Penny on the phone, then glanced up to see if the cab driver had heard.

At their last stop, she'd asked him to drive around the block a few times until she came out. It was just as she'd just exited the front door that he'd driven by, so she'd flagged him down. Now she was in the back seat, on her way to the next destination. Suddenly aware that he could hear every word, she lowered her voice to a whisper. "Our undead guest, Gate Westrum."

"So, he is alive and well."

"Very much so."

"Then how can the cops not know that?" Penny asked, incredulous. "How can Jennifer Reels have not figured that out? And how can the guy be happily tripping all over the country and no one knows? It just doesn't make sense."

"Preaching to the choir here."

"And how come if our airport security is so great, with all their fingerprinting and iris scans at every international airport, why haven't they picked him up when he came in?"

"Exactly the same thing occurred to me. Then again, maybe they have. Let's face it, it's probably not the Cleveland cops or the Boston police who are watching him. It'll be the FBI."

"Or the CIA," Penny said solemnly.

"Could be."

"They could be waiting for bigger fish. You could be walking straight into Organized Crime Central. You could wind up arrested as one of their cohorts. Or worse. You could wind up one of their victims. Stay right out of there, Elizabeth. Believe me, if these people are half as bad as Delaney said, you need to keep right away."

"Believe me, I don't intend to get involved. And I don't intend to wind up dead."

"So, where are you now?"

Elizabeth turned to the window where the passing streets of beautiful Victorian homes had turned to cityscape: tall buildings and traffic lights, neon flashing over street-level stores and restaurants.

"The cab driver knows of two other places where Laney could have gone. I'm following up on an old hotel that's owned by the same syndicate. He says it's a known brothel with an illegal high-roller casino in back."

Penny sounded like a horrified mother. "So, what did we just talk about? You said you're not getting involved."

"I'm not getting involved."

"And how are you planning on getting in there? Wearing a halter top, a pair of Daisy Dukes, and six-inch heels?"

"Not a plan. The heels would kill me," Elizabeth replied. "Don't worry, I'll think of something."

Penny's voice rose even higher in shock. "And once you're in, how do you plan to get out? Elizabeth, these are known criminals and you're walking right into their domain. Turn around, right now. Go somewhere safe. Then call the cops. Tell them there are two missing women and you believe they're in one of these places." The line went silent. "Are you listening to me?"

"Yes, of course."

"Then just do as I say. Turn around and leave. Right now."

The cab slowed and pulled into a parking slot. The driver turned to speak over this shoulder. "We're here. The North City Club."

Elizabeth ducked to view the building in its entirety. Twenty-odd stories. Gray concrete construction. "Listen, I'm here now. It would be stupid to turn around at this point."

"Seriously, Elizabeth. There is no sane reason you should go into that place."

"All I plan to do is ask if they've seen Laney. I promise I won't do anything more than that. If I get the feeling she's here, I'll consider my next move. If they say they've seen her, I'll leave."

"Either way, call me before you do anything else, okay? Don't go anywhere or do anything without consulting me first."

Elizabeth smiled. "Yes, boss. Give me fifteen minutes." She hung up.

Across the street through floor-to-ceiling glass doors she could just make out a dimly lit reception area. Faded gold lettering over the doorway announced the building as *The North City Hotel.*

Elizabeth peered back and forth down the narrow street. Cars were parked on either side. Nowhere were there available slots. "Drive around the block until I come out," she said to the driver. "I won't be long."

***

The Associate

What the hell did Westrum think he was doing?

After Elizabeth left, he'd remained sitting outside the Hyde Park address waiting for Westrum to head back to the North City. That was the only way this plan was going to work. So, he'd called him.

"Where are you now?" he'd demanded. "Do you still have Elaine Donohue in the Studio like I asked?"

Westrum had hesitated before replying. Not because he didn't know. A clear warning lay in the silence. *You're on thin ice*, it said.

He didn't care. All he needed to do was ensure the murdering bastard got back to the North City Hotel, back to the Studio behind that ugly freezer door. All he had to do was have the girl in there with him. Then he'd head straight over and complete the task.

By the time he'd finished, he'd be rid of the pair of them. Then he could leave his life of boredom. He could leave his dreary hag of a wife. What did he need her money for? He'd saved enough of his own. From today, he'd have a whole new life and a whole new identity. He'd be spending every day with Katarina, lavishing her with gifts. Loving her the way she deserved.

But Westrum's presence at the Beaconsfield had been a problem. No way could he go in and take Katarina. Not with Westrum there. He'd have to wait until they were safely out of the way before he could do that.

"What time will you be back at the North City?" he asked.

The sound of a closing door, and the hiss of a breeze into the phone. "I'm on my way now. This had better be worth my time."

He peered through the branches of the shrub to see the asshole and his entourage descending the front stairs of the brothel and heading to the car.

"Oh, believe me," he said, shrugging back out of sight and returning to the waiting cab, "you'll think all your Christmases have come at once."

CHAPTER FIFTY
DAY THREE—6:23 PM—LANEY

Laney felt like she'd been locked in this cage for weeks. Her knees had gone numb and her back ached. Added to that, her face had ballooned out and throbbed from where Fatso had hit her back at the first basement. She kept pressing her fingers to her swollen cheek to see if it still ached. Which it did.

Still on her elbows and knees, she dropped her head, with forehead on her hands, and closed her eyes. "Listen, I'm dying of thirst here," she told Fatso, then looked up.

His irritation was obvious. He'd been pacing the floor, checking his watch every few seconds. This time he huffed aloud, then went across to the surgical trolley where he moved a couple of items. Then he picked one up, holding it high as if to check his reflection in it. When his phone rang, he dropped the instrument back on the trolley with a clatter, and fished the phone out of his pocket. He listened, then spoke a few words and hung up.

Suddenly he seemed more animated. Whoever was on the phone must have given him an order. As he ambled over to her, he dug a keyring from his pocket, scrambled through it to find the small gold key, then bent to unlock the cage door.

"At last," she sighed. "You're letting me go, right?"

After removing the padlock, he yanked the cage door open and stood back. "Boss is coming. Get out." He stepped forward to grab her.

"Wait, wait! I can get out on my own."

He paused, straightened, and stepped back again. "Then hurry."

Slowly, she crawled backwards out of the cage and climbed painfully to her feet using the frame of the cage to steady herself.

Fatso pointed across the room to where the manacles dangled from bolts on the tiled walls. "Over there."

"You are shitting me."

"Move!"

Her shoulders fell. "Oh, c'mon! What am I going to do? Attack you? Overpower you?"

He pointed. "Go!"

Groaning like a reluctant teen, she shambled across to the manacles and stood against the wall. He snapped a pair of bracelets onto her wrists, and two thick leather cuffs onto her ankles. Once she was secured, he sauntered across to the freezer door, moved up the few steps, and unlocked the padlock.

"I can never understand why guys like you do this shit," she told Fatso. "It's not like you're getting paid, is it?"

He slipped the lock from the handle and opened the freezer door, seemingly ignoring her. But she could feel the tension crackle in the room; could feel him listening. This was his Achilles' heel. She'd learnt all about it in prison. Not from any book, either. From Julie Hester and her dirty fighting tactics. It was only now she was realizing how much she'd learned. So she tried again.

"This guy Jerko can't go on forever, you know. You're in America. We have laws."

A soft snort from Fatso as he descended the stairs again.

"You wanna wind up in an American prison the rest of your life? Shit," she muttered. "Better you than me. Being shut up all day like that just about sent me batshit crazy. And I was only inside for, like, six months. And that was in a women's prison," she told him pointedly. "Imagine how bad a men's prison is."

"What do you want?" he asked her with his arms wide. "You think if you talk I will let you go? Answer to Njerku when he gets here?"

Frantic to keep the conversation going, determined to use everything she had, she said, "I could help you."

His head snapped back, incredulous. "Help me? How do you help me?"

Was that a crack in his armor? Was he seriously asking her how he could get out of this? If she had a plan?

If so, she had to keep him talking, find what to work on. After racking her brain for an answer, she ran with, "Do as I say, and you could get out of this clean as a whistle."

Cynical amusement. "Sure I could."

"I'm serious."

Chuckling. "Sure you are."

"I know how you could walk away—no one would even know you'd been here."

He took a few steps closer, eyes narrowed, head tilted. But the amusement had gone.

"So, tell me big plan."

"Okay. But you gotta undo these first." She shook the manacles.

"No. You don't need hands. You talk with your mouth. Then maybe I let you go."

"Okay," she said again, feverishly searching for anything that resembled a sensible solution. "How about you turn state's evidence?"

He blinked at her in either confusion or disbelief.

She held her breath, then said, "You know what that is, right?"

No reply, just a dubious glare.

"You turn yourself in, then give the police what they want in return for your freedom."

He chortled. "Yes, of course that will happen."

"I'm serious. You think the cops won't be after him? A place like this? They'll be all over his ass. He probably doesn't even know."

Still grinning and nodding, but no response.

"You have one chance to do this. Just one. You could walk away. Go have a normal life. You wanna live like this forever?" She shook the manacles, indicating the room. "You wanna be one of Jerko's minions for the rest of your life? *He doesn't even pay you*," she added.

The grin evaporated and his expression cooled.

"All you have to do is let me go. I could tell the cops you helped me."

"No. I let you go, then I never see you again. Njerku ask me, 'Where is she? Why do you let her go?' What do I say?"

Was he serious? Was he feeling out the plan? Searching for an alternative? Or telling her it was out of the question?

She had to test it out.

"Then come with me," she said, kicking herself and mentally running through snap follow-up plans to turn him in to the police. "I'm serious. I'll go straight to the cops, tell them what I know. All about Jerko. About all this shit. I'll tell them he kills people. That he's got all these girls held prisoner. I can tell them he brings them in from other countries and uses them for his brothels. He'd be in prison for the rest of his life. He'd never, ever get out. And if you're worried, seriously, you could just disappear. Walk out of here and I won't even mention you."

Was she winning him over? Could she see the cogs turning behind those greedy little eyes? Weighing up the possibility, perhaps?

She was about to go in for another attempt when his phone rang again. She grunted in frustration as he lifted it and turned away. At the snapped comments she could hear coming across the line, her hopes rose again. In response, his voice rose too, long sentences delivered in vitriolic streams. Maybe he'd told Jerko to go screw himself. Maybe he was about to cut a deal with her; to run with her, turn state's evidence.

He stabbed the screen of the phone to end the call, then turned to her.

"Boss is here."

She shook her restraints. "Please, just cut me down. It's not too late."

"For me, it is not too late. But for you, my friend, I'm sorry. This is the end."

***

The Associate

He'd given Westrum a head start, timing it so that he himself would have made it out to the North City Club, then ridden the elevator to the nineteenth floor before the bastard turned up. He had to be sure Westrum and the Donohue girl were in the same place. Those were the two birds. One stone and he'd be rid of both of them. If he timed it right.

So as the cab slowed in front of their destination, he sat up, craning to see over the driver's shoulder. No sign of Elizabeth. Thank God. There was no way she would have known about this place. But he'd worried, all the same.

"Go down into the parking garage. It's at the end of the block," he said.

The driver maneuvered past the front entrance of the building to where a ramp led down into the basement parking, hit the turn signal, and slowed. A couple of cars passed and he swerved across the street and down the ramp to where a keypad was mounted on a pole in front of a heavy grille door.

"You got a password?" asked the driver.

"Key in the word *Njerku*," he said, and spelled it out.

The grille door gave a shudder as if waking from a deep sleep, then clanked and rattled as it rolled up. As soon as it had risen high enough, the driver eased the car down into the gloom of the basement, tires squealing on the surface as they took the first sharp corner.

After winding around a few bends that led them almost back to the grille again, the driver said, "Where will I park?"

"Over there," he said, pointing to a slot next to Westrum's black Cadillac that was huddled in the far corner, Celtics plates clearly visible even from this distance.

The cab turned into the adjacent slot as requested and came to a stop.

"You want me to wait again?"

"Not this time. There's a button near the exit. Just press that to get out."

The driver twisted in his seat with his hand out.

Infuriated, he cut a sour look up at him. "How much?"

"Six hundred." Not even a flinch. The bare-faced audacity of the man.

He flicked the clasps on his briefcase to check the contents, lifted his eyes to the driver, and froze as the amount sank in. "Don't be ridiculous."

"Six hundred is what I have on the meter."

"You didn't use the meter."

"I calculated it in my head. And because I like you, I even gave you a discount."

The hand was still out. No sign of humor in his face. What was the point in sitting here arguing with this cretin? He dug three hundreds from his pocket and shoved them angrily into the man's hand.

The driver parted the three notes between his fingers and thumb, counting them, and looked back. "I said six."

"That's all I've got. Be happy you got that much."

The greedy asshole gave him a long, bitter stare, then stuffed the crumpled notes into his shirt pocket. "Don't call me to pick you up."

"You can be sure I won't." Dragging his briefcase along the seat after him, he got out and stood watching, one hand in his coat pocket, briefcase in the other, as the driver swerved the car in a tight circle, missing him by an inch, then floored it back to the grille door. The shriek of the tires cut through the silence and echoed off the concrete walls as he accelerated to the door. Another screech as the car came to an abrupt stop in front of the grille, and a hand came out of the window. He could see the finger stabbing repeatedly at the exit button until the door went up. As soon as the door was high enough, the driver planted his foot on the accelerator, and the car lurched over the grate onto the incline, then shot up the ramp and back out onto the street.

As soon as it was out of sight and the grille was rolling back down, he turned for the elevator with the bitter taste of anger in his mouth. Inevitability pressed down on him like a weight. There were two avenues out of this. Which one he took depended entirely on the fates.

Steeling himself, he pressed the button to the lower basement floor, and waited. Whatever the outcome, by tonight it would be all over. Never would he be swindled by idiots like that driver again. Never would he be manipulated, used like some kind of cheap lackey as he had been over these past months. Never again would he have to answer to this predatory brute he was about to destroy.

He could hardly wait.

After directing the driver to a side street, Elizabeth gathered her purse and opened the car door.

"If you can't find a parking slot, drive around until I come back out. I won't be long."

She got out, waited for a couple of cars to pass, then crossed to the hotel, where a sign affixed to the façade advised potential guests there were no vacancies.

"Yeah, sure you don't," she muttered as she pushed her way in through the heavy glass front doors and ran a calculating eye over the place. Inside it looked as dreary as it had from the outside—like a four-star hotel in desperate need of a makeover: blue zigzag-patterned carpet, dim overhead lights that shone down on groups of strategically placed brown leather armchairs, shadowed corners in which bouquets of dusty artificial flowers stood on wooden plinths. Overhead, soft music of no specific melody wafted from speakers set in the ceiling; the smell of furniture polish overlaid with a faint whiff of some essential oils, possibly musk, gave the place an even drearier atmosphere.

Apart from the music, the only sound was the click of her heels echoing off the marble floor as she stalked across to the dark wooden reception desk and peered back and forth, searching for an attendant. When no one appeared, she hit the small dome bell set on the side next to a large vase of fresh white lilies and a phone—an old model, Elizabeth noted, with the corkscrew cord from the receiver. As if she'd stepped straight back into the early eighties.

After almost two minutes of her standing there and wondering if the cab driver had brought her to the right place, a girl entered through a door to Elizabeth's left. The instant she saw Elizabeth, she faltered in surprise and pulled her kimono-style robe tightly in around her. Without speaking, she darted a look out the front window to the street, as if that might offer an explanation as to Elizabeth's presence.

Still not convinced this was the upmarket brothel and casino it was supposed to be, Elizabeth wondered briefly if the girl was simply a guest who'd inadvertently wandered into the reception area of the hotel, or maybe one of the employees.

She took a cautious step closer to the girl. "Excuse me, I wonder if you can help me. I'm looking for—"

But the girl cut her off, saying, "Please wait." And she quickly retreated back through the door from which she'd come.

"Wait!" Elizabeth called after her, then sighed because she'd already gone.

Feeling like an intruder, she strolled over to a coffee urn sitting on a dated wooden buffet where a visitors' book lay closed at an angle on the surface. After a quick glance around, she furtively used the nail of her index finger to lift the cover, then peeped inside to find the first two pages blank. With another quick check over her shoulder to ensure she wasn't about to get caught snooping, she lifted the next page. Also blank. It wasn't until she turned to the final page in the book that she found a column of scribbled names and dates listed from top to bottom. Twisting the book towards her, she leaned over, eyes narrowed as she tried to decipher the squiggled words. Nothing she recognized. Only the dates, the last two of which were today's. So she started with the most recent and went from one to the next, searching for Laney's name.

So engrossed was she that when a man's voice behind her said, "Madam, what can I do for you?" she visibly jumped and spun around guiltily, to find a heavyset man watching her.

His thick black hair, dark eyes, black-rimmed sunglasses set on top of his head, and the tattoo on his inner wrist that disappeared up under his suit jacket sleeve gave him the look of a villain's henchman in some B-movie spy thriller.

After scrambling to close the book, she straightened to face him and lifted her chin. But as she did so she heard the book fall, the slap of the cover on the floor. Ignoring it, she said, "Yes, I hope you can."

He smiled as he approached, bent next to her to retrieve the book. Despite the mild manner, confidence and threat radiated as he brushed past her to replace it on the buffet, then remained next to her, uncomfortably close.

"Then what can I do for you?" A heavy accent. Probably Albanian, although Elizabeth wasn't entirely sure. Conscious of his proximity, she stepped back, giving herself a little distance.

But when the front door opened again and a second man dressed in the same way as the first entered, Elizabeth recognized that one immediately. He was one of Westrum's hoods. The one who had met her at the door of the previous place. An involuntary swallow tightened her throat while a shiver of fear ran down her spine.

Realization sent a blinding message: She'd made a monumental mistake in coming here.

Now she had to get out.

The second guy said nothing. Just stood between her and door with his hands clasped loosely in front, feet astride, head angled. As if ready for action.

With her exit cut off, a second bolt of adrenaline hit her system.

Keeping her composure and gripping her purse tightly to stop her hands from shaking, she addressed the first guy. "I'm wondering if you can you tell me if a girl had come by here?"

A frown, a slight shake of the head. Face set in fake incomprehension. "A girl?"

"Her name is Elaine Donohue. I thought she might come this way." When he gave a little shrug of denial, she added, "Then clearly, my information was incorrect."

The two thugs exchanged a glance that Elizabeth couldn't read and didn't particularly want to. By now her heart was pounding in her ears. She could feel the blood thudding in her ears and the skin on her face and hands prickling, fear sitting in the pit of her stomach and Delaney's warning ringing through her head.

Determined to stay calm, she said, "Then if you'll excuse me, gentlemen, I'll be on my way."

As she went to move towards the front door, the second guy stepped across into her path.

She flicked a questioning look back at the first guy, heard the rise in her voice. "If you don't mind, I need to leave."

Instead of ordering the second thug to step aside, the first one strolled casually towards her. "My apologies, Mrs. McClaine, but my boss has given me orders to take you upstairs."

A blast of terror burst in her chest. "Tell your boss that I have meetings to attend and that I don't have time right now. Perhaps we can meet another time. Right now, I'd like to leave, thank you." Even she could hear the tremor in her voice contradicting the self-assured tone.

This time, the second guy moved in, standing so close behind her she could feel the heat of his body under his shirt. Again, her heart surged and her throat contracted as she took one small step aside. Nothing she could do but go with the pretense, fake the confidence until she figured a way out. Because it wasn't going to be through the front door.

"If you'd please come this way," the first guy said, stepping back to gesture through the open doorway behind him.

Elizabeth shot a look at the guy behind her. "I find this very irregular," she said, then kicked herself for coming up with such an absurd line.

Bristling with indignation and fear, she followed him as he ushered her through the doorway to a hallway to the elevator area. She stopped short, determined not to be led on like a lamb to the slaughter. "Where are you taking me?"

Neither of them replied. She had to talk her way out. She had no idea how.

"This is unacceptable. Tell Mr. Westrum I want to see him. Right now." It was all bluff. Which clearly didn't work.

The first guy walked a few more steps and paused in front of a door where he gave a gentle knock.

"Yes?" A man's voice from inside. Westrum. She knew it before she even saw him. The guy in front of her peered into the room, nodded, and stepped back.

Elizabeth wanted to turn and run.

Still running with the front of indignation, she stepped into the room with her head high. A simple desk, set next to a king-sized bed in what must have once been a hotel suite. Now it served as his office.

She strode across to where he was signing documents with an expensive-looking fountain pen, leaving the two thugs at the door. "Mr. Westrum, what is the meaning of this?"

He swiveled on his leather chair to face her. "Mrs. McClaine, I might ask you the same thing."

"I've already told you what I'm doing here. I came here looking for Elaine Donohue. I believe she may have come to this establishment. Now I find myself detained by your…" She flicked a dismissive hand at them, quelling the urge to say something unflattering. "…*employees*."

"My employees have orders to bring potential problems to my attention."

"And I'm a problem? Is that what you're saying?"

"Certainly not. However, I have already told you we haven't seen this girl. Your repeated questioning and your appearance here may change that."

"I wouldn't be a problem if you'd let me leave."

A half-smile. "Ah, but if you leave right now, then I would have a greater problem." He casually reached over to place the fountain pen to the side of a document on his desk. "And now what am I to do with you?"

"May I remind you that Charles McClaine is my father-in-law." She let that one sit for a while, watching for a reaction.

The smile widened. "I know who you are, Mrs. McClaine. And as such, you will be my guest for a short while. Take her upstairs," he told Thug One.

Thug One went to take her arm but she shook him off. "You're holding me against my will?"

"Please, Mrs. McClaine. I am simply offering you my hospitality until I speak with Charles." The smile dropped. "Room 409," he told the guy to her left.

This time, both thugs moved in on each side of her. Not touching her. Just close enough for discomfort. One opened the door and gestured. So she lifted her head and walked out.

***

The Associate

No matter what Westrum eventually did to refurbish the upper levels of the North City Hotel, it was down here in the bowels of the building that the structure showed its age. Down here was the detritus of decades of good times and bad: discarded furniture and building materials, paint pails, and tools. All from a bygone age and left down here to rot.

He followed the path through the labyrinth of dust-covered shelves with the constant hum of boilers and machinery throbbing through the thick concrete walls like a heartbeat, until he came to the recently installed server room.

Shiny and new among the decrepit surroundings, it hummed and blinked with activity. He tried the door and it opened. Hot air wafted out to meet him while inside, lights flashed on and off in red, blue, and green. This was the internal hub of the building. All communications flowed through here. But before he started work here, he had to ensure he could get to the target area.

Exiting the server room, he followed the concrete path past the old wooden reception desk, stacks of battered sofas and furniture, all ripped out during the last renovation and stored down here to collect dust. Shaking his head at the stupidity and waste, he continued on until he came to a set of four concrete steps leading down to a plain wooden door set into the east-facing concrete wall.

A quick glance around to ensure he was alone. Stepping down to the lower stair, he tried the door handle. It creaked under pressure, until he pushed the door open.

Perfect, he thought as he stepped into the gloom. Beside the doorway inside, he felt down the wall until he found the switch and clicked it on.

In here, the air was hot and thick with the smell of damp and mold.

And there, sitting alongside the throbbing machinery of the internal workings of the building, was what he came for.

At a business party some years ago, one of their contractors had told him he could bring down a thirty-story building with a minimum of strategically placed explosives. That had always stayed with him.

At such short notice, there was no way he could get his hands on such explosives. And besides, why would he let anyone else know his plan? After all, that's how he got into this mess in the first place.

But he had a variation on the same theme. Right here in the basement of the old '60s hotel Westrum had turned into a high-class brothel was an old gasoline-powered backup generator. He'd seen it on his first visit and questioned the wisdom of storing such large quantities of gasoline on-site.

Westrum had arrogantly brushed off the notion of potential danger, saying that in his country having no generator meant no power for most of the night. And that gasoline in America was so cheap, why would you use anything else?

Just the dismissive way Westrum had spoken to him still brought bile in the back of his throat. After all their business dealings. After all the lies and subterfuges he'd had to carry out. Just to keep this bastard safe.

If only he could be around to see the look on Westrum's face when the whole building went up in flames. If only he could say, "Didn't I tell you that those tanks of gasoline were a bad idea?"

He could just see him hammering his fists at that locked freezer door, knowing that a raging inferno was about to engulf him from the basement up.

By that time, he'd be miles away. And he'd be with Katarina. And all this would be behind him.

First, however, he had one vital task to complete. Because of the specific construction that had gone into the Studio, cellphone communication from up there had been compromised. To overcome the problem, a signal booster had been set inside the room, all connected to and controlled from down here.

The last thing he wanted was for Westrum to call for help. One thing he did know was that despite the inferno, one of his loyal thugs would almost certainly rush to his aid.

So, he made his way back to the server room and stepped inside, leaving the door open.

Despite the cool breeze circulating through the room from the AC unit high on the wall, sweat beaded on his forehead and his underarms felt wet. Heat radiated from high racks of computers as he moved between them. Finally, he saw what he'd been aiming for—the main server cabinet with cables sprouting from it and leading up the walls, though holes, and disappearing throughout the building like a network of arteries.

For the briefest moment, he hesitated. Up until now, if he was discovered, perhaps he could have explained his way out. Once he embarked on his plan, however, there was no turning back. This very act would tar him as Westrum's enemy—something he'd turned his life upside down to avoid.

Until now.

Swallowing hard, he splayed both hands in front of him to find them trembling. Redoubling his resolve, he clenched both fists briefly, then reached for the first cable. Holding his breath, he jerked hard on the cable, felt the release as he yanked it out. The tiny light adjacent turned red, so he moved to the next and yanked it out. Again, the light switched to red so he moved on, wrenching out cables one after the other until loose ends dangled like severed blood vessels.

Now he'd crossed the line. This was the point of no return. He had to be quick. In no time, the communications failure would alert Westrum's IT specialists. They'd check all the systems from their third-floor office, then dispatch a tech to the basement—another event he'd pre-planned for. So he set to work disabling the mail servers, the backup servers, everything he could find.

Just as he tugged the final cable out, the faint ding of the elevator bell sounded followed by the clunk of the doors opening.

His heart flipped. That was way faster than he'd expected.

He quickly exited the server room and hurried to hide behind a nearby concrete pillar. No sooner had he pivoted behind the pillar with his back pressed to it than he heard the sound of rapid footsteps and men's voices. Two of them. Words urgently spat out in Albanian.

He froze in place as they approached the server room and stopped short. Probably at seeing the door left open. Maybe from there they'd seen the cables dangling loose. Taking a gamble, he peeked around the pillar to see one enter the room, then quickly ducked back as the man returned to the doorway.

Clearly sensing imminent danger, their voices dropped.

If he was going to do it, it had to be now!

Swiveling on one foot, he stepped out in front of them. Both looked up, surprise registering.

On recognizing him, the first man stepped forward with a puzzled expression. "Sir, what are you doing here?"

He ambled across to get closer. "My Internet connection failed. I came to see what had happened. When I got here, this is what I found." He nodded at the server room.

Both guys frowned. The explanation made no sense. Yet both of them turned to peer back into the room at the cables. In that moment, he yanked the gun from his jacket pocket and shot the first guy in the head. Before that one had even hit the floor, he shot the second guy in the chest. The impact sent him reeling back, reaching for his gun. But too late. The second shot hit him in the forehead. His head jerked back and he crashed to the floor.

Hands shaking, breath ragged, he moved across to the bodies. Both stared blankly into nothingness. Neither of them moved. With that last blast of adrenaline still aching in his muscles, gun dangling by his side, he backed away.

Now he had to get back to the generator. Sooner or later, someone would call the two dead IT guys to see what they'd found. He figured that would be in around one minute. By the time the first match was lit, he had around four minutes to reach the Studio, four minutes to get out of the building. That meant fast action upstairs.

It would be touch and go. So he tucked the gun back into his pocket, collected the IT guys' weapons and phones, then quickly retraced his steps.

CHAPTER FIFTY-TWO
DAY THREE—7:38 PM—ELIZABETH

Growing more furious by the minute at such treatment, Elizabeth marched into the room ahead of the two thugs, and turned to face them with purse clutched in tight, head high. As soon as they left, she'd simply call Penny and ask her to send help. But her mouth dropped open when one of the men sauntered over, snatched her purse from her grasp, and opened it. He fished out her phone, inspected it, then slipped it into his pocket.

"How dare you!"

As he snapped the purse closed the first man pointed to where a phone sat on the nightstand next to the bed. The other man went over, bent beside it, and unplugged it from the wall. He coiled up the cable and tucked the phone under one meaty arm.

"May I at least have my purse back?"

The one who'd taken it simply snorted. The two of them exchanged amused looks, then turned and left. A second rush of fury hit her when the click of the door lock sounded in their wake. In horror, she raced to the door and tried the handle—locked.

"You bastard!" she screamed and pounded one fist on the upper wooden panel.

Only now did the real terror of her position begin to dawn. Why didn't she listen to Delaney? Surely, she could have simply demanded that the Boston police search for Laney. Had she been so arrogant that she didn't believe they'd harm her?

Determined she wouldn't be subject to the whims of a madman, she went to the window. The floor she was on was at least four stories up and the window was fixed. No way out that way. So she began frantically searching the room.

Inside the bedside cabinet she found a Bible, and a selection of brochures. Each of the shiny pamphlets advertised a different girl posing in a revealing costume. Sickened, Elizabeth flicked through them until she came to one that caught her breath in her throat. The girl was strawberry blonde, long hair cascading over her shoulder, freckles dotting her nose and cheeks, pale almond-shaped eyes. And according to the short description beneath, she could be ordered to the room by dialing number 420 on the bedside phone.

Elizabeth didn't even need to read the description to know this was Wendy O'Dell. Since her last photograph, she'd clearly changed. Her cheeks had hollowed, and a look of despair and dread radiated from her blue eyes.

A scowl of contempt tweaked at Elizabeth's upper lip. "You disgusting…" she spat out in utter contempt. She flicked through a couple of others, then realized that each of the phone numbers on the brochures related to a room number. So, if she was on the fourth floor, there was a chance she could expect to find Wendy O'Dell on the same floor. If that was the case, there was a chance—infinitesimally small as it might be—that she might also know where Laney was. If so, then perhaps she could get them both out of here. So she began to search.

In the top drawer of the nightstand was the Bible. The second was empty, as was the third. In the opposite nightstand was a ready supply of condoms in packets, along with massage oils and instruments Elizabeth pushed to the back of the drawer with the edge of a brochure. Nothing she could use to get out of this room.

But a desk over by the window caught her eye and she went straight to it. In the top right drawer, she found a pen, a writing pad, and a dagger-like letter opener. She touched her finger to the tip. It wasn't sharp, but the blade was narrow enough that it just might work.

She returned to the locked door and tried to insert the blade into the gap where the latch bolt crossed into the opposing plate. Finding the blade was too thick, she tried the blade in the keyhole. No use. In frustration, she stabbed the knife tip repeatedly at the edge of the lock. With her arm aching, she stood back to inspect the damage, and groaned. All she'd achieved were a few gouges in the surrounding wood.

But she wasn't done yet.

After searching the closets and bar, she returned to the desk, wrenching out the remaining drawers and leaving them open. Still nothing. Next, she went to the bathroom. Nothing in there except the usual small packets of shampoo and soap.

In rising agitation, she yanked all the drawers open. Still nothing. Then she remembered Stacy, one of her clients, telling her how she'd once taken the handle off a locked door to escape. Elizabeth went back for the letter opener and inserted it into the handle screws—but couldn't turn it.

The nightstand.

In furious determination, she brushed the clock and brochures to the floor and hoisted the table with both hands. It had some weight, but not so much she couldn't swing it. Back at the door, she hoisted it precariously over her head and slammed the edge of the tabletop down on the door handle. The handle held, but now a small gap had opened at the upper edge of the plate. So she raised the table and brought it down again and again until her arms ached and exhaustion doubled her over, and she dropped the table.

She rattled the handle. Still, the lock held. Infuriated, muscles twitching, her mouth dry, she growled in frustration and drew back. Overcome now with fatigue and emotion, her face crumpled and all those regrets for her foolish decisions washed over her.

Why didn't she listen to that tiny voice of warning in her head? How had she let herself get into this situation?

Was this it? Would she die here? Never to be found?

Would she never see her beloved Holly again?

She squeezed her eyes shut, desperate to shut out the rain of self-recrimination. But just as she folded over with her face in her hands, a black cloud of hopelessness pressing down on her, a tiny knock came at the door.

Elizabeth's head jerked up. Had she really heard it? Or was it her mind playing tricks on her?

"Hello?" said a voice from outside the door. A girl's voice. She sounded young. And frightened.

Elizabeth flew to the door and hammered on the wooden panel with the side of her fist. "Hello! I'm locked in here. Please, I need to get out."

"Wait there," said the voice. "I'll be right back."

"No, please don't leave me!" Elizabeth screamed. "Please! Let me out!"

But the girl had already gone.

***

The Associate

Back at the generator room once more, he opened the screw cap on the side of the gasoline-driven machine, then tapped the side until he found the level. It was only about half full. But that would be fine. He took off his tie, then fished out one of his two handkerchiefs. Tying them together at the ends, he twisted them into a rope. Dangling one end of the tie into the tank, he jiggled it up and down, then withdrew it.

The tip came out wet and oily with gasoline. Perfect. So he lowered it back into the tank, flared the exposed end of the handkerchief out so it would ignite quickly, and gently positioned it down the side of the tank. Once that caught, the whole machine would go up in one blast. The perfect Molotov cocktail. The trick would now be to set the seat of the fire far enough away that he had time to escape.

Adjacent to the machine, two large tanks stood side by side. A disaster waiting to happen. Even after he'd warned the conceited idiot, the tanks were still in the same perilous location.

Not for long. The explosion from the generator would rapidly take out one tank after the other. From then on, there would be no stopping the blaze.

With nothing else to fashion a fuse line from, he took off his jacket and tore a sleeve from the shoulder. A gasoline canister used to fill the generator stood rusting in the corner, so he snatched it up, and held the plastic pipe steady as he screwed the cap off. Fumes rose from the liquid, stinging his eyes as he sucked on the end of the hose. When the putrid taste hit his mouth, he switched the tip of the hose into the canister. As soon as he had enough, he extracted the hose and screwed the cap back on.

Now, where to start? The obvious place was back along the rear wall where the wooden framework of the old wine cellar formed a grid backing onto this area. The downside was that the alcohol from the wine would escalate the path and increase the intensity of the fire, and this was directly below the floor of the main lobby. That could make escape more difficult.

So he'd have to move fast.

After dragging an old table covered in drop cloths into place, he jerked the can at the surface, sloshing gasoline over the table and cloth. Satisfied he'd washed it with enough fuel, he reversed towards the exit to the stairway, angling the can and splashing the remaining gasoline in a line. At the stairway door, he took out a book of matches and struck the first.

"Adios, asshole. May you burn in hell."

He tossed the lighted match. A tiny line of blue flame sputtered before taking hold. It followed the path to the first puddle, and suddenly the PHWOOF of flame and heat burst into the room.

He backed up, wiping his face on the remaining sleeve of his shirt, scooped up his jacket, then hurried for the elevator.

CHAPTER FIFTY-THREE
DAY THREE—7:59 PM—LANEY

"How long's this guy gonna be?" Laney complained. Whereas in the cage her knees were killing her, now the restraints were cutting into her wrists. "I've been strung up here so long I can't feel my fingers anymore."

Patently fed up with the time he'd been there, Fatso looked at his watch for the millionth time, checked it with the clock on the wall, and huffed.

"You could have let me out hours ago. We could have both been long gone by now. But no, you wanna stay and get treated like shit. That's your business. You coulda let me go."

Once again, he turned his back on her and strode to the far side of the room, up the steps, and checked the door lock.

"Can you just loosen my arms? I'm gonna wind up with arms like a gorilla."

He cut her an acid look, licked his lips, and followed the line of the rear wall around to the corner, only to start back again.

"And I'll bet you must be really hungry by now…" She was about to run off a list of her favorite foods to tempt him into action when the door clicked open.

Fatso spun around and snapped to attention.

Still in his shirtsleeves, still looking cool and dapper, Jerko reentered followed by the two thugs. He skipped down the four steps then sauntered across to the surgical table without acknowledging either Laney or Fatso. After selecting a pair of white rubber gloves, he stretched them in a line, shook them out, then slipped them on. This time, he turned and smiled.

Laney's heart skipped into double-time and her knees went weak.

"My apologies for the delay," Jerko said. "We're waiting for my colleague. He tells me he's in the building."

She didn't want to know but she had to ask. "Why? What's he gonna do?"

Jerko strolled across in a leisurely manner to stand in front of her. "He tells me you have some valuable information."

Laney's eyes cut to the door. Hadn't she told him that? But what information did she have that was so secret even she couldn't put her finger on it?

Finally, the freezer door swung open and there he was—the old guy from the house in Cleveland.

"You again," she said with a groan. "What do you want from me? I don't know anything."

"Did you get the things I asked for?" he asked Jerko.

"You're late," Jerko told him.

The old guy spread his hands and cast a look down at his crumpled suit. "My rental car ran out of gas. I spent twenty minutes walking to the next gas station."

Which probably explained the faint whiff of gasoline that had accompanied him into the room.

"How unfortunate. We've been waiting," Jerko told him, then swept a hand in her direction. As if to say, *She's all yours.* The gesture looked gentlemanly, almost gracious. But it crackled with menace.

Another flash of heat burst on Laney's cheeks. "What's going on? What do you want?"

"Let me get my briefcase," the man said, and turned to leave.

A thug who'd been standing behind him stepped into his path.

Jerko frowned, fake bemusement radiating from his smile. "You left it behind? How very remiss of you."

The old guy turned to face him, sweat beading his flushed face. Even from here Laney could practically hear his heart pounding in his chest. Suddenly, inexplicably, she feared for him.

What the hell is going on?

"Tell me," Jerko said, walking casually over to him. "Do you think I am stupid?"

The old guy's gaze flicked to the thug in his way, then back. "Not at all. I needed to be sure you were here."

Oh, no. The old guy's gonna get it.

Laney wanted to shut her eyes. She wanted to disappear, but it was like watching an impending train wreck and she had to see what happened next.

The silence that followed hung in the air like a poison cloud. Jerko dropped his head as if considering his options, then nodded. "Then I will have Grigori accompany you."

The old guy looked back at the seven-foot-tall thug, who nodded down at him with a self-satisfied smirk.

"Sure. Whatever you want."

"And perhaps if the information is as I expect, I'll allow you some time with Katarina."

The man's face switched in an instant from flushed pink to a mask of pale gray. He looked ill. "Katarina? Where is she?"

"She's downstairs, waiting for you." A wide grin on Jerko's face. "Your reward for your loyalty."

Almost the moment his words were out, a vibration cut through the building. It shook the floor and the walls like a shockwave, followed by the sound of an alarm.

Jerko cut a questioning scowl to his thugs, who shrugged in wide-eyed wonder.

"Go see what it was," Jerko shouted, then spat out a string of orders in his own language.

"I'll go," the old guy volunteered.

"You stay here," Jerko ordered.

An expression of terror froze on the old guy's face. His horrified gaze switched from Jerko to Laney.

"I'm sorry," he told Laney. In that split second, he spun, drew out a gun, and shot the thug behind him once in the chest, the second in the thigh In a cacophony of shouts and gunfire Jerko did a duck-and-run out of range, pulling a gun as he moved. As the old man snatched the lock from the door and ducked back, Jerko fired three times. The bullets hit the door with three metallic cracks, leaving only three small dents in the steel as it slammed shut. He raced up the stairs and grabbed the handle and yanked, but the sound of the lock clicking into place beat him to it.

***

The Associate

With his heart thudding painfully in his chest, the burning sensation from the bullet that had grazed his wrist, and the sting of sweat on his brow, he hurried back to the twentieth-floor elevator.

Damn his stiff old joints. Damn his decrepit body.

Pausing at the elevator to catch his breath, he pounded on the button with the side of his fist and swiped the sweat from his face. The second the elevator doors opened, he shouldered his way in and thumped the close button. But just as the doors met, a figure in his peripheral vision made him physically jump. In the mirrored walls of the car, the aghast expression of a gray-haired, parchment-faced old man stared back at him. From nowhere, a rush of reality hit him like a train.

In the all-too-familiar form before him, all he could see was a man he barely even recognized. Who in God's name had he turned into? Where was the sweet-mannered man he'd always been? What faced him now was nothing but a criminal no better than those he'd repeatedly railed against. A monster every bit as vile as the one who had tormented him.

This wasn't him. Before this, he'd never raised his hand to another man. He'd never even raised his voice to his children.

A sweet man. Isn't that what Elizabeth had called him?

You are a slave to your emotions. Even a monster had seen that.

Both knew him better than he knew himself.

In all his sixty-five years, he'd been the perfect gentleman, a pacifist, a wonderful father and dutiful husband. The real him was the respected VP of

Finance to one of Cleveland's largest construction conglomerates. In truth, he was just another old fool with a hopeless crush on a woman young enough to be his granddaughter. Why couldn't he have seen that earlier? And how could he have ever been so stupid?

And yet, in these past few days he had murdered *five people*! And what had he achieved? Five people dead. Five lives lost in his juvenile quest to be with a girl young enough to be his granddaughter. And what could he possibly hope to achieve now? To wind up dying in this God-forsaken cesspit that was the cause of his fall from grace in the first place? To be carted home in an unmarked box and buried in shame?

Not this day. Not while he still had breath in his body.

If he hurried, he still had time to turn this disastrous situation around. He could still be a man of honor in Katarina's eyes. Even if he had to let her go. He could do so knowing she could still respect him. But first, he had to save her.

Holding his hand to the aching breath in his chest, he raised his eyes to the light panel to discover the car hadn't moved. It was only when he jabbed the button again for the next floor that he realized the panel lights had gone out. And now, when he thumped the open button the doors remained shut. The power to the elevators must have been cut.

Shit! That meant the stairs. He didn't even know what floor Katarina was on.

He squeezed his fingers into the gap between the doors, and pried them apart, feeling every muscle in his arms and shoulders complain at the effort. Ignoring the pain, he shouldered his way out and made for the stairwell. Bursting through the stairwell door he hurried on trembling legs, down the first flight, then the second. At the sixteenth-floor landing, he paused to catch his breath, then shoved through the smoke door to be met by the scream of the alarm and a gaggle of frightened girls staring wide-eyed at him from the halfway along the hallway.

After a brief discussion among themselves, one girl in a bathrobe hurried up to him. "What is happening? What will we do?"

He glanced up at the siren speaker and pressed one hand to his ear, grimacing at the noise.

"Go downstairs," he shouted, pointing toward the stairwell, then realized the body of the fire could be racing through the lobby by now and heading up through the lower floors. "No, wait! Stay here. I'll come back for you. Just stay here," he said, patting the air downwards so they'd understand.

Despite the utter terror in her eyes, the first girl nodded, hugged herself, and shouted something to the others, who also nodded in terrified compliance.

He took the girl by the shoulders, fixed her gaze, and spoke slowly and clearly. "Tell me: Katarina. Do you know where Katarina is?"

Her desperate gaze cut to where wisps of smoke were now curling from beneath the closed elevator doors and her expression grew more desperate.

"I won't leave you here," he assured her. "I promise I'll get you out of here. Just tell me where Katarina is."

"She is on the sixth floor," she said.

CHAPTER FIFTY-FOUR
DAY THREE—7:38 PM—ELIZABETH

Elizabeth had been pacing the fourth-floor hotel room, silently praying the girl outside wouldn't desert her, when a distant explosion shook the building like an earthquake and an alarm burst into life. It shrieked through the room at a deafening volume forcing her to clap both hands over her ears. Any minute she'd been expecting the sprinklers to go on, but when she scanned the ceiling, nothing happened. Almost at once, she detected the faintest hint of smoke spiraling from the air-conditioning unit.

She raced to the door and pounded on it.

"Help! I'm in here!"

Almost at once, she heard the insistent rattle of a key in the lock and the door swung in on her. Outside was the girl she recognized immediately from the photo as Wendy O'Dell.

"Come this way," Wendy said. "We have to get everyone out."

She hooked Elizabeth around the shoulders and drew her out into the hallway, shooting glances back and forth.

"They took my purse. They locked me in," Elizabeth babbled in shock and confusion as Wendy released her.

"I know. Come this way." Walking quickly now, Wendy led her along the hallway, speaking over her shoulder. "We have to move quickly. A fire's broken out in the basement on the east wall of the building. I have to get as many people out as I can. This way," she said and turned in the next hallway.

Gathering her senses, Elizabeth scurried after her, grabbed her sleeve and jerked her around to face her. "Are you Wendy? Wendy O'Dell?"

"Correct," she replied and looked feverishly around. "Listen, it's a long story, Mrs. McClaine. I've got you and twenty-two girls to get out of this place. Come this way."

She went to grab Elizabeth but she jerked out of Wendy's grip.

"I can't. Somewhere in this stinking dump is Laney Donohue. I can't leave her here."

For a second, Wendy blinked in confusion. Then she jerked her head towards the stairway and started walking again. "Laney Donohue. She's the sister of the disabled girl Katarina was caring for, right?"

Elizabeth hurried after her. "Um…I guess so, but—"

"An older man fell in love with Katarina and tried to help her escape. He used my identity to hide her at Sunny Springs."

"An older man?"

"He met her here."

"But why didn't he—"

"I'm sorry, it's a long story and I don't have time to explain. I need to start clearing people from the ground floor up. We'll have helicopters waiting on the roof."

This whole turn of events had thrown Elizabeth. "*We? On the roof?*" Gathering her thoughts, she paused to shout after her. "Wait! Who *are* you?"

Wendy spun around, trotting backwards as she spoke, "Like I said, no time to explain. I need to get you to safety. How fast can you run on the stairs?"

For a second, all Elizabeth could do was blink at her. There was no way she could walk out of this building and leave others to die. No matter what. So she steadied herself with one hand on the wall, wrenched both shoes off, and cast them aside. "As fast as I need to. But I'm helping you evacuate this building."

Wendy hesitated, then kept walking. "You don't have to, you know."

"Where do we start?" Elizabeth said as she hurried after her. When she caught up, they strode out shoulder-to-shoulder. Wendy glanced across at her.

"Are you sure about this?"

"Sure as I'll ever be."

"Okay. You ready?"

"You lead the way," she said.

With Wendy trotting ahead, they charged through the stairwell door and headed downstairs.

***

The Associate

He was leaning heavily on the railing at the fourteenth-floor landing, catching his breath, when the distant sound of a slamming door echoed up the stairwell over the shriek of the alarm. It had come from way down below. Maybe several flights.

He leaned right over the railing, peering down. All he could see was the gathering haze of smoke obscuring the lower floors of the stairwell.

Could it have been Katarina?

Desperate now, he ignored the aches and pains racking his frame and hurried down the next flight. At the thirteenth floor, he paused again. Sweat ran into his eyes. His breath burned in his lungs. His old legs throbbed. And whereas his aging body complained at the sudden exertion, now a dull ache crept from his shoulder to the elbow of his left arm. How he'd ever get back upstairs was anybody's guess. But he could not stop now. He had to find Katarina.

Forcing himself into motion, his feet stumbled from one step to the next, descending as quickly as he could.

Twelve…eleven…ten…

On the ninth-floor landing, he collapsed against the wall with his hands on his knees until the burning in his thighs and the knife-like pain in his chest abated. After getting his breath, he removed his jacket, bunched it into a ball, and pressed it to his face. Still, the smoke stung his eyes and prickled his nose until he sneezed. On the eighth floor, with his vision blurred by tears and his nose streaming, he paused to gulp in whatever air he could. But at the first gasp, smoke caught in his throat and sent him into a coughing spasm that wrung his lungs like a sponge. He fought for control but a second coughing fit folded him right over, gasping for air with tears streaking his face and a stream of mucus dangling from his nose. Even more determined now, he swiped it away with his sleeve, dashed his jacket across his face, and pushed on.

He had to get to Katarina. Or he'd die trying.

CHAPTER FIFTY-FIVE
DAY THREE—7:59 PM—LANEY

Laney felt like a hunk of meat in the butcher's shop window. With the manacles cutting into her flesh and her feet barely touching the floor, the sound of the alarm had brought her a glimmer of hope. At last, surely he'd release her.

Now, she realized that hope had been in vain. Jerko was only intent on saving his own crazy-as-shit ass and leaving her to die.

"Just cut me down. That's all I'm asking!" she shouted for what felt like the millionth time.

No way was he listening. It seemed like from the moment the old guy had slammed the door shut, she'd evaporated from his mind. Even Fatso was stuck in indecision, shouting panic-filled questions in his own language and casting questioning looks at Laney when he got no reply.

Jerko had gone straight to the top of the stairs and rattled the freezer door handle. Finding it locked tight, he'd stepped back, taken out the handgun, and aimed at the door. After he fired four shots that simply pinged off the door, a bullet hit the handle. He dashed over, ignoring Fatso shouting questions in his wake, only to find the handle wouldn't budge. As Fatso marched up behind him, demanding attention, Jerko stepped aside and aimed at the handle again. Three shots pinged, ricocheted off the metal, but the fourth thunked into the handle. Behind him, Fatso fell back, going down like a tree and hitting the floor on the flat of his back with a perfect black dot of a gunshot wound right between the eyes.

"You killed him," Laney yelled, surprised by her own anger and resentment.

Again, Jerko tried the handle. Still nothing.

A surge of rage burst in Laney's chest. "Did you hear me? You *killed* the guy."

Racing back to the surgical table, Jerko hauled out a drawer and upended it on the floor with a crash of steel on marble. Kicking instruments aside, he snatched up a bone saw and a pair of long-handled metal cutters and returned to the door.

At the door again, he inserted the back of the sawblade into a gap around the metal housing of the handle. Gripping it with both hands, he threw all his weight onto it. Amid the din of the siren it let out a pained groan, and a yawning gap opening up in the uppermost edge of the faceplate. Readjusting his position, he thrust downwards over and over, until the handle broke away from the steel door and a wisp of smoke drifted in through the hole.

Laney could just see him taking off and leaving her here to die.

"Please, please, *please cut me down,*" she begged.

When he shifted position to get a better angle on the steel door, she thought he was going to shoot, so she shrugged her head down and squeezed her eyes shut. Instead, Jerko snatched up the cutters, latched them onto something in the mechanism, and used all his strength to snap them shut. Even over the shriek of the alarm, the clack of snapping metal echoed off the white tiled walls.

Jerko yanked something out of the hole in the door, then swung it open. A whiff of smoke whirled in through the open door on a wave of hot air. Casting the cutters aside, he twirled around, aiming the gun at her. She hunched to make herself a smaller target, eyes closed until she heard the click of the empty chamber. She opened her eyes.

"You're in luck. You live a little longer," he said, pocketing the gun. Next thing, he was gone.

Rattling the restraints in a mix of rage and terror, she screamed at the top of her lungs. "Come back, you asshole! Just cut me down!" Realizing he'd gone, she shouted, "Thanks a bunch, Jerk-off," after him as a visible wisp of smoke snaked in through the open door.

Oh shit!

Now, all she could do was scream and pray someone would hear her. Because she didn't even want to think about what happened next.

CHAPTER FIFTY-SIX
DAY THREE—7:59 PM—ELIZABETH

Wendy charged for the stairwell door, shouldering it open onto the ground floor landing, only to fall straight back in the face of a churning wall of thick, black smoke that rolled out to meet her. She hauled the door shut, but not before raging drafts of boiling air and ash roared through the gap. It swirled on the hot air then streamed upwards like a wraith searching for freedom in the upper reaches of the stairwell. As if to block the advance of an oncoming enemy, Wendy turned and leaned her back on the door, her expression grim.

"There's no way we're going in there."

Elizabeth shot an aching look at the door, but Wendy pushed off it and grabbed her arm.

"No one could survive in there," she said, and tugged her up the stairway.

On the first-floor landing, she repeated the exercise. "No one's going in there, either. It's too dangerous," she said and went to move on.

But Elizabeth hesitated, desperately wondering if they were leaving innocent people to their deaths.

"What if there are people in there?" Elizabeth called after her. "I'll go."

Wendy paused on the stairway, then hurried back. "You can't. I won't let you."

"I'm not moving until I know we're not leaving anyone behind."

Wendy shot a look up the stairway, then back at the door. "Wait here," she commanded, then began unbuttoning her shirt.

Realizing what she was about to do, Elizabeth stopped her. "Wait." She shrugged out of her jacket, and handed it to Wendy. "Use this."

Wendy nodded and bunched the jacket at her mouth and nose, took a deep breath, then punched her way in through the doorway again. Ducking against another wave of boiling smoke that rolled into the stairwell, she yelled a muffled, "Is anybody in here? Shout if you can hear me!"

Nothing but the sound of crackling flame and the alarms.

In the face of the billowing heat and choking black air swirling out, Elizabeth gathered the front of her blouse, pressed it to her face, and pushed into the room behind Wendy. The fumes burned her eyes and blistered her throat. Through the tears, she could just make out the décor. The room looked like the entrance of a casino.

"What if they can't call out?" she shouted.

Wendy returned to the door and pulled it open, sucking in air from outside. Then she grabbed Elizabeth and drew her back into the stairwell. Just as the gap in the door narrowed in their wake, the muffled sound of a voice cut through the wail of the siren.

"Someone's in there," Elizabeth said urgently.

"We can't go in."

"Who's likely to be on this floor?"

Wendy bunched her mouth while she thought. Then she gave Elizabeth a pained look. "The croupiers. Any of the bosses would have run at the first hint of trouble."

"Then let's get him."

"It's too dangerous."

Elizabeth stabbed a finger back at the door. "I'm not leaving someone to die in this building."

She turned and went to push back in through the doorway, but Wendy grabbed the back of her blouse, stopping her.

"Then we'll go together. Here, you'll need something." She offered Elizabeth the jacket

"Keep it." Elizabeth unzipped her skirt, and shimmied it to the floor, leaving her only in her blouse, slip, and stockings. She balled up the skirt and pressed it to her face, and together they pushed through into the casino again.

The inside of the room was black with smoke. Elizabeth's eyes streamed against the thick choking blanket, cheeks flushed from the heat. On this level, they found one enormous open area, the space once conference rooms, now filled with gambling tables and bars. Broken glass now lay in pools of alcohol, obviously having been knocked from the shelves with the first explosion.

"Where are you?" Wendy yelled.

"We're here," called a man's voice. "Please help us!"

With the balled-up garments pressed to their faces, they raced to where a heavy free-standing pillar in the center of the room had toppled onto an oak roulette table, scattering chips and counters over the floor like a tawdry shower of confetti. Beneath the pillar, twisted at an odd angle, was a small man dressed in a suit and tie, black smudges of soot already marking his cheeks, both legs pinned under the weight. Two men, one on either side, were trying to lift the pillar but each seemed almost overcome by the smoke and heat, their energies spent.

One of them reached out to them. "Help us. Please."

Elizabeth and Wendy hunched against the heat and rushed to each side of the downed man.

Wendy gave the situation a snap assessment. "Is there anyone else in here?"

"Everyone ran when the building shook," one man said. "We couldn't leave him here."

"You two go that side. You," Wendy told the second man as she searched the room, "come help me on this side. The fire's going up the east side of the building. It's moving fast and everything on that side of the building's going up. We have to be quick. Ready?"

"Ready? Go," said Elizabeth.

Each of them threw their shoulder to the pillar. It felt like lifting a ten-ton truck. Finally, Elizabeth felt it move. She readjusted her grip, grimaced, and let out a guttural howl of determination until she felt it lift.

The physical strain and the choking heat tightened Wendy's throat to a growl. "We'll hold it. You pull him out."

Dropping the skirt, Elizabeth held her breath and squeezed her eyes shut as she hooked the fallen man under the arms. Leaning back and scrabbling under the weight, she wrenched with all her might while the man pedaled backward. The second he was clear, the three of them dropped the pillar with a thud, then grabbed the injured man by the arms, jerking him clear. A blast of adrenaline surged as Elizabeth snatched up the skirt again, this time wrapping her face to just below her eyes and tying it roughly at the back while the man staggered, then stood.

"Can you walk?"

With his two companions on either side of him, he hobbled a couple of steps. "I think so."

"This way."

They dragged him to the smoke door and shouldered their way through, Wendy swiveling in through the doorway first and holding it as Elizabeth and the three men followed. In the stairwell the air was clearer, but smoke had billowed out after them and was now rushing upwards, carried on a scorching blast of air from somewhere below.

"Is there anyone else down here?" Wendy shouted as they hurried to the third floor.

"They all ran. Soon as they saw the smoke. The explosion tipped everything over and I couldn't get out," the man wailed.

This time, Elizabeth shouted. "Where are the girls?"

He swallowed back the grit in his mouth and grimaced. "On the seventeenth floor. But there's one girl on the sixth—Katarina. Please help her."

"We will. Can you walk?"

The guy nodded.

"You go with them, Mrs. McClaine," Wendy said. "Get them all up to the twentieth."

At that moment, the wail of sirens filtered through the sound of sirens from the street below.

"Fire trucks. It'll take them awhile to assess the situation and get in," Wendy said. "Just go."

"What about you?"

She signaled for Elizabeth and the men to move ahead. "I'm searching the sixth."

Suddenly, the screech of alarms ceased, and the building fell into a splintering silence, the only sound the crackle of the raging fire and the odd creak of falling fixtures.

Elizabeth turned to Wendy. "The fire crew must have entered the building. I'm searching the upper floors with you. Are you okay to go on your own?" Elizabeth asked the men.

"We'll be okay." With that, they started on ahead. "Please be careful," one man called back.

"Just go," Elizabeth told him. "Find the girls on the seventeenth floor and take them with you. Don't wait for us. Just get them to the roof."

They watched the three men disappear up the next flight of stairs. Then Wendy said, "Okay, let's do this. Ready?"

"I'm ready," said Elizabeth.

***

The Associate

Acid boiled up from his gut and burned in his chest. His muscles in his legs screamed for respite, and his head throbbed as he clambered down the next two flights. But he couldn't stop now.

Soon, very soon, he'd see her. That thought was the only thing driving him on. So he ignored the pain, swallowed back the bile, and pushed himself onward. Hands gripping the hot rail, he merely guided his feet as they stumbled from one step down to the next. When he reached the seventh floor, he leaned over the railing. Below, he could hear the distant sound of women's voices and the clatter of footsteps.

Can it be Katarina? Oh please, God. Let it be Katarina.

"Hello!" he called.

"Hello!" A man's voice. "Who's down there?"

"Is that you, sir?"

Shocked by the familiarity of the voice, he shouted, "Miguel! It's me. Who's down there?"

He ducked back, and more rapid footsteps echoed up until the croupier appeared on the landing below, supported by two men, one on each side, all clambering up towards him.

"Wendy. She's searching for survivors. She's with a lady named Mrs. McClaine."

The words hit him like a hammer to the chest. "Elizabeth? But what's she…? How long has…? Never mind. You get upstairs. The fire's taken hold downstairs. The fire crew won't get in for some time. The internal structure will hold, but there's no way out down there. Our only hope is the roof."

He sent up a silent prayer that was true.

"But—"

"Just go," he ordered.

Miguel broke from the grip of his compatriots and scampered up the steps, touching a hand to his forearm as the two others passed. A gesture of friendship. A mark of respect.

Respect I don't deserve. Respect that the man before you has yet to earn, he thought bitterly. He clapped a hand over Miguel's, squeezed momentarily, then pointed upward. "Go."

As soon as the three men disappeared up onto the next floor, he launched himself with renewed vigor at the stairway below, his feet falling down each step, the shock of each footfall jarring throughout his old frame, his breath burning in his chest. He'd seen the original blueprints of this building when Westrum first bought it. He knew the structure inside out. The way he'd set the fire meant it would take root in the east side of the building, then move to the south driven by the outside prevailing wind. That should have given him his escape. That was before he'd discovered she was in here.

Only a short distance now. His beloved Katarina was almost within his reach. At the next floor landing, he leaned hard against the upper panel of the sixth-floor smoke door, breath wheezing in his chest from the exertion. Already the heat from the fire had scorched the wood, causing small bubbles to erupt in the paintwork. He grabbed the handle, ready to force his way in, when he heard a door slam from somewhere below, and the sound of a voice he recognized.

She was heading up toward him, shouting, "Come on. The smoke's getting too thick. We have to move."

What was he to do now?

CHAPTER FIFTY-SEVEN
DAY THREE—7:59 PM—ELIZABETH

Once again, Elizabeth followed Wendy to the next floor, then stopped short at the sight of the man on the sixth-floor landing—Kyle Hendry, Charles McClaine's long-time friend and financial advisor. His face was ashen, the remains of one shirtsleeve hanging from one shoulder. Soot and grease had merged with sweat to run down his face, and the dirt-stained fabric of his shirt showed damp rings across his chest and under his arms.

The second she saw him, her heart just about stopped. In that one clanging moment, everything came together: Gate Westrum's meeting at her party. It was Kyle he'd been talking to. Could he have been involved in the body of the young woman in the cemetery? Or Velma Stanford's murder? Was Kyle the man who had fallen in love with Katarina, and hidden her at Sunny Springs? So many unanswered questions, so many loose connections yet to be made.

But this wasn't the time.

"Elizabeth, let me explain…" he began, as if desperate to explain his presence there.

Angry and confused, she said, "Not now, Kyle. Where's Laney Donohue?"

His features flinched, as if the very question bought him physical pain.

"She's upstairs. She's safe for now."

Elizabeth glowered at him. "And what about Katarina?"

Still reeling from his admissions, he turned his attention to the smoke door leading to the sixth floor. "I can't find her anywhere else. I'm praying she's in here."

Wendy pushed past Elizabeth and went for the door, covering her nose and mouth with the jacket as she leaned her shoulder to the metal panel.

"Where are the rest of the girls?" she demanded of him.

"Upstairs. On the seventeenth floor," he said. "They're safe."

"They won't be for long. The fire's spreading fast," Wendy said. "You ready?" she asked Elizabeth.

"I'm right behind you," she replied, darting Kyle a stinging look.

Wendy jerked down the handle and shouldered her way from the landing in through the doorway. Elizabeth followed, peeling off to the right-hand side of a hallway once tastefully decorated with potted palms and wood paneling. The temperature in here was like a furnace, hot drafts blasting from the air ducts, wilting the potted plants and lifting the wallpaper at the corners. A shroud of black smoke had gathered along the hallway ceiling, twisting and undulating like a Chinese dragon. And now it was rolling down the walls, sending wisps like fingers, searching for escape and filling the hallway.

With Kyle following Elizabeth on one side, Wendy on the other, they hunched to escape the thickening cloud and hurried from room to room, banging on doors and peering into rooms, shouting for survivors before moving to the next. "Is anybody here?" they called in turn until Elizabeth came to a locked door.

She rattled the handle and pounded on the upper panel. "Is anyone in there?" she yelled.

Kyle, who had hurried on ahead, turned and came back with his remaining shirtsleeve pressed to his face. "It is her? Is it Katarina?"

A tiny voice replied. "Help me. Please, help me."

He pushed past her, shoulder to the door. "It's her," he told Elizabeth in desperation. "That's Katarina."

"She's in here!" Elizabeth shouted.

Wendy abandoned the storeroom closet she'd just opened, and rushed over.

"Katarina! Is that you?" she shouted.

"Kyle, help me. Please help me."

He angled himself around and slammed one shoulder into the door panel.

"It's locked!" Wendy barked at him in frustration. "The doors are reinforced. You'll never break it down."

Anger and hardened resolve flashed in his eyes. "Katarina's in there. I'm not leaving her."

"What about the locks? Can we bypass them?" asked Elizabeth.

Wendy shot a fevered look at the gathering smoke overhead. "Electronic. You can't pick them. Wait here," she said and hurried back to the storeroom and searched the shelves. She dragged spare blankets and sheets from the stacks, yanking out boxes of soaps and shampoos, condoms and oils unpacked in cartons, leaving them in a heap. She was about to give up when she dived down behind a trolley set with towels and came up with what she was searching for—an electrical cable. She tugged the power cable from where it was plugged into the wall and returned to the locked door.

"Stand back." She jammed the pins of the power lead over the handle so it clung to it like a set of jaws. Then she shoved a potted palm aside and plugged the end into the wall socket.

"Katarina! Stay back from the door!" Kyle yelled.

"Ready?" Wendy asked. They nodded so she hit the switch.

A crack of electricity was followed by the snick of the lock. Wendy pulled the cable from the socket. "Try it now."

Kyle ripped the cable from the handle, shoved past Elizabeth, and plunged into the smoke-filled room.

Elizabeth stood in the open doorway, waving back the black clouds rolling out to find Kyle inside with a young woman enfolded in his arms. He kissed the top of her head with a tenderness that sent a crack through Elizabeth's heart, and now she knew what all this had been about. The love of a man for a woman. The strength of his commitment to her. Something she'd almost forgotten.

"We have to go," Wendy yelled.

Elizabeth stood aside to let Kyle usher the girl out, his arm protectively around her. Despite the soot on her cheeks and her disheveled hair, her beauty radiated.

But they had to get out. And she had yet to find Laney Donohue.

CHAPTER FIFTY-EIGHT
DAY THREE—8:32 PM—ELIZABETH

By the time they hit the tenth floor, Elizabeth's muscles burned and the heat and fumes caught in her throat. She clamped the skirt to her throat but couldn't fight off the coughing fit that folded her over with her eyes watering and her lungs wringing.

"Keep going," Wendy yelled at Kyle, who was now leaning heavily on Katarina as they trudged from one floor to the next.

Unable to speak through the spasms in her throat, Elizabeth motioned for them to go on, but Wendy scampered back down the stairs to her, hoisted her under one arm, and dragged her up the next flight.

When she finally regained control, she gasped a thank you, and stumbled on.

"Go, go!" Wendy shouted up the stairway at Kyle and Katarina, who had paused to look back after them. "Keep going up!"

"How far now?" Elizabeth asked.

"Eight," Wendy replied apologetically. "We'll get there."

Elizabeth swallowed back the grit in her mouth, straightened out of Wendy's grip, and forced herself onwards. "I need to find Laney. I won't go home without her."

They clambered up two more floors, pulling themselves up on the railing, mouths and noses covered until a crash below them was followed by the FWOOM of escaping flame. Elizabeth paused to dash a look back, but the burst of heat from below told them everything—the fire had burst through one of the smoke doors and was now pursuing them up the fire escape.

Wendy hiked a shoulder up under Elizabeth's arm, and drew her up the next few stairs. "Hurry! We have to keep going."

With a second surge of searing heat, Elizabeth felt as if the very gates of hell were on her tail. "I am, I am." When she glanced back, already she could see the glow of the flames reflected on the walls behind them. Once again, a blast of adrenaline surged through her veins and renewed her energy. She put her head down and scampered up another flight until she rounded onto the next floor to find Kyle slumped on the landing.

"Help me," pleaded Katarina. "I can't lift him."

Kyle's face was twisted in pain, his hand clutched to his chest.

"Kyle," Elizabeth shouted and rushed to him.

"You," Wendy ordered, pointing to Katarina, "keep going. Leave him to me. And you," she told Elizabeth, "make sure she gets to the roof."

Elizabeth said, "I'm not leaving you—"

But Wendy cut her off. "Go! Now!" Then she turned her attention to Kyle.

Seeing the determination in her eye, Elizabeth hooked Katarina under the arm, but the girl slipped free and scurried back to kneel beside Kyle, weeping openly.

"Kyle. Don't leave me."

He clutched her hand, drew it to his lips and kissed it. "Go."

"I won't. I won't leave you here."

His face squeezed in agony.

Wendy grabbed him by the wrist and jerked him to his feet. "Get up, or die here. That's your choice." With another heave, she angled sharply into his side, shoulder wedged under his arm. "Go, go, go." She motioned forward like a cavalry officer.

Again, they lurched forward from floor to floor until they came to the seventeenth floor.

Kyle pulled free of Wendy, and staggered up the next flight to lean his shoulder to the smoke door of the eighteenth floor. "You go. I'll get Laney."

"You're dead on your feet," Wendy said. "I'll go."

But fury flared in his eyes. He stabbed himself in the chest with his thumb. "I'm the reason she's here. Me. I'm the one who left her to die, and I'm damned if I'm leaving her again."

"Then I'm staying to help," Elizabeth told Wendy.

"No. You go. Get Katarina to safety."

Elizabeth responded sharply. "I'm the reason Laney came looking for this girl in the first place. I'm not leaving any of you."

But Kyle had already shoved open the door and disappeared inside.

"Will somebody help me, for cryin' out loud," Laney's voice echoed out of the open freezer door.

"Laney?" Relief flooded her. She shared a joyous though somewhat dubious look with Wendy.

"Sounds like she's alive and well," Wendy said, also with palpable relief.

"Thank God."

They filed into the room to find Kyle scooping up the cutters where Westrum had dropped them, then making for Laney, who was manacled to the wall. He angled the cutter onto the restraints on Laney's left wrist just as another blast of hot air burst from the stairwell behind them.

Laney's face glowed scarlet, sweat running down her temples. She glared at Kyle who worked to free her. "Who the hell are you? Why didn't you let me go earlier, you asshole?"

"I'm sorry. I'll explain later," he told her brusquely.

"Laney," called Elizabeth as she rushed over. "Are you okay?"

"What are you doing here? What the hell is going on?"

Wendy responded, saying, "You'll be told everything later. Right now we have to get out. The building's on fire."

"No shit," Laney snapped back, massaging the welts on her wrists left by the restraints.

"This way," Elizabeth said, and made for the door with Laney right behind her. Striding towards the stairs again she glanced back to find Laney heading for the elevator.

"You can't," she called after her, pointing. We're going up to the roof."

Laney spread her hands wide. "Why the roof? Shouldn't we be going down?"

Wendy jumped in, answering as she ushered Kyle from the Studio. "I have a chopper up there. Now, everyone out. Get to the roof." Taking up Elizabeth's position at the doorway, she ushered Laney, then Katarina past her and up to the next floor. When she came to Kyle, he paused next to her.

"I'm so sorry. I never meant to—"

"Just go."

"Please…" He shook his head in despair while his gaze followed Laney and Katarina up the stairway. "If I could just—"

Elizabeth placed a hand on his shoulder. "Let's go, Kyle."

Wendy closed the door behind them and followed as they hurried to the twentieth floor. At the rooftop door, Katarina burst out onto the rooftop, where a downward blast of air from the overhead chopper buffeted her, yanking at her hair and threatening to topple her in the harsh glare of the spotlight. For a moment it hovered in a deafening thud of rotor blades and engine noise, then dropped to a point just above them. A harness fell from the open door and an amplified man's voice shouted for one of them to secure themselves in it for airlift.

"Katarina, you first," Wendy shouted over the din. She helped the girl into the harness, then each of them stood back to watch as she was winched into the waiting helicopter, her body stiff, fingers spread in terror, and her face a mask of dread.

Behind them, another rolling wave of heat and smoke burst from the open rooftop door, so Laney dashed over and slammed it shut, shoulder against it while Wendy shouted for Elizabeth to be ready. Moments after Katarina was hauled aboard the chopper, the winch let out again and the harness dropped with a radio attached, swinging like a pendulum in and out of the spotlight until Wendy snatched it out of the air.

Flicking a switch on the radio, she barked out a few orders, then motioned Elizabeth over. "You're next."

Elizabeth ducked her head and scurried over, using her fingers to rake back the hair whipping her face and eyes. Squinting against the glare and the dust riding the hot air boiling up around them, she met Wendy's gaze.

"What about you? What about Laney?"

Wendy lowered the radio and glanced behind her to where the two were hunched in the shadows against the blasts of hot air. "I'll get Kyle up there first. Then Laney."

From where she stood, Laney sent a determined look up to the helicopter, then yelled to Elizabeth. "Just go. We'll be fine."

With her heart in her mouth, Elizabeth stood with her features tight and her hands and knees trembling as Wendy adjusted and tightened the harness on her.

Wendy placed one hand on her shoulder. "Don't look so worried. You'll be fine."

Steeling herself, Elizabeth took a ragged breath and gave one tiny nod. "I know."

Twenty floors down she could see the lit-up windows of the surrounding buildings, the flash of red and blue from the rescue vehicles lighting up the streets while the headlights of tiny cars inched along the distant streets like toys. Once before she'd been on a building rooftop. That time she'd meant to jump. She'd meant to end her life. This time, she just wanted to live. She needed to see Holly again; to hold her in her arms and tell her how much she loved her. She needed to see Lance, to tell him she was sorry, that she'll never defy him again, to tell him how she felt about him. So many people she loved. And yet, so much she'd left unsaid to them.

As the chopper rose higher and higher, she clung to the harness and closed her eyes until she felt the slack in the cable taken up and her feet lift.

"Stay safe. All of you," she called back, but no one would have heard because they were swallowed up in the distance below while the yawning mouth of the chopper door loomed.

Clinging to the leather straps across her chest, Elizabeth sent up a tiny prayer, begging for all their lives, for the lives of anyone left in the building, begging God to let her see Holly just once, *Please God, if not forever, then just once more.*

For what felt like an eternity, she spun and twirled like a fish on the line. When the noise from the engine throbbed right next to her, she opened her eyes to find a man in military uniform leaning out of the helicopter with his hand out to her. She reached out, felt his hand grasp hers, and the jar of metal against her shins as he hauled her to the side of the chopper. She clambered inside door and flopped to the floor. Rolling to her back, she unclasped the harness with a groan of relief, and sat up. Inches from her was the door to the outside, where the distant ground below swayed this way and that like some kind of fairground ride, so she crabbed back on her butt, away from the open door.

"Where are the other girls? The three men?"

"We got them," the man said. "They're on the ground."

But the helicopter rose and the rooftop swung out of view and she knew they were moving away.

"What about Wendy and Laney? You can't leave them there."

The airman gathered up the cable, preparing another harness drop. "Don't worry, we're going back. The fire's caused an updraft on the east side of the building and we had to shift position. Hold on."

Sure enough, as she scuttled over next to Katarina in the rear of the craft, clinging to handholds on the frame, she felt the chopper swerve, and bank around. Once again, she held her breath as the airman angled himself at the open doorway and spooled out the harness.

This time, amid the staccato of radio communication and the throb of the helicopter engine, it was Kyle who was winched to safety. He clambered aboard, but his face was gray, his breathing shallow. He lay on the floor of the chopper, sweat glistening on his forehead as he stared heavenward. Katarina scrambled to his side, clutching his hand in hers, stroking his brow and calling his name over and over.

For the fourth time, the harness was let out.

But a squawk from the airman's radio cut through the throb of the engines. A man's voice. Probably the pilot. "Hold on, folks, we're not out of the woods here."

"Why? What's happening?" Elizabeth demanded.

The airman clinging to the side of the door leaned to look out as they lifted and pointed to the building below. "Who's that?"

Elizabeth scooted forward, clinging to any handhold she could find, narrowing her eyes against the blast of hot air until she caught sight of Wendy still on the roof…

…and Gate Westrum with a handgun at her head.

CHAPTER FIFTY-NINE
DAY THREE—9:16 PM—LANEY

They'd watched Kyle, the old guy, scramble into the open door of the helicopter and disappear. But as Wendy stood with her hand shielding her eyes and gazing up at the chopper, Laney glanced back just in time to see the rooftop door swing open. She was about to hurry over and help whoever they'd mistakenly left behind, when a form burst onto the roof and in a blinding sweep of the helicopter spotlight, she recognized Jerko.

The instant she saw him, she ducked back, hiding behind a boiling-hot air-vent next to her. She went to cry out, to warn Wendy, but in an instant Jerko drew his gun and lunged, grabbing Wendy and locking one arm around her throat, his gun to her head.

Laney ducked down and shrank back into the shadows.

What now?

Was it the same gun he'd had downstairs? The one he'd emptied on the door?

She couldn't be certain.

As Jerko and Wendy stood locked together, watching the helicopter lift and bank around again, Jerko put his lips to Wendy's ear and spoke.

Clearly furious, Wendy reluctantly put the radio to her lips, relaying the message.

Laney didn't have to hear the words. He was negotiating. His life—or Wendy's. Decision time. If Laney read it correctly, he was probably telling them he'd spare Wendy if they airlifted him to somewhere safe. He'd negotiate some deal where he'd be free to escape the police. At least that's what she figured.

But she was damned if she'd let him get away with it. The memory of the callous way he'd killed Fatso and left his body crumpled in a heap in the Studio; the terrifying way he'd spoken to the old guy; the arrogant swagger as he selected his instruments of torture. Probably just as he'd done to the girl in the basement. Ripping out her fingernails with those pliers. How could anyone do that?

Hatred for all that evil boiled in her gut. Blinded by determination and rage, she burst from her hiding spot, head down, and rocketed into the back of him, shoulder-charging him until the three of them stumbled forward and Wendy slipped from his grasp.

Barely maintaining his balance, Jerko spun around, leveling the gun at Laney now.

She stepped back, hands in the air. "Same gun, Jerko? Same one you ran out of bullets with downstairs?" she said. Then she gasped when the first shot whizzed past her ear.

Shock jarred her to her very bones. How stupid could she be?

But behind him, Wendy had leapt to her feet. With lightning speed, she twirled on one foot, delivering a roundhouse kick to the back of his head. Jerko stumbled sideways, firing off another wild round that pinged off the air vent, but stayed on his feet. Laney ducked and twisted in a full circle, this time rushing him while Wendy latched onto him, one arm around his neck, the other snatching for the gun. Together they clung to him, wrestling him this way and that until he swung around, shoulder-slamming Wendy into the corner of the air vent until she yelped in pain and let go.

A smug smile tweaked back his lips as he stepped wide, the gun swinging from Laney to her.

"Well played, my dear. You had us all fooled. Shame I never got to find out who put you up to this," he said. "Unfortunately, you'll never be able to tell me."

He raised the gun, finger wrapping around the trigger, and aimed. But a shot rang out from the open doorway of the helicopter and Jerko stumbled back. He clapped a hand over the bloodied wound to his shoulder, and glared up at the helicopter through the hot swirling wind and gathering smoke, his face set in a mask of disbelief.

Wendy scurried across and yanked the gun from him grasping it in both hands as she pointed it at him.

"One move, you're dead," she shouted.

A bolt of determination filled his eyes. Cradling his wounded arm, he spun on the spot and ran for the rooftop door. Wendy fired off two shots, the first thudding into his upper arm, the second thudding into his back. He stopped short, as if caught in freeze-frame animation while a dark stain widened between his shoulders. For a moment, he remained rooted to the spot, standing rigidly in the doorway as if nothing had happened.

With her gun still on him, Wendy moved slowly towards him. "Put your hands in the air."

He turned slowly, eyeing her with that same defiant determination, then collapsed in the doorway.

Wendy rushed over and knelt beside him, two fingers pressed to his neck. Slowly, she got to her feet and turned to Laney. "He's dead."

"What now?" Laney shouted as the helicopter descended once more. Her hair whipped her face and flew wild as she blinked against the dust and heat.

"Let's go," Wendy yelled. "The support crew can pick his body up and take him to the morgue." As the helicopter approached, she motioned the harness down and secured it around Laney.

"Don't let them drop me," she said.

"They haven't dropped anyone yet." Wendy gave her shoulder a squeeze, then backed away and gave the signal.

Laney gasped and held her breath. Then grinned as she drew back and the city lights filled the night, winking and sparkling far below.

"Well. Holy. Shit," she said.

CHAPTER SIXTY
DAY THREE—10:59 PM—ELIZABETH

Elizabeth watched as the ground below loomed closer and closer. Everywhere was alive with flashing lights and rescue vehicles, all circled by a swelling crowd.

"They'll take you to the hospital," Wendy told her.

"I don't need—" Elizabeth began

But Wendy cut her off. "It's a precaution."

The helicopter hovered over the heliport of a nearby building.

"We're landing here in a couple of minutes," Wendy said.

As the chopper angled around preparing to touch down, Elizabeth turned to her. "I need to ask you. How…?" She shook her head, wondering which question to ask first.

"I'm Special Agent Wendy O'Dell. The FBI recruited me because of my languages. And," she said with a hint of a smile, "the martial arts kind of sealed the job for me. I was brought in here to bring down Gate Westrum's people-smuggling racket. And it's not just this operation. There are others."

"You mean he has other businesses?"

"He's been importing women for the past two years. We'd almost gotten enough to bring down the whole network when Kyle here smuggled Katarina out. He hid her the only place he could think of—Sunny Springs."

"Why did he use your name?"

She grinned. "That was my idea. That way we could trace her movements.

We didn't want her to disappear because we knew she'd be a valuable information source. Then Velma Stanford was shot dead. We weren't sure initially who killed her. We think we know now."

"You think it was Kyle, right?"

Katarina interrupted, her voice insistent. "Kyle would not hurt anyone. He is a good man."

Elizabeth and Wendy shared a troubled look. It wasn't something they were prepared to debate in front of Katarina.

Instead, Laney filled the silence, saying, "Yeah, real good. *He tried to kill me.*"

"He would never do that. He saved you," Katarina said. "He saved all the women there—all my friends. They would be dead if it weren't for him." She sent a glance of appeal across the group of women. Finding no support, she dropped her attention back to the man in question.

Kyle's face squeezed in pain and his eyes opened on her. "I'm sorry. I'm so sorry."

"Hush," Katarina said, stroking his face. She bent her head and placed a gentle kiss on his forehead, holding it tenderly until he closed his eyes again.

"I think it's better left to the police," Elizabeth told Laney. "They'll decide who did what."

"So, how come you ended up here?" Laney asked Elizabeth angrily.

"I came looking for you. If someone had told me your aunt had been available, Kimmy would never have gone into Sunny Springs. She'd have been there. None of this would have happened."

For a second, Laney looked furious but lost for words. She swiped a knuckle under her nose and looked away. "Okay, so I guess that's it. We all nearly get killed, and for what?"

"A lot of women were saved because of you," Elizabeth told her.

Begrudgingly, she met Elizabeth's gaze again. "What'll happen to Katarina now?"

"I guess she'll be sent home, back to Bosnia," Elizabeth said.

Laney's mouth dropped open. "What? She can't stay? Why not?"

Wendy answered, her voice firm. "She was brought here illegally. Besides, she'll want to be with her own family."

The pain in Katarina's heart reflected in her face. She folded over Kyle, cupping his face in her hands. "With all my heart I want to stay."

He placed a gentle hand over hers. "Oh, my sweet girl. You have to go home, be with your family. I love you more than you'll ever know, but you were never meant to be here. I'm sorry." He lifted her hand and kissed it.

Tears glistened in her eyes as she turned to Wendy. "Will I be charged by the police?"

"I doubt it," said Wendy. "It was through no fault of yours. And besides, I think you've been through enough."

As the helicopter touched down, a saddened gaze ran between each of the women; each knowing their experiences over the past days had brought them close to death, and some closer to each other. But each knowing that in the end, they would part.

"Okay, ladies," the chopper pilot said as the rotors wound down and the background din faded. "We've got paramedics coming in for the wounded. Watch your step as you get out."

Elizabeth drew back and watched two paramedics position a gurney at the open door of the helicopter, watched as Kyle was shifted onto it. As they wheeled him away, Katarina got out. Before disappearing, she paused and turned to Elizabeth. "Thank you. For everything."

When she'd gone, Laney cut Elizabeth an accusing glance. "Yeah, thanks for everything," she muttered sourly, and followed.

"Laney! I just…" she called after her. But Laney was gone without a backward glance.

"Sometimes, you can't please 'em all," Wendy told her.

The encounter had left Elizabeth feeling as though a heavy stone had settled in her chest. After all she'd done, everything she'd gone through, she hadn't once considered how Laney felt. "Yeah, but sometimes you have to try."

Elizabeth followed, scooting over to the doorway on her butt to where she looked out into the glaring lights. Out there amid a flurry of rescuers and paramedics, she spotted a familiar form waiting for her. Despite her reservations, she couldn't contain the smile that broke across her face.

As the airman took her hand and assisted her from the doorway, Delaney ducked his head and hurried over. Just as her stockinged feet touched the ground, his arm circled her waist and he drew her in.

"Are you okay?"

"I'm fine."

He hurriedly escorted her back to the circle of rescuers awaiting casualties. As they stood on the fringe, watching Wendy alight from the helicopter, Elizabeth said, "And there she is…our missing Wendy O'Dell. And she's an FBI special agent. Who knew?" she asked Delaney, then she lifted her eyes to him, only to find him with his mouth open, eyes searching the air for an answer.

"You knew," she said and went to push him away. "You knew she was an FBI agent the whole time."

"What was I supposed to tell you?"

"Well…that you knew?" she said, aghast, before the reality of his position hit her. "Then again, I guess you couldn't. Because you're a cop, right. I had to go and find out myself."

"Do you know that you are the most… infuriating…frustrating…hard-headed… woman I've ever known? Do you?"

For a moment she froze in shock, until he pulled her in once more and his arms tightened around her.

"I thought I'd lost you," he said and pressed a firm kiss to the top of her head, held her close for a moment, then released her. As if embarrassed by the display of emotion, he shook it away and stepped back to look her over with his eyebrows up.

She dropped her eyes to take in her ragged blouse and half-slip. She'd almost forgotten she'd stripped off the skirt and jacket.

"May I ask what's with the outfit?"

"Oh, Lord. Where do I even begin?"

A smile tweaked the corners of his mouth as he tucked a lock of her bedraggled hair behind her ear. "You're okay, though?"

She nodded. "I am."

"Then let's get you back to Cleveland. I've got some serious questions to ask you, young lady," he said.

"And I think I might have the answers," she replied.

CHAPTER SIXTY-ONE
THREE DAYS LATER—ELIZABETH

Elizabeth stood on the front porch of Janelle Hooper's house at exactly the arranged time, fist clenched and ready to knock at the door. After her last encounter with Laney Donohue, Elizabeth had her heart in her mouth. She hadn't exactly expected friendship after all her foundation had put her through. Hell, she hadn't expected thanks. After all, she was the one responsible for Kimmy's care. But she hadn't expected the blatant fury Laney had cast upon her. She hadn't expected the hate she'd seen in the girl's eyes. Now, all she had to do was knock on the door, face the music, and try to make amends. All she had to do was present the offer and leave.

So why was it so hard?

After noting Elizabeth's hand hovering at the panel, Penny said, "You want me to?" and gestured at the door.

Elizabeth shook her head sharply. "I'm good." Although she was anything but. All night she'd practiced her speech, framing and reframing the apologies to be delivered to Laney. Telling her how sorry she was, that a simple software glitch had been responsible.

But then the question had rearisen with every rendering: Why hadn't anyone else caught the glitch? Why did fifteen young people have to suffer?

Swallowing back the bile in her throat, Elizabeth rapped three times on the upper glass door panel and the door opened almost immediately.

Once again, Janelle Hooper stood framed in the doorway, glaring out.

"Wondered how long it was gonna take for you to knock."

"You knew we were here?" Penny asked.

"Saw your car." Janelle stepped back, widening the door. "Now you're here, you might as well come in."

Elizabeth drew in a breath, held it as she stepped over the threshold. "We won't stay long."

"The hell you won't," Janelle said, closing the door behind Penny. "I spent all morning making lunch. You can stay, can't you?"

For a second, Elizabeth blinked in confusion. "Lunch? But…"

Janelle's expression softened. "It's all we can do to thank you. Come on in. Laney here has something to say to you."

Janelle ushered them to the living room where Laney rose from where she'd been seated on the sofa, and was now wiping both hands down the fronts of her jeans in obvious discomfiture.

No eye contact, Elizabeth noticed.

"Mrs. McClaine? Um…first up, I want to apologize to you," Laney began, and nodded down at the floor.

"Well, go on, get on with it," barked Janelle. "Lunch ain't gonna serve itself."

Laney shuffled awkwardly and cleared her throat. "Ah, yeah. I shouldn't have been so…"

"Ungrateful," Janelle butted in again.

Laney gave her a stinging look, but said, "I shouldn't have been so…*ungrateful*, when you came all the way over to Boston to find me." She gestured clumsily, then rubbed her hands together while picking out the right words. "I shoulda been more…well, grateful."

Elizabeth eased out the breath she'd been holding and crossed directly to Laney. Gently placing one hand on the girl's shoulder, she ducked her head to catch her eye. "Laney, I came here to apologize to you, to Janelle, and to Kimmy. Over the past few days, I've hated myself for what's happened. I cannot tell you how sorry I am."

Laney blinked in confusion. "But…shouldn't I be apologizing to you?"

"What for? I'm the one who put Kimmy into Sunny Springs. I should have investigated other avenues."

"Yeah, well, if I hadn't screwed up so bad, she wouldn't have had to go anywhere."

"Okay, that's it," Janelle butted in, hands spread as if she was parting two adversaries in the boxing ring. "Apologies are over. Mrs. McClaine, Laney here's got a stubborn streak. Takes after her mom like that."

"I do not," she said, but the grin said something else.

"Quit arguing. We only got so much time before Katarina has to leave."

"She's leaving?" asked Penny.

Laney replied. "In two hours. They're sending her back home."

"Where is she now?"

"She's upstairs with Kimmy. She's helping her get into her best dress for lunch."

"Then let's get this over with," Elizabeth said, and drew a nervous breath. "Laney, I've made arrangements with the trust, and we can offer you a place for you and Kimmy. The rent is low, and it's in a good neighborhood near a workshop she can attend. And I know," she quickly added before Laney could interrupt, "this will still be tough, so I can put together a package so you can work and have someone caring for Kimmy when you're not home."

No one replied for the longest time.

Then Janelle said, "They're staying with me."

"Janelle told me we can stay as long as we need," Laney said. "But thank you."

"The offer for funds for additional care still stands," Elizabeth said. "But I'm so pleased for you all."

Almost at once, footsteps on the stairs drew their attention and there they were—Kimmy dressed in a blue wrap-around dress and makeup, Katarina in a black skirt, loose-fitting cream blouse and shawl. Despite the drab colors, she still radiated beauty and vitality.

Kimmy wrapped both arms around Katarina's waist and hugged her. In response, Katarina pulled her in, kissing her on the head.

A grin broke across Kimmy's face as she gazed up in idolization. "Wendy."

"I keep telling you, her name's Katarina," Laney said.

"Wendy," Kimmy insisted.

"Okay, have it your way."

"Right," said Janelle. "Looks like we're all here. Who's hungry?"

Penny blew out a breath and turned to Elizabeth. "Don't know about you, but I could eat a horse."

"Well, thankfully, I think my appetite just came back," she replied.

***

Cleveland Clinic Hospital

He loathed hospitals. He'd been in too many to count. This time was no different. Confidence, that was the key. You walk with the right kind of confidence, no one sees you. Smiling, he glanced up at the security camera set high on the wall overlooking the corridor. Didn't matter. By the time anyone had noticed, he would have walked right out of here and disappeared into thin air. Not a soul would know where he went.

Despite the pain across his shoulders, he turned the last corner and strode down the corridor, past doctors and nurses, visitors with faces etched with grief. As far as they were concerned, he was just another of them—invisible against the backdrop of their own anguish. Halfway along, he checked the sign to his left, indicating wards and room numbers.

Almost there.

When he came to the door, he peeked through the glass window set in the upper half. There she was, sitting next to the bed, her face impassive, unreadable.

Perhaps sensing his presence, she looked up, gave him the briefest tilt of her head, permission to enter. Flicking a glance along the hallway each way, he pushed open the door and stepped inside.

For one long moment, he stood with his hands clasped loosely in front of him, waiting while her eyes went back to her husband.

Not one sign of emotion. Not one jot of sorrow. Only that same dead-eyed stare of disappointment; of utter hatred.

Without a word, Celeste Hendry got up, gathered her purse and left without a backward look.

The moment the door hissed closed, he lifted the lapel of his jacket and took out the syringe. Moving quickly now, he uncapped the needle and laid it on the bed while he disconnected the IV line from the lure in the back of Kyle's hand.

Kyle's eyes flickered open and his head turned on the pillow. The moment their eyes met, realization and panic flared. A terror-ridden glance down at his hand told him everything.

As Kyle's questioning gaze rose to his again, he pressed hard on the plunger and the solution flooded Kyle's veins.

Kyle flinched. "Why?"

A thousand replies flooded his mind, but he didn't offer one. Betrayal was betrayal in any man's language. Kyle of all people should have understood that.

Without offering a word, he tucked the syringe back in his jacket pocket and left the room.

As he strode back down the corridor to the exit, the sound of alarms had already set doctors and nurses scurrying. They rushed past him in the hallway, rushing to his aid.

They would never get to him in time.

Kyle Hendry would already be dead.

CHAPTER SIXTY-TWO
LATER THAT EVENING—ELIZABETH

On Elizabeth's way home from Janelle's, she'd gotten a phone call from Charles. Initially, she was reluctant to pick it up. Then she thought, *What the hell*, and hit the answer key.

She'd been ready for the onslaught, ready to defend her decisions, and challenge him on her authority, but from the moment she'd answered, his tone was amiable and calm.

"I'd like to take Holly out to dinner, if that's okay," he'd said.

No mention of the past few days. Not a word about her direct defiance of his orders. Just the mild manner, the way he'd always been. So she'd agreed.

Now, here she was at home with Holly kneeling on the sofa by the front window, dressed in her best dress and shoes, and peering out the window waiting for him.

"Where will he take me, Mommy?"

"I think that might be a surprise."

She chuckled and bounced in excitement. "I like surpwises."

"So do I," Elizabeth said, a little skeptically. "Sometimes."

"Here he is!" Holly shouted, scrambling from the sofa and running to the front door.

Elizabeth followed to where Holly had pulled open the front door and was hopping up and down on the spot as she waited for Charles to get out of the car and stride up to the house.

"How's my favorite girl?" he asked as Holly threw herself at him, jumping up and down and shouting, "Grampa! Where are we going, Grampa?"

Charles dipped his head to her. "Didn't your mommy tell you that's a surprise?"

For a split second, Elizabeth's heart seized. Surely, he wouldn't take her away from her now. He couldn't.

Reading the look on Elizabeth's face, he smiled. "You don't have to worry. I'll have her back by eight."

Feeling a little foolish, she smiled and shook it away. "I wasn't. But thank you." Just as he was about to turn away, she said, "Charles? Any word about Kyle?"

He paused, seemingly subdued by the question, and let his gaze drift to where Holly was already getting into his car. "He died this morning."

Elizabeth gasped. "Oh my God, I had no idea. I'm so sorry. I thought he was improving."

He nodded, visually rocked by the loss. "We all thought that. He was a good man, Elizabeth. I don't know what got into him."

"We all make mistakes. Are the police—?"

"No," he interrupted. As if the very thought of sullying Kyle's reputation drove a dagger into his heart. "They said there's not enough evidence."

"What about Laney? She said he locked her in that basement."

"Katarina said she was willing to testify that he did that to help her. Said he did the same to her."

"And they believed that?"

He shrugged. "We've lost a big part of the company...of the family. I've been with Celeste. Naturally, she's devastated...as we all are." He turned to her, looked her in the eye. "He was a good friend. I'll miss him."

He went to walk away, but she called after him. "Wait."

He paused, turned.

"Did you mean what you said? That you'd...?" She couldn't even bring herself to say the words.

But he knew. He walked slowly back to her. "Never. The police were already interviewing us about our connections with Westrum. They were close to arresting him when the body turned up in the dumpster. I was…helping with their enquiries," he said, quoting the police rhetoric. "I'm sorry I frightened you. I had no other way to keep you out of it."

"And look how that worked out," she said sheepishly, just as another car pulled up behind Charles's.

Charles turned towards the street. "Looks like you have a caller. I'll see you at eight."

Elizabeth folded her arms, a little hesitant now, nerves jangling as she watched Charles and Holly pull away, and Lance Delaney walk up the front path, looking after them.

"I guess I can't pretend I'm not at home," she said.

"You mind if I come in?"

She stepped back while he crossed in front of her, hands in his pockets and looking around as if he'd never been here before.

Leaning against the open front door with her arms crossed defensively, she said, "You knew all along. You knew that Wendy was an FBI agent, and that Kyle was involved. And you also knew that Gate Westrum was alive and well and happily running a thriving organized crime syndicate over in Boston. Thanks for the heads-up."

"I can explain, Elizabeth."

Before he could, she said, "And what about the girl in the cemetery? I suppose you're also going to tell me you knew all along who she was?"

Delaney paused a moment, looking around while he gathered his thoughts and figured out which accusation to address first.

"We found a notebook under the girl's body, so yes. We figured out pretty quickly that she'd escaped from the Boston brothel and come searching for Katarina."

"Well, that was convenient."

Shuffling as he held back the caustic answer she'd been expecting, he mildly said, "We think it must have dropped out of the pocket of whoever dumped her."

"And who do you think dumped her?"

He blinked at her a long while, then said, "There's evidence to suggest it was Kyle Hendry."

"I don't believe it. He would never have killed her." Although from what she'd seen now, the conviction in her voice was lacking.

"Elizabeth, I don't have enough evidence to prove what he did or didn't do. The man is dead. There's no point in pursuing it now."

Elizabeth frowned down, wondering how so many people got it so wrong.

"What was this all about, Lance? Okay, so I know it was about Gate Westrum trying to avoid arrest and keeping his businesses going, but why murder Velma Stanford? Who was the body in the dumpster that was supposed to be Gate Westrum?"

"Velma's husband was admitted to a private hospital. She couldn't afford the fees and rather than take him somewhere else, she found another way to pay."

"Blackmail?"

"We believe she discovered the secret behind why Kyle turned up with Katarina, trying to hide her. Velma agreed. And suddenly she realized she had a potential income source and she wasn't about to let that go. It was only when you started asking questions, she knew she couldn't stop you."

"So she set her sister, Jennifer Reels, onto me."

"Like you said, it's an old and well-established method of deflecting a line of enquiry."

"And the body? The one in the dumpster?"

"A college graduate who got himself into too much debt. Gate murdered him and used the opportunity to stage his own death."

"But you weren't fooled, of course."

"Oh, he did a great job. We have no dental records to identify him, and somehow, he'd managed to evade arrest so supposedly we didn't even have his prints on file."

"Except…?" Her eyebrows went up.

"At immigration. Last time he entered the country."

"So, you knew right off the bat it was a set-up."

He shrugged. "Soon as we started asking questions, we had the FBI on our doorstep, warning us off the case."

"Would have been great if you'd been able to tell me."

"Wouldn't it, though?" he said with a sardonic smile. "But then, would you have listened?"

She hugged herself and dropped her head, not quite knowing where to go with this. Not knowing how to keep the connection that was forming. A connection different from the one they'd had when he'd arrived. This one was something new. A closeness she hadn't had with him before.

"So, I guess that's it."

"I guess so."

She drew a breath and glanced past him and out the open door. "So. What about…?" She gestured awkwardly between them.

"Us…?" he said.

She looked up, straight into his eyes.

He gestured back to the street. "I see Holly's out."

"Gone to dinner with Charles. Be at least a couple of hours, I guess."

"I see. Then, why don't you and I see what we can work out?"

She nodded. "We could. Where do you think we should start?" she asked.

"How about at the beginning?" he asked.

She nodded. "I think that works for me. I'll put the coffee on," she said, and closed the front door.

THE END

Read an excerpt from the first book in the *McClaine and Delaney*
series of thrillers by Catherine Lea

THE CANDIDATE'S DAUGHTER

CHAPTER ONE
DAY ONE—2:24 PM—KELSEY

Six years old. Even from here the kid looked small for her age.

Kelsey lowered the binoculars and squinted off down the street.

"Is that her?" Lionel asked and reached back. Kelsey handed him the binoculars while Matt shifted forward in his seat and rested both arms across the steering wheel, his attention on the child.

"That's her," he said.

They'd been sitting in this junker Camry for half an hour now, freezing their asses off while they waited for school to finish and the last remaining students to leave. November in Cleveland and no functioning heater, the car was an ice-box. The instant Kelsey saw the kid, it was like someone had flicked on a switch. Now all she could feel was heat flashing down her back and sweat prickling under the wig. She adjusted her jacket and loosened her collar, watching the woman and the child exit the Special Children's Center and make their way to the street.

"Ready?" Lionel said.

Matt checked the street front and back. "Not yet. Wait for it …"

Kelsey lifted the binoculars again, leaning forward so she could get a clear view of the kid. Holly McClaine's mousey brown hair was cut into a bob and secured back from her face with a headband; she wore a windbreaker two sizes too big over a checked pinafore dress, fawn-colored tights and plain brown shoes. Her left hand was on the strap of her Dora the Explorer backpack, her right one in the grip of a woman Kelsey recognized as her teacher, Audrey Patterson. While Holly stared straight ahead, a worried frown creased the teacher's brow. She pulled the child's hood up, then turned and shrugged her shoulders against the icy wind, searching the street for a car that was never going to come.

Matt checked his watch. "Okay," he said. "Now! Go, go, go."

Kelsey opened the left rear door, got out and headed down the street, drawing the collar of her jacket up over the dagger tattoo on her neck. "Hi," she called, flipping back a strand of her long brown hair and smiling as she crossed and trotted towards the teacher and the kid.

Audrey Patterson gave her the brief smile, but otherwise ignored her and continued scanning the street, until Kelsey paused next to Holly, dropped to one knee, and said, "Hey, Holly, I'm taking you home, baby."

The teacher swung on her, automatically gripping the child's shoulders and pulling her in, saying, "Excuse me?"

Kelsey straightened, offered her hand. "Oh, I'm sorry. I'm Amy, Lizzie's sister. You must be Audrey. Lizzie told me all about you. Says you're a terrific teacher."

Audrey's frown softened but the skepticism remained. She took the proffered hand. "Nice to meet you," she said, although the snap visual she gave Kelsey's jeans, Metallica tee-shirt and fringed suede jacket told her something entirely different.

"Oh, yeah, I didn't have time to change. Airports, huh?" Their eyes met, locked. Right there Kelsey saw the distrust and her heart did a flip.

Audrey flashed another zero-degree smile. "Thank you for coming, but Holly's car will be right along." Then she turned her attention back to the empty street.

Kelsey followed the teacher's gaze. "Oh, so Lizzie didn't call?"

"Elizabeth? No. Was she supposed to?"

Kelsey gave her a lopsided grin. "Jeez, I swear she'll forget her damn head one of these days. She's been so busy with all that campaign sh … stuff with Richard and all, and yeah …" She shrugged.

Another tight smile. "So I believe. And I think he'll be a great state senator."

"Yeah well, he'll have to get voted in first. Way he's going, that'll never happen. Anyhow, everything back home's gone all to hell. That's why I'm here." She smiled down at the kid. "Oh yeah, and Sienna. Y'know, like the nanny? Lizzie told me she's gone to her mother's. Yeah, so anyway, she told me to pick Holly up—Lizzie, that is, y'know."

Holly looked up at Kelsey, open-mouthed and without a hint of expression. Her puffy eyes were red-rimmed and lightly crusted with the yellow flakes of pinkeye. They were set in a round, flat face that bore the trademark scar of a cleft lip running from just under her nose to her upper lip like a jagged crack. Below that, her round pink tongue peeked from her open mouth. Apart from the scar, she looked like any other Down syndrome kid Kelsey had ever seen.

"I'm sorry but that's out of the question," Audrey told Kelsey, like she was speaking to an idiot. "School policy dictates that we secure confirmation from the parents before we release any child into the custody of anyone other than his or her authorized guardians."

Kelsey stuck her hands on her hips and shifted her weight. "Oh, right." It pissed her off when teachers and rich assholes talked down to her like this. "Well, I guess Lizzie should have told me that before I drove all the way across town," she said, a little more sharply than she'd meant to.

Audrey stepped back and pulled Holly in a little closer. "I'm sorry, what did you say your name was?"

"Amy. Amy Pace. I just flew in yesterday from Idaho. Shit of a place," she added and grinned. When nothing came back she directed a smile down at Holly, and said, "Well, I guess there's nothing I can do but go home and wait."

Audrey said nothing, just stared at her, both hands still firmly on the child.

"So, I guess I'll have to see you back at your mom's, huh?" she told Holly.

Audrey's flinty glare never faltered, so Kelsey tipped her head, said, "Fine," in a *have it your way* tone, then turned and started walking away.

This was the part where Audrey Patterson was supposed to call her back. According to Matt, she'd be relieved the sister had come to take the kid home so she could run along to the phony meeting he'd set up for her. That wasn't happening. Kelsey crossed the street, shaking her head and wondering yet again why she'd let Matt and Lionel talk her into this dumbass plan. When she glanced back, Audrey was watching her, only now she had her cell phone to her ear and was talking on it.

"*Shit.*" Now Kelsey didn't know what to do. Matt and Lionel would be watching her from the car and going nuts. She spun on her heel, and crossed the street again, trotting back towards Audrey Patterson and Holly.

"Y'know, if you phone the house," she called as she approached again, "Sienna could tell you who I am. I mean, if that's what you need. That's all you have to do." She shrugged; cool, casual.

Then remembered she'd just told her the nanny wasn't there.

When the teacher turned back to her this time, the tilt of her head, the sharp, knowing little smile all told Kelsey one thing—Audrey Patterson knew something was going on, but she was the one in control here. "That won't be necessary," Audrey said as her eyes went straight to the uncovered tattoo. "I'm sure Holly's car will be right along." Then she angled the child around and began shuffling her back up the path toward the school.

Kelsey turned, gave the street another once-over, wondering what the hell to do next. By the time she came to a decision, a couple of cars had gone by and Audrey Patterson had steered Holly halfway back to the front door. Once they got inside it would be too late. So, she went after them.

Audrey had just got to the door when Kelsey threw her arm across, barring their way. "Give her to me," she said quietly. "I'll take her now."

"Excuse me—" Audrey began, and tried to push Kelsey aside. Without even thinking, Kelsey gave her a shove that sent the teacher reeling backwards and crashing into a trash can beside the door. For the briefest moment, Kelsey hesitated and thought, *What the hell am I doing?* Her first instinct was to stop and check that she was okay. Instead, she grabbed Holly by the hand, scooped her up like a sack of potatoes, and ran for the car. The backpack fell to the ground with a clatter of pens but Kelsey didn't look back. All she could hear was Audrey Patterson screaming for her to stop.

Kelsey leaped out into the road with the kid in her arms, but a car appeared from nowhere with a screech of brakes and a blast of its horn. She twirled away, looked right and left, then ran for the car. She ripped open the door and tossed the kid in as Matt started it up, yelling, "Get in!" Kelsey jumped in after Holly but just as she reached to close the door, a hand grabbed her arm, and there was Audrey Patterson, teeth bared, eyes wide, clinging on like her life depended on it. Kelsey jerked away, trying to break Audrey's grip while Lionel leaned over and swatted her. Matt hit the gas, grinding through the gears, swearing and yelling, but Audrey Patterson held on even tighter.

Kelsey tried prying the woman's hand off, but she had a fist like a bear trap and her fingers wouldn't budge. "Slow the fuck down," Kelsey yelled to Matt, but he wasn't listening.

Audrey stumbled, almost fell, and Matt screamed, "Shut the fuckin' door," and swung the car left then right.

Still Audrey Patterson hung on. But now they were dragging her along, her feet pedaling against the speeding blacktop, trying to keep up.

At the corner Matt spun the wheel so hard Kelsey almost went out the door and Holly wound up in her lap. When Audrey Patterson finally lost her grip, Kelsey reached out, grabbed the swinging door and slammed it. Matt hit the gas again, but almost at once they heard a bumping on the side of the car.

Matt yelled, "Open the door!" His eyes were riveted to the side mirror. "She's caught in the fuckin' door. Open the door."

Kelsey threw open the door, then immediately slammed it again. She turned just in time to see Audrey Patterson tumbling over and over on the blacktop as they sped away.

"Mitha Pannathon," said Holly. She looked like she'd taken the whole experience like a routine trip to the mall.

Kelsey's heart was pounding, her hands shaking. She ripped off the wig and raked her nails through her short-cropped blond curls. "Huh? Oh, Mrs.

Patterson, yeah, sure." Through the rear window she could see Audrey Patterson lying in a heap on the roadway while people rushed toward her. "Yeah, she's fine," she told Holly. "She's waving goodbye."

"Holy shit," said Lionel. "Holy fuckin' shit."

Matt's eyes were switching from the road to the rear-view mirror. "Everybody just stay calm. Just stay ..."

Behind them the wail of a siren split the air.

"Oh Jesus! Hang on tight," said Matt. He swung hard right at the next street, then took a left, smashing the stick-shift through the gears. "This piece of shit ..."

Kelsey leaned forward, gripping the front seats. "Go down the Theatre route. Two blocks in there's a shortcut to the parking building."

"I know, I know," said Matt. He twisted the wheel and the tires screeched as they flew around the next corner then spun into the next. The left wheels mounted the curb and they flew down between stopped cars and terrified pedestrians, but the cop did the same. People jumped out of the way and shouted abuse after them. Kelsey grabbed the armrest with one hand and Holly with the other. When she looked down, the kid smiled up at her.

Suddenly Matt swerved and they all rode air as the car flew over the first incline and crashed down on the underground ramp. Tires squealed as they twisted and turned deeper and deeper into the parking garage. The cop drove straight past but in a matter of seconds he backed up and Kelsey knew he'd soon be behind them again.

But now there were two sirens.

They hit the fourth level down just as a car pulled out and cut the cop off. On the fifth level Matt slammed on the brakes and twisted the wheel, skidding sideways to pull into a slot. Kelsey grabbed Holly, hugging her close as they all leaped out. Matt fumbled in his pocket for a key, unlocked a blue Ford SUV and they jumped in. Matt fired up the engine while Lionel twisted in his seat, searching for the cop. Kelsey buckled Holly up and turned her attention to the rear window.

"All clear," said Lionel, so Matt slammed the truck into reverse, swung it around and threw it into first. They shot forward to the end of the row, and stopped. Then, calmly, quietly, he drove out of the building while three cop cars went screaming past. "Everybody okay?"

"I think I'm gonna throw up," said Kelsey.

CHAPTER TWO
DAY ONE: 3:09 PM

The SUV turned into the driveway and the instant it came to a halt, three doors flew open. Kelsey waited for Holly to scoot across the seat towards her, and lifted her out while Matt waited with the blanket. He tossed it over the child in Kelsey's arms, and guided them to the house. Lionel opened the front door, checking the street for prying eyes, and slipped in behind them, shutting the door and locking it.

"Wah-hoo!" Lionel yelled. "Blue skies, crystal clear waters, here we come." He and Matt bumped fists while Kelsey pulled the blanket off Holly and brushed her hair back from her face.

"You okay?" Kelsey asked her.

"Holy shit," said Lionel, staring down at the girl for the first time. "Holy shit, you see this?" he asked Matt and pointed. "She looks like a gopher."

"Shut up, Lionel," Kelsey said, wheeling Holly around and steering her toward the stairs.

Behind them he was laughing and saying, "Oh man, she's like one of those Goofy Gophers from the cartoon show—we got us a Goofy Gopher," he said, and laughed so hard he doubled over with his hands on his knees.

Even from the bedroom upstairs, Kelsey could hear Lionel braying like the jackass he was.

"Naff," said Holly. "Naff an' naff."

Kelsey opened the Walmart shopping bag and searched through the children's clothes they'd bought the day before. They all looked too big. "Huh?"

"Nine-a naff."

"*Nine-a naff?* Oh! Oh yeah, Lionel's laughing. Whole street can hear Lionel laugh. He's an idiot. Here, try this on." She took out a crumpled tracksuit and shook it out.

"No naff a' me," Holly said, shaking a little finger. The words came out so fiercely, they made Kelsey look up.

"Hey, nobody's laughing at you. Ignore Lionel. He's an asshole."

"Ah-ho."

Kelsey gave her a half grin. "Okay, so maybe not that word. Maybe we'll stick with 'jackass.'"

"Nack-an."

"Yeah, a nack-an. And we'll keep that between you and me. Here, take your dress off. We don't want your expensive clothes getting all mussed up, do we?" She slipped the dress up over the child's head and checked the label. "Target. Oh, wow. So, no expense spared, huh? Oh," she said and stopped short when she saw the wet patch on the child's leggings. "I see you had a little accident, too, huh? Take off your undershirt and panties and I'll get 'em changed." She peeled Holly's soiled clothing off, noting the yellow coloration of faded bruising across her buttocks. "What happened there? Huh? Did you fall down?"

Holly looked up at her and said nothing, the emptiness of her stare so deep it almost echoed. But out of nowhere, a smile bloomed across her face. She bunched her little fists to her mouth and folded over laughing. To Kelsey the transformation was so stark, so sudden, it was like looking at a different child.

"Fah down. Oopny oop. Ah fah down," Holly said, and giggled all the harder.

"Oopty, oop's right." A smile caught the corners of Kelsey's mouth. And when the kid doubled over helpless with laughter, Kelsey found herself chuckling along with her. She was still smiling and stepping the child into a pair of clean panties when the door opened and Lionel leaned in. His eyes went straight to Holly. "So, what's happening?"

Conscious of his gaze, Kelsey angled herself between Holly and Lionel and pulled the panties up. "What do you want?" she said as she reached for the track pants.

He leaned on the door frame, grinning. "Well, look at you. Little mama, huh?" he said, angling his head to look around her. "Little mama and the Goofy Gopher."

Kelsey pulled Holly in close. "Get out, Lionel." Still shielding Holly from his gaze, she pulled the sweater over the child's head and tugged it into place.

"You got a new mama there, huh, Goof?" He folded his arms and leaned a shoulder into the door frame. "Hey, Goofy, are you deaf or somethin'?"

Kelsey felt an instant flash of irritation. "Don't call her that. And she isn't deaf."

Lionel's grin solidified and his expression switched to something more calculating. "Aw, shit, she don't know what I'm sayin'. Do ya, Goof?"

Kelsey tucked in the child's undershirt and adjusted the sweater. Then, she shuffled Holly in behind her and turned to face him. "Was there something you wanted?"

Lionel said nothing. Just looked from Holly to Kelsey.

"Then get out."

He gave her a wink, shut the door as he left.

Kelsey clamped her mouth shut, holding back the torrent of words she would have let go if there wasn't a child present. She pulled back the comforter on the bed and waited for Holly to climb in. Now, staring down at the kid who looked back up at her with her pink eyes and open-mouthed wonder, she couldn't help but smile. "You snuggle down there, missy. Try to get some sleep. It's nap time."

Holly wiggled into the bed but just as Kelsey tucked the comforter around her, a little hand popped out, snatching at the air. "Ninny, Ninny," she pleaded.

"Ninny? What's a ninny?"

"Ninny Nion," Holly said and snatched at the air again. "Wah Ninny Nion."

"You want your nanny? You mean Sienna …?" But before Kelsey could finish, Holly's eyes widened and she let out a howl that made Kelsey jump.

"Hey, hey," she said, but Holly sucked in another breath and howled even louder. Her arms flayed and feet kicked, and all Kelsey could do was grab her wrists and pin her down. "Hey, whoa there. Sienna's not here. You hear me? She's not here. She's all gone."

Holly fell silent. She sucked in one long hiccupping breath and drew the back of her sleeve across her eyes. "Nenna ah gong?" she asked. "No Nenna?"

"Nope, no Sienna. She's way gone. And she ain't comin' back."

Holly reached out again. "Wah Ninny Nion."

"Oh, I got it. You mean *Lilly Lion*." When Holly's eyes lit up and she snapped her hand again, Kelsey said, "Okay, so Lilly must be your favorite toy, right?" She touched her finger to the end of Holly's nose. "Well, I'm sorry, but I don't have your Lilly Lion. Listen, though, I'll make you a deal—"

But before she could finish, the door behind her opened and Matt leaned in. "What the hell's goin' on? Why's she yelling like that?"

Kelsey tucked the comforter up around the child, then turned. "Nothing. Everything's fine."

Matt regarded them both, and dropped his shoulders. Twenty-four years old, Matt was as good-looking as the day Kelsey met him—maybe better. Thick brown hair, strong white teeth, great body. He was the one who had planned all this. Right down to the last detail. He had covered bases no one else even thought of. Like mailing the ransom note out the day before so it got there at the perfect time. Kelsey would never have thought of that. She would have just called on the phone like you see in the movies. Matt told her the cops could track you down if you called on the phone. But how many people passed through a different part of town one day and were gone the next? So if you posted a letter from any particular part of town, how would the cops ever trace it? The rest was in the timing. That's what he'd said.

Even now she still didn't understand why they couldn't just call on the phone. But there you had it. Matt was the smart one. Kelsey's old man always said she was dumb as a sack of hammers. But she had enough clues to know smart when she saw it. And Matt's ingenuity, his cleverness, his ability to make something out of any situation; those were the things she loved most about him. Though lately, he had so much on his mind he hardly seemed like the same guy.

He raked his fingers through his hair and said, "I'm going to get something to eat. You want something?"

"I'll go," she said.

"We'll both go."

"No," she replied so sharply that he shot her a look. "I'm not leaving her with Lionel."

"I don't know why you don't like him."

"It's not that," she lied. "It's just … what if he gets strung out? He can't look after her if he's out of it. Anyway, she needs some shit for her eyes. They're all red and itchy. They're driving her nuts."

Matt spread his hands and let his gaze circle the room in exaggerated wonderment. "So, why's that our problem? Why do we have to get it? Why can't her rich parents shell out their money for it? It's not like they can't afford it."

"Well, maybe they would. Only they're not exactly here."

He considered it. "Okay. You go. Don't talk to anyone, keep your head down and stay low. Don't go blowing this. We've come way too far to screw it up now."

"Just keep an eye on her."

Kelsey followed him to the door and looked back. Holly lay tucked under the covers, grinding her little fists into her eyes. "Just keep checking on her. Make sure she's okay," she said and pulled the door closed.

Downstairs Matt dug in his pocket and came up with ten dollars. "Quit worrying, will you? We'll take good care of her."

Matt was Kelsey's world. She never trusted anyone like she trusted him. She'd trust him with her life. She wouldn't trust Lionel to butter her toast. If she'd had the choice, she'd have taken Holly with her. That option wasn't on the table. So she'd have to move fast.

To read more, visit http://geni.us/B3FU

Read an excerpt from the second book in the *McClaine and Delaney* series of thrillers by Catherine Lea

CHILD OF THE STATE

PROLOGUE
CARRINGWAY WOMEN'S PRISON, OHIO—AMY

Amy knew she should have gone to Stacy the second she'd opened the box. All night she'd lain there in her cot, listening to every sound, frightened they'd come after her, and wondering who else knew. Because somebody did.

Why she'd even gotten stuck in that stupid job was anybody's guess. She'd applied for the prison sewing program. Would have helped if she knew how to sew, but others on the same work scheme didn't know how to sew when they started, either. They got lessons.

Amy still couldn't make a buttonhole worth a damn so she got stuck in dispatch, sending out boxes of garments in the truck that turned up twice a week. Her job was to pack the boxes, check the details on the packing slip, seal the boxes up. Most boring job on the planet—or it was until that particular box came back, returned from wherever and marked Attention Dispatch Department. The only person around with any authority to accept the box was Trish Tomes, the prison officer overseeing the project.

Amy had been going through the contents of the box, looking at every item. She was just holding a silk blouse up to the light, checking she wasn't imagining things, when Officer Tomes appeared behind her. Amy just about peed her pants. She yelped and pressed the blouse to her chest to try and slow her heart down. The woman had the stealth of a cat. Didn't matter how hard you listened, you'd turn around and there she was, standing right behind you.

Officer Tomes took the blouse from Amy, holding it up to the light while she looked it over. Then she dug through the box, frowning as she brought out other garments and checked them.

"I'll take care of this," she told Amy.

"But these are ours."

"I said I'll take care of it. Now go back, seal up the last of those boxes." Her tone implied she wasn't going to say it again. She gathered up the returned box and took it back to her office. When Amy looked up the next time, she could see her on the phone, talking to someone with that sour look on her face, every now and then glancing accusingly across at Amy.

But Amy wasn't stupid. She'd already tucked one of blouses down the front of her prison jumpsuit, then slept all night with it tucked under her mattress. Now here she was standing in line for breakfast with the blouse down the front of her jumpsuit while she waited for Stacy. What she'd discovered was something big—she just knew it was, and Stacy was the only one in this joint Amy could trust. She was also the one who'd know exactly what to do.

After several minutes, the doors opened and Stacy's crew entered, lining up for their breakfast trays, all chattering and checking out the tables to see whether anyone had been stupid enough to sit in their seat, then looking back down the line to see who they might be eating with. Amy fell into line with her heart jumping and her hands shaking. She waited until her oatmeal and juice box had been set on her tray, and when she turned, she caught Stacy's eye, indicating for her to sit with her.

Soon as Stacy came over, slid her tray onto the table and sat down, Amy looked left and right, and said, "Gotta talk."

Stacy dug her spoon into her oatmeal, screwed her face up in disgust as she stirred it around. "Sure. Go ahead."

Amy leaned forward and hissed, "I'm talking *real talk*. In private."

Stacy looked up from her tray, her expression grim. "Are you okay?"

Amy gave the adjacent tables another furtive once-over. Satisfied they weren't being overheard she leaned forward again. "I found something."

Stacy straightened in her seat, lifting her head and letting her gaze casually navigate the room before settling back on Amy. "Go on."

Amy took another quick glance back over her shoulder. "Can't. Have to show you. Bathroom."

Stacy got up and returned her tray to the counter along with her uneaten oatmeal, and pushed through the swing doors, heading in the direction of the bathroom. No point in leaving the meal until she got back. You leave your food unattended in this place, you never knew what might have been added to it while you were gone. Amy followed, placing her food tray back with her breakfast untouched, giving the area another wary scan before following Stacy.

When she got to the bathroom, two stalls were closed. A toilet flushed and Nyla Guthrie stepped out and looked from Stacy to Amy and back. "What?" she said in an accusing tone.

"Nothin'," said Amy.

"It's nothing. Don't worry about it," Stacy told her.

Nyla gave Amy a sour once up and down, then pushed through the bathroom door going back to the dining room, leaving Stacy and Amy both watching the second stall.

Impatient, Stacy went across and banged on the door with the side of her fist. "Hey, hurry it up, will ya?"

The toilet flushed and Cissy Pettameyer stepped out, a picture of ingratiating sweetness. "Good morning, ladies," she said with a sly smile as she moved to the basin and washed her hands, checking her face in the mirror.

Neither of them spoke, just watched her.

"Be like that then," Cissy told their reflections, and ran a smoothing finger along one eyebrow. "I'm just trying to be polite."

Neither Amy nor Stacy was taken in. Cissy was a poisonous, two-faced gossip who spread stories at a rate that would make the black plague look slow.

Stacy stuck one hand on her hip and shifted her weight. "You done?"

Cissy turned and ran her eyes right down to Stacy's prison issue shoes and back. "I guess."

She jerked her head towards the door. "Then get out."

After Cissy had gone, Stacy opened the door and peered out, then closed it, leaning against it so no one else could enter.

"So, what's so important? Are you okay, Amy? Is someone giving you a hard time?"

"No, it's not like that. I'm fine. But when I was working today, a box came, addressed to the prison, like they do sometimes. It had a Faulty Goods sticker on the side, so I figured it was just stuff coming back that had stitching problems with them or something." She paused and dropped her voice to a whisper. "But this was in it." She reached down into the front of her jumpsuit, pulled the blouse out, and handed it to Stacy.

"What is it?"

"You look," Amy said, hugging herself and jerking her chin toward the blouse in Stacy's hands. "I didn't know else who to tell."

Stacy checked the seams, the sleeves, the buttonholes and her eyes came back up to Amy, questioning.

"Keep lookin'," she said.

Stacy turned the garment, checking the collar, then the neckline. Her jaw dropped and she looked up, eyes wide.

"Well, holy shit," she said.

CHAPTER ONE
FOUR MONTHS LATER
DAY ONE: 1:56 AM—STACY

The car rounded the last bend into Becker Street and came to an abrupt halt. Right in front of them was a pack of reporters and TV crews surrounding the front gate and stretching halfway down the street. By the look of them, they must have had the place staked out since dawn. The instant the first person spotted the car, the crowd was in motion. In a matter of seconds the car was swamped, microphones and cameras pressed to the windows, reporters and news anchors pushing and elbowing each other and yelling questions while a couple of cops tried unsuccessfully to hold them back.

Stacy sat up in the back seat, peering out at the commotion. This was something she hadn't expected. This could be a problem.

She twisted around, looking out the side and rear windows, watching the chaos outside while Mrs. McClaine, who was sitting next to her, leaned forward, directing the driver to pull in as close to the front gate as possible. Meanwhile, Penny Rickman, Mrs. McClaine's secretary, got out of the car behind them and cut her way through the crowd, also pointing and yelling over the rabble, ordering security to push the media back, and to form a guard around the car while Stacy and Mrs. McClaine got out.

There was nothing like this when Stacy was sentenced three years ago. As she'd left the courthouse that day, a handful of supporters had lined up along the front steps, shouting and waving placards that said things like: "No mother should be in prison for wanting her child," and "Where's the justice in this country?"

Didn't make one iota of difference because she'd already been tried and sentenced. Seventeen years old she was, and on her way to Carringway Women's Correctional Facility for assaulting the social services lady who'd taken her baby away. And that was the last she'd seen of the outside world—would have been for the next two years, if it hadn't been for the Governor's new early release program.

Now, here she was free again—or at least, she would be if all these reporters weren't surrounding the place.

The car door opened to a semi-circle of space made by a wall of security guards. Stacy flashed Mrs. McClaine a glance, and when she got the "okay" Stacy got out, head down, hand shielding her face from the flash of cameras. The security guards closed in, forming one compact unit, and together they moved in through the front gate, up the front steps, and onto the porch.

While Mrs. McClaine turned to answer questions and pose for the cameras, Stacy took a second to ease the tension out of her shoulders, look the place over. Seemed kind of ironic that after all these years, here she was back at the very house she'd run away from.

Gayleen Charms, never would have made Mother of the Year. Child Services knew the house better than the mailman. Having a child at fifteen might have been the best thing that ever happened to Stacy, but being a teen mom hadn't been top of Gayleen's list of career choices. Gayleen had wanted to be a dancer. She wanted to live in the big city under the bright lights.

From the minute Stacy was born she knew she'd been the biggest mistake Gayleen ever made, that she'd ruined her mother's life. Fourteen years of being made to feel like trash finally made life on the streets a way more attractive prospect. Which was why Stacy had run away.

Standing here now, the place looked no different—same crappy house with the same dirty white paintwork, same clutter all over the front porch, same broken railing her mother still hadn't fixed in all the time she'd lived here. One of the conditions of Stacy's release was that she must live at this address for a minimum period of six months.

Like hell.

Stacy didn't intend staying six minutes.

To read more, visit http://geni.us/vYGfGI